The Rift

*Also by Tommie Lee and available in paperback
and a variety of eBook formats:*

Mulligan

For Four Players

NoThing

Chair de ma Chair

Mulligan's Daughters

The Mayor of Seventeenth Avenue

These titles are available at *The Hammes Notre
Dame* bookstore, *Smashwords*, the *Amazon Kindle*
store, *Barnes & Noble's NOOK* store,
and many online retailers.

Find all of them via tkcbooks.com

First Print Edition
Published by Tommie Closson, Jr.
Distributed by CreateSpace

First Print Edition
ISBN-13 978-0-6159-2361-1
ISBN 0615923615

eBook Edition
ISBN pending

Printed in the United States of America

For Peart and Ellison, for Verne and Pratchett,
and for all the others who made it look fun...

And for Kim. ALWAYS for Kim.

The Rift

The First Novel of *The ReYear,* by

Tommie Lee

Contents

Prologue
There Must Have Been Some Magic

Peterson Air Force Base, Colorado Springs
December 2
6 months before The Event

The first days of December in Colorado had begun to spill across the wall calendar in Helen Pemberton's kitchen.

A peek through the curtains suggested the weather might finally be ready to become season-appropriate. There had been a few weeks of unusually warm weather here at the foot of the Front Range of the Rocky Mountains.

Each year, this was roughly the time that Helen would have the boys drag the Christmas decorations out of the basement and get to work.

This year though, there was no urge to decorate.

She had no desire to put an ounce of Christmas in the house. Failure to do so, however, would drag the boys down to her depths of despair. Helen could not let that happen. There would have to be decorating. It might as well happen today.

Helen Pemberton stood at the bottom of the stairs with her arms crossed. She stared at the large red plastic tubs with the green lids in the corner under the stairwell. There was so much Christmas there to be put together, and there was hardly a single trace of motivation to do it.

This wasn't just any Christmas.

This was Helen's first Christmas after losing her eldest son.

The chill of the basement caused her hands to absent-mindedly rub a little warmth and comfort into her arms. She paused in that process and squeezed, giving herself a small hug.

She couldn't see it from the basement but the first snow of the season began falling outside. Having grown up in the Florida Panhandle, she always enjoyed watching the snow fall. She especially liked the first snow of each winter, something her military marriage had afforded her an opportunity to see in several spots all over the world. When she had been a little girl there had never been a first snow of the season. A childhood on the Florida Panhandle meant the first snow every winter was always something you saw on TV.

If the *Frosty the Snowman* story was to be believed, there was magic in the first snow of the season.

Her life could use a little magic right now.

Helen was only one week into the process of trying to absorb the news of the death of her Billy. She was only a couple of days removed from his funeral. Coming down these basement stairs had been the first real movement she had made since the ceremony.

Now, her own internal timetable stated that she was supposed to care about Christmas. It was what was expected of her. If she was going to make The Colonel and everyone else try to act normal, then she had to do it, too.

Wild Bill wasn't home. Her husband, Colonel William Pemberton, had gone back to work. He had done this because that was *who* he was, and that was *what* he was. She had pushed him to do it though, despite his protests. Moping around the house with her wasn't going to help anything. Likewise, Little Sammy was in school today, his first day back. Danny, the middle child, was at home and waiting to ship out to a war she didn't want him to go to. Danny was pretending not to be as low as she was. He was checking on her every now and then and pretending not to have a head cold.

Helen wanted everyone's routines to get up and running again as soon as possible, including her own. She wanted everyone to have the distraction of normalcy after the horrifying Thanksgiving news their family had been blindsided with.

To that end...here she stood. She was frozen in place, rubbing her arms, staring at Christmas as if it were a worthy opponent that was waiting for the first opportunity to attack.

There were two trees to put up. The first was in the one of the tubs in front of her. The other was a live one they bought each year when they bought the two they would donate. They hadn't gone out to find that tree yet. It hadn't seemed like much of a priority up to this point.

In the other tubs and boxes were an entire North Pole workshop's-worth of things that blinked, smiled, sang, danced, and did all the other things that made it the most decorative and festive time of the year.

It would all have to come upstairs to be placed around the house with her painstaking precision. And the thought of doing that right now was like a hundred-pound lead weight hanging off of her heart; A holiday albatross slung around her neck by a crew as cold and unforgiving as the usual Colorado winter.

The act of carrying it upstairs would not be the hard part. She had Danny for that. His routine at the moment was waiting to go off to combat. He was upstairs somewhere. He had taken to sitting around the house doing far too much heavy thinking about his big brother Billy than could possibly be healthy.

Decorating for the holiday…pretending to *care* about the holiday in a world without Billy…*that* was going to require a Christmas miracle, a bit of holiday magic, and God knows what else.

"Mom?"

The voice of Daniel drifted down from the top of the basement stairs.

She wiped her eyes, realizing that she had been crying again. Actually, she realized that a lot lately. Daniel pretended not to notice, trying to spare her the discomfort. It didn't work.

"Yes?"

"UPS truck just pulled up."

Helen Pemberton shook her head and sighed. "Okay," she said as she wiped a hand across her proud black face to break up her pooling tears. "Hey, baby?"

Danny had been turning around in the doorway above her. He paused.

"Yeah mom?"

"Christmas has to come up today, if you would."

"No problem," Daniel replied. He heard his mother start climbing the creaky stairs.

When she reached the top, he gave her a hug.

They held onto each other until the doorbell rang. Her usual delivery person, a short, round black woman named Shannon, stood there with a small box.

"Good morning, Helen. Overseas package for Sam here."

"For Sam, huh?" Helen smiled. She shook off the heaviness with a façade. "Come in, girl. It's good to see you."

"Good to see you too, ma'am. Hey, Danny."

Daniel stepped out of the basement doorway, his arms wrapped around the first two of several boxes of decorations he would have to maneuver around the basement stairs today.

"Hi, Shannon," he responded, and smiled weakly. He carted the boxes into the living room.

Shannon took a chocolate chip cookie that

Helen offered with a gesture of her hand. Usually, she didn't accept things like that from her customers, not even from the regular stops that she had gotten to know a bit over the years, such as the Colonel's family.

Helen Pemberton wasn't just anyone though. She was the Base Commander's wife, and Shannon's husband was a Staff Sergeant on the flight line who turned wrenches on airplanes. It seemed rude not to accept. Besides...Helen's cookies were so good they were practically their own food group.

Helen signed for the package and handed the digital clipboard back to Shannon.

"Well, thanks for the cookie. I gotta get going before the snow gets too bad today."

Helen looked past her to the kitchen window, noticing the snow for the first time. It hadn't even registered with her when she had answered the door. "Absolutely," she replied. "We can gab next time, girl."

"You bet," Shannon said. An awkward pair of seconds passed between them before Shannon silently placed a hand on Helen's arm.

They shared a sad smile and a nod.

Shannon turned and walked out of the front door. "Thanks again," she called, and waved as she walked to the brown delivery van.

Hang in there, Helen, she wanted to say, or possibly *Sistahs gotta stick together, and you can talk to me about what happened.*

She didn't say any of that. There was no way to say much of anything without making the poor woman even less comfortable than she already was in her grief. They weren't exactly friends, but Shannon knew Helen well enough to not want to cause the woman any discomfort at all in a difficult time. Everything was still too fresh for that family.

Shannon was just thankful that her husband had never had to go overseas. She couldn't imagine how she might cope with something like this.

She twisted the key in the brown van's ignition and drove down the circle.

In the house, Helen watched Shannon drive away. She liked Shannon. She reminded her of the girls in the little social group she had grown up with.

Helen watched the snow for a second, listening to Daniel make another trip up the stairs, struggling with one of the larger plastic tubs. She dumped a cold cup of coffee into the sink and turned around to look at the package Shannon had delivered.

She held the box up and looked carefully at the markings. A moment later, she dropped it softly back onto the kitchen table with a dull thud.

It was from Billy.

The package said *Merry Christmas Sam* in one corner, written in her late son's unmistakably bad handwriting.

As far as she was concerned though, what it actually said was *Make Christmas, Momma. You guys are still alive.*

So Helen spent the day making Christmas

once Danny brought up the last of the boxes and tubs from the basement.

She put on holiday movies that had a better chance at making her laugh than cry, and she set about her work.

Daniel took DayQuil and helped her.

Wild Bill showed up in time for the last of the tree-trimming in the middle of the afternoon. Around two o'clock he had decided that he'd worked enough for today, and he was the boss.

The afternoon was a busy one, the sort of afternoon that flies by. Before she knew it, Helen heard the squeaking brakes of a school bus rolling to a stop in front of the house. By that point, there was a single inch of white, fluffy snow on the ground.

When Sam walked into the house and started shedding his book bag and coat, he saw that the family had accomplished a lot of their traditional Christmas set-up. The fake tree was up, the one that faced the bay window at the front of the house. It was always the first one to go up. When they got their real one...something they typically did by the end of the first weekend in December...*that* would be the tree the gifts went under. Such was their tradition.

Sam was therefore surprised to see a wrapped gift under the window tree when he kicked off his boots. Being a kid, he couldn't help but also notice that it had his name on it.

The *from* part of the label was left blank.

"Mom?"

"Be right there, baby," Helen said.

Upstairs, the Colonel gave his wife a kiss on the cheek and knocked on Danny's door.

Danny muted his stereo, silencing Wiz Khalifa for a moment.

"He's home," the Colonel said to his son, "Let's go."

"All right, Dad." He thumped the POWER button on the system and swung his legs around the bed, jumping up to join his parents in the hallway. He loosed another weighty sneeze, courtesy of his head cold.

Danny wiped his nose, balled up the tissue, and shot it at his old Denver Nuggets trashcan with the little plastic basketball hoop over it. He missed, like many of the members of the team had done with their shots this season.

Sammy was sitting on the couch, starting to dig his homework out of the book bag he had dragged in from the hallway, when his parents and his sole surviving brother suddenly appeared in the hallway from the stairs. Startled, concerned…afraid of what else could possibly have gone wrong so soon after losing his big brother Billy…he dropped the bag.

"Shit. Now what? Is it Gramma?"

The Colonel, Helen, and Daniel all started to laugh. Whether it was at the absurdity of the question, the tension of the last several days, or the fact that young Sammy had just said *shit*, no one could say. It was obvious that the laugh had been needed. Sam laughed with them after a few seconds.

The Colonel put his arm around his son.

"Your Grandmother is just fine. Everything's fine, boy. We just thought you, uh...we just...there's a package that came for you today. We didn't think you should wait until Christmas to open it."

"Oh-kayyyy..." Sam said, a little confused.

Daniel handed him the box from under the tree.

"Go ahead, baby," Helen said, wiping her big brown eyes. "It's from..."

"Billy," Sam interrupted, figuring this out. "Billy sent me a package from Africa, didn't he?"

Helen nodded at her little boy. Sam held the box in his hands for a moment and then smiled.

The smile spread warmly across his face and quickly sprouted three colonies on his family's faces.

Sam un-wrapped the package with great care, his concentration not unlike that of a watchmaker with a dozen gears on black velvet. He intended to save the paper. His brother had written it out by hand sometime in the last few weeks of his life. It was something to cherish, every bit as much as whatever was inside of it. The label had a colorful border and postmarks from stops in Ethiopia, Kenya, and Aviano Air Base in Italy. It would be a bad thing to allow it to rip in the slightest.

The box was heavy but not big. Something of decent weight rattled around in it. From the sound of things, it did so in a forest of packing peanuts. Once he split the tape and peeled apart the middle of the top, he confirmed this. Light green packing peanuts that looked like little Ss began to jump toward the open air.

Sam popped the scotch tape on the end of the box open with his index finger and pulled the flaps all the way open.

Their dog Duke had come over to inspect the business going on at the base of what it knew as The First Unpeeable Tree, which sat by the window. There were two trees every year that The Food Lady would set up, trees he was not allowed to mess around with. Shushed away from the Styrofoam packing peanuts, the beagle tottered off to another room to sulk at the injustice of it all.

Whatever it was, it was wrapped in a gray cloth that was tapered off with two heavy-duty rubber bands on either end. Sam pulled it out of the box and turned it over, feeling a piece of paper between the rubber bands on the other side.

RUB FOR THE DJINNI.
MERRY CHRISTMAS, BABY BRO.
– B.

Sam pulled the rubber bands off and unrolled the cloth.

A somewhat cylindrical brass lamp sat in the middle of the cloth, shining up at him as well as it was able given its considerable weathering and age.

It looked exactly like the lamp on the cover of Sam's favorite book, *Aladdin,* which Billy would read to him night after night when Sam was very little and Dad was working late.

The entire family looked down at it. A

spreading feeling in Helen's chest finally started to feel like Christmas for the first time this season. She hoped the others felt it, too, but she said nothing about it. There was no way to articulate it.

There was also no need to do so, as she was not alone in this.

The Pembertons had Billy home, if only for a moment. The moment was enough. They all knew that the emptiness that had been in the background for a couple of days would charge back into the room again, powering itself back to the front and center like the proverbial elephant. For the moment, however, there was peace in the Pemberton house.

The television began singing *It's beginning to look a lot like Christmas.*

Part One

Reset,

Rewind,

Recall,

Re-Year.

One
Unexpected Visitors

Somewhere in Ethiopia
June 1
4:26 PM local time
Less than a day before the event

Perhaps, if he is finally able to kill today, he will get a chance to see his mother again.

The afternoon sun is still hot under a clear blue sky in the Rift Valley. The wind is absent today. The wind spends little time here.

The sand is bleaching underfoot, and the areas of exposed rock in this part of the country are hot enough to scorch any hand foolishly laid upon them.

Sand whips around him and his comrades. *There are worse places to be,* he thinks to himself. Places with even more sand, more heat, more glaring sun. There are worse assignments than this one for men like him. He is thankful to God for his part in this. It could be so much worse.

Balah pushes the clip into his rifle and snaps it into readiness with a click. His rifle is the most important thing in his life right now, so it is well lubricated and cared for every day. It sings out proudly with each clean, rehearsed movement, trumpeting that it is now armed and ready to go. The sound makes him smile a row of shiny white teeth, and he looks up into the sky to share his smile with God.

It was not so long ago that his country suffered the pitiful stares of the rest of the world, a time when disease and starvation were the real gods here. Then the government found the yellow stones, which men turned into gold. Gold has forged a new God for his people in King Roti. King Roti has led them all to a greater future. He put rifles in their hands and food in their bellies and water in their throats and said to his people, "You can have *more*. You can *be* more."

He made the same offer to the godless heathens of Somalia and joined their countries together. When Kenya would not accept his generosity, Roti forced himself upon them. That had been some time ago. Balah had only been a boy when that happened.

Balah has a birthday tomorrow and will turn 15 years old. He is nearing his second year in Roti's Royal Army.

There are many strange visitors these days in his country. He knows in his heart that they must look up at this hot sky and marvel at its purity. So blue, this sky. So beautiful and healthy.

The visitors must do this because most of them have come here from America. Every schoolchild in Ethiopia grows up knowing that the Americans live under skies choked with chemicals, ruined by their corporate flatulence and their ill-intended attempts at mastering the entire world. They breathe in the evil vapors of excess and grow obese and disgusting under their poisoned sky. They throw away perfectly good food without reason because they can.

The eerie silence of the flat, sun-baked sand with its sparse vegetation is broken with a series of clicks from his fellow soldiers. Nineteen other rifles are snapped into readiness around him. They will be there in about 40 minutes.

This war is not over until their King orders them to stand down. The reporters from the West who say the war is lost for Great East Africa and her people...they are not as smart as they think they are.

The men of the Royal Army all know what is expected of them. They all know what to do.

Colorado Springs
June 1
7:10 AM Mountain time

The sun begins to pour into the windows of her home.

The house is nice. Better than modest in size, but it is still a military house, and therefore lacks a little character. It sits impressively at the precise middle of the circle street where the most powerful officers of the base reside.

Military housing means the walls are gray

and lifeless when they are bare. No different from the walls of the barracks where the unmarried enlisted men live. No different from the walls in the homes of the soldiers that aren't the Base Commander. The clothing is not the only thing that can be labeled *uniform* in the military life.

This house, however, has a painted wooden sign in the yard that reads COL WM PEMBERTON JR and BASE COMMANDER with the logo of Peterson Air Force Base between the two lines.

Helen goes out of her way to wrench life out of the drab walls. Covering lifeless walls with life is a tradition in military families. She has done this at every Air Force Base her family has served at for the last 31 and one-half years.

There are photos of her boys. When she says *her boys*, she refers to her three sons *and* the Colonel.

She dusts the pictures, taking special care to dust the frame containing the photo of her eldest son, named for his father, in his dress uniform. Billy is gone now. She has held that frame to her heart when alone in the house many times. Quiet moments spent crying and mourning.

Billy has been dead for several months now. The pain in her heart, however, remains fresh. She holds it close. Even though it hurts, the pain is one of the few things she has left of her oldest son that has tangible heft and is real.

There are also happier things to be dusted. Like the paintings done by her sister, many of them featuring the horses they grew up with in the Florida Panhandle. There is a large and formidable cross, heavy oak with shiny brass. It sits next to a traditional painting of the Virgin Mary. There is the typical compliment of mirrors. There are also expensive draperies that she frets and fusses over with far more energy than they need or deserve.

She's up most days around a quarter after six in the morning. Her husband wakes even earlier. Helen keeps herself very busy running the house.

Her home is kept neat. It is kept neat because her mother's home was always kept neat. Mother's obsession with neatness…and she was *Mother*, not *Mom*…is something that rubbed off on both of her daughters. They both grew up with it, and they were both berated and scolded about it. They both still cringe at the thought of it to this day. Mother was the youngest daughter of a prominent Black Catholic family in Florida. Mother was always trying to outdo her two sisters and grab the lion's share of her parents' approval. Helen and her sister did much the same with their mother when they came along.

In Helen's case, the obsession with cleaning that was passed down to her by her mother has been more of a blessing than a curse. She married a career military officer who was also something of a social climber.

The combination of the two has never been easy for an African-American family in some circles, but for them, the Air Force has almost always been devoid of racism.

They have always entertained and rubbed

elbows with powerful people so they could make the right connections and work their way up the ladder. It paid off insofar as it eventually landed him a Base Commandership in his 24th year of service. However, his brown-nosing has yet to push him up far enough to achieve his first star. They continue to entertain the right people and host the right kinds of parties, stretching the wings of the silver bird on his epilates as far as they can reach. There is that hope, however vain, that those wings will eventually turn their shiny pinions into the points of a Brigadier General's star.

Always prepared to host an event or an impromptu meeting at the drop of a hat, Mrs. Helen Pemberton keeps her home immaculate. One might think that a challenge with three boys running around for the past couple of decades, but they learned early on that they needed to keep the house clean or face their mother's wrath.

Back in Panama City, Florida, her sister Tara has another reason for carrying on the cleanliness curse. She now runs the old family estate. She cleans it maniacally as if the ghost of their late mother will glower at her from any possibly dirty corner of the 18 rooms. Her mother had a stare that always reminded her daughters that in centuries past in that part of the country, a house like theirs was only owned by people of a different color. It was a well-learned look she had picked up from her own mother. Helen went to great lengths to not give it to her sons, but she was certain she failed to do so.

Despite her often stern and distant mother, there were very few bad memories for Helen associated with that big Florida house. In fact, she had been living there when she met her husband.

The Colonel came into her life when he was a Lieutenant, stationed at Tyndall Air Force Base more than 30 years ago. He was handsome and gallant, a gentleman whom her father got along with. Their courtship was fast, perhaps too fast for her traditional family's liking, but the love was real and it deepened quickly. They were married after only a few months; they were moving on to a new duty station a year after that; and several years would go by before they became parents themselves.

By that time, she had seen much of the world. She had lived in far-flung, exotic places. Her husband continued to be promoted.

She had always been happy. The military gave much...until it finally took something away.

Visible through the windows in the early morning sunlight is Helen's well-kept backyard. It has several strong trees filled with the life of late spring, a garden, and a lush lawn trimmed to golf-course perfection with decorative ornaments. There is enough color in the backyard to rival Monet.

The phone rings a few minutes after seven in the morning. As it rings, she just has a feeling it is her son Daniel. She figures it to be evening in Ethiopia. She still has trouble remembering if it's tonight or last night there. *Maybe it's tomorrow night.*

Whatever.

She is never certain because it never matters to her on a personal level. She hates Ethiopia. She *hates* Ethiopia. She just knows she needs Daniel to come home, and Daniel is determined to do his duty.

These weren't things she ever had to think about with her husband. He never had any long deployments overseas without her where she would have to think about things like his being in harm's way or what time zone he was in when he called her.

In her capacity as the Base Commander's wife, she knows as much as she needs to when the airmen under her husband's command go to war. This is a very rare occurrence. This particular Air Force Base has a focus that is more domestic and research-based.

Her two older sons, though, both joined the Army. The two of them couldn't wait to get on the ground in East Africa. Only the eldest son became an officer.

And the eldest son doesn't call her anymore because he can't. He's under a headstone.

"Danny Boy," she sings into the phone to her middle child. She doesn't sing it to the familiar tune though. She has just always had a way of singing the names of her sons to them. There is a quality in her voice that makes the most important words sound like a song. No words are more important to her than the names of her three sons.

In the other room, the cat has jumped up onto the mantle. She hears the glass break and wrinkles her eyes as she sees that the cat has knocked over Billy's frame and broken the glass. She bites her tongue and closes her eyes with anger. That anger is quickly squelched as Danny starts to talk to her.

Her conversation with Daniel is light and pleasant. Active combat operations have ceased in The Rift Valley War. Danny spends most of his time delivering aid and being bored and hot. He is given the opportunity to call home often.

However, neither side is aware that this will be the last time Daniel calls home. If Helen knew that, she might have been more invested in their conversation.

This will be the last time they will speak before it happens.

Before the madness begins.

Helen is unaware of it, but company is coming this afternoon.

The house is always ready for company, and she might think that she is ready as well. No one, however, can ever be prepared for the visitors she will be receiving later today.

Camp Tango
Awasa, Ethiopia
June 1
5:48 PM local time

Roughly a half-hour after his ten-minute call back home, Private First Class Daniel Pemberton is racked out.

His unit has been enjoying the relative quiet of the base for about two weeks now, and he relishes every opportunity to grab some sleep before the next day's duty. In the field, they pretty much had to take turns sleeping. This is time to read mail, go online, sleep…and reflect.

The war has all but ended. Ethiopia's king has been deposed, his Royal Army hides scattered and disorganized in the mountains of the Great Rift Valley, and the shaky union with Somalia has already crumbled. This put Somalia back into the same chaotic state it had been before this mess began 18 months ago.

Daniel's older brother was among the casualties in the first full year of the war. A few of his friends here knew the story of how Lt. William Pemberton III led a squad into battle in the early weeks of the mission. Ethiopian and Somali forces had crossed into Kenya and run amok for months, pushing their border into the middle of the country before the tide turned…with help from units like Billy's.

Billy's troops were among those that pushed the Royal Army back into the mountains of Ethiopia, pushing toward the capital. In a city called Sodo, not far from where Daniel's current base is located, they met the enemy.

Billy came down from the mountain in a medevac helicopter. He already wore a toe tag by the time the wheels touched down at the forward medical unit.

This happened about a week before

Thanksgiving. At that point Danny had been only a month or so away from shipping out to Africa himself.

Just last month, the self-styled king of Greater East Africa found himself in a cell in The Hague awaiting trial on war crimes. It was a far better fate than traditionally awaited most African politicians when their rule came to an abrupt end. However, the depths of his particular fate had yet to be fathomed. When they were, it would happen in front of a global television audience.

For now, Daniel Pemberton sleeps. Dreams do not typically come to him here in Africa. Time spent in combat...brief, though it was...has taught Daniel to sleep lightly. Part of his mind is always focused on what's going on around him, even if nothing is. He wonders how long it will take him to get out of that habit when he rotates back to the world when his year is up in January.

It's another of those things he would have liked to discuss with his brother when he returned home. There was a laundry list of things he wanted to talk to Billy about.

Daniel wakes up when he hears the first rifle shot from the northeast corner of the base. He reacts to it before the klaxon alarm starts to whine across the base. He leaps out of his bed and grabs his rifle. It only takes a single step for him to realize he's in his underwear.

Outside someone pounds on the sheet-metal wall and shouts "Skinnies at the gate! Get your asses in gear!" to anyone who might still be in the barracks.

He sets the rifle down on his bed for a moment to pull his pants on. He quickly picks the weapon back up and hits the door with five other men who had been in bed.

He is at his position when it occurs to him that he forgot his helmet.

"Dumbass," grunts Sgt. Bryce, as he jumps beside him. He slaps Daniel's helmet onto his head and gives him half a smile.

"Sorry, Sarge," Daniel says. Bryce smacks the back of his helmet.

Daniel looks in the direction of the North gate. He's watching, waiting.

The klaxon dies out and everything becomes silent with anticipation. The last of the American, British, Kenyan, and Qatari soldiers that share this occupation base on Ethiopian soil fall into their positions and wait. Most of them have dinners getting cold, or at least as cold as anything can get this close to the Equator in the beginning of June. At the very least their dinners are being visited by flies in the chow hall.

Bryce taps his wrist and gestures over to the wall. Daniel nods and checks the readiness of his rifle. His sergeant climbs past him and moves toward the new spot.

Daniel hears the shot, and he freezes in place.

His first instinct is to look in the direction the shot seemed to come from. His second is to check on Sergeant Bryce.

Bryce is coming back in a big hurry but moving almost in slow motion. Daniel can't quite figure that out at first. It's like a scene from a movie, a dramatic shot that looks out-of-place without some kind of musical accompaniment.

On the other side of the gate, the young man called Balah is absolutely certain he hit the man he had in his rifle-sights. What he doesn't understand is why the man didn't drop right away. He doesn't have the opportunity to wonder this for long.

Within a few seconds of his lucky shot, the sparse vegetation he was hiding in is being shredded by gunfire. The last things Balah sees are the orange bursts of fire from a dozen rifles. Each of the men holding one noticed the wisp of smoke that came from Balah's rifle and is answering in kind. He feels at least three different shots enter his body before they stop registering with his pain center. He falls onto his back with a shocked look on his face. Shot to death a day shy of his fifteenth birthday.

Daniel attempts to raise his rifle to join in the melee that has suddenly broken out around him. For some reason, he finds his arms filled with lead, and he cannot lift his weapon.

In an instant, Sergeant Bryce is back at his side. Thankfully, he seems to be unhurt. Daniel is relieved and smiles.

The smile hurts, a lot.

Bryce is yelling something at him, but his voice is really far away. In fact, he notices all of the noises around him starting to slip behind some kind of wall. Not necessarily gone, but muted like when he would wedge that red-tipped white mute into the bell of his coronet in band class.

Band class.

9th grade.

Mary.

Ellen.

Ayres.

The woman he loved. The girl he had seen since high school, who kissed him goodbye at the airport.

Mary was the younger sister of his brother's girlfriend. The two of them were fortunate to have grown up in a military society, one that didn't languish under a lot of racism, one that would not find reasons to create problems for two black brothers dating two white sisters.

Mary had a field of amazing raven hair on her head and deep hazel eyes and a dazzling smile that made him shiver a little. It all came together into a package that had hypnotized him when he was 14. There was the homecoming dance where she let him touch her bra. There was sneaking off at band camp to kiss by the river. There had been so many amazing times.

Mary Ellen Ayres. *God* how he loved that girl. She dumped him at one point in their junior year because he was a jackass...but he rallied and won her back. She would always be his first *real* love. You never forget about the first *real* love. You don't give up on that love.

He can almost see her. He can almost see her smile, almost smell that sweet little perfume she wore, almost taste her lips...

"Pem!"

Bryce is screaming at him, but the words don't register that well. Daniel Pemberton squints at him. A bullet sings in the air over their heads. It sounds like a cartoon gunshot to Danny, as if it should have a face drawn on it and smoke trailing behind it...

"Hold on goddamnit!"

The kid from Nebraska they all call Moose leans over Danny and fires several rounds in the direction that last bullet seemed to come from. After a moment, he gets up and moves to a forward position.

Daniel feels himself drop his rifle, which he has been gripping tightly since the confusion of the original shot. Only now does he notice that he's on his back. Three of his brothers in arms are hovering over him, pulling him down into a safer spot.

Something's wrong.

He finally feels it, and his face immediately collapses into agony. The left side of his face actually feels paralyzed as if he's had a stroke or something. It isn't responding, and it hurts in a strange, almost deadened way.

An attempt to call out in pain fails as wind escapes from the gaping hole in his throat. The whistling sound it makes is sickly, and for a moment, it becomes the only thing Danny Pemberton can focus on.

Balah's shot had been impressive. It was his first and last shot at another human being with his rifle. He had just the right angle for a head shot, but his sights were just off enough to affect his accuracy.

The round struck Daniel Pemberton in the

left side of his neck, tearing away everything it came into contact with.

It came into contact with *a lot*.

Doc, an Army medic from Maine who has been with this group since they shipped out, works the bandage around the wound under Danny's field of vision. Danny feels a tear start to build in his right eye and feels the rush of fluids starting to drown him as he tries in vain to breathe.

Mary Ellen Ayres is standing over Doc's shoulder as Daniel looks up at him. She's faint, but he can see that she's standing there. She smiles at him.

He tries to smile back, but the seizure hits too quickly for him to be able to pull it off. She begins to fade, her smile turning into a frown.

Daniel Pemberton stares up at the sky where she had been, his mouth agape, his fists clenched at the wrists of two of his closest friends.

He stares up at the sun without wincing, fails to draw a final breath of any true value, and dies hard.

Colorado Springs
June 1
1:20 PM Mountain time

Colonel "Wild" Bill Pemberton is not sure if he is more concerned or annoyed. He marches out to his Hyundai in a huff, his low-quarter shoes echoing in the quiet parking lot until the whine of jet engines in the distance drown them out.

He is the Base Commander here at Peterson. He does not typically *receive* orders. He gives them.

REPORT TO YOUR HOME IMMEDIATELY, the piece of paper had said, and it was written in all CAPS.

The message had come directly from the Division Commander's office. That was it. No further explanation had been given.

He turns the key, and pulls the silver-green sedan out of the lot. His house is exactly four minutes away from his office.

Halfway to the house, he realizes something that hadn't occurred to him at first. He takes a deep breath as he executes a left turn.

The last time he was told to report home was when Billy was killed in Ethiopia.

Shit. Shit. Shiiiiiiit.

He looks at his iPhone and picks it up.

Within a second of sliding it unlocked, he puts it back down in the cup holder. If he's right, the last thing he needs to do is upset Helen before he gets there.

Raising children at the tail end of the Cold War, Wild Bill had always had the mind-set that if the nukes were on their way to whatever Base they were living on...he would not call home. It wasn't as if he would be able to do anything to save his family. Better to let them all die without fear and dread. What he wasn't sure about was whether or not he would have abandoned his post to join them at the house.

Fear and dread.

Here those two bastard emotions were again, dripping their acid on his life, his family; eating away at the flesh of their rebuilt lives.

Shit.

He pulls into his driveway and quickly exits the car. Walking up to the house, he hears another vehicle coming up the street.

Colonel William Pemberton fears that he knows who and what that vehicle is, and he ignores it. He walks through the front door.

"Helen?"

"Bi-ill? Out ba-ack," is the musical reply. She sang his name to him a bit when she said it, like she always does with the boys. By now, his heart is already aching in his chest.

Helen has been gardening. The weather is perfect today, although there is a hint of rain in the dark clouds pouring over the Front Range of the Rockies. This is typical of most June afternoons in Colorado Springs.

"What brings you home?" she asks with a smile. The smile quickly vanishes when she sees him standing in the back doorway, looking deflated. She did not marry a man that spends a lot of time ever looking deflated.

The doorbell rings. The Division Commander is standing there with the Base Chaplain, a senior JAG officer, and a man they sadly remember to be the Base Mortuary Officer.

Helen Pemberton sees them over her husband's shoulder and drops her trowel.

A rumble of thunder comes from the direction of Pikes Peak.

They stand on either side of the wide granite steps, stoic and silent. They're a great pair of terrible stone sentinels, vigilant in their duty with unwavering and savage stares. They are the proud British Lions of Trafalgar Square.

Every day she sits between them. She does this for as many hours as she can, until her wrists begin to ache or the hard steps make her butt hurt. Her hair is long and greasy and it hangs in stiff tangles in front of her grooved face. Her smile is genuine and ever-present. She loves her work.

The children who regularly shuffle their feet in this part of the square all know her, and they call her The Grey Lady. Many of the adults of the neighborhood do as well, because she has sat on the steps between the lions for many years.

The Grey Lady likes the lions. They make her feel safe. They remind her of her childhood, of King George the Sixth. Of Churchill's stout rhetoric on the radio and the way the island pulled together and thumbed its collective nose at the Fuehrer.

The Grey Lady flips to a fresh page in her sketchbook and pulls out a piece of charcoal. She holds the cover over the page because a light sprinkle of rain is falling under the cloudy sky.

She takes a deep breath and begins.

The tourists love her as much as the locals do. The Grey Lady sits almost every day on the steps of the library at Trafalgar Square between the two huge statues of the lions. Today she is sitting all the way over to the right, next to that lion. She is almost always on these steps at mid-day, looking for people that catch her eye.

She sketches and paints the people that do so with a deftness of hand that betrays her years. It's as if she sees past the surface of people, finding an emotional depth that she reflects in her work. The eyes of the people she sketches stare back at you from the paper as if they know something you do not.

She mutters quietly when she sketches, dressed every day in her gray smock. What people don't realize is that she is actually talking to someone.

"Mayhap the little girl over yon, smiling and singing to the finches upon the tree. A grand subject! Have you sufficient purple for her dress?"

"That's who I was looking at as well. Thank you, Doctor. I'm only sketching today. It is too wet to paint."

Doctor William Harvey, dressed like any

gentleman of the early 17th Century would be dressed, smiles at her.

Only she can see him, but that's how it always is.

"Remember to make the blood move like a river under the skin. Thy subject must live and breathe."

"Always, Doctor Harvey. Always."

She pushes the charcoal for a moment, capturing the little girl's smile forever. One of the birds is teasing her in the drawing, flittering just out of reach. Doctor William Harvey peeks over her shoulder.

"Your dexterity today is exemplary, Lady."

"Thank you." She looks up at him for a moment. "I just can't seem to get her hair right."

Big Ben begins to strike the noon hour.

She looks back down at the drawing, and it changes as she looks at it. It is now a drawing of a young couple who are suddenly standing in front of her looking very confused.

The Grey Lady finds herself exhaling when she was inhaling, and it forces her to let out a cough. She feels her heart rush into the next beat as if she were trying to experience two heartbeats simultaneously.

To her left, Doctor William Harvey is missing. In fact, she is startled to see she is now sitting on the left side of the steps beside the other lion. She is no longer wearing the hat that she left home with today. The gray dress she was wearing is gone, replaced with one of her gray tops and a pair of black jeans. All at once, the sun is shining without a trace of the clouds that had been in the sky moments ago over London. There is no evidence whatsoever of the light rain that had been falling just now.

Trafalgar Square is suddenly filled with screams. The sounds of auto accidents are everywhere.

The Grey Lady is an expert with faces. Every face she sees as she stands up and looks around Trafalgar is frightened and confused. Some are even sobbing. A few move their hands over themselves as if in total surprise to be in their own bodies.

The young couple her paper now claims she had been sketching stands there before her. They are looking around at their surroundings disoriented and lost. They pull each other a little closer.

The woman looks frightened and begins to cry. The man looks fretfully around the square, confused.

Doctor William Harvey walks up to the steps looking every bit as puzzled and confused as the people who are actually around her in the physical sense.

"Something has happened."

Two
Back

For the second time in Helen's life, she wakes up early on the morning that came after she lost one of her sons.

Numb, she climbs out of the bed where her husband sleeps. He will also wake up early. He usually does.

With her heart full of stones she pulls her light blue bathrobe over herself and steps barefoot into the hallway.

She walks over to Daniel's bedroom and opens the door.

Sam lays curled up in the blankets atop his brother's bed. Her youngest son. Her only surviving son.

The TV spills blue light into the room from the screen. He had fallen asleep to a videotape of Daniel playing high school baseball.

Helen smiles and begins to cry. She leaves

the room without turning off the television, closing the door quietly behind her.

Her bare feet walk down the steps on autopilot. She hears rain tapping on the skylight, steady and strong, but it doesn't really register with her.

She has to cook for the Colonel. He will be up soon. He won't be going into work today but he will still rise early like she did to begin the long process of welcoming Daniel home for the last time. Danny's body should be back in a couple of days.

The Colonel almost always wakes up at five no matter what's going on. Therefore, at five in the morning, she is usually already making his breakfast. It has been that way for many years now, since he became a senior officer and had hours that were more regular. She has developed an internal alarm clock that goes off 10 or 15 minutes before his does.

The rain stops abruptly, and she finds herself with her back leaning against the sink. A moment ago, she could swear she had just been getting the bacon out of the fridge.

Now, however, the bacon is already cooking. She closes her eyes and puts her head in her hands. *Must have zoned out for a second. It's understandable,* she decides. It's early and it's going to be a horrible day.

She sighs and tends to the bacon in the dimly lit kitchen. The smell of it has summoned Duke, their beagle, from a sound sleep on his favorite couch in the family room.

She fails to notice that she is wearing slippers now. She is also wearing different pajamas under her light blue robe. This, too, escapes her notice.

From the street, there is a faint thump and the breaking of glass. It doesn't register either. There is only the noise of the bacon and the depths of her thoughts on this sad morning.

Helen is unaware of much of anything. She contemplates the injustice of it all. The cruelty of God. This goddamned war. How easily the military gave her a strong, happy family...just so it could strip it away from her a piece at a time.

She opens the fridge and absent-mindedly reaches for the eggs. Nothing is where she remembers it being on the shelves last night. She smirks and pulls the eggs out. There are only four left in a carton she could swear she just bought yesterday.

She begins cracking the eggs into a mixing bowl. If there are only four left, she might as well use them all. The Colonel is going to have a nice big omelet today, whether he feels hungry or not.

Helen cooks in silence.

Flint, Michigan
June 2
7:00 AM

The alarm beeps. It beeps because it is not set to play a song. When she wakes to the radio her first subconscious instinct is always to incorporate the music into whatever dream she's having. The result is that she stays asleep. So the damned thing beeps, filling the room with an annoying noise.

Anne slaps the snooze bar on the top of the alarm clock and waits for the second alarm. The one on the bedside table is always the warm-up act for the one in her cell phone at 7:15.

The sounds of a car accident on the street below her window force her to get out of bed. Horns and screams draw her to the window, and she sees a few people running around below. They look agitated or confused, and they aren't shouting at each other so much as they are just shouting in general.

She pulls on an old *Ramones* T-shirt and walks out of her bedroom.

The first thing to catch her eye is that her couch is gone. The old leather couch from her former roommate is in its place; the one she had to replace when Jena got married and moved out. She stares at it for a second and then steps back to her bedroom door.

To her surprise, she does not see herself still lying there sleeping. She was kind of hoping that she was somehow dreaming this whole thing. That would explain it.

A sound from the other bedroom turns her head. Snoring.

Anne walks down the short hallway and knocks softly on the door.

"Val?"

The snoring continues. It sounds masculine, and Anne feels a little chill in her spine. Valerie doesn't usually snore anyway, and she hadn't said anything about bringing a guy home last night. It wouldn't be like her to do that on a whim.

She opens the door softly and knocks again.

"Va -- ?" she starts to say, and stops herself.

Jena and her husband Kyle are in the room. They are fast asleep in Jena's old bed, holding each other.

Kyle Jacobs is snoring like a man trying to rattle the weather-stripping off the windows. Either Jena does not hear it, or time has kindly taught her how to block the sound out completely.

Anne hears someone shouting in the street from below Jena's window. It isn't angry shouting. It's the mournful, confused shouting of someone who sounds lost. She can feel the wispy hairs on her arm standing up.

"What the...?"

Jena is sitting up in bed staring at her in the dark. They can barely make out the features of each other's face in the light that peeks in from the street.

Anne puts her hand over her forehead. "What are you guys doing here? Where's Valerie?"

Kyle snorts. Jena elbows him in the ribs. He stops snoring but simply smiles and continues sleeping.

"He can sleep through anything," she says, with a tone that suggests it isn't something about him that she enjoys. Jena climbs out of bed and walks over to the doorway. She gives her friend a hug.

Anne hugs back. "I thought you guys were in

Boston 'til next week."

Jena holds her tighter. "We are. Or, were. What the hell is going on?"

She lets go and goes to her dresser. She reaches for her phone.

"My *old* phone," Jena says. Anne watches as she picks it up. It is indeed the phone she used last year until Kyle got her the new one for Christmas.

Jena presses a couple of buttons on the phone and then draws a sharp breath as she stares at her left hand.

"Oh God! My wedding ring is gone!" Jena is rubbing her ring finger with the pinky and middle fingers on either side of her left index finger. Her engagement ring is there, but the gold band is absent.

Jena springs back to the bed and starts looking frantically for her wedding band. She pulls back the sheets and the blanket, exposing Kyle in his boxer shorts. This still fails to wake him up, but he rolls over to his side and puts his left hand over his face.

His ring is also missing. It becomes apparent quickly that neither ring is in the bed. Jena covers Kyle back up. In her state of adrenaline it does not occur to Jena to try harder to wake him up.

"Wait a minute," Anne says suddenly, "c'mere."

She leads her out of the bedroom into the living room they had shared as roommates. Entering the room, Anne clicks on a tall floor lamp as they walk past it.

The room is different than it had been last

night. Jena's stuff is everywhere. There is no trace of anything that belongs to Valerie.

Jena closes her eyes, takes a long breath through her nose, and shakes her head lightly back and forth.

"What the hell are we doing back here?" she asks.

"I don't know. This doesn't make any sense at all."

The little ceramic kangaroo Anne made in her ceramics class years ago in Colorado is on the entertainment center. She lifts it up and pulls out the little felt box.

Anne opens it and glances at it before she snaps it back shut. She tosses it over to Jena who catches it in the thin light of the lamp.

In the box, both her wedding band and Kyle's are in their slots. They sit there as they did while they waited to be put to use in July of last year.

"Why...what...?"

Jena turns around and sees the huge maroon-colored plastic folder that served as her wedding planner. It is bloated with notes and business cards, and it sits on the coffee table.

She sits down and opens it.

The last date marked off on the calendar inside it is June 1, of last year. She distinctly remembers marking off each of the days in that folder as the wedding came closer and closer.

Jena is still holding her cell phone. She looks at the screen, and her eyes go wide.

It shows the right day, June the 2nd. But it

shows the wrong year, claiming it to be last year. It also says that today is Monday, when it should be Tuesday. Yesterday had been a particularly long and rotten day for Jena, a proud representative of Mondays. She wasn't exactly wanting to live that day over again.

"Anne? What the hell?"

"I have no idea."

They stand in silence for a moment, desperate to get their bearings.

Down the hallway, Anne's cell phone begins to beep.

The time has come to wake up.

Colorado Springs
June 2
5:00 AM

Daniel Pemberton is about to open his eyes.

He gives them both a rub first and then opens them. He sees a ceiling bathed in the thin light of predawn, which creeps in through the edges of a window. The sun is about thirty minutes away from rising. There is a light fixture in the ceiling, and the shape of it suggests that he is in his old bed back home.

He is back in Colorado.

A turn of his head has the red numbers of his old alarm clock spelling out 5:00. Above it, there is a poster celebrating an Avalanche Stanley Cup victory from when he was a small boy.

He sits up and stares at it. This alarm clock stopped working around Christmas, and he bought a new one shortly before he shipped out for Kenya.

He isn't sure how he came to be here. He can't remember anything after the firefight at the gate.

There is a crash of glass and metal from the street, and Daniel hops out of his bed with more than a little surprise that he is able to do so. He steps to his window in time to see someone completely dazed step out of a car and collapse into what appear to be frustrated tears. No one else is on the street. The driver struck the light pole at the entrance to the Circle, which bows slightly at a new bend.

Overhead, he hears the powerful engines of a refueling tanker plane, the type that is usually referred to as a flying gas station. There is nothing unusual about this over an Air Force Base, but what he wouldn't have been able to see from his angle is that the plane is tilting its wings back and forth, straightening itself out, as if it had temporarily lost its bearings.

His nose tells him bacon is frying.

Bacon shouldn't be frying. Hell, he shouldn't even be here.

He knows. He knows he died. He's sure of it.

Daniel remembers each sensation that accompanied what happened to him in Ethiopia.

I blacked out, he thinks to himself. *They sent me home. Maybe I've been in a coma.*

He looks back at the bed. There is not a single

piece of medical equipment next to his bed, nothing anywhere in the room that would be used to monitor him. There's no way he was in a coma in his old bedroom in Colorado.

As he sits back down on his bed, letting the curtain fall back over the window, he realizes that the sensation of dying in Ethiopia is suddenly the foremost feeling he has. In his mind, it happened moments ago, right before he rubbed his eyes and opened them to find he was back home.

He looks at his hands and walks over to the mirror. He tilts his head back and to the right.

One spot on his neck is getting the bulk of his scrutiny as he looks at is reflection. He alternates running his fingers over it and looking closely at it.

There is nothing on his throat. No scar, not even a scratch. There is no indication that he was ever even wounded.

I'm not dreaming. I'm dead.

I'm not dead. I can't be dead. I'm home.

How can I be dreaming if I'm dead? Is that what death is?

Do you just…dream?

He pulls on a pair of sweatpants with the word ARMY screen printed on the middle of the thigh and walks down the stairs.

Daniel walks carefully and quietly, not knowing what to expect. His heart is racing at the prospect of seeing his mother again.

No.

This is wrong.

He's dead. He's sure of it.

Daniel tiptoes into the kitchen.

Helen is facing the counter next to the oven. Bacon is frying, and she is stirring eggs, milk, and other things together in a clear glass bowl.

A floorboard creaks, and she stops whisking.

Helen Pemberton, not usually prone to panic or surprise, turns around.

She sees her son Daniel, and she screams.

The whisk drops from her hands and clatters to the floor as her hands rush to cover her shocked mouth. Her eyes are wild and confused. The terror painted on her face is pure and genuine.

Daniel runs to her and holds her close. She is shaking.

He grasps his mother tightly, then shudders once and feels himself shiver twice. He tries to pull himself away but Helen is not going to let go of him any time soon.

"How are you here?" She whispers this softly into his ear. Even her whisper falters as she hugs him even tighter and repeats the question.

Confused and unsure of his surroundings, even though they are those of his home, Daniel Pemberton is surprised to hear himself ask her an awkward, genuine question.

"Mom? Is this Hell?"

She squeezes him even tighter, still unable to articulate any further words. Tears begin to flood her eyes as she opens them wide, wondering why the boy who used to hold onto her apron strings when he was smaller would say such a thing.

There is a thunder of footsteps on the stairs behind them. The Colonel and young Sam are racing down the stairs to see what is wrong with Helen in the kitchen. Her scream woke Sam from a deep sleep, and the youngster shot out of his bed before his brain even registered why.

Daniel's little brother stops at the foot of the stairs next to his father. Both of them look confused and disoriented.

They are only seeing the person Helen is embracing from the back, but there is no mistaking who it is.

"Danny!" Sam shouts, and he runs to his brother and mother. The Colonel stands there in shock. He's turning his head back and forth slowly in an effort to shake cobwebs from inside his head.

The bacon is turning black on the stove. Duke the beagle and a cat named Prince lick uncooked egg off the linoleum as it oozes out of the metal wires of the whisk.

10 miles south of Yreka, California
June 2
4:00 AM

Francis Guagenti should not be here.

He suddenly appears on a moving bus that is swerving violently on a highway. He's not aware of that at first because he has been asleep. As the driver attempts to correct the swerve, he finds himself on the floor of the little cabin in the back. That wakes him up.

He recognizes the bus. The last time he was

on it, it was painted up with his face on one side and the words *Promise Express* in a big, friendly font on the other. Both sides also bore his name.

Only a few moments ago, he was running around the track on the grounds of the White House, getting a bit of exercise before a meeting. It had been lightly sprinkling in D.C. He had been wearing a blue Yale sweatshirt and shorts. He had resisted the urge to grab a doughnut from the kitchen on his way through the residence. His wife would reward him for that later when she checked up on him with the members of his Secret Service team, who were wisely more afraid of the First Lady than they were of the President.

Now, as he woke up with a start, he wondered if he had only been dreaming about jogging around the White House grounds. He found the prospect of dream-jogging very sad, for the briefest of moments that it was there. Realizing he was on this bus had fixed that.

Guagenti had been sleeping, just as he had been doing a year ago in this same exact situation. He slept under direct orders of his wife soon after the bus pulled out of Eugene, Oregon on its way south to Sacramento. He had a full day and night planned all along California's great Central Valley, from Yuba City to Bakersfield. Concerned for the dark circles her husband the candidate was developing under his eyes, and knowing he would be standing next to Hollywood's beautiful people around 36 hours later, she had demanded bed for him and plenty of it. The candidate slept in the back of his bus, and his spouse sat outside the door, reading a book with some coffee. She was therefore in a position to growl at anyone who dared attempt to approach the door.

As he hits the floor, he hears the First Lady scream on the other side of the door. The door to his little mobile sanctuary bursts open, and his agents rush into the room. There are only a few of them because at this moment in time Guagenti hasn't been elected yet. Still, they are men he knows well.

"He's secure," the senior agent says into his collar. Senior Agent Bickell lowers his weapon and the others follow suit.

"What the hell's going on here, Bicks?"

"I have no idea, Mister President."

The bus finally rolls to a safe stop on the side of the highway. All around it are the sounds of multiple automobile accidents that have just happened in the pre-dawn darkness. There seem to have been a lot of them.

Just south of Gore, Ethiopia
June 2
3:00 PM

Balah finds himself sitting in his mother's home, surrounded by several members of his family. Everyone looks surprised to suddenly be there together.

If the meal on the table is any indication, it is his birthday. No one looks much like they have anything to celebrate as panic begins to thread itself through each of them.

His mother is talking a blue streak in the kitchen. Each sentence is louder and faster than the one before it. Everyone else is yelling, too, in Amharic.

"Where did you all come from?"

"Why am I here?"

"What is going on?"

"How did I come to be in this house?"

It takes Balah a moment to notice that his father is there, standing outside the window in the yard. He jumps up and pushes through the door to his father.

No one has seen his father since he was sent to hold the Blue Nile in Benishangul by King Roti's Royal Army, one year and three months ago.

No one realizes it yet, but it was only three months before this day.

His mother notices him run to the door. "Balah!" she shouts, and then she sees who he is running out to see. "Phillipe!" she screams as she runs to her husband.

Most of the family stares after her in stunned silence.

Phillipe holds his wife close and stares at his son.

In an instant, Balah understands. There is a look in his father's eyes, and somehow Balah recognizes it as the look of a man who has seen and felt the same thing he has.

It is the look of a man who has died and suddenly finds himself alive in some kind of impossible dream.

Balah is very certain that he has the same look on his face, and that his father Phillipe has noticed and recognized it as well.

Suddenly, there is a panicked chorus of voices outside of their home. The road is filled with other families who have suddenly found themselves in the wrong places.

Balah goes to the door and looks out, walking right past his father. He is happy to see him, but he is in shock like everyone else.

He sees at least two faces right away that belong to people who have died in the past year.

The war has been unkind to their village.

He and his father make seven who were believed to be dead.

"We are truly...here?" Phillipe whispers to his son, as he steps beside him at the door.

"I think we are in Heaven, father. I think we are in The Glory."

Phillipe smiles at his son and says nothing. In that moment he understands, without having to say the words out loud, that his son has experienced the same misfortune that he did.

Phillipe pulls his son closer. Balah tightens at first and then softens. His father was never one to embrace his children. Balah has only ever wanted to be held by him, and here it is. They both had to die first, but here it is.

Balah feels the sudden push of his family crowding around them. Everyone has assumed for some time that Phillipe was dead. His sudden reappearance is nothing short of a miracle of God.

Balah wonders if the family had been told yet that he has died. If he had to guess, he would say that the news had not reached them yet.

Perhaps he didn't die. If this is his birthday, perhaps he never joined the attack on the Americans.

None of this makes any sense.

He looks at the members of his family who have gathered here for his birthday. It is the same group of people who attended his birthday last year. The last one he figured he was going to have.

He frowns at the thought that he was right about that.

Balah pulls his smile back up as the family embraces Phillipe. This is not a time for them to see him sad.

Balah weeps. He cries and cries hard, as does the rest of his excited, confused family.

Balah pretends that his tears are tears of joy.

Inside the house the frosting is melting on a cake with a large 14 on it.

Three
Two-Headed Eagle

Flint, Michigan
June 2
7:21 AM

"So," he begins. Then he inhales and says, "what do we know?" as he exhales.

Ron is the News Director, and he is smoking in the newsroom. This is illegal in the workplace because this is not the 1960s. At the moment Ron doesn't care and no one is stupid enough to call him out on it. Even the rabid anti-smokers are still in deep enough shock over the morning's events that they aren't complaining.

Everyone is still freaking out about the strange teleportation and time shift as it becomes more and more obvious that it was global. Being professionals they are doing their best to freak out quietly and privately, typically away from everyone else. The people in this room are doing their best to pull themselves together. They do this because they are in a newsroom.

This is the shared information nerve center of two radio stations, a television station, and a newspaper. They are the award-winning staff that makes it function. If there is any one place in their collective world where they can get answers to this insane mystery...this is that place. They do not have the luxury of freaking out right now. They have a job to do.

Their job is to cope as best they can and try to make sense out of all of this. Ron's nature, in particular, *demands* that he find a way to make sense of this. Almost nothing in the last 21 minutes has made any sense at all.

Ron quit smoking as a New Year's Resolution; the first such resolution he had ever managed to hang onto to the month of June. However, he suddenly found that he had blinked into existence at his desk for no reason, having been at home in bed. He had been sleeping in...truly a rare thing for him...before his annual check-up with his doctor to check on his stress levels. Those stress levels are off the charts at the moment.

The entire world seems to have been tampered with. As far as they are able to make sense of the incoming information, the effects of this occurrence are being felt everywhere. This happened suddenly in a way that defies speculation or explanation.

Reports have been coming in over the wire services from sources just as confused as Ron and his staff are. A great number of people seem to be dying all over the world as a result of it.

Through the haze of it all, he managed to find an opened pack of his old favorite brand sitting there on his desk. They were still fresh, most of the pack was still there, and they were right next to his old flip-top lighter.

Familiarity, in the form of smoke, is breeding a little bit of sanity for Ron in a situation more insane than a dog show at a steakhouse. The cigarettes are familiar. They have not been around for the last six months, but they had been a key part of his life for the 240 or so months before them.

Most days, there are five other people in the newsroom at this hour. This is the case right now.

One of them is a woman named Valerie. She no longer works the morning shift and is none too impressed to suddenly find herself at work instead of home in bed. She is the next person to speak up in the newsroom.

"Atomic clock in Boulder says the time is accurate, the date...seems to be right, too. The only discrepancy is the year. It has the same mistake everything else has. Our phones are right, too, according to Boulder."

"So...so far as we can tell..."

"Yeah," Valerie says.

The entire room falls silent, listening to what she says next.

Ron walks over to a huge map of the world that dominates one wall. "Somebody wants us to think that everyone everywhere went back in time together. Exactly one year. And for some reason, we all ended up where we were at that moment, doing what we were doing. Some kind of weird teleportation thing. Or maybe some kind of chemical attack to make us think it happened."

"My mother called me, Ron," a man at one of the desks says. "My sister is pregnant again, and they can't find any sign of my little niece."

"So it looks like this...really happened?" Ron asks. He takes another long drag from the cigarette. He had missed cigarettes - a lot.

"And we all remember the missing year."

"Every bit of it."

"Especially moving to the afternoon desk," adds Valerie. Valerie has always used mistimed humor as a coping mechanism.

"Did we get a hold of your friend at the observatory?"

The woman he posed the question to is holding up her index finger at him, and finishing her goodbyes with someone on the other end of a phone call.

"It's still dark in Hawaii," says the woman, named Tina, as she hangs up. "They're confirming star positions, comets...all matter of trackable space junk. They say everything matches June second of last year. Whatever happened here happened everywhere. That includes...up there. The whole universe looks like it backed up exactly one earth year."

Ron blinks slowly. When his eyes are open, they are wide...processing...

This is too big. This is too much. This is impossible...

"And there's no word from the White House yet?" he finally asks. He stubs out his cigarette.

"It's last June, Ron. The President is on the

campaign trail. Former President Wolcott probably would be, too."

"Wonderful," Ron groans.

"So, we can assume that Wolcott's staff is running a very confused West Wing right now, if I had to guess. The wrong staff is there, the wrong portrait is on the wall. Vice President Delahanty could very well be in the Situation Room with the Joint Chiefs. If *he* was in Washington."

"Someone find out if he was," Ron says.

"What was he doing a year ago?" Tina asks.

"He was the Vice President. What was he doing yesterday?" Valerie says.

"Think about it," says the morning show co-anchor. She has just walked in from the set to see if there is anything new. Her suit is neat, her hair is an immaculate blond haystack, and she is wearing the strange makeup that news anchors have to put on for HD cameras. "It has to be total chaos at The White House right now."

"Near as we can tell, this happened everywhere," Val adds. "So the people in the West Wing right now are all people who got on with their lives back in January after Guagenti was sworn in."

"That's true," Ron says, nodding.

The anchor starts to put her hand on her forehead but stops before she makes contact with her makeup. "We won't hear from them until they get a handle on what's happened. That could be a while. It's only been…what…a half-hour?"

The anchor sighs and blinks very slowly before she adds another morsel of food for thought. "Which begs the question…" she tilts her head slightly, "…who *is* the President right now?"

The room is silent for a few seconds.

"Guagenti," Ron says emphatically. "We all remember his election. We all covered the race. We all watched the inauguration right here in the news room with eighty dollars worth of pizza and beer."

"Which we got on trade, right?" Valerie is smiling as she says it. It is the first smile anyone has had since this happened this morning. She seems to be the only person in the room taking this whole thing in stride. No one can understand how she can, but she is.

"But now it's a year ago, Ron," Tina says, ignoring Valerie. "He hasn't won yet. Hell, he just won his delegate race, what, last week?"

The Democratic Nomination had been quite a bitter fight. It eventually proved to be a precursor for an even more tempestuous Presidential race that followed. Tina had gone to Los Angeles to cover the convention in August for their broadcast cluster.

Valerie glances up at a television and suddenly falls silent.

"That's right," Tina continues. "Oregon put him over the top at the end of May. Your old stomping grounds, right Val?"

Valerie has not responded and is still fixated on what she sees on the TV. Everyone notices this and looks up to see what's so fascinating.

An official statement from the French Government is being carried on CNN.

However, the *late* Prime Minister of France is reading it.

Ron grabs the remote and turns up the volume on that particular screen.

The statement is being carried live. Prime Minister Michel, a shocked look on his face, is reading a statement about the strange event. He is fighting back tears, and he is flanked by his replacement, Prime Minister Larienne. She looks just as confused as her predecessor.

They had been friends, and Minister Michel's death on the Autobahn only 11 months after leaving office was one of the worst days of her life, and one of the saddest of their nation's history.

Then came the event, a short time ago.

Suddenly, Michel had appeared in his former office at one in the afternoon. It was decorated the way he had always kept it decorated, and Larienne found herself in a different suit, sitting on the other side of the desk.

"Michel died a month ago, right?" Valerie almost whispered the question.

Ron, never taking his eyes from the screen, snuffs out his cigarette and lights another. "Right."

The news ticker on the bottom of the screen is suddenly full of stories about people who had died in the past year now suddenly having returned, no doubt a part of whatever it is that has happened.

"I'll be right back," Valerie says, rising suddenly. She leaves the newsroom without another word.

Valerie runs out of the room and down the long hallway, past Studio A, and into the fancy break room no one really uses. She walks over to the windows and presses a couple of buttons on her cell phone. She puts it up to her ear, her pulse quickening like an excited hummingbird.

It rings six times before a confused voice answers on the other end.

Oregon City, Oregon
June 2
4:27 AM

Pamela Harrison wakes up to the bedside phone.

She starts to reach for the phone and then stops.

It rings a second time, and she shakes the cobweb of sleep out of her head. The phone shouldn't be ringing right now.

A third ring. It shouldn't be ringing because she's dead. She shouldn't be here to hear it.

A fourth ring. There was a hospital room. Why had she been in that room? It was sudden. There was a pain, a sharp, sudden pain in her chest..."

It rings for a fifth time. Instinctively, she grabs it from the rocker and looks at the digital display.

VAL CELL

As the sixth ring ends, she presses the green

button on the phone.

"Valerie?"

In Flint, Michigan, Valerie begins to cry. "Oh my God. Mom...you're...alive." She smiles, and her mother starts to cry with her. "Oh my god, Mom, you're alive."

Her mother is crying with her on the phone.

"What...wh...am I having a dream?"

"Mom. Listen carefully. I'm at work. I know this sounds crazy, but hear me out. No one knows why, but for some reason...everybody went back in time exactly one year about half an hour ago. Everybody remembers the year we lost. But it's like it never happened. I was asleep in my apartment one minute and wide awake here at work the next. I was doing mornings a year ago."

Pamela says nothing.

"Mom...stay with me Mom. Say something."

"Honey, you're not making any sense."

"Mom, do you remember...dying?"

There is continued silence from her end of the phone as Pamela turns on the lamp next to the bed.

Her room is exactly how she remembers it. With the exception of the lamp, which she just turned on. She remembers it shattering as she reached for the phone as the heart attack began. She had been sitting up in bed, reading before she went to sleep. It had been Groundhog's Day. She remembered being angry that this happened because she ate right and worked out regularly.

Finally, she says..."yes."

Valerie sniffles on her end of this bizarre,

unexpected conversation. "Mom," she wipes her nose, "you have to go see your doctor this week. You have a second chance, Mom. I can't lose you like that again."

Pamela is bawling now. This can't be real. Everything feels real, but this can't be real.

"Valerie, I…"

"I'll be back home as quick as I can, Mom. I suspect the airlines are going to be crazy for a few days. But I'm coming home as soon as I can get there."

Pamela smiles so wide that Valerie can feel it through her cell phone.

"Just hurry."

"I love you, Mom."

"I love you too, Vally. I…I just hope this is…real."

Valerie smiles.

"I do, too, Mom. I really do."

Pamela wipes her eyes. "Get back to work, Vally. Find out what's going on and call me later. Hopefully you can explain it when you do."

Valerie sniffs loudly with what feels like a pint of liquid draining out of the front of her face.

"I will. Count on it."

"Goodbye, sweetheart."

"Don't say that, Mom. Say you'll talk to me later." Her voice is shaking.

Pamela smiles and wipes more tears. "Talk to you later then."

She hangs up the phone in its cradle next to the bed and looks over at what used to be John's side of the bed.

Her face sighs, and her eyes fill with even more tears.

She wonders why, if this is real, was it only *one* year. If it could have been four years more, she would have been able to hold John again.

If this is some kind of joke, that alone makes it an especially cruel one.

Cleveland, Ohio
June 2
7:01 AM

Oliver Wolcott wakes to a brusque knock at his door, which then opens abruptly and loudly.

"Mr. President!" It is an excited exclamation, not a question.

Immediately, Wolcott is aware of a number of things. His wife is not beside him. He is not in his bedroom at the family manor in Windsor, Connecticut. He appears to be in a rather nice hotel room. He feels the unmistakable ache of jet lag, and he sees his old, thickly embroidered Air Force One jacket sitting on a chair opposite the bed.

Furthermore, he cannot help but notice that he has far more agents in his room right now than are typically assigned to his detail now that he is out of office. Each of the men looks confused, and they are armed. That combination of factors is disquieting. Each of them had been assigned to his detail when he had been the Commander in Chief.

The senior agent assigned to him, though, remains the same. The man got along very well with Wolcott, and therefore had the opportunity to stay on as the senior agent in charge of his security detail when Oliver Wolcott failed to win reelection.

The air in the room is thick with tension and a firm layer of panic.

"What the hell is going on, Steve?"

Senior Agent Steven Hawking, who has heard every possible joke about his name, looks incredibly agitated. He also looks like he has had either 700 cups of coffee or a fresh set of batteries inserted into him somewhere.

"Mr. President...all of us just sort of appeared here, sir."

"Appeared...appeared where...what the hell are you talking about, Steve?"

"Sir...we...for lack of a better term...we all just...teleported, or something. I don't know. Like Star Trek without the beam and the Scottish guy in the red shirt."

"Whatever each of us was doing...we were interrupted and just appeared here. I was in the gym at the mansion. You were upstairs sleeping."

Agent Sayers is at the door, her eyes darting around the room, taking it all in. "I was in D.C.," she says, "sitting outside the Oval, minding the President. What about you, Hendricks?

A third agent holsters his weapon. "The residence," he says. "First Lady's morning detail. Waiting for her to come out of the residence to head off to a breakfast meeting with the Young

Democrats."

We were all somewhere else, sir, and now we're all here."

"Where's here?"

Hawking drops the newspaper on the bed that had been sitting in the hallway on the other side of the former President's door.

"We appear to be in Cleveland, sir. Presidential Suite of the hotel we stayed at when we were campaigning last year. Why we're here again, I couldn't say...but we are...uh...working on that."

Agent Sayers hands her phone to Hawking. "I'm through to the White House."

"This is Agent Hawking. Nutmeg is secure...repeat...Nutmeg is secure."

He pauses and listens. He listens for almost a full minute before he says "Understood. Standing by," and hands the phone back to Agent Linda Sayers.

"Mr. President...this is going to sound unbelievable..."

Just north of Redding, California
June 2
5:56 AM

"We should be at the airport in about 15, sir."

Working their way through the snarls on the I-5 took a hell of a lot longer than any of them would have preferred. There were traffic accidents everywhere, and judging by what they were hearing from Washington that story was the same all over the country.

There had been no request for a police escort. The police were more than a little busy this morning.

Cars, semis, SUVs...there were piles of twisted steel all over the country. Given the time differences the scenarios had to be far worse all over the world. Much of the United States west of the Mississippi had still been in bed when The Event occurred. For that small favor of timing, the President was grateful.

President Guagenti had once had the opportunity to drive the Autobahn deep in the mountains of Germany. He remembered how fast everyone, including himself, drove on it. He shuddered to think about the number of people that undoubtedly died in fiery wrecks all along the length of that scenic, fabled roadway. People killed when they suddenly found themselves behind the wheel at an incredible rate of speed, not unlike his own bus driver. Guagenti knew he was incredibly fortunate to be numbered among the living right now, instead of the dead.

The chaos on one of California's busiest highways was heart-wrenching. They had stopped at first because they were forced to do so when they went off the road. It quickly became clear to President Guagenti that there was nothing he could do here but be in the way. They had to leave the scenes of the multiple accidents that had happened around him. The only place he could be useful right now was in Washington. It was a cruel reality to face.

He had spent much of the last hour avoiding the windows of the bus. There was nothing out there he wanted to see. His wife, on the other hand, couldn't help but stare.

How, she wondered as she glanced over her husband, *does he* fix *this?* His eyes met hers, and she forced herself to smile.

Without a word, he gathered what looked important into his briefcase. In this strange situation, he had no idea what papers might be important, so he would leave almost all of them behind. They would be well protected anyway.

There would be a Department of Defense plane waiting for them on the strip in Redding. It would get the President, the First Lady, and the key elements of his White House that were with him back to Washington as quickly as possible to try and make some sense out of all of this.

What he hadn't been able to do during what had become the longest bus ride of his life was contact three of his Senior Staff. Those calls continued as the bus moved off the Interstate and made a beeline for the airport at Redding. For the final leg of the trip they had as much police escort as the State Police were able to muster given the situation in the past two hours. He had not requested it, but an aide had.

Guagenti's nerves caused him to fidget with his Yale ring with the fingers on either side of it.

The world was a mess, and technically he might not be the president right now if all of this was indeed real. Fortunately for him, everyone continued to act like he *was* in fact the president. He was certainly going to continue to act the part.

His phone rang. The number belonged to the White House Switchboard.

"Hello," he said, with more urgency than he intended.

"Your Deputy Chief of Staff has been located, Mr. President, and he is on his way in from New York."

"Thank you," he said, and hung up the phone. There were only a couple to go, and his Chief of Staff was one of them.

He was kicking himself now for insisting after they won Oregon that Walt take some time off from the campaign and do some hiking. Hiking relaxed the man, and he sorely needed to relax before the convention and the final push.

The unfortunate truth to that was that where Walt was hiking, he was unreachable. He was likely to be unreachable for another few hours before he would be close enough to civilization to touch base with him. With all the chaos breaking out across the country, they were having a hell of a time putting together a search party to find the man and get him to the White House as quickly as possible.

There was a feeling in the pit of President Francis Guagenti's stomach that he was going to need Walt's wisdom to get through this. It was right next to another feeling, one that suggested his predecessor, old Wolcott, might try to find a way to hang on to the West Wing if it really was last year again. There was no better man to have in your corner in a fight than Walter Randall. No matter which of the two fights...or both...he might face.

The First Lady squeezed his hand.

"Have everything, hon?" she asked. She smiled, betraying the dread she felt after absorbing all the horrors of a body-strewn highway for two hours.

"Almost," he replied softly, smiling. He took a deep breath. "Almost."

The White House
June 2
9:25 AM

"We have confirmation that Air Force One is in the air."

"I know," Denise Tycheson barked at the runner from the Communications Office. "His flight should be arriving from Ohio any time now."

"Um, not *that* Air Force One, ma'am. President *Guagenti's* plane. It became Air Force One as soon as he climbed aboard, correct? They took off from Redding about 15 minutes ago."

Denise took a deep breath and tilted her head back. "You're right, I'm sorry. Guagenti's the President now. It just...it just seems..."

"I know, ma'am. It seems weird to all of us to be here when our guy isn't technically in charge."

"Isn't he?" asked the former Chief of Staff for former Vice President Delahanty. "We're all here, hardly anyone from the Guagenti administration is, and so far there is no official documentation anywhere that proves the man won an election. An election, I remind you, that apparently hasn't happened yet. Am I wrong?"

Denise Tycheson decided to ignore the little worm's comment since her gut told her it bordered on treason, especially since she agreed, on some level, with the premise of his statement. She turned instead to face the communications runner and saw that he had been joined by the Assistant Communications Director.

He was looking at her expectantly. She frowned, shut her eyes for a moment, and then glared back at him.

"Tony, tell Charlie to continue to say absolutely nothing. No one from the Press Room gets back here, I don't care who they are or how many favors they think they're owed. We have no comment, including the fact that we have no comment. I'm not releasing anything until we've had a chance to sit down with Guagenti's people and figure out what the hell is going on here."

She looked at the rest of the senior staff, a collection of people who had worked together for four years, had hoped for four more, and been denied. Here they were playing the strangest coda she'd ever heard of. And she had the conductor's baton.

"Everyone start tapping on the old spider webs. I need some answers. I need to know what the hell is going on here."

This didn't happen on our watch, she thought to herself, *and I still have to clean it up.*

She picked up her coffee cup and found it empty. She shouted back over her shoulder as she prepared to close the door behind her as she ducked into her former office. It was decorated in her style from a year ago. This whole thing was so stupid. Stupid and impossible.

"And somebody get me Walter Randall, and a cup of coffee…in whatever order you can!"

Entering Washington, D.C. Airspace
June 2
9:31 AM

Oliver Wolcott is 66 years old as he sees Washington D.C. appear below him from the office suite of Air Force One.

Or…is he 65 again? If the people who have tried to explain this situation to him are correct, then he and everyone else are physically a year younger. That possibility seems both incredible and impossible.

The phone on the desk rings. It's a sound he hasn't heard since his last flight on this plane six months ago.

"Sir, we have President Guagenti's aircraft on the line now."

"Go ahead," Wolcott says.

"Connecting you now, sir."

After a second or two and an unquiet click, he hears the voice of his most bitter political rival on the other end of the phone.

"Joyriding in my plane again, Ollie?"

"I'd say 'good morning', Mister President, but we both know better."

"That we do, Mister President. I understand you're about to land at Reagan?"

"Yes. I'd like to offer you some help, sir. My staff will be the ones in the building. It could take the better part of a day to get your people back in place. I can focus on the background noise and help them make a clean transitio…"

"Ollie," Guagenti says, cutting him off. "I think I'd like a little more help from you than that. There's a lot of work to do, a lot to consider, and a country that could get pretty ugly in the coming days if we don't play our cards right. I'd like to have us work together here at the beginning of this mess, trying to show that the government is putting aside party squabbles and trying…no, *making* the absolute best effort to get everything to make sense again."

Wolcott considers this for a split-second, trying to decide just exactly what the man is asking him to do. He allows himself a few seconds to smile and think to himself that he knew this man was not up to the job. Wolcott's ancestors were counted among the founding fathers. An Oliver Wolcott signed the Declaration of Independence. Oliver Wolcott Junior served as the Treasury Secretary for the first two presidents. America needed a Wolcott again. They would regret not giving him his second term.

"Ollie," the president's voice says from the phone speaker, "I'm looking to present a united front here, trying to make sure things don't get out of hand. Are you in?"

Wolcott turns his head, deep in thought as his plane begins its descent on the approach to a very locked-down airport.

It was not so long ago...

"I serve at the will and pleasure of the office, Mister President."

"Thank you, Ollie. Step one...don't do anything with the press until I get there. We say nothing until we know what we're going to say."

"Do you have any idea what that might be yet, Mister President?"

Francis Guagenti took a deep breath.

"Not as such, no."

Flint, Michigan
June 2
10:06 AM

Ron is mesmerized by it.

His news room staff, the morning and noon anchors...everyone in the building...they are all mesmerized by it. Everyone around him is doing the same thing people are doing in every other news room around the world.

They are watching the network carry the unbelievable story. Ron watches the network anchors closely as they deliver the improbable updates to his audience in the Tri-Cities area and beyond. There is nothing for him to add right now on the local level as the story unfolds and enters its third hour of existence. There is nothing else for anyone to do except make certain nothing happens to the feed.

Ron sits in his office and smokes the last cigarette in the pack while watching the wide screen TVs affixed to one wall of the room. He, like most people, finds himself in a mild state of shock, trying to get his bearings. And he, like most people, is failing.

It has reached the point now where he's only hearing snippets of the sentences the network anchors are delivering. All three screens are set up to run off the same remote depending on which box he points it at. He is tapping his way through the channels on each TV.

It's as if he's hoping one of them will start to make sense.

It's confusing for most people to listen to, but the volume is turned up on all three screens. Ron's brain has always managed to differentiate the audio from up to three channels at the same time.

"...believed that the worldwide death toll could be in the millions..."

"...impossible as it is to believe, that the entire world could have somehow traveled..."

"...Tropical Storm Beatrice, which had been expected to strengthen as it approached the Carolinas overnight, has instead disappeared completely off the map..."

He changes all three channels.

"...widespread panic and rioting being reported everywhere..."

"...nearly every government has had nothing official to say yet, except to call for calm while they attempt to ascertain exactly *what* has..."

"...the woman with the gun has been identified, but her name is being withheld for the time being. An eyewitness who knows the suspect claims that she had been pregnant...*very* pregnant, she said, before the event...reportedly expecting a child next month in fact."

The woman on the screen was shouting something to someone off-camera. She was wearing a half-shirt.

"As you can see," the announcer continued, "she is clearly *not* pregnant as her standoff with the Massachusetts State Police enters its third..."

With one tap of his thumb, Ron mutes all three screens at once.

He buries his face in his hands, the cigarette smoldering in front of his forehead between two fingers.

The Hague, The Netherlands
June 2
1:00 PM

Hans digs in his ear canal with a pinky finger. He is at his guard station, reading a book as usual when the words on the page change and frighten the hell out of him.

He sits up in a hurry, pushing his folding chair back against the wall, and dropping the book onto the desk. It closes itself as he does so, the cover revealing it to be a book he finished reading some time ago. The book he has been reading today is gone.

Hans reaches toward the book and is just short of touching it when he hears the shouting down the main cell block outside of his office.

He yanks the nightstick out of his belt with so much force that it nearly flies up and smacks him in the face. He fumbles with his keys and opens the door, steps through, and locks it behind him. This is the policy, and he never breaks it.

No one goes in or out of this hall without his knowledge and approval. This is a high-security detention facility used by the United Nations for the highest-profile prisoners awaiting hearings and transfers.

There are only two prisoners in the hall. One is a Belgian finance minister, Harold DeCreste, who stands accused of sex crimes. The other is the Ethiopian King, Roti. Roti faces war crimes, and accusations of genocide. The African has only been here for a couple of months.

Hans walks down the hall, which has only six cells in it. All six cells are empty.

Somehow Hans just knows that he is going to be blamed for this.

Four
Proud Sons of Africa

Kitale, in the Rift Valley
Kenya
June 2
3:00 PM

In the cradle of civilization, not far from a dig site where some of the earliest skeletal remains of human beings were dug up...Billy Pemberton suddenly finds himself on one knee firing his M4.

A fierce firefight is underway, although he isn't sure at first who he is shooting at, and so he drops to the ground ceasing his firing. From the sudden absence of noise and projectiles everyone else has had the same instinct as well.

He rolls to a safe spot behind a wrecked jeep that lies on its side. At some point it was on fire, but that was some time ago. Now it lies ruined, pocked with dents and bullet holes. It sits on the side of an abandoned street in a non-descript town surrounded by tan and yellow buildings.

The air is hot, and it reeks of garbage and rot. Everything has become quiet as a tomb now, which makes him nervous. The only sound is the buzzing of insects around an abandoned fruit market at the corner of the street. He doesn't see anyone else, but he hears panicked breathing all around the area. There is the occasional cough from the dust.

An open door behind him would grant him an opportunity to find a better vantage point. Such a nest would likely help him to get his bearings. Billy climbs the steps carefully, his weapon at the ready, his ears tuned to every cough and creak and slip that happens around him. There are no shots being fired.

He's halfway up the stairs before it occurs to him that he isn't supposed to be here.

He's dead.

Billy remembers dying. It isn't the sort of thing you would forget if you were aware enough when it happened. He remembers the whistle of the incoming projectile, whatever it was. A grenade, a bomb, a rocket...the possibilities are endless and he isn't sure at all. What it *was*, was now a moot point. It was the next-to-last-thing he would ever hear. The *last* thing, of course, was the explosion itself.

The explosion that killed him.

He doesn't remember any pain, and for that he is thankful. He doesn't like the idea of spending eternity reliving battles, possibly as a ghost, and feeling the pain of his own death.

He is certain that he died. He remembers clinching up, bracing for the explosion that he had no time to dive away from. Instead he dove toward it, trying to shield Sgt. Harris. He was successful in that effort, even though he never knew it.

Yet here he is. Doubt, therefore, is starting to creep into his mind about the events of that day.

Did he, in fact, die? Has he been unconscious for a time, and then woke up in the middle of...

...no.

He was suddenly firing his weapon. Out of nowhere. There had been no awakening in a hospital bed. He had been on one knee opening fire. He was just...*there*. He was *in the act*. There was no return to consciousness. There was just this battle, and he was suddenly in the city fighting in it, moments after feeling himself being blown up on the side of the mountain.

He snaps out of the thoughts. He knows he's exposed on this stairwell and needs to find a safer spot. Priorities.

The stairs lead to a second floor and then a third. No one else seems to be in the building, and he selects a room that offers an excellent view of the street he had suddenly appeared on with his rifle.

He glances at the balconies and visible windows of neighboring windows. Someone is in a window across the street, but he appears to be American. They lock eyes for a moment and exchange hand signals. They also exchange confused looks with each other before they melt into the darkness of their respective rooms.

That's when Billy notices it.

A mountain rises up above the forest of roofs on the other side of the building in the direction his compass tells him is due west. It looms over the city in a way that isn't right.

Billy furrows his brow. They weren't next to a mountain in a city when he remembers being hit. They were *on* a mountain, several clicks away from a city. Furthermore, they had been surrounded by thin, ugly trees and dry shrubs. Not thin, ugly buildings.

Men are starting to fill the street below. Some are Americans, and some are skinnies. Everyone has their rifle slung over a shoulder and their hands either up in the air or out in front of them.

Billy looks across at his mirror in the other building. The man nods at him and turns to walk out of his room. Billy does the same, curious.

On his way down the stairs, he meets up with Pvt. Henry Cooper. He's sitting on the stairs, holding his weapon tightly.

"Coop?" he says, trying not to frighten the kid.

Cooper looks up, his hand on the stock of his gun. He jumps up and turns to face Billy, pulling his hand away from the weapon's trigger. The Private is jumpy and confused...like everyone else.

"Private Cooper sir as ord...Lieutenant? Is that you?"

"What are we doing here, Coop?"

"What are *you* doing here, sir? You're," he breathes in and out rapidly, confused and nervous, "you're freakin' *dead*, sir."

Billy says nothing, but pauses on the stairs for a moment to look at the young kid. Then he descends the rest of the way down.

"Your GPS running, Coop?"

Private Cooper stares at him without moving.

"COOP?" Billy Pemberton doesn't mean to shout that, but he does.

Cooper looks down for a second and presses a button on a piece of his gear. "Yes sir. Buffering."

"I want to know where we are, right the hell now."

"You died, Lieutenant," he says. He is tapping the screen of his GPS, waiting for it to latch onto the nearest satellite. "I was there. It was around Thanksgiving, north of The Bor. Mount Damot."

"I remember. But here I am."

"Here we all are, sir. I was on R&R at Mombasa, swimming in the ocean. Next thing I know, I'm..."

His GPS beeps.

"We're just north of the Equator in Kitale. This...is this the Battle of Kitale? Oh man...look at the date!"

He hands the GPS to Billy. The display claims that the date is June 2nd of last year. A day about four and one-half months before he remembers being killed.

Coop stands up and looks around, sheltered by a disabled truck. He takes a deep breath and says what everyone has been thinking.

"We already fought this battle. We wiped out 100 Ugandans that were holding the city. The rest of them slipped back around Mt. Elgon and went back across their own border."

Billy points at the mountain visible through the doorway.

"That's Mt. Elgon then," Billy replies. "It looks too lush to be one of those rocky bastards I remember from Ethiopia."

Cooper closes his eyes. "We were done with those rocky sons-of-bitches six months ago, sir. We breeched Addis Ababa back in March."

"Back in March?"

"It's June, sir, or…at least it *was* June. According to this," he took his GPS back, "it still is June, but it's the wrong year."

"And I died in November? And you remember that?"

"How is this possible, sir? How can we be back here and remember everything that happened in the last year? How can you be standing here in the first place? You were dead, sir. You were…you were really, *really* dead, sir. That damn shell landed right next to you and you dove on top of it."

"Lieutenant?"

The question comes from the door.

Both men look up to see Sergeant Harris standing there, alternating looks between the two of them and at the strange scene playing out on the street between men who were shooting at each other just minutes ago.

"Sarge?"

"I'm not a sergeant yet." He taps his arms, which carry two stripes each. "You either, by the way, Coop. I'm glad to see you're back, too, lieutenant."

"Back, too?" Billy coughs.

Harris waves them out to the street. "I've counted three guys out here who've died in the last year. You make four. We're in Kitale, Kenya. And it looks like we're here where we were last June.

"Who's back?"

"We have the unit we had exactly one year ago. You're back, Crazy's back, Elvis, and the kid, Timmy."

Crazy and Elvis are talking to each other behind a truck. Billy realizes that Elvis, the talkative kid from Memphis, was his mirror in the other building.

Billy shakes his head a little, trying to place the name Timmy. And then it hits him.

Oh yeah. Tim McClare.

"Timmy's over there freaking out." He points at a young red-haired kid huddled next to a bench in front of the next building.

Private Tim McClare. Billy remembers him now, all too well and for the wrong reason.

Tim was a new kid. He had only been a part of their unit for less than a week, hardly enough time for them all to get to know him. He was their only casualty in Kitale, on the last night of fighting. Maybe it was tonight. He doesn't remember the exact date. All he remembers is that Tim was only the second man to die in his unit. The second of five over the course of the year, a number that included him.

He remembers every one of the faces of the

soldiers he lost, and he remembers them all very well. Tim was fresh in-country from the reserves. He'd been in West Kenya for all of five days when he was assigned to the unit for the siege of Kitale. Tim McClure was around just long enough to joint them at the outskirts of the city, to get shot in the belly, and to bleed out on a dirty restaurant table on the north side of this town.

"The lieutenant's back, too!" someone shouts. Those members of his unit that are coherent right now surround him.

Billy looks into the eyes of the three he knows to have died in the coming months before his own exit in the Ethiopian Highlands.

Each of them has a particular look in their eyes, as if they had seen something that defied description.

Billy wonders if he has the same stare. He embraces them all, saying nothing.

He glances over at the Ugandans on the other end of the street. No one on either side has made any aggressive movements since the firing stopped a few seconds after they all blinked into existence.

Without another word, he walks away from his men. They fall in behind him, ready for anything.

The leader of the Ugandans notices this and starts walking toward them. His men follow him as well.

Billy notices that Private McClare holds his position, silently lost in his own thoughts.

Billy stops a few feet away from the best-dressed soldier, likely the leader.

"English?" he ventures, hopeful.

"Thank you a little bit," the man replies. It's something Billy noticed when he first arrived in this area. Ugandans say 'hello' in English by saying either 'thank you a little bit', or 'well done'.

"English very much," the man continues. "I am Captain Turagini of the Ugandan Republican Army."

"Lieutenant William Pemberton, U.S. Army. Did you just get here, too?"

"Yes."

"Do you remember what happened the last time we were all here?"

Billy looks into the man's eyes and knows that he does. He has the same look. He was dead before this strange moment in time, perhaps even killed here in this city, in this battle.

"What is happening here? Why are we back here?" He pulls out a simple cell phone. "Why does the screen tell me I have lost a day?"

Billy shrugs. "My men tell me we actually lost a year. Exactly one year. But we all remember as much as we can. As much as we were alive for."

Turagini looks into Billy's eyes. "You died too, then. When?"

Billy pulls a pack of cigarettes out and slips one between his lips before holding the pack out to his counterpart.

"November," he says, flicking his lighter open and lighting his smoke. He leaves the lighter blazing and holds it out to light Turagini's cigarette. The Ugandan leans in to light it.

"Almost six months from now, in Ethiopia."

"Ethiopia? Your army made it so far in six months?"

"We did," Billy replies, blowing smoke from the corner of his mouth. "Your country bowed out early, and from what I hear, the war is pretty much over a year from now."

"Good," Turagini says, and he smiles. "This is not my war, Pemberton. This is their war. I was simply ordered to go and fight in it."

"Which brings us back to the here and the now, Turagini."

"Ah yes," the Ugandan says, looking back at his men. They all wear expectant faces. "The here, and the now. Or the *then*, as it were." He smiles a mouth full of ivory teeth. "What do you propose?"

"I propose that we've been given a second chance here. I have no interest in shooting at you."

"Nor I you, good Pemberton. Nor I you."

"So what do you think?"

Turagini ponders this for only a moment, rubbing his scruffy beard. "I know you to have the upper hand in terms of how many men you have brought into Kitale. I think my men will hand over this city without a fight, good Pemberton. I think we will march back around the mountain and live to fight another day."

Billy smiles.

"However," Turagini says, "I would request that you allow us to keep our guns, good Pemberton. I have no idea what waits for us on the road back to our country."

Billy nods and takes a long drag from his

cigarette. He smiles at the thought that he hasn't had one since yesterday, even though his yesterday was several months ago to everyone else. Nothing about this makes any damn sense at all.

Sergeant/Corporal Harris walks up and places an electronic device in Billy's hand. The screen has a coded message.

ALL UNITS, VICTORIA THEATER. REPORT IN AT ONCE ON CHANNEL 11-38.

Turagini raises an eyebrow. "Your Generals?"

Billy nods. "Something like that, yeah."

"I suspect mine will be looking for me as well."

Billy offers the man his hand. "I wish you luck, Captain Turagini."

"And I you, Lieutenant Pemberton. Health and prosperity to you and your men. If we should meet again, let us hope we are holding beer, not guns."

Not so different, Billy thinks to himself. *Not so different at all.*

"I'll drink to that."

"So will I," Turagini says, with another wide smile." The moment I arrive home."

Turagini turns around and whistles at his troops. He taps his wrist and points at the mountain.

Ten minutes later, all of the Ugandans have left the city.

"Thank you a little bit," Billy says to Sgt. Harris. He says it in an almost perfect mimicry of the Ugandan's accent. Billy always had a gift for imitating accents. Harris always found it amusing.

The Americans follow suit, and begin to walk southeast toward Nairobi. Smiles are one thing, but there's no guarantee of anything right now. There is especially no guarantee that this city will be safe tonight. No matter how much his heart tells him to trust Turagini...he is not willing to gamble the lives of his men on it.

The Hague, The Netherlands
June 2
12:59 PM
One minute before The Event

Roti is restless, listening to the sounds of the only other occupant of the hallway of his prison.

The man weeps a lot. The man is weak.

"Oh, be quiet, you little girl!" His voice echoes down the hallway. His voice is the sort of voice that would carry even without the acoustics of a room lending themselves to it.

Minister DeCreste wipes his nose and silences himself. He has no interest in getting on the nerves of the only person he is able to talk to these days.

"I am sorry," he says.

After a beat he quickly adds, "Your Majesty."

He learned very quickly that Roti's temper faded quickly when one addressed him by his royal title - even if it was a title that he had given to himself.

Roti lies down on the bed of what is a very plush cell but is a cell just the same. He had hoped to be incarcerated in a suite somewhere, under guard, while awaiting his farce of a trial. However, Time Magazine had to have their photo of him behind actual bars, didn't they?

He closes his eyes, and then they are open again...without him being the one who actually did the opening.

Addis Ababa, Great East Africa
June 2
3:00 PM

Involuntarily, Roti's body jerks and shakes at the shock of suddenly finding himself standing up. His eyes are open, and he doesn't remember opening them.

You would never know it to look at him because he displays cool confidence in every situation, but Roti is frightened for a moment.

He is standing in a field of lush green grass, and he is talking on his private Blackberry.

"Hello?" the voice on the other end says gingerly. It is the voice of his Defense Minister.

Roti looks around as he responds in query. "Tafi? What is going on?"

"I...I do not know, Your Majesty. I suddenly find myself in a strange place on the phone with you. Where are you?"

Roti looks over his shoulder, confirming what he assumed. "I am on the lawn behind my palace. Why, I do not know. Where are you?"

"I am walking to my car from what I think is our embassy in Kampala. It is certainly hot enough to be Kampala. How did I get here, sir?"

"Where were you?"

Tafi looks around before he answers. The last couple of months have taught him to trust no one but himself and his friend General Dikir. They have also taught him to anticipate ears are listening in everywhere he goes. General Dikir, in fact, had just been with him and is now nowhere to be found.

"I have been hiding in The Sudan since your arrest, Your Majesty. Some distance from Uganda, I assure you. Yet here I am, and my driver looks as confused as I do."

"Get on a plane, Tafi. Return to Addis Ababa as quickly as possible."

Roti hangs up the phone without another word and looks back toward the Palace. His wife, Fedens, might be in there with his children. There is something he must do first, however.

He kicks off his shoes and digs the heel of each foot into the toes of the other in succession to pull off his socks.

He walks in the cool, lush grass with his bare feet. It is a wonderful feeling for a man who has been in a cage for a couple of months.

Just in case this is all a dream, he wants to do this first.

The blades of grass feel wonderful, and his

tranquility is interrupted by the overjoyed shouts of his confused personal guards running to him from the palace.

"We saw you from the windows, Your Majesty!" His head of security wears the widest of smiles and might be suppressing a tear. "I do not understand the miracle that has brought you to us, but welcome back! What has happened?"

"I do not know, Benji. Let us find a television and see if it has any clues to give us."

He walks to the palace in his bare feet. His shoes and socks, he decides, can remain there in the sunlight.

Benji flanks Roti while wearing a generous blend of unfettered joy and total confusion. Since his King's arrest and his subsequent questioning by both the UN and Ethiopia's new government, Benji has been the head of security for the largest bank in Ghana, thanks to a friend with influence there. It was a good job, a quiet job, where no one talks about his time with the Royal Security Staff in the failed Kingdom of Great East Africa. In Accra, he is just a wise man named Benji.

He's very curious why he isn't there right now. He is curious why both he and mad old Roti, to whom he was loyal even when he didn't believe in his cause, are here in Addis Ababa again.

The barefoot steps of King Roti make a thick and oddly pleasant sound as they echo around the Great Hall of the Palace.

King Roti smiles and continues to enjoy the feeling of the cool tiles on his feet as they walk toward the entertainment room.

A large screen is already firing up with the international news. It will provide the King with just as many questions as it does answers.

Wajir, Kenya
June 2
4:03 PM
One hour after The Event

Colonel Paul Kabinda has had little more than an hour to adjust to suddenly finding himself alive again.

He has seen no news reports and has no clue that the rest of the world is experiencing the same strange circumstance that he is. Aside from the two soldiers with which he travels, he has scarcely had any contact with another human being. There was a confused old woman on the outskirts of the ruined and abandoned airport, but she had paid him no mind.

"Hello, mother," he had said to her, gently trying to appeal to her maternal instincts. He only wanted to afford her some respect in order to try to reach out and help her.

The old woman said not a word to him in response. She clutched a bundle to her breast and staggered slowly out of the city.

"Hello, mother," he attempted again, this time in what he could manage of Arabic.

Again, there was no response, nor would she accept any effort of assistance as he and his men attempted to get closer to her. Dazed and silent, she had just wandered off into the plains toward the dried up bed of the Laga Bor.

He worried after the old woman, who was now beyond his sight. There were plenty of wild dogs in this part of the savannah. A few large cats skulked in the grasses as well. She resisted their efforts to keep her safe, and they were in no position to insist, given their own circumstances in this city of the dead.

Kabinda remembers his visit to Wajir. With UN Sanction, he and the other volunteer officers from the United African Alliance had come here to look for evidence of genocide.

The town of Wajir sits at the crossroads of the two major roads in the northeast corner of the Kenyan lowlands. The small airport it boasts is more of a glorified airstrip, really. It sits perhaps 150 kilometers from what used to be the agreed-upon border with the former nation of Somalia before this mess began. During the course of his investigation process, Wajir had been the second town he had seen with obvious signs of war crimes committed by the invaders from the east.

The fact that he is suddenly alive again through some strange miracle and has traveled back in time does not faze him in the least. If anything, the situation has been far more disturbing for the two UAA soldiers that accompany him. They fail to understand why they have returned to this fetid pit of despair to repeat one of the most disturbing assignments of their careers.

Paul Kabinda, however, is a man of missions. He accepts the miracle at face value, decides he will have time to explore the reasons for it later, and returns to the work he has to do. If it is real, he will adjust. Perhaps he did not die after all. Perhaps he had merely lost his memory after being shot and only just regained it. It seems unlikely but so does a return to Wajir. He can't imagine a reason why he would have come back to this place by choice.

The oddest part of this situation filled with oddities, however, is that he remembers having already done this work. He remembers the mass grave that he is about to stumble upon at the southwest corner of the airport where the air is still thick with lime and corpses. He remembers meeting up with his partner in the delegation, Major Hamambwe of Tanzania, tomorrow. They come together again in what remains of the town called Dif, right on the border itself. It was the last of the towns to be freed during the May Offensive that drove the Somalis of Great East Africa back across the frontier. He remembers the other mass grave they uncovered together in Dif. He remembers it teeming with the bodies of more than a thousand innocent Kenyan civilians, all growing foul in the equatorial sun.

He especially remembers the children. How the sight of their ruined little bodies made his blood boil. He remembers how he drove to the border soon after, crossed it, and urinated on the sand of Somalia, promising to make the bastards pay for this. A promise upon which Kabinda made good.

Colonel Kabinda remembers all of this. Most especially, as these minutes have passed by him, he remembers the circumstances of his own death.

He recalls that he died in February, a month after the media credited him with capturing Mogadishu. *The Liberator of Muqdisho*, they called him in the African press, and the Liberator nickname followed him for the last month of his life. He had become a celebrity, a war hero. Nothing he had wanted to become. The United African Alliance took that option away from him. They were eager to trumpet their first true war hero to the world press as the war was ending. Most of the faces of victory had been white and European or American. Kabinda was Congolese, by way of South Sudan. He had the potential to be the new face of Africa. If the powers that be could market him correctly...he would be. Kabinda was a proud son of Africa who had cast off the chains of oppression in his childhood and then ripped those chains off the backs of a culture as a man of power. He was the perfect poster boy for African strength.

He never really had an opportunity to diminish the spotlight that had lit his work. In fact, Kabinda knew nothing about the extent of his celebrity until a week before he died, when he happened to catch a glimpse of his own face on a television and stopped to watch the story.

From that moment to the moment of his death, everything happened to him very quickly. Soon after the day he learned of his infamy he found himself traveling up the coast from Mogadishu to the city of Cadale. Here, he was to meet with the Pirate Warlord that the UAA was grooming as a possible Provincial Governor. He was not particularly happy with the United African Alliance's choice, but the name had the silent approval of the United Nations. Sadly, there was a dearth of trustworthy Somali leaders from which to choose. It was one of the many reasons why the unification of Somalia and Ethiopia, despite the vast religious differences between them, had happened so easily.

On his way up the coast, a faction of Roti's rapidly deteriorating Royal Army attacked Kabinda's convoy.

The troops that struck at them did so quickly and ruthlessly. They made their play under the perfect conditions of ambush in one of the few tree- and hill-laden spots along the coastal road. These were salty men, angry that the war had gone so poorly for them. It was a great betrayal that Somalia was now going to have to stand alone again. Like many of their countrymen, the soldiers had enjoyed being a part of a greater Ethiopia.

Their unit had still held the inland stretches of the Shebele River and was branching out to raid the cities along the coast for supplies. "Supplies" included whatever wealth, food, and water they could find. When they found Kabinda, one of the last four survivors of a group of 20, they had no idea who he was.

Kabinda found himself dragged from the wreckage of his Humvee under a canopy of stars that winked at him in the darkness overhead. He was quickly hoodwinked, kicked a few times, and made to kneel.

Then he was shot in the head, execution-style.

Kabinda remembers the smell of the hood. It is a fresh memory, an hour after it became the last thing he can remember. The hood smelled slightly of vinegar as if it had recently been used to clean something.

His hand explores the spot on the back of his skull where he felt the shot splinter the bone in the instant of his death.

There is no indentation, no scar, not even a sore spot that reels at the touch of his fingers.

The only conclusion he can come to is that he has not been shot. He remembers it, but it appears that it did not happen.

He goes to the place where he knows the burial site to be and takes his pictures of the dead who were not as lucky as he was.

They are all still there. For whatever reason, they are still dead. Why he should be so much more fortunate than they is a question for which he has no answer. Kabinda does not understand why he is standing here drawing breath after breath. What makes him more valuable than all of these people in the eyes of God?

Kabinda closes his eyes, inhales deeply, and says a prayer for the poor citizens of Wajir that did not make it out of their city in time. There are so many of them. There will be more in Dif, like there had been in the town of Garissa a week before his trip here. The Somali contingent of the G.E.A. Royal Army may have been shoved back across their border, but they have left a mess in their wake.

Kabinda intends to clean it up, all over again.

Flint, Michigan
June 2
12:04 PM

Valerie had no family in the area and was one of the volunteers to work the newsroom for the entire morning. She did this on the condition that she would return to her regular schedule tomorrow. She waited for Anne to arrive at work before she left, though the two of them didn't really say much to each other. What was there to say? None of this made sense and it wasn't as if Anne needed any instructions on what stories to follow today.

She worked until about 10:45 and went out to grab something to eat before heading home. She was unpleasantly surprised to find that the gas tank she had filled the night before was now sitting just above empty again, as it had apparently been on June 2nd, one year before. She had no cash but a credit card in her wallet...one that had been cut up several months ago because she hadn't made the payments on it...was only too happy to allow her to fill the tank. It also bought her a nice lunch at Tim Horton's. It did these things because it was not maxed out anymore.

Right around noon she pulled into the carport at the apartment she shared with her friend and coworker, Anne Ayres. She just wanted a shower and a nice quiet lay-about in her bed for a good think. She walked up the steps and searched through her keys with her fingers to find the one for the door.

She did so in vain. She didn't have a key for this door.

She didn't live here yet.

"Shit."

Her keys rattled as she dropped her arms at her sides.

"I still live in Davison," she said with a sigh of frustration.

As she stood there shaking her head for a moment, the door suddenly flew open before her. Jena stood there in a Ramones t-shirt and cutoff shorts. She had been packing all morning, trying to separate her stuff from Anne's again. Her husband...or perhaps fiancé...had left a few hours ago. Like everyone else in the world these last few hours, he had to try and make his little corner of this chaos make sense at the place where he worked.

"Hey Val," Jena said with a smile. "I suppose you'd like to come in...maybe live here again."

They didn't really know each other all that well, but just the same, Valerie reached out and shared a hug with Jena. Both of them were shaking a bit.

In that moment this entire situation became a

little more real for both of them. Not that it had been lacking in reality to begin with.

Lieutenant William Pemberton III stared up at the moon. It was beautiful here in the Rift Valley of Africa. It had incredible shine and vibrant color. It lit the corners of the valley and provided light for the night hunters and their prey alike.

Billy had seen the moon all over the world. He saw it in England and South Korea and Iceland when he was a kid and his father had been stationed at each of these places. He had seen it in Florida and New Jersey when visiting his grandparents. He had gotten to know it well at Air Force Bases in Louisiana, California, and Colorado while he was growing up. Every time his family had gotten comfortable somewhere, Dad would get new orders and they would have to move again. He would complain at first, but later he would come to appreciate another new view of the moon.

The moon was always the same, but it always seemed a little different to him. No matter where he lived, the moon stared back at him with the same cold, dusty indifference. Sometimes, when he was very little, he imagined the moon was following their car as he stared up through the rear windows.

Here, under the broad and unspoiled sky over Kenya, it shone down upon him like a spotlight and regarded him like the eye of God.

I have given you a second chance, William Pemberton, the moon seemed to say. *What are you going to do with it?*

Billy realized he didn't have an answer for that question just yet. It wasn't a question he had really pondered in the handful of hours since his strange return.

"Sixteen delta, report," the radio suddenly says, breaking his train of thought.

Coop is their radioman, and he double-times it up to Billy and passes him the handset. Billy checks his GPS. They are closing in on the outskirts of the city of Nakuru.

"Approaching position Charlie Tango Seven, and we are on foot. Current location iiiiiiiiiis…" he clicked over to a quick map on the GPS… "Charlie Sapper Five."

Their unit has passed over some rough mountain road through the uncomfortably quiet town of Eldoret in the last hour. They were still moving at quite a healthy pace as they came out of the mountains. The road did not improve as it carved its way through the Rift Valley.

"That's where we have you, too. How many are you?"

"Still six, sir."

"Understood. Be advised that Charlie Tango Seven is no longer friendly. The heat is turned up, and you will be coming in heavy to back up two units on the south and west. Be further advised that we have no transport for you."

"Sixteen Delta copy." Billy hands the handset back to Private Cooper.

"Everyone look sharp and check ammo. Skinnies have the city."

"Good," says the guy from Montana they call Crazy. "I ain't shot nobody yet since I've been back."

Billy smiles at Crazy.

"I'm sure we can do something about that. Double-time it, boys. They're waiting for us to join the party."

Washington, D.C.
June 2
7:07 PM

Presidents Wolcott and Guagenti both sit at the table with the Joint Chiefs. It's a little unclear which of them actually is the President right now in the strictest legal terms.

The constitution didn't make any provisions for unexpected global time travel.

Both men have only just returned to the White House within the last couple of hours. They made the decision to try and sort this mess of messes out together. This is a huge step for two men who truly do not like each other. They have also agreed that Guagenti is the President, and

Wolcott is something of an *advisor emeritus*.

"Okay," Guagenti says. "Go."

The Chairman turns to the large backlit screens that display a map of the world. He is an Admiral, a portly man with a crew cut you could possibly shave with. He looks like he just stepped out of a 1950s parade film, and that he should be holding a cigar in one hand and a gin martini with two olives in the other. "All troop positions are as they were one year ago, both ours and theirs. The same is true everywhere. Anywhere we have troops, they are exactly where they were a year ago."

"That means," the Secretary of State says, "that the chess board in Kenya is set to one year ago today."

Both Presidents rub their eyes slowly, in the exact same way as they absorb the information. Everyone sitting at the table notes how odd that visual is. How two bitter political rivals can put aside their differences and sit here so calmly together, listening to this improbable briefing and reacting like synchronized swimmers.

A year ago, Wolcott's Vice President was a man named Patrick Delahanty. He was minding the store here on Pennsylvania Avenue while both Presidential candidates were out on the campaign trail. He spent a long afternoon waiting for them to arrive, and he too is sitting at the table. Vice President Rollins is still on his way to Washington. A year ago, he was on a Congressional visit to Indonesia. He's still out of radio range over the Pacific.

"And the dead from the last year…?"

"All of them, sir," says the sole woman in uniform, Air Force Lieutenant General Harriet Bellingshausen. She holds her hands up and shakes her head in disbelief at the words as she says them. "They're all back, Mr. President. That situation has not changed since whatever happened 12 hours ago…happened."

Another man chimes in, the Secretary of Defense. He's an incredibly nervous looking black man with a southern accent. "We figure roughly 56 million people came back worldwide. Probably two-and-a-half-million of them Americans, Mister President. We're still trying to get a handle on how many have been lost again right away. Worldwide, a lot of people died almost instantly from the shock of it, accidents and so on. That number is smaller here in the U.S., because so many people were still asleep."

The room is silent for a beat, and then the Secretary adds, "My aide broke his nose when he suddenly found himself running on a treadmill this morning."

Many of the brass in the room fight the urge to smile at the visual. It is a beacon of crude humor in a very dark situation.

Guagenti's Chief of Staff, Walter Randall, comes into the secure room. Walter is tall and thin and always serious. His face does not have worry lines…it bears thoroughfares. A year ago, he was on a break from the campaign hiking in the Appalachians. It took a while for him to get to a spot where he could be airlifted out of there.

Wolcott's Chief of Staff, a woman named Denise Tycheson, welcomes him into the room by getting out of the Chief of Staff's seat at the table and gesturing toward it.

To everyone in the room, it's a welcome sight. It's a bit of verification that the Guagenti administration, perhaps not technically in power at what seems to be a repeated moment in time, *should* be in power and making the decisions.

That has been the consensus around the building for the last 12 hours. This is in spite of the fact that the staff in the West Wing are Wolcott's, because he was the sitting President a year ago. The election may not have technically happened yet, but everyone knows that it did, in fact, happen. More than a few of the people at the table, however, are silently contemplating the legal angles of what has happened here.

Guagenti continues, grim-faced. "And…the other side of that return coin…the babies."

"Yes, Mr. President," Tycheson replies, as she looks for a corner to stand in. "Every child born in the last 12 months has disappeared."

Guagenti closes his eyes and shakes his head. *"Every* child?"

"Yes, Mister President. Four million in the U.S. alone."

President Guagenti crosses himself, a good Catholic struggling to understand this strange new world he is suddenly faced with.

"Christ," he says. "The vice president's new grandson."

The room falls silent.

There really isn't anything to add to that statement.

Colonel Kabinda arrives early at the rally point with Major Hamambwe. He does this because there had been no good reason for him to remain in the graveyard that was once called Wajir. Not that the city of Dif promises to be much of an improvement.

He did the work quickly in Wajir because he had done it once before. He knew where to look. He probably didn't have to do the sad work again, but nothing makes sense right now. It is better to assume he has to create the record again, than not do so and have to come back to this horrible place a third time.

The graves at Wajir Airport had now carried the ghosts of his childhood back to him, twice.

Kabinda grew up in the Congo, when it had been called Zaire. In his childhood, his country's cruel leader Mobutu had long arms. Those arms reached into every corner of the modestly large country and held it in a dark embrace. This included Paul Kabinda's small town of Kasenye, which had enjoyed many years of relative safety, tucked away on the other side of an uncomfortable

- 124 -

mountain road from the city of Bunia.

Kasenye sat on the shores of Lake Albert with Uganda on the other side of the shimmering water, water that brought life to their town, and that fed one of the smaller branches of the Nile. The trees around the town teemed with apes; the water teemed with delicious fish.

In Paul Kabinda's youth, his father had been a cattle man. He kept his family healthy and alive by way of his toils with beef and milk. For this reason, he had the trust of their neighbors. In return, he respected and protected them. His father went to great lengths to keep his young son out of the army in a country where children were conscripted as an unofficial policy. By some miracle, he had been successful in doing so.

When Kabinda was in his 20s, ethnic bloodshed between the tribes spilled into Kivu province. This was not far from their mountain town, and the madness of the western cities spread quickly to their region in the waning years of Mobutu. Kabinda found himself forced to flee the country with his ailing parents and sister. They abandoned their farm and traveled north on the Nile through Northwest Uganda on a boat. Paul Kabinda traded all of their cattle for the boat, a decision that enraged his father.

Looking to the east as the lake prepared to tighten into a river, he gazed for what he feared would be the last time at the majestic beauty of the Murchison Falls. Those falls dropped the headwaters of the Victoria Nile 130 feet into a rapid that fed the watery path that lay before his family. The falls stirred that river up into a rapid that would propel them quickly through the unstable piece of Uganda they would have to travel through.

They crossed into Sudan as another unwanted family of refugees in a land that couldn't support them, and they found a way to scratch an existence along the river. They settled in the northern outskirts of the river city of Juba. His parents would die there, exiles from the land of their bloodlines, which to this day remained too dangerous and unpredictable for any of them to return to.

Kabinda worked at the airfield until he had enough money to buy a better boat than the one they had escaped with. His charming smile and impressive command of the English language that was spoken here, which he studied as a small boy in Zaire, made him a successful tour guide and smuggler. He was equally adept at both vocations.

Soon after the fever deaths of his parents, which came within a month of each other, Civil War tainted their new homeland. It was something the Sudanese had become accustomed to for generations, but the fighting had always remained far enough to the north that it didn't encroach on their lives on the upper stretches of the White Nile. This time, though, it was different. This time the people of the South were seeking to establish their own country.

Kabinda had made powerful friends by this time, mostly through his illegal activities. Additionally, his sister had married a powerful landowner. It became obvious to Kabinda that neutrality would not be the clothes he should continue to wear if he hoped to continue to make a living on the Nile.

So, the independence movement in the South Sudan found a firm advocate in Paul Kabinda. He joined the rebel army, despite his years, and spent time fighting with his adopted countrymen with a noteworthy, passionate fire. When independence came in 2011, he celebrated the country's birth with his neighbors and looked to a hopeful new dawn in the world's newest nation.

As a reward for his loyalty, he was made a full citizen. He quickly found himself appointed a regional Marshall in Juba. In this ancient city in a fresh nation, he began to build some real political influence.

He found an early ally in the man who would rise to become the Minister of Defense, Henry Akela.

When Juba was selected to be the capital, over the more popular but less easy to defend cities like Malakal and Waw, Kabinda found himself suddenly flush with even more clout in the right circles.

Then came Roti.

When Roti defied the odds and united Christian Ethiopia with Muslim Somalia, he did more than proclaim a new Kingdom. Flush with newfound mineral wealth, he dangled just the right bauble in front of young South Sudan. *Support me*, he said, *and I will support you against the North. Support my idealism, and I will teach you to unify your 10 provinces.*

Those were the right promises to make. The shaky treaties signed with Sudan were rife with instabilities. Bad blood remained after the South broke away. The 10 states of South Sudan, though united in the new nation, still had factional conflict. Like Kenya, the key to politics here was tribalism.

An alliance with the powerful new Great East Africa was wise. Independence remained a fresh, ripe fruit. It was also probably the best way to make sure Roti's new GEA would not violate their border.

Paul Kabinda was one of two votes of dissent in the People's Parliament.

Roti honored his side of the agreement. However, the neighboring king dreamed of empire. He attacked Kenya and called on his allies in South Sudan and Uganda to stand with him and sweep into the Great Rift Valley to aid him. Fearful of reprisals if they refused, both nations answered that call.

Kabinda was called up to command a battalion that would be tasked with taking and holding the swamp of the Elemi Triangle. The triangle had been disputed for some time and administered by Kenya for decades.

It wasn't particularly important real estate, but it sent a message that Kenya was not something the tiny nation would fear.

Kabinda wrote a letter to his friend the Defense Minister. In it, he resigned his military commission. He sent it by courier *after* his sister's family and he were safely in the air over Kenya. They made their way to the Kenyan capital of Nairobi fearful that they would be shot out of the sky at any time, by either side.

It was a hell of a risk, but Kabinda knew there was no other way to escape. It felt familiar to him, reminding him of his family's escape from Zaire on a beaten-up boat.

His family was granted asylum as Paul Kabinda took on a new command. He was made a full Colonel in the hastily assembled United African Alliance, and given one of three regiments comprised of soldiers from various African nations. A number of them were lining up to assist Kenya in their time of need, taking a stand against the first domestic expansion threat any of them could remember. The continent agreed on very little, but each of the houses of government agreed that the new Great East Africa was unlikely to stop at Kenya if it went unchecked.

Kabinda enjoyed great success as he pushed the Somali units out of the East country. The GEA Somalis never made it farther into the country than the Tana River in the South. They also failed to link up with the GEA Ethiopians in the Northeastern plains.

The eastern front was a failure for the invaders. Roti's anger was evenly distributed between the Somalis who had let him down and the treacherous Paul Kabinda, whom his intelligence suggested had stood directly in his way.

Roti ordered the men to slash their way out

in retreat, and they butchered many innocent civilians as they abandoned their new real estate.

This had all ended a handful of months before this time to which Kabinda has found himself returned.

They crest a hill and spot the Government Review Station. It sits right on the border where his small band of wanderers agreed to meet Major Hamambwe's delegation.

Dif is a lush yet dusty city. It has belonged to both countries over the years as the border between Kenya and Somalia has been drawn again and again, over and over, for decades. The British, the Italians, the Kenyans and Somalis and the United Nations have drawn it. Most recently the king of the new Great East Africa has tried to say which way the wind blows at one time or another and over what invisible line in the sandy underbrush of the frontier.

Yesterday morning the wind was blowing from Kenya and her allies. The war was over, the invaders driven out. Now everything was likely a mystery again.

Kenya's reclaimed border, whether it was still a true line today or not, was thanks in no small part to the efforts of the man approaching the Government Review Station. Kabinda walks into the building with his small cadre of guards to wait for his ally. No wait will be necessary.

"Colonel! Come! Sit!"

The Major has also managed to arrive here a day ahead of schedule.

Major Hamambwe is sitting at the bar

sipping single malt Glenmorangie Scotch. As Kabinda sits on the stool next to him, the Major leans over to reach under the bar, producing a clean glass. He pours an inch or so of the scotch into it for Kabinda and gives it to him with a smile.

The two men who were traveling with Hamambwe have found some beer in a refrigerator and bring four of them to a table to enjoy with Kabinda's guards.

"I am afraid there is no ice, Paul. But there is scotch. You prefer it neat anyway, as I recall."

"I do."

"I thought so. Forgive me, but I was not certain." He smiles. "You have been dead for some time."

Kabinda smiles. "That must be why I feel so awake now. I am rested. So, what news?"

"The Somalis, or the bigger picture?"

Colonel Kabinda takes a sip and savors the sharp stinging flavor on his lips and tongue. The scotch is a wonderful sensation for someone who never expected to taste anything again. By Paul's way of thinking, he has only just died and reappeared.

Setting aside how strange it is to think of his own death, it is stranger still to think of his death in terms of something that actually happened three or four months ago for everyone else. This must be the way Major Hamambwe views it. For Kabinda, however, those months do not exist. The more he thinks about this, the more it makes his brain hurt.

"Tell me what you know of the big picture. There was not much of an opportunity to watch CNN when I was in Wajir, and the radio has been silent."

Hamambwe sighs. "It sounds fantastic, and it sounds impossible, but I swear to you that it is all true." Every word is drawn out slow and deliberate by his accent.

They both take a drink before he continues.

"No one knows how it has happened, Paul. But it has happened everywhere. Everyone and everything went back in time exactly one year."

Kabinda enjoys listening to the Major's accent. Hamambwe struggles with English, but you would never know it to hear him speak it. He speaks like a school teacher who has only just learned the material himself and would struggle with the exam. He speaks with polished clarity.

"That means that old Roti is still in control of most of Kenya. If we crossed the savannah due west from here, we would be in enemy territory until we reached the mountains."

"Early June, I assume?" Kabinda asks.

"It is June the third." He looks at his watch. "It has just become the third. It happened at 3 o'clock."

"Yes, that part I knew." Kabinda thinks for a moment. "Did it happen at three o'clock everywhere or when each place reached three o'clock?"

"Three here, Noon in England, early in the morning in America. It was everyone, everywhere, at the same time. No one knows why."

"Amazing."

"Those who died in the last year, like you, have all returned. The babies from the past year have vanished, and if they were close enough to the day they were born, they are once more inside their mothers."

"So Roti is in his capital, a free man?"

"Yes, Colonel. It is so. And there is more."

"Go on," Kabinda says, intrigued. At the other table, the younger men enjoy their beer and speak of lighter things, not wanting to address the elephant in the room with one another. Kabinda envies them that freedom.

"The last report I saw on the news said they believe one of every 200 people, on average, died soon after they returned. So many of them died suddenly in the places where it was daylight, as it was here."

Kabinda plucked up the bottle and poured another inch of scotch for each of them. "Why so many?"

Hamambwe took a sip. "Shock, for some. There were many heart attacks. Hospitals all over the world have been overwhelmed in the hours since this has happened. Many others died in accidents. Still others were people who were suddenly driving or in delicate surgeries or flying in planes that crashed. Others were suddenly in life-threatening situations where they did not have the benefit of their attention in the vital preceding seconds leading up to the moment they returned. This means there are 300 million or so fewer people on the Earth than were there before the rift in time occurred."

"My God," Kabinda says, his voice more numb than a limb awaiting a surgeon. "So many."

"The entire world is in shock, and all we can do is work to rebuild our part of it as best we can."

He paused and took a deep breath before continuing. There was so much to take in.

"My recommendation, Colonel, is that we return at once to Nairobi and see what becomes of the Rift Valley War. Perhaps it will end in light of what the global community must face."

"Perhaps," Kabinda agrees.

Both men know, however, that this is unlikely.

The Road to Nakuru, Kenya
June 3
2:55 AM

Billy sweats in his armor and leans against the sign. In English, Kiswahili and French the sign indicated they were all standing on the equator at this very moment.

The road they had walked and run on together for the many miles since Kitale came to an abrupt end here, meeting another road that ran almost due north-south.

Sgt. Harris sits on the ground with his legs crossed and leans forward to catch his breath. The high mountain road has extracted a toll from each man. "There's a town just north of here on the map, Lieutenant."

"Timboroa," Billy manages to say without gasping, "yeah. But that's the wrong way, Sergeant. If we go farther south we'll hit Londiani. We can rest there, and we'll be almost to Nakuru."

"Londiani used to be a rally point, but I'm trying to remember when. And I'm not a sergeant yet, sir."

Billy shakes his head. "As far as I'm concerned, you're all the rank you were when I died. Just shut up and accept it." He says this in an imitation of Tony Soprano, with the New Jersey accent he learned to mimic when his family was stationed at McGuire Air Force Base, outside of Trenton. Harris grins at this accent, and the men share a much needed laugh to boost their morale.

"We all missed that, sir," Harris says. "You and your voices. It's damn good to have you back."

Everyone knows they aren't going to rest for long. They are getting close to Nakuru, and if the Royal Army has come as far south as the city, then it likely could be anywhere on this road along the north face of Mt. Lumbwa.

Each of the men is sharp and salty, with the notable exception of Private Tim McClare.

McClare has been led, nearly by the hand, through these mountains by Harris. Time has not healed Tim's mind. He's responsive, but only barely, and he hasn't spoken a word since the event. That was roughly 12 hours ago.

Billy sweats in his helmet and removes it to wipe down his hair with a cloth from his pocket.

With his very dark complexion, he looks like a native in the moonlight.

"I remember this road from our trip into Kitale. It's old, Billy, and it sucks. But it's passable. It won't be a very popular road for the skinnies if they're in the neighborhood. It's too rough for their tires."

Everyone frowns at the thought of running all night in the thin moonlight on a mountain road that probably hasn't been paved since LBJ was in the White House back home.

"I know you're all tired, but we ain't safe yet. Let's get to Londiani and we can find a building to hole up in for a few hours. Hu-ah?"

"Hu-ah," all but one of them responds. McClare continues to stare into the darkness on the north side of the road. He seems intensely focused on something. None of the other five in the unit notice this.

McClare's stare is hyper focused, as if he's trying to tune in to another mind out ahead of him.

There.

This time he's sure he caught a glimpse of it. He can hear the oncoming thump on the road, can feel the slight approach of the vibration getting stronger.

"Guys," he says, but he says it too quietly and no one hears him.

"Gear up, let's go," Billy says, "We…"

He stops. Everyone has stopped making noise.

There's a sound approaching from the

northern end of the road, something beating against the cracked pavement like the hooves of a giant horse.

"Guys?" Private McClare says again, and he begins to run toward them before diving off the side of the road at the last possible moment.

It is hard to tell if the rhino is agitated or frightened as it lopes past McClare. Whatever the reason, it is galloping full bore to the south, heading toward Londiani as fast as it can move. It's hard to believe something that large can move that swiftly, but it does.

The men all jump out of the way as it charges toward them and crosses over into the Southern Hemisphere with a full head of steam.

"Holy…" Crazy says, stepping back onto the road. He could hear it wheezing as it went by, as if it had been running at full bore for quite a while. He wonders for a moment if the event confused the animals like it did human beings.

"Yep. *Holy* indeed," Billy concurs. "Welcome back, Private. Thanks for the heads-up."

Tim McClare nods.

Billy puts his helmet back on his head. "So I don't really want to stick around and see what he was running away from. Agreed?"

Everyone voices their assent, including McClare.

"Follow that rhino," Billy says, smiling at how insane that sounds.

The unit begins walking again toward Londiani.

**Cairo, Egypt
June 2
2:00 PM**

One moment, Kari is tuning a guitar on the balcony of her apartment in the bright sunshine trying to improve her mood.

The next, she suddenly finds herself on her back, her legs elevated in cold steel stirrups of a heavily air-conditioned room.

And she is in labor.

Everyone in the delivery room pauses for a moment, and Kari begins to scream in terror. The medical professionals in the room all jump in surprise, both at her scream, and the fact that they are all suddenly in this delivery room.

Kari's estranged husband Peter is standing next to her. He was holding her hand but has let go in a hurry, startled, as if the hand were white-hot.

In a matter of seconds, everyone in the room understands what's happening. As the seconds tick off, they all assess the situation quickly and make the decision to act on it.

They have all come to realize something together.

This is a birth from some time ago. Furthermore, it was a birth that did not end well.

No one understands how this has happened or why they are all suddenly here again. There is an unspoken understanding between them all though. There is no doubt that *this* is that same expectant mother. Her baby's death has haunted everyone in the room.

Dr. Al-Hayat is the doctor in charge. He looks over all of the instrumentation. He closes his eyes and shakes his head, remembering all of this quite clearly. He can almost recognize the features of her birth canal.

Dr. Al-Hayat is able to do this in a matter of seconds, despite his confusion, because he remembers every birth in his career that had a negative outcome. This one went very wrong. It was last June, he is sure of it. Why he is dreaming about it again, he does not know, especially since he is dreaming about it in the middle of the day, when moments ago he had been on a golf course in Alexandria.

It feels entirely too real, however, to be a dream.

Kari screams again, and Al-Hayat reconnects his train of thought.

He searches his memory. *What went wrong with this one?*

He begins barking orders to the stunned team of three nurses around him. "Your name is Kali, yes?"

"Kari," she shouts at him, wracked with pain and with panic in her eyes. "What is happening to me?"

"I do not know. I do not know why any of us are back here. But here we are. I know we all remember what happened last time. I do not intend to let it happen again. Work with me, Kari. Breathe with me, please."

"Oh God, Peter," she shouts to her husband, squeezing his hand so hard he can feel the circulation waning. "I cannot lose this baby a second time. I cannot. I cannot take this."

She sobs and takes in a pair of huge, gasping breaths.

"Why are we here again? Why is this happening?"

Peter says nothing. Peter has not been her husband for a few months now.

His leaving had been more than her idea. It had been her demand. Kari's depression after the stillbirth of their baby last June took a horrible toll on their marriage, and she pushed him away.

Peter is in complete emotional shutdown at the moment and begins to hold her hand in both of his.

"Breathe, my love. Just breathe, and try to calm down. Let Dr. Al-Hayat do what he must."

With that, the battle begins.

It is difficult to keep their heads in their work. Everyone is confused but determined to do whatever they can to not make the same decisions they are able to recall from a year ago.

Kari knows with absolute certainty that it

was a year ago. She has been obsessing about it all day. It was a year ago today, around two in the afternoon, when they lost the heartbeat and worked as quickly as possible to deliver her baby. It was about 2:15 when they told her that her baby was dead, and her entire world came crashing down.

For the next five minutes, Dr. Al-Hayat is silent, except when barking terse orders to the nurses or gentle ones to the patient and her husband.

The baby comes into the world after much pushing and shouting and squeezing and praying. Immediately, the doctor rushes it over to the birthing table and begins to work.

Kari is in agony, her mind and body constricted and exhausted. She is one clenched muscle, crying…waiting…listening. She can't believe she is back here. Just this morning she had toyed with the idea of *if I had another chance to do it again…*

Her son begins to cry, and the nurses all gasp.

"He has opened his eyes," one of them says to the new parents. "It is a rare thing for them to open their eyes so quickly."

"His eyes are pure and perfect," one of the nurses beams through her mask, "like a miracle." The young woman's smile can be seen clearly in her eyes.

The duty nurse wraps him in a warm blanket and carries him over to Kari and Peter.

The two of them have no words.

They don't need words.

They have each other, and they have their son.

They huddle together, confused, shocked, and elated for the first time since they found out about the baby. It was only a year and a half ago, but it feels like a lifetime away from the room where they sit together now and listen to their son cry.

Five
Lt. Billy and His Howling Commandos

Colorado Springs
June 2
10:56 AM

Young Sam is hypnotized by what he's seeing on the screen.

His least favorite part of school is when they have to do Current Events. He hates having to watch the news or go online to read the Gazette or the Times-Dispatch to get his homework done. Now he understands why it's important that they learn about the news in the classroom. It's something all of his friends from school are suddenly realizing as well.

His mother is struggling with Sam's fascination with the coverage. On the one hand, Helen is very nervous at the thought of her youngest watching too much of the often disturbing footage. On the other, she has never hidden the realities of the world from her boys. She doesn't feel she should start now. Not when the reality of the world seems so historic, so improbable, so likely to dictate the rest of their lives. Besides, if she sends him away from the television…he'll only follow the news on his phone anyway.

"Does this mean he's back to stay, Momma?" he asks, his eyes never leaving the screen. "Does this mean Billy's coming home to stay, too?"

"I don't know, baby. All we can do is wait to find out."

Helen is having a very early glass of wine to calm her nerves. She's amazed she went this far into the day before having one. Helen used to drink a lot, and her husband spent a lot of time early in their marriage getting her straight. Only in the last few years or so has she dared have a drop again when she knew she would have better control over it. She proved that last year when Billy died. She proved it again just this week with the news about Danny. The news that at least one of her boys is no longer dead, though, was a little more than she could take, especially since she still hasn't heard anything about the other one yet.

This morning though, she's having a glass to keep her from shaking. Wild Bill, to his credit, said nothing to his wife about it. He didn't even raise an eyebrow at her, even opened the bottle for her when she fumbled with their wine key and couldn't get the corkscrew part of it to open.

She is very glad the Colonel came home after only an hour at the office. She needs him more than the Air Force does right now, no matter what the Air Force might think.

The Colonel was at the office for a while, of course, listening to his Generals in Washington pretend they had any way to react to this situation that would make sense from a military standpoint.

None came. So, Wild Bill has come back home. He has come home to be with his sons and his wife. There is little he can do now anyway beyond putting the base on alert and canceling all leaves until there is more information to base a decision on. His superiors have a direct, secure line to him here at the house. They have families too. His brass isn't brassy enough to force him to sit at his duty station and make any important decisions. The Wing Commander is calling all of the shots at this point based on the trickle of information coming out of Washington.

The news coverage continues to get weirder and more disturbing. There is little discussion of the war, but a great deal of speculation about what's happening with Roti. The deposed despot of eastern Africa, it seems, has vanished from his cell in Europe.

The Colonel stares at the phone waiting for it to ring.

Ring, he thinks to it, a scowl painted on his face.

To his surprise, it rings.

The entire family jumps as if the phone were an intruder, which at this moment, in a way, it is.

Without even looking at the caller ID, Wild Bill picks up the handset.

"Pemberton," he says, devoid of emotion.

"Mr. Pemberton..." a small voice says on the other end of the line, "...it's me. It's...Anne."

"Anne...Anne Ayres?" he says, confused and

taken off guard. He was hoping for a call...but had never expected it to be his eldest son's ex-girlfriend. Helen and Daniel turn their heads toward him, taking their eyes off the television for the first time in a while. Young Sam's eyes remain focused on the family flatscreen, observing and absorbing.

"Yeah...yes, sir," she says, meek as a mouse and twice as nervous. "I was...I was just wondering if..."

She pauses. After about five seconds, the Colonel puts it together and bails her out.

"No, sweetheart. We haven't heard anything. We don't know if he's back or not."

"Is Danny back? My sister heard that he..."

"He's right here, hold on, Anne." The Colonel hands the phone to Daniel. Daniel doesn't know what to say any more than his father does.

"Anne?"

"Danny! I heard you were dead! You're back and you're home...that's so great!"

"I'm...I'm fine. I...give me your number, and I'll let you know the moment we hear anything about my brother, okay?"

"Okay," she says, suddenly feeling like she has picked exactly the wrong moment to reach out to her late-boyfriend's family.

Danny reaches for a pad of paper and a pen and scribbles down Anne's number in Michigan. The conversation ends abruptly when the phone line dumps the call. A lot of calls are being dropped sporadically right now. Lines and towers are being overwhelmed all over the world right now.

In Michigan, Anne tries to dial them back and hangs up after she hears silence on the line as the call fails to connect. It was an awkward call, but she just didn't know what else to do. She was rapidly approaching the point where she would finally have to call her own father and sister.

Assuming she could get a line again.

One mile west of Nakuru, Kenya
June 3
6:56 AM

As they approached, they could hear the unmistakable sounds of battle. It would appear that the war is, in fact, still going on.

Lieutenant Billy Pemberton and his unit have just completed a walk, jog, and run of 100 miles. They have done this along a difficult mountain road, occasionally in the rain, in less than 17 hours.

Most of them feel like they would like to die now.

For some of them, this would be a second attempt at dying. Deep down, of course, each of them knows to be careful what they wish for.

They have stopped before entering the city, trying to catch their collective breath, listening to the battle up the road. A few are removing their boots, discovering black toenails and angry blisters. Everyone is dizzy, thirsty, and hungry.

Crazy is vomiting, but he seems to be enjoying it.

Billy is dreading the thought of removing his boots. His feet feel completely shredded after their unexpected ultra-marathon, and he's pretty sure that if he removes his boots…he'll never get them back on his feet.

Harris, the best athlete among them, is sitting on the ground. He gasps slightly less than the rest of them but is fighting for his air just the same. Back in the world Harris is a cop and a personal trainer. He was the unit's biggest motivator during this "little hike" to the city from the high mountain pass.

At the very least, he was the biggest motivator other than the indigenous creatures in the area…the ones watching them from the darkness that enjoy the taste of running humans. Kenya has plenty of those, and each of the men could hear them in the distance every now and then, no doubt sniffing the air and licking their lips.

Along the way, Sgt. Harris has spent a lot of time with Timmy McClare in order to make sure the new guy didn't lag behind. Tired soldiers who lag behind in Kenya are always in danger of being picked off by animals when traveling on the roads of the Rift Valley. Such a thing had been reported twice during the first week of the war in their part of the war.

It has been a long day and a longer night. No one has anything left in the tank, and still the six of them are already starting to obey the order before Billy gives it.

"Check 'em."

Everyone's gear is combat-ready, as are they themselves.

They pause as a Kenyan family, thin and terrified, passes by them in the morning light. Like many of the city's sixty-five thousand people, they are fleeing into the valley to the west. It seems odd that they are the first ones Billy has noticed on this road. It is also a little disconcerting.

The father of the family gives Billy a long look. There is a wordless sentence spoken there that is more of a paragraph really, one that transcends words or even language. Confusion is paramount in the sentence, yes. Also fear and panic and a complete lack of understanding of why they are back here in this place which they have now had to abandon all over again. Why the city, peaceful for months, is suddenly under siege once more. Why they have all returned to this grueling moment in time they have all lived once before. This is a grim moment his family had left behind them, so long ago. Without uttering a sound, the man's look asks Billy *why has this happened to us?*

Billy nods at the man, understanding, agreeing...empathizing. There is no answer in the nod, though. Billy has none to give.

The unit moves on with a quickness that betrays how tired they are after the long walk from the mountains. They stay low and move in spurts as their training tells them to do. A few more refugees pass them by, and Harris watches them closely from the rear. He sees no indication that anyone makes any attempt to use some form of communication to warn the city of the approaching Americans. That sort of technology remains beyond the general population in this part of the world.

There is shouting on the wind. Loud voices are coming from just within the city on the other side of the closest buildings. The shouting is in Amharic rather than English and sounds like orders being barked by a soldier. That particular tone is identifiable in any language.

Billy throws a nod and a gesture to Harris who passes the expressions and hand-signals on to the others. From this point, there will be no further words until they have passed through the street.

More refugees stream past them. The Kenyans scarcely seem to notice the American soldiers at all in their haste to leave the city.

After they have all passed, Billy and his men disappear into the rubble and secret themselves in places off the road. Any of the Kenyans who might have bothered to turn and look for Lt. Pemberton's men after passing them by would not see them. It's a moot point, as none of them do so. The Americans are not on their radar at the moment. Billy's unit did not have to bother hiding.

Timmy gets the signal first, and he swallows with a nervous smile.

He scans the environment until he finds a nice spot by the first real structure of the city where he can safely be invisible. This is his first chance to really prove himself in combat, all over again. His other first chance had resulted in his death. He would like to think that he has learned from that.

His training says to wait until there is a break in the flow of civilian refugees moving out of the city. The sheer numbers of them suggest that he could be waiting for a while, so he will have to potentially endanger some of them if he is attacked early. He creeps into the building from the rear entrance, quiet as a mouse, and is surprised to find that he has selected the Royal unit's temporary base of operations for the west side of the city.

The fact that they chose this building, exposed to everything, tells him everything he needs to know about the strategic intelligence of the men they will face. No one else is in the downstairs area, and he works his way up the stairs as quietly as their construction allows.

As invisible as a raindrop in a river, he peers out at the street from a high perch and makes his count of the Ethiopians in this Kenyan city. They are easy to differentiate from the Kenyans. The Ethiopians are the ones with rifles, and they are not trying to leave.

They are the ones with smiles on their faces.

Four of them are on the street, another three are being yelled at by an officer who looks puffed up and imposing as he stalks back and forth like a riled bear. He is spitting in the street after each sentence, so he is probably chewing khat and therefore more than a little bit stoned. Timmy knows that isn't necessarily a good thing. His training tells him most khat chewers are jumpy and impulsive.

The officer is also the only one wearing a proper uniform. Conscriptions tend to happen rather quickly in Roti's kingdom.

Two are on the opposite roof, and one of those is still asleep despite the rain and the nearby gunshots. He is a young man, obviously used to hearing the sounds of battle. He appears to be about he same age as Timmy himself. Timmy may be the one in the uniform, but of the two of them, he is certain that he is probably not the one that truly understands what war is.

It is an easy assumption that on the roof above him, there would be another two Royal soldiers.

Timmy goes to the window in the back and signals. A minute later, Harris is next to him.

"Eight," Timmy whispers, "assuming two upstairs. Pretty sure I heard 'em a minute ago, Sarg'nt."

Harris holds a finger to his lips three times and then points upstairs. Timmy nods and goes into the stairwell, climbing with every bit of stealth his gear will allow.

As with the other roof, there are two. One is watching the street, the other is sleeping. The one sleeping is perhaps 13 or 14 years old, and beside him is an AK-47 with the safety off.

Timmy takes no pleasure in clamping his hand firmly over the boy's mouth and sticking his knife into him.

The boy is the first kill Tim has ever made.

His time in the war before he came back was incredibly short, and he had barely fired a shot before he died.

In his training, he was told that the rush of adrenaline that floods his arteries needs to be counterbalanced with something, perhaps shallower breaths or a clenched fist. They told him first is always difficult, and it becomes easier with the second.

Tim is certain; no matter how long he is allowed to live this time, he will never forget the look in that child's eyes when he stabbed him, nor how his entire face squinted in pain right before he slipped away. The wrinkles in his forehead and in the corners of his eyes made him look like an old man at the end.

War, Tim McClare has just realized, makes old men of us all in the end.

His second kill did not hear him finish off the first because Tim, though inexperienced, was trained by the best. He accomplishes the kill very quietly and quickly.

It is completely by chance that the other man, who has still been looking down at the street, turns around as Tim is about to stab him.

His eyes wide, the man raises his AK-47 up to his hip with his right arm as his left instinctively goes to his throat, trying to protect himself from the flash of the blade. He is a heartbeat too slow though, and Tim's knife slices through the front of his throat.

The man attempts to shout. However, the sound is like air escaping from a pressurized hose that has been severed…which in essence is the truth. The sound is nearly as desperate as the look on the man's face, the hollow whistling of hoses hooked up to nothing. They send a shiver down Tim's spine, and then the sound coming from those hoses disappears.

The dead man squeezes the trigger as he falls, a flinch at the end of a long electrical impulse through his nervous system as it prepares to shut down.

Everyone hears the resulting shot, and time stands still for a moment for Private Tim McClure as the shot whizzes past him and embeds itself in the wall beside the door he had crept in through.

Down below, Harris looks up at the ceiling and rolls his eyes skyward.

"Damnit."

Behind the building, crouched behind a utility shed, Billy says, "Damnit," and waves everyone up.

The initiative is lost.

As the bullets begin to fly, Billy signals Coop to hit the propane tank next to the building on the other side of the street.

Cooper nods and moves into position quickly. By now the rest of the unit has swept into their advance positions and are selecting their first targets. Harris pats Coop on the shoulder and moves off to his left, leaving the young man to his aim.

Cooper's rocket strikes the tank, filling the air with a sound like a hammer striking the middle keys of a piano.

The sound still rings in every ear as the explosion turns all of the oxygen around the Royal troops a bright orange.

Just like that, a new front has opened up in the Battle of Nakuru.

Colorado Springs
June 2
12:05 PM

The initial shock seems to have worn off for the four of them. Hearing a familiar voice from the past might have had a little something to do with that, even if that nice young white girl who had dated their eldest son was only confused and lonely.

Now, watching the screen, there is only the prolonged shock of the situation as it continues to unravel, layer by layer.

The news is like a huge basket of incestuous puppies...confused, random, and chaotic. The stories climb over each other. They blend and spin at great speeds. Every now and then one of the stories goes flying off to one side and isn't revisited. For the audience in the United States it is eerily reminiscent of the initial coverage of 9-11.

News anchors in studios everywhere clearly have no idea how to try and organize so much information. It's like a tap dance in front of a camera with music that keeps changing every 60 seconds or so.

What can you possibly do when every single thing in the world is your top story?

Most of the local stations are doing nothing but watching the network feeds with everyone else.

The Colonel grabs his phone and dials the same phone number he has dialed several times today already.

"Anything?" he asks curtly, before the voice on the other end has a chance to say a word after connecting the call.

"No sir," says the voice on the other end of the line. "Nairobi isn't saying much on the official channels. They're still getting their bearings on *who* they've got *where*, sir. I swear to you, Colonel, you are my *first* phone call the instant there is anything."

Colonel Pemberton says nothing and hangs up. His Base Information Officer is far too busy for his constant interruptions. And yet, he continues to make them. And will again in the next half-hour or so.

A couple of miles away at Base Ops, the woman hangs up her phone and smiles, shaking her head. She understands. She's staying as patient as she can with the man on the phone. She just wants to go home right now, too. Not everyone can be as fortunate as Colonel Wild Bill Pemberton apparently was to be able to go home to his family. Lieutenant Jackie Fisher's family, however, is in West Virginia. So she has her job to do, and she's doing it.

Fisher is beginning to realize that when you

take a step back and piece the whole thing together, the news is starting to make a little bit of sense, even though you have no idea why it happened.

Everyone who was alive a year ago came back. Unfortunately, as the news has said, some of them were only alive again for a moment because things happened to them right away that were beyond their control.

Everyone knows the Colonel's oldest son was a casualty during the push into Ethiopia. No one's quite certain yet where his unit was located on this date a year ago, but a lot of people are looking into it. There are bigger fish to fry in Washington at the moment.

Colonel Pemberton understands that reality, but he hates it all the same. He knows how the process works, and he is going to operate around it as best he can, anyway.

At his home on the Circle, there are far too many questions right now and almost no answers. The Colonel is getting tired of that. He has given an awful lot to the military in his life, and it has taken far more from him in the last year than he ever imagined would be possible.

Half of what this war took away from him has come home. He wants the other half back. And he wants it *now*.

Nakuru, Kenya
June 3
7:31 AM

"I have no idea why."

"Keep checking, Coop" Billy says. "Let me know when comm is back up."

"Hu-ah."

Billy looks around at the scorched patch of street they are leaving in their wake strewn with the bodies of dead enemy soldiers. They pride themselves, Deltas, in their ability to work quickly and quietly. Ruthless efficiency. That they were efficient in their initial incursion into the city, there is no doubt. Nor can it be denied that they worked quickly here.

Quietly, though...no.

Billy regrets the decision to order the explosion. Nevertheless, he had to distract the men on the other roof from spotting Private Tim McClare. And it worked. It worked well enough that Royal Army regulars are quickly moving toward their position to back up the unit that had been watching the western edge of the city.

When Sergeant Harris pointed this out to Billy, he gave him a shrug and a grin.

"In my defense, Sergeant," Billy had said...in the King's English style of John Cleese..."I *was stone dead* for a while. I'm out of practice!"

Harris returned the smile and nodded, clicking a new magazine into his M4. "Fair enough."

Later on, as they watch the Ethiopian RA reinforcements creep into the street below them, the two men both mull the absurdity of that comment. Dead is dead. It's pretty much the first rule of what these men do. That rule has been thrown out the window.

All six of the members of the unit, from safe positions over and around the street, are watching and counting. They are smiling because they are soldiers with a set goal in front of them. The other factors, including the strange circumstances that have brought them back here are completely beside the point. There is a job to do. They will do it. It's what they do. And they do it very well.

There are 36 Ethiopians taking up positions in the streets of the west side in reaction to this new threat that none of them have managed to spot yet.

Billy's unit is a little disappointed. They had hoped there would be more.

"Lieutenant," Private Henry Cooper says. "Radio's up."

"Thank God. Get Nairobi and tell 'em where the hell we are…"

"Sir, yes, sir," he says, and he starts talking in the background.

Billy scratches his chin and looks over at Sgt. Harris who is unscrewing his canteen.

"For all we know the war is still over. I don't want to be responsible for starting it back up again."

"I get it, sir," Harris says. "I'm just enjoying the rest."

"What? You too good to run 100 miles, Sarn't?"

Harris takes a drink.

"Too good, sir? No, sir."

He takes another drink and smiles as he wipes his mouth with the back of his gritty hand. It leaves a smear of grime across his face.

"What I am is too goddamn old."

Colorado Springs
June 2
10:35 PM

The phone finally rings. It is not Base Ops. The ID on his phone says only *Gil*.

"Bill? Jack."

"Sir," the Colonel replies, unable to hide his urgent nervousness.

"Your boy *is* back, Bill. His unit resurfaced in West Kenya fighting a Ugandan unit. Both sides walked away, and he's hoofing it to Nairobi to await further orders. I'll make sure his C.O. has him call you the moment he's able."

Wild Bill smiles and nods at Helen. She holds her other two sons close, and they collectively sigh in relief. Their family is whole again less than a day after it had been torn apart for a second time.

"I'm not gonna lie to ya, Bill. He's got some bad bush to go through before he gets to Nairobi. There's a good-sized city on the road, Nakuru, and we're fighting over it again right now. He's walking right into that."

"Understood, thanks, Gil."

"Just stay within shouting distance of your

cell phone," the General says. "And by the way, congratulations. I was going to call you today to tell you how sorry I was to hear about Daniel. Instead, I'm doing the exact opposite about Billy. Daniel's home, right?"

"He is. Thanks again Jack. I'm a lucky man."

"You're welcome, and yes you are." General Jack Gilmour hangs up the phone.

Jack and Bill have known each other since the Academy. In fact one threw passes to the other on the Falcons football team, many more years ago than either would care to admit.

"General." a young Captain says, opening the door. It's raining in Washington D.C. and General Gilmour is huddling under a canopy enjoying the fresh air. The Captain is in uniform and throwing a salute. He is surprised to have found a general lingering in the unofficial smoking area this late in the evening, in the rain.

"Out for a smoke, Captain?"

"Yes sir."

"Good. You can bum me one. I left mine in my truck about a year from now."

"Yes, sir."

Nakuru, Kenya
June 3
8:19 AM

The soldier known to his unit as Crazy has gotten his hands on an M-134.

- 163 -

He can barely hold it when he fires it, but he manages. He wields it like a poet with a pen, truth told, right down to his concentrated smile of purest joy.

Billy isn't sure where Crazy picked up the monstrous thing or the ammo to fit it...but it makes Crazy happy, and that's good enough for Billy. Crazy being happy is always something he used to strive for.

For the better part of an hour, Lt. William Pemberton III and his men have weaved their way up the street through dozens of Royal Army regulars.

This far south in the theater of operations, being a Royal Army regular is best defined as being someone with a rifle who is willing to go on long walks when he's told. Billy can't believe an army this poorly prepared has swept so deeply into Kenya. Roti was fortunate. In fact...Roti was beyond lucky. Kenya was truly unprepared.

The unfortunate truth though, the more Billy thinks about it...is that Roti is now a year smarter.

They run out of skinnies to shoot at after a while and reach the Sarova Lion Hill Game Lodge. They find the allied command there. The city of Nakuru is almost completely devoid of Kenyans now, and the RARs stopped bothering to fire at the locals about 10 minutes ago when they realized the cause was a lost one.

The Sarova Lodge has no remaining guests, and only a few of the staff have lingered to serve the soldiers who swept in and kept Roti's men from taking the place for their own.

Billy approaches a man with a gold leaf on his helmet and gives him a salute.

The Major returns it. "Mornin', Lieutenant. Major Maddox, Fourth Infantry."

His accent is 100% Texas, and his smile is infectious. Billy thinks Maddox looks like he should be on a screen with Henry Fonda or John Wayne crawling under barbed wire somewhere in Southern Germany dodging Nazis.

"Lieutenant Pemberton, sir. We're Delta." Part of his mind begins dissecting the Major's accent. *Panhandle*, he decides. *Probably Amarillo.* Billy has a gift for tongues and accents. He volunteered for linguistics and ended up with a rifle instead. Such is life in the army.

"Y'all the boys that cleaned all them skinnies out the west side then?"

Billy and Sgt. Harris smile in reply.

"Well, thank you."

"Our pleasure, sir," Harris says, and leaves the officers to talk among themselves.

"So where'd y'all pop up yesterday?"

"Kitale. Given the circumstances, it seemed to make a lot more sense for us to double back this way, check in in-person, get fresh orders and a hot meal before heading back out."

Major Maddox takes off his helmet and wipes his brow with a handkerchief. "Kitale. Quite a haul. So, who dropped you off and didn't stick around?"

"No one. We walked it, sir. Hard to get a cab in this part of the war."

Maddox tilts his head at an angle. "Hell of a

stroll. Bet'chu boys could use a bed and some good food. We can take care of half of that anyway. Sergeant," he says to the man behind him, "square these men away in the hotel."

"Yessir," the man replies, in an accent from the deep south. Billy's men turn to follow him into the lodge.

"We could also use a lift to The Robe, sir."

Maddox presses his lips together and nods. "Can do. Nairobi's only a two-hour drive from here assuming the road stays friendly. The way these boys abandoned Nakuru, I'm thinkin' it probably will. They're all just as confused as us, an' it's a lot easier for them to run home to their mamas than it is for our boys. We've been sending our wounded straight to The Robe since we're so close. I'm planning to pop down to visit them tonight and check in. You boys are more than welcome to tag along."

"Thank you, sir."

"Come with me, Lieutenant," he gestures toward a little hut. It was probably a visitor's center before the invasion came.

As they walk in, it's obvious to Billy that the Major has been using it for his quarters. He can't blame him...it's nice and cozy and in the middle of everything. Not to mention the fantastic view it offers overlooking the park.

An elephant strolls slowly across the savannah, and Billy allows himself a moment to wonder how the animal kingdom coped with the time-slip. Or if they even noticed it at all.

"So," the Major says, opening a mini-fridge

and pulling out a couple of beers, "When did you die?"

Billy takes a can and opens it. "Sir?"

"Don't bullshit me, troop. You have the stare. I've been seeing it on people all damn day, people that used to be dead. When and where?"

Billy takes a sip before he responds. It's the first beer he can remember in a long time.

He sighs. "November. North of the Bor, up in Sodo. Way up in the mountains."

"You just missed it then," Maddox says with a smile. "We took Addis Ababa pretty soon after that."

"So I've heard. I don't intend to miss it a second time."

"I'll drink to that," Maddox says, and they clink their cans together.

"I just hope it still rolls out that way."

Maddox squints at him. "Whad'ya mean?"

"Well, I keep thinkin' about Roti."

"What about him?"

Billy takes a long sip and puts the sweating can down. *Beer tastes better now,* he thinks to himself. "He's got the last year to do over. He knows every mistake he's made."

"More than that," Maddox says, "he knows how we countered his invasion of Kenya and how we took the Ugandans and the Sudanese out of it. He knows what Kabinda's guys did to the Somalis before they got to him…"

"Who?" Billy interrups.

"Colonel Kabinda from the UAA. That's somethin' else you missed."

"I'd love to hear it, sir. Plus, Roti knows how every single battle played out. Who's to say he'll do it all the same way? Would we?"

"Good point," Maddox says.

"My Dad used to kick my ass in chess. I can't help but think about how much better of a chess player I became over the years after so many losses."

"I hear what you're saying, Lieutenant."

Billy takes a pull from the can. "Roti has spent the better part of the last year losing chess game after chess game."

"So, you're thinking stalemate?"

Billy takes another long sip. "Maybe. Unless we can figure out how to put pressure on the King the board could end looking radically different than it used to."

Maddox nods and closes his eyes. Billy works to stifle a burp.

Sgt. Franklin Bosworth is waiting to wake up.

This is the most intense dream about his time in Ethiopia that he has had since he came home to his wife and kids and moved to Fresno.

He doesn't dream about his experience as a prisoner of war all that often. When he does, the dreams are always intense.

This one however has an entirely different feel to it. It seems incredibly realistic, and he just wants to wake up from it. He can feel the thin twine wrapped far too tightly around his hands making his circulation weak and his hands ache.

Franklin is back in his cell, a little 5x5x5 box hanging from a thin, rubbery tree of a species he couldn't identify if he were given a million guesses. He remembers the tree well though. He remembers the texture of it. He remembers the smell of it and the way it swayed in the wind. He remembers the trips his little cage made on the

- 169 -

end of the rope...up, down, up down, up down...whenever his captors felt the need to question him. Or whenever they felt the need to just beat him again for their own amusement.

He spent a month in that cage, listening to the groans of his fellow prisoners as they gradually numbered fewer and fewer as they were gradually killed off.

The guards are shouting below, agitated. They have been shouting at one another since he reappeared in the cage in this dream. They haven't noticed him yet: an advantage to being tied up overhead in an ugly tree.

It is raining. It almost never rained in this part of the Rift Valley. But it is raining today, which is unusual for his dreams about this place.

Sgt. Bosworth has been aware of the cage around him for only a handful of minutes.

He is looking forward to waking up.

The agitated shouting below him comes to an end. He is pretty sure the one in charge, the only one he ever remembers having seen in a full uniform during his time there, has ordered them all to shut up and get back to work. Odge, his name was, although Franklin is sure that wasn't how it was spelled. Odge was the one who spoke English, and the one who asked the questions.

Time passes. Long, boring stretches of time. The sort of time he hasn't experienced since his time in the cage. His afternoon grows darker, and the shadows that used to leak into his box diminish. Evening has come. He is still having the same dream. He can't wake up from it, for some reason. And the sensations continue to be intense and realistic.

Night falls. He has been perfectly still in the cage for several hours, and he is getting a leg cramp. Finally, it forces him to shift, and in doing so, the box swings on its creaky rope.

Shouting begins underneath him, and a few seconds later Franklin feels the cage shudder as it is untied and hastily lowered to the ground.

The lock is fiddled with, and the face of Odge peers in and sees him.

Odge is confused and surprised, and then smiling.

"Mister Bosworth. What you doing in there?"

Pushing into view to take a look is a young soldier whose face Franklin will always remember. The young man in his old and faded Ethiopian Army uniform shirt and jean shorts is the guard that Franklin killed the night he escaped.

Sgt. Franklin Bosworth is still waiting to wake up.

The soldier he killed on that dry, hot night in late June when he escaped from the camp grabs him by both of his ears and pulls him out of the box. His shoulders ache at the awkward motion like they did every time he was yanked from his cell. His hands hang limp and useless in their bindings.

"We never expect to see you again, Mister Bosworth. Why you come back here, ah?"

Odge smiles. His teeth are discolored from chewing khat leaves. He is chewing them now. He was always chewing them. He has that crazed look in those bright, round eyes of his, eyes that Franklin can still see sometimes when he closes his own.

"You remember, ah? You remember when you go away from here? You the only man who ever escaped from here, Mister Bosworth. We remember you very, very well."

Odge pulls Franklin up to his feet. Franklin is not surprised at how thin he is. He was always thin here. It makes sense that he should have such thin legs again in this far too vivid dream.

"Jody here has just come back to us today, too. You left him for dead in the grass where the cheetahs and the dogs all took turns picking at him before we finally find him. I think to myself 'maybe he desert' at first. But then, here we all are back in the camp together, even Jody. He come back just like you. And you know what he tell me?"

Bosworth says nothing.

"Jody tell me 'Sir, the American drag me away and choke me.'

Franklin Bosworth remembers choking Jody. He remembers how it felt when he did it. He remembers how he has felt about it every day since. And he is very certain how he feels about it tonight.

There is anger and rage on Jody's face as he stares into the eyes of the man that once strangled the life out of him. He looks like he is just waiting for the command.

It comes.

Franklin remembers the word, though he has no idea what it is or what it means. When the soldiers heard it, they were free to beat him.

The one Odge called Jody…the one Franklin killed…he is the first one on him. Jody rushes at him like a junkyard dog whose collar just broke under the strain and he slams into him, knocking him to the ground.

Franklin feels his shoulder give as his hits the ground, and the searing pain makes him think for the first time that maybe; just maybe, this really isn't a dream after all.

Jody is screaming at him in a high pitched voice, his emotions getting the better of him as he slaps and punches Franklin repeatedly around the face and head. He is flailing madly and shouting in a language Franklin doesn't understand. Despite this language barrier, Franklin is sure he gets the gist of what the man is saying with his shrieks.

After several seconds of this, the others begin working his midsection and back and legs with their boots. The pain is overwhelming, and he has no opportunity to scream or shout about it between the nonstop grunts of pain.

This is not like his usual dreams. It is far more vivid.

Odge shouts something that Franklin can't make out, and they all stop. Several hands grab him and set him up on his knees, facing Odge and Jody.

"Sergeant Bosworth of the Army of the United States. You are charged with the crime of escape from our facility and of the murder of a Royal Soldier of the Kingdom of Great East Africa."

Odge hands a pistol to Jody.

"You are sentenced to execution, to be carried out immediately."

Jody levels the gun to the back of Frank's head.

There are shouts from the two 5x5x5 boxes directly above him. He glances up and sees white fingers pounding at the spaces between the wooden bars in protest.

"You sons-of..." are the last words he hears, shouted from above him, as a pistol fires and a bullet turns his lights out.

Sgt. Franklin Bosworth is no longer waiting to wake up.

Six
Storms and Hurricanes

Colorado Springs
June 3
9:16 AM

Heading in for the second day of the strange new world, the Colonel is running late.

He is about to step through the door when he hears the phone ring. He pauses at the door and turns to look at Helen who is rushing into the kitchen to grab the handset.

"Hello?"

"Hey, Mom." She can hear the smile so clearly that she can picture it as if he were standing right in front of her.

"Billy!" she shouts, and suddenly the rest of her boys are all in the kitchen. "Oh my God, I can't believe this!" She slaps the speaker button and Billy's next words fill the kitchen, ringing off the hanging pots and pans, bouncing around the room with love.

"I'm okay, Mom. I'm okay."

Sam, who hasn't much to say to anyone since the rift in time happened, brightens up at hearing the voice of his oldest brother again.

The Colonel slumps into a cherry-wood chair at the small kitchen table. He is doing his best not to cry in front of his other two sons. There is a huge smile of relief on his face.

"Mom, I'm sorry it took so long to call you…I had to travel to get to a phone."

"Where are you, son?" asks the Colonel. His voice is cracking with joy.

"Nairobi, sir. Awaiting further orders."

Helen screws up her face in disappointment. The Colonel, Daniel, and Sam all recognize that look. Billy would, too, were he able to see it. He practically can when she speaks again.

"You're not coming home?" she asks.

The Colonel says nothing. Awaiting further orders sounds awfully familiar to him right now. He's been doing it for most of his life. Actually, when he considers his childhood…he's been doing it for pretty much his *entire* life.

Helen amends her question before Billy has had the chance to respond.

"Why aren't you coming home?"

"I still have work to do, Mom. If we all came home, we might as well kill these people on our way out."

"I really need to talk to you," Danny says. "I need to see you, man."

"That's gonna have to wait, Danny, unless you're still coming out here."

"Wait for me," Daniel says. "Don't do anything stupid."

"I will. Danny…you gotta call her for me,

and let her know I'm back, okay?"

Daniel sighs. "I will."

"Mom?"

"Yes, Billy?"

"I'll be home as soon as I can be home."

Helen feels her heart fall all over again.

Washington, D.C.
June 3
10:49 AM

The note had been passed to the former President covertly and casually during the morning briefing. It was unlikely that anyone else saw it being pressed into his hand by his former Deputy Press Secretary.

"Later," had been whispered in his ear, and Oliver Wolcott stuffed it into his pocket without attracting any attention to it. He continued to listen to the Joint Chiefs and shot a quick glance at his former deputy that didn't have the slightest nod of acknowledgment.

Around 10 o'clock, in the washroom, he'd finally found a moment for himself. He fished the note out of his pocket and unfolded it.

EARLY LUNCH? 11? – B.

By the time his car came to pick him up, his driver had already been informed where to deliver him. They drove to a parking garage in Georgetown where Wolcott was transferred to another car and driven directly to the home of the

Speaker of the House, Bruce Dumont.

He and the Speaker had worked together very closely during his sole term in the Oval Office. They had managed to pass a great deal of legislation together, made easier by their party controlling both the White House and the Senate. For Wolcott's last two years in the Oval their party held the House, as well.

Oliver Wolcott liked Speaker Dumont. The man was a shrewd politician, a good Christian and a devoted family man. These were all character traits Wolcott liked to ascribe to himself as well.

"Ollie! Come, sit!" the Speaker bellowed from the open door of the back porch of the house. His hands were stretched out to shake Wolcott's in both of his own.

"Good to see you, Bruce." The former President shook his head. "Can you believe all of this?"

"I know," Dumont said, "I don't really know what to say." He gestured at an empty chair at his patio table that sat under a huge umbrella.

"None of us do," Wolcott replied, and he sat. The Speaker did as well.

Speaker Dumont pointed toward the kitchen. Through the window, a trio of his staff could be seen craning their necks, looking up at an angle to the spot where a small television was located. "Everyone seems to be in a shocked sort-of trance now," he said, "staring at the television, absorbing every new layer of this mess. I thought if we sat out here we could avoid having to listen to it for a little while."

"It's difficult to digest something like this after a day, Bruce. I haven't managed it myself. All I can do is try to help out. That's all any of us in our position can do at this point."

Lunch was served, and the Speaker waited to respond until the kitchen staff had walked back into the house, and the Secret Service had closed the doors behind the last server.

"That's just it, Ollie. If I can be frank..."

"...when have you ever not?" Wolcott asked, and he cut into his chicken.

"To be honest, Ollie...it isn't your job anymore. The perception isn't that you two are working together. It looks more like you're spoon-feeding that dago son of a bitch in a moment of global crisis."

"Come on, Bruce, you..."

"Ollie," the Speaker says abruptly, "one of the reasons I got where I am is because I know how to read the spin and take the pulse. You want to hear what I have to say, or not?"

By way of reply, Wolcott said nothing.

"The spin is you're the wiser man, the guy who knows what he's doing...and you're letting the clueless young kid take all the credit. You're doing everything you can to make his life easier."

"Isn't that what I *should* be doing, Bruce? What we *all* should be doing in this situation until we can get a handle on this...this mess? What are you getting at?"

"What I'm saying is it looks to our people like you're maybe being..." he waved a hand as if searching for the right words…"a little *too* helpful. The better you make the President look in this…the more difficult it is for our side to win back the White House in the next election."

Wolcott chewed, swallowed, and took a drink as he considered this.

"So, you want me to back away, let the President do his job."

"Exactly. Let Guagenti suffer his own fallout from this. His administration has a lot of work ahead of it, a disaster that can't help but taint every government that touches it. Already there are reports of rioting. Here…let's take our food in the sitting room." He gestured at his bodyguards, who opened the door and motioned for a small cadre of young men and women in crisp white uniforms.

Even in a crisis situation, Bruce makes sure his key staff show up for work, Wolcott noted.

Their meals were swept up by the staff and walked carefully to the sitting room where Dumont thumbed a silver remote that had been sitting at his bar until the news was on the large screen in the center of one wall. It appeared that he had changed his mind about watching the coverage.

The Speaker stayed at that bar and worked a little alcoholic alchemy before he sat down. Wolcott was already sitting by this point, cutting into his chicken again. Dumont's kitchen staff did amazing things with chicken. Even on days when they should have been home with their families.

Wolcott was about to say something until the

Speaker interrupted his thought process by handing him a highball glass. Jack Daniels, pair of rocks. *A little early in the day, perhaps,* Oliver thought to himself, *but under the circumstances...*

Speaker Dumont is a drinking man, and he never forgets the preferred libation of anyone he deems to be important.

"Educational television," the Speaker says after a savoring sip of his own glass. Southern Comfort, sweet, two cherries, no ice.

Wolcott looks at the screen. A woman in a thin cotton dress clutches a baby to her chest, crying, standing in front of the charred ruins of a neighborhood store of some kind. The caption line at the bottom of the screen says **Maureen Lorman, Store looted in Denton, Texas.**

Oliver Wolcott heaves a heavy sigh.

"You know as well as I do that this is going to get far worse before it gets better. It will affect every man, woman, and child in the U.S. in ways they can't even imagine yet. We may never know what happened to us. We may never know if it will happen again. We may never know a lot of things," the Speaker says.

"What are you getting at, Bruce." Wolcott puts down his silverware as he asks. His appetite is failing, watching the woman cry on television live via satellite.

"One of the biggest issues about this is data. Data is truth, Ollie. Every piece of data from the last year has completely disappeared. It's as if we are really, truly back at the point we were a year ago."

"So…"

"So that means there is not one piece of legal evidence anywhere in existence that says Guagenti is actually the President of the United States."

Flint
June 3
11:25 AM

"Lunch," Valerie says. She is resting her arms on the top of Anne's cubicle. "In thirty minutes. You and me at Five Guys."

Anne looks up from her keyboard. "I have a ton…"

"…you have the same work the rest of us have. You also have a best friend who wants to pay way too much for a burger and get way too many Cajun fries. You're going to Five Guys with her. She's buying."

"Fine," Anne says with a smile. Her phone starts to ring. "Now if you'll excuse me, I'm sure this is a far more interesting person who would like some of my valuable time."

Valerie smiles at her. "You hurt me right there, Anne Ayres. You hurt me real bad."

"I'm sure you'll…" Anne stops talking when she looks at the screen on her phone. She taps the green button.

"Hello?"

"Anne…it's Danny. We just heard from Billy. He's still over there, but…but he's back."

She smiles and starts to cry, and Valerie walks around to put a hand on her shoulder.

Anne swallows hard. "He's...he's okay?"

"He's fine, Anne. He's safe right now. But he says he's gonna stay over there...for now."

Anne sticks an arm out in frustration, balls the hand into a fist, and swings it down on her desk with a crash. "Of course he is."

They are silent for a few seconds, which feel like an hour.

"I...I'll be in touch, Danny. I gotta go. Thanks for calling me. I really mean it."

She disconnects before he can respond or ask her to say hello to her sister for him.

Valerie looks in the direction of the News Director's office.

"Ron, we're going to lunch."

"Val, I..." he says, but he's cut off.

"Ron! We're going to lunch right now!"

Ron waves and returns to his website work.

"Usually I have to give someone a ring before they yell at me with that tone of voice," he mumbles to himself.

Tampa, Florida
June 3
11:25 AM

The Vice President is sitting in a dark room in his house in Florida.

Only the sunlight through the curtains

provides any light, as Rollins wonders what he could have done to deserve this. His secret service detail remains vigilant, and silent.

Rollins has been given time to take care of his personal business in Florida. Back at the White House, no doubt, President Guagenti has to be contemplating the mass funerals and memorial services being planned all over the world. He would like to be helping him, but his friend Francis sent him home.

I'm going to need you focused, Tony. Take some time.

Every nation on Earth is attempting to deal with the massive number of people who died at the moment the press is calling "the Rift Event" for the time being.

The aftermath has been bad enough in the U.S., but in Europe, Africa, Asia...it had been a daytime occurrence. The death toll had been far greater there from Rift-related accidents than in America. Most Americans had either just been waking up on the East Coast, or had been deep asleep in the West.

For Rollins, it is far more personal. This is why the President is operating a man down at the moment.

While on his flight across the Pacific, once communication was finally established with Washington, Rollins absorbed all of the strange and improbable truths. As they continued to unfold over the line, he began to draw conclusions of his own.

Rollins is a man with almost no family. He is

a widower and has had no one but his son, his daughter-in-law, and their two children.

Somewhere over the Pacific it hit him: If the babies were all gone, so was his new grandson, Brandon.

Many of the babies that are missing, at least the older ones, are back in-uteri. Their mothers will have to give birth to them all over again, but they should see them again. Judging by what he has been hearing on the news, those older babies will be back. Or so it is hoped, this early in the situation.

The youngest ones, however, have not yet been conceived under these circumstances.

Those babies seem to be lost forever. Included in their number is little Brandon Anthony Rollins, who had only been 10 weeks old.

The Vice President dwelled on that grief until he was finally in a position during his flight across the Pacific to contact his only son's family. He had tried for hours without success, which said a lot given that he had some of the most reliable communications apparatuses at his disposal. In those first hours everything was a mess in the world. Communication was complicated.

He didn't care.

Vice President Rollins was now just a man who wanted to find his family. The fact that he was the Vice President meant that in a nation of grounded flights, he had a flight to Florida ready to go as soon as he checked in with The White House.

The head of his security detail on the flight

with him was the one to deliver the grim news. They had been due to land in roughly a half-hour at LAX where they would switch aircraft and board Air Force Two.

Rollins listened to the man break the story down.

Like everyone else in the world...young Tony Rollins, his wife Chris, and their daughter April, had suddenly found themselves doing what they had been doing exactly one year prior to that very morning.

At that time, on that date, they had just gotten on the road shortly before seven for a long road trip. They were headed up to Tennessee to visit Chris' parents for a short vacation.

A 7 a.m. the previous June 2nd Tony, Chris, and April had been heading northeast on the long I-4/I-75 bridge between Tampa and their home in St. Petersburg. Chris had been trying her best to stay awake and keep Tony's mind sharp for driving, but she had already drifted back to sleep. April, all of three years old, was asleep in the backseat. Tony had been singing along to a CCR song on the radio.

They were starting the trip where Brandon was conceived, actually. It had happened during a brief moment of privacy at the end of the trip when Chris' parents took April into town for ice cream on the second day of the visit.

Shortly before they instantly reappeared on the road, all three of them had been home in bed. Tony was shocked to find himself suddenly driving, in what he was certain was not a dream, and doing 75 miles per hour on the bridge over northernmost Tampa Bay.

Tony swerved with panic in his eyes from the shock of suddenly finding himself on the road. He was able to regain control of their Nissan Murano and right it in their lane in the space of three seconds.

Beside him, though, was a large tractor-trailer carrying dozens of pallets of gallon-sized orange juice jugs. The driver of that vehicle swerved when the event happened, like millions of people all over the world had done. He was just as panicked as Tony, the people ahead of them, and the people behind. It was a scene of chaos and shock playing out at that instant all over the world.

Tony's wife and daughter awoke with a scream as the Orange Juice semi truck slammed into the side of their SUV. They weren't in bed anymore and were barely given any time to freak out about that.

Tony could not recover from the second swerve after they were hit. They spun and plowed into the guardrail with such an angle and amount of force that they flipped over it and rolled off the bridge.

The three of them could do nothing but scream as their vehicle plunged into the warm waters below.

All told, of the nearly 1 million people living in the Bay area, 418 died during the Rift Event. The percentage was typical across the United States where most people had been asleep when the event occurred. Other parts of the world had been far less fortunate.

The world prepared to bury a horrifying number of dead...all the while, dealing with a large number of people who had returned.

Vice President Anthony Rollins, already a widower, now prepared to bury the last of his family.

Washington D.C.
June 3
11:25 AM

It's extraordinary, he thinks, that he is only five minutes off-schedule at this point.

Wolcott continues to stick around and consult for him, and President Guagenti isn't entirely sure how he feels about the idea. He feels less good about that idea with each passing hour.

The campaign was a tempestuous one; one of the ugliest in recent memory. On the one hand, having all the help he can get lightens the burden a little as he faces the most unbelievable scenario any sitting President has ever faced.

On the other, having a predecessor with whom he is so diametrically opposed putting his hand in just doesn't ring well in Francis Guagenti's mind.

Additionally, a member of his speech team just told him this morning that the Speaker of the House let something slip to an aide about the constitutional question of running the election again in November. That's the last possible bit of whispered susurrus Guagenti wants to have out there right now.

Complicating matters even further, Vice-President Anthony Rollins is not in his office.

The President sat and thought about the reasons for the Vice President's absence as he stared at a folder with an intelligence briefing on The Rift Valley War.

Rollins had become more than a running mate, more than a second-in-command. He had become a friend. There was no time to spend consoling his friend right now, something President Francis Guagenti tried very hard to not consider a personal failure.

"Mister President?"

Guagenti looked up and saw his Chief of Staff in the doorway.

"Walt," The President says, "how are we doing on our staff?"

"All of the key people came back, sir, even Renate. A few stragglers at the support level, and a scant few who have begged off. Not too shabby, given how many people work here. Some of Wolcott's people are sticking around to help out where we've been thin."

"It's your staff, Walt, I trust you."

"Thank you, sir. The reason I came in is Roti."

Guagenti lifted up the folder. "Someone just handed me this a few minutes ago. What's he doing?"

"We need you in the room, sir."

Guagenti got up from his desk and walked with Walter Randall down to the Situation Room.

"Do you think we're all being punished for something, Walt?"

"I wouldn't presume to have any kind of guess about why this happened, Mister President. I can't help but be furious that it happened on our watch though."

"I can appreciate that," Guagenti says. "However, I like to think this happened for a reason. I aim to find out that reason and make sure we all make the most of our response to it."

"Yes, sir."

Neither of them said anything further as they passed through the armed security of the Sit Room. Any silence between them was unusual, which served to make these particular moments very uncomfortable. They took their seats at the large and deeply waxed table with the Joint Chiefs, and Guagenti poured himself a glass of water from the pitcher in front of him.

"Let's have it," he says.

"Mister President," the Secretary of Defense begins, "Roti has pulled completely out of the western mountains of Kenya. It looks like the Ugandans and the South Sudanese have had a change of heart in light of the new circumstances and are no longer supporting Roti's campaign in West Kenya. We're also getting intel that suggests the Somalis might be leaning toward separation."

The President purses his lips. "So, the Rift Valley War could turn into a Civil War in Great

East Africa?"

"There is a very strong possibility," a general says, folding his hands on the table. "We think a far more likely scenario though, is one where Roti redoubles his efforts in East Kenya and keeps the Somalis on board. His troop movements in the last 24 hours suggest that might be what he's thinking."

The Chief of Staff considers the map for a second. "It hasn't become obvious to him yet that the war is unwinnable, especially without his alliance in the West?"

"Our hope is that he will come around to that way of thinking quickly. The quicker, the better."

Guagenti closes his eyes for a moment. "He was in a cell, in The Hague, ladies and gentlemen. He was a prisoner. He was as low as you can be. And now fate, or whatever, has given him a second chance. I don't expect he's going to quit. I don't think our military should expect him to either. I want that man back in his cell."

He stands up, and the room rises with him. The President of the United States buttons his jacket and walks out of the room without another word.

Addis Ababa
June 3
7:25 PM

The room is filled with people, yet quiet as a

grave.

Roti is late, but he is the King. For the most part the King sets his own schedule. It's one of the many perks.

His Ministers wait for him in silence. No one is chatting about their families, or the extraordinary circumstances of the last couple of days that have brought them back to this place and this time with a new opportunity to craft Roti's empire. The Ministers have learned that light conversation has no place here in this room. Roti has never cared for it. He has cared for it even less since his miraculous return.

None of them have had their supper yet. Their stomachs are beginning to remind each of them of this fact as they sit, and wait. Many of these men are Ethiopians, though. Hunger is not a stranger to them.

Roti enters the room smiling brightly like a prisoner on furlough, which in essence he is. He is in his uniform because he feels a King should always wear one during the day when his country is at war. And he is pleased that he has his war back.

Benji is the chief bodyguard, and he walks in with the King. Benji looks like a man who feels he has been given another chance to not fail a man he fears and admires. There is a lot of that sentiment in the room tonight.

The Ministers all rise when Roti comes into the room.

Roti looks around the room. The Ugandan ambassador is conspicuous by his absence.

"So it is true then."

"It is so, Your Majesty. Dr. Eniridi has returned to Kampala."

"No matter," Roti says with a dismissive wave of his swollen hand. "The hearts of Uganda's people were never in it from the start. The impact they brought to bear was minimal at best the first time. What of our neighbors in the South Sudan?"

The Press Minister responds. "The world media are reporting that they too have abandoned the alliance. This is of course not the case. They have withdrawn from Kenya per your morning instructions and await the orders that follow our reevaluation."

"Excellent," Roti says. "Everyone sit. I will share with you our first priority."

Everyone sits and begins flipping the pages on their agendas.

"You will not find it there. Close them, please."

The Ministers respond in kind.

"Our first priority must be to strengthen our own Kingdom," Roti begins. "We began to lose the savannah territory quickly once Kabinda sowed disdain for the Kingdom in Mogadishu. We need to remind the Somali people of the miseries visited on them by the warlords and pirates before they joined our Kingdom. I propose we cut the head off the asp before it can bite us."

The Ministers nod and begin to look around the table at one another. *So, the old man wants Kabinda to be the first trophy of his return.*

"Early June was when he was uncovering the graves in the border area," the Intelligence Minister says. "He should be in Dif or on the road back to the airport at Wajir. There is no passable road south toward Nairobi unless he crosses the frontier onto our soil. He would be a fool to do so."

"Would he?" Roti barks tersely. "Does our army still choke that road to the Giuba?"

"We hold everything between our border and the river, Your Majesty, yes."

"Force his hand," Roti says, smiling. "Snare him. I want the road to Wajir shelled and carpet-bombed until the holes outnumber the smooth parts."

The Minister of Armies is scribbling this down.

"Are we still using the airport at Wajir for a forward operations base?"

"We are not, Your Majesty. We have quit Wajir completely. We had done so a week before when the north side of the Somali line collapsed."

"Retake it. Retake it now. I want Kabinda brought to me here at the Palace. Send the units in El Wak and Sarinleey to Wajir, and have them hold it. It is to be our new foothold for the savannah. Tell them that is the line, and they are to draw it with a firm hand. Not so much as a gazelle is to enter the city if it is not flying our Kingdom's flag."

Roti flips open his copy of the agenda.

"Now. Let us address the financial questions. I want my Royal Army to be happy. They are going to win, and when they do, they are going to have money in their pockets to celebrate.

Sam Pemberton hasn't had much to say since the event happened.

Mostly, he has spent the past two days staring at the phone, waiting for Billy to call back again.

"Hey," Danny says to his little brother from the doorway of his room, "Check it out."

Danny holds up a pair of tickets and waves them. The thick paper crackles as they bend in mid-air. Danny is smiling.

"Sky Sox. You and me. They're still trying to figure out what they're doing about the seasons. Boise's players are stuck in town because their plane is grounded. Our team is here too. The teams decided to play an exhibition game and make a distraction for everybody. The tickets were cheap. Grab your mitt."

Sam smiles, something Danny always likes to see. Sam is blessed to have two exceptionally cool older brothers.

Sam grabs his mitt, lingering for a moment at the spot on the dresser where it had been sitting. After Christmas, it was the spot where his gift from Billy would be kept. That gift hasn't come yet. That Christmas hasn't come yet. It's too confusing to think about.

He shudders a little. He loves that gift, but now…now he is more than a little afraid of it. And it isn't even here anymore.

He needs that gift. He's sure it can fix everything.

Daniel fails to notice his brother's confusion and conflict, grabbing his ball cap out of the closet for him.

"Here," Daniel says, tossing a baseball jersey on a hanger onto the bed. "Don't take too long or we'll miss batting practice."

Sam nods. He still hasn't said anything, but he is smiling as he nods. Daniel makes the decision that that will do for now.

Perhaps a hot dog and a soft pretzel with cheese and jalapeños will get a few words out of him.

He walks back downstairs and smiles at his mother.

"Thank you," Helen says to him. "Good luck."

"I'm just amazed there's a game today," he says.

Helen shrugs. "The teams were here. They probably didn't know what else to do."

She points at the TV.

"They're starting to talk about shutting down all the airlines."

Daniel glances at the screen. "Probably not a bad idea. You know, you should stop watching this coverage all day, Mom."

She smiles at her son. She feels so fortunate to have him back in her life, a handful of days after hearing that he was dead, half the world away.

"Yeah," she says, "that's probably not a bad idea, either."

West of Afmadu, Great East Africa
June 4
1:51 AM

They can hear the thundering of the bombs shaking the African soil in the distance behind them across the Kenyan border. Their echoes bully their way over the wind that blows past them as they drive the rut-filled Somali highway. The flashes of light are like lightning across the plains in the mirrors of the vehicle.

The bombing competes tonight with actual thunder and lightning as one of the annual spring storms pours a hard rain over the dry brush in this part of the former Somalia.

"Afmadu is 20 kilometers more, Major."

Major Hamambwe frowns at him, the stern look his inferior officers back home have come to find disquieting over the years.

Hamambwe is driving the old Mercedes truck along the rutted road that runs along the swelling river bed of the Lagh Bor. The rain has been persistent for a day now, and this is the time of year when the river is vibrant. For that reason, they drive as slowly as they dare. It would be as equally bad to run into a herd of elephants headed to drink at the shoreline as it would to come across an RA patrol with a chain gun.

Major Hamambwe is not happy.

"This is a stupid idea."

"Not if we continue to get assistance from the rain," Kabinda replies. "And from the look of that sky, we will."

They drive in silence for another minute.

"It is a stupid idea," Hamambwe repeats.

The idea, stupid or not, is the only option the two men truly have. Dif will surely be the next target of the bombing, and there is no other passable road that will carry them into Kenya. They have no choice but to cross the border.

Dressed as civilians, the two men are racing to Afmadu in order to loop back and slam their way back to the border and a straight road to the British, Qatari, and United African Alliance units that are supposedly holding the border town of Liboi. The men who had accompanied them on their UN-sanctioned mission had stayed behind after Hamambwe suggested that Kabinda was likely to be a target of the Royal Army and perhaps a covert departure was the better option.

Afmadu is the only worrisome stop along the way. There is another town on the road before they make the border, but it has been abandoned for several years. At worst, it will have some stragglers from a Royal unit. There has been little there left to loot however, for a generation. So the chances of running into anyone in the tiny town are slim.

The radio finally roars to life, their first contact with the outside world since the two of them suddenly found themselves in the borderlands again almost two days ago.

"Safari...to...the...Mathematicians," says the radio. The voice that said this is unsure, as if it belongs to someone rocking back in forth in a radio room somewhere. The operator's fingers are crossed, hoping that a hunch is correct.

Kabinda grabs the handset. They were sent without support teams to do the initial genocide observations as covertly as possible for the UN and the Allies. They were the "mathematicians." The code name was established a year ago, but it was ridiculous enough that it has stuck in their minds.

"Mathematicians," Kabinda says, keying the mic, "we read you, Safari."

The woman's voice is relieved but urgent. "We have been unable to reach you. Are you well?"

"We are well. We have not been near a city, Safari, until now. We are approaching..."

Kabinda pauses for a moment. He is not all that interested in broadcasting their location.

"...we are moving to the east."

"Turn around," the woman's voice says. Return to your rendezvous point and await support approaching on foot from the south. Confirm."

Hamambwe has stopped the truck. "I told you it was a stupid idea."

Another clap of thunder accentuates the

morning storm, and the rain is pounding hard on the roof of their truck. It has to be thunder since it came from east.

Kabinda keys the mic again. "Very well, Safari. We will return to the rendezvous point and await support."

"Be advised of heavy shelling in that area as well."

"Oh," Kabinda says, "we're aware of it."

"Understood. Just keep your heads about you, Mathematicians."

"Yes, we will. Mathematicians out."

By this point, Hamambwe has already turned the truck around, and they are following the river road back out of Somalia.

In the distance, hopefully far beyond the city of Dif, they can see a glow from fires set in the brush by incendiary bombs. Fires the rainstorm cannot hope to smother.

"Perhaps," Kabinda says, "it was a stupid idea."

Valery Konopilov wakes up with a level of sore and tired that usually comes the morning after a tough practice skate. His team's season, however, ended three weeks ago in the semi-finals. This means that as he lies there with his eyes closed, he is wondering if he is finally reaching the age where, skate or no skate, he is still sore each morning. Every player gets there eventually. He had hoped he still had a few more quality years left before that hit him.

There is no mistaking it. He is sore as he rolls over in bed…sore in the specific way he would be after a late practice. Not just any practice though. One of those monster skates they always take before a particularly important game…the sort of practice where he and the rest of the Carolina Hurricanes would check each other a little harder during practice, or face the wrath of Coach for taking it too easy.

To make matters worse, even his bed seems

far less comfortable than usual. That could just be his aches and pains, though.

His eyes are still closed as he lies there, debating whether or not to get up and put on the Weather Channel.

Tropical Storm Beatrice is bearing down on the Carolinas and might be a hurricane by now. Since he lives in Wilmington, right on the coast, he has a vested interest in putting on the Weather Channel. After all, Beatrice is expected to make landfall in the next few days and might choose his part of the coastline.

The bed, though…it just feels wrong this morning. He's sure of it. It's not just his usual aches and pains. The room doesn't *feel* like his room.

Something's not right.

He opens his eyes, lifts his head, and cocks an eyebrow.

The pillow hadn't *smelled* right to him, for a start, and now he realizes that it's because it isn't his pillow. The bed itself is also too firm. It isn't his bed.

He sits up, and begins hearing noises from outside the window. It isn't the window of his bedroom because that isn't where he is right now. This is a hotel room, and the sounds on the street seem to be coming from several floors down.

He rubs his eyes and jumps out of bed as quickly as his 33 year-old professional hockey-playing knees will permit. He pulls the drapes aside and sees that the street is probably 18 stories down, perhaps more.

From his vantage point on this floor he sees numerous automobile accidents and hears many people screaming. He watches a number of people scurry and run around on the street below in confusion.

He can relate. He feels more than a little confused right now, too.

A glance in the direction of the television shows one of those folded laminated signs. They are the typical advertising stuck to hotel televisions that promote whatever movies are on HBO this month and possibly a local channel.

This ad has a local channel on it.

09 WGN.

"Chicago?" he asks aloud, pretty much to himself.

He turns on the TV and sees a reporter staring blankly at the camera looking very lost.

"Um," she says, and struggles to find something to say.

He bumps the channel to CNN.

"Uh..."

Channel after channel, he sees faces that wear the same confused look. The same one he sees in the tall mirror above the dresser, actually, beside the television.

"Kons?" says a voice from the other bed.

Valery turns around quickly and sees his old teammate Travis Otto.

"What the hell, Ott? What are we doing here?"

Hockey players have a habit of shortening each other's names to a single syllable, something easy to shout on the ice.

Both men stare at each other for a confused moment, and then laugh. It's a nervous laugh because they have no idea how else to react. They were always roommates during road games. Carolina traded Otto to the Flames for a bigger and younger defenseman after last year's Stanley Cup loss.

The Stanley Cup loss in…Chicago.

"We're in Chicago, Ott. Look." He tosses the laminated TV ad on Travis Otto's bed.

"Dude, this is…I…" he shuffles quickly out of his bed… "I…I went to bed at my place in Calgary last night."

"Yes. I fell asleep in my living room looking out on the ocean last night. We were watching the first clouds of the storm roll in. Oh! The Weather Channel…"

He turns on *Wake Up With Al* and sees the same confused looks on their faces there that the news reporters were wearing on the other networks. They are standing in front of superimposed radar pictures. Tropical Storm Beatrice is not in the Atlantic anymore. It had been there only minutes before. Everything, in fact, had looked different on the maps a few minutes ago.

"Kons, look." Otto holds his Droid phone up to Valery."

"It is 6:02 in the morning."

"Look at the date, Kons."

"It is…last year?"

"So…what?" Otto asks, indignant. "We have to play the damn Cup Final again? Detroit and the

Jets will be pissed to hear that they've been preempted for reruns."

"Bad dream? I know I've had a few about the Final."

"How are we both having it?"

"Good point," the Russian concedes.

The sounds of confusion outside on the street in front of the hotel are increasing and are now mixing with police sirens. Otto and Konopilov go to the window and look down.

Mesmerized by what they see, they barely register the sound of shouting in the hallway and nearly fail to notice the knock at the door at 10 minutes after six.

"Team meeting. Five minutes. Room 1601. Got it?"

The voice belongs to Assistant Coach Giribaldi. Instinctively, both men say, "Got it, Coach."

Giribaldi knocks on the next door. It opens.

Goalie Tim McManus, the hero of the Canadian Olympic Team a few winters ago, stands before the coach. He is ashen faced and confused.

"I was pretty sure I was losing my mind, Coach," he says with great solemnity. "I woke up in this room, not knowing where I was, and…"

McManus grabs Giribaldi by the collar suddenly and pulls him into the hotel room.

"…look," he says.

Sitting on the bed, facing the mirror, a man is lost in his own face. His hands are on either cheek, and he is feeling his own skin. He is muttering to himself in a low voice.

The man is backup goalie Jonathon Idler.

Idler died in a car crash, hit by a drunk driver about a month before the season began. The other driver, ironically, was a season-ticket holder for the Hurricanes. Both the city and the league took Idler's tragic loss especially hard.

Idler looks at himself in the mirror, unsure what to think, mumbling gibberish under his breath in shock.

Giribaldi and McManus can do nothing but stare at him.

Seven
A Second Chance to Go Wrong

Flint
June 3
12:41 PM

Lunch has been going on for an hour now. It shows no signs of stopping anytime soon.

A simple round of burgers at Five Guys had been the original plan, but as they approached that part of town their decision was overruled by a desire to find a place where they could enjoy wine with lunch.

There had been food at first, but the last 30 minutes have been dominated by a pair of bottles of Pinot Grigio.

"It's agreed then," Anne says. "We're going."

"We're going," Valerie agrees. "To going!"

"To going." They clink their glasses together.

The collective decision to take some personal time was easy. Many people have reached the same decision in the last 24 hours at the company, and they know that Ron is not going to be happy at the thought of losing two more of his newsroom staff at the same time. Ron, they have decided, will just have to get over it.

Valerie is going to fly home to see her mom in Oregon. Anne is going to go with her and fly to Colorado to see her family and visit Billy's.

Anne has an idea though. She will follow the wires, file reports during their trip, and keep her part of the interactive media content flowing for the radio and print side. She just won't be sitting in the radio anchor chair any more to deliver it. The opinion at the table...that is, the collective decision between Anne, Valerie, and the Pinot...is that Ron can't say no to that. If he knows what's good for him.

Oregon City
June 3
2:19 PM

The nurse opens the door and steps into the waiting room.

"Pamela?"

The room is fairly full, with a lot of people trying to see their doctor today. Pamela Harrison imagines that she can't be the only person who has come back from the dead looking for answers. She notices a lot of people staring ahead quietly rather than reading as they wait to go back to the exam rooms.

Pamela stands up, smiles, and walks to the door. Her appointment had been set for 1:30, and she is finally going back to wait for her doctor.

She doesn't recognize the nurse from her time with this doctor. Nurse Julia must have left after the event. She doesn't bother to ask this new nurse just how many people have flooded back to their doctors like she did, after suddenly finding themselves alive again. She's willing to bet it's a fairly large number. It's also likely why her appointment is running so late when Doctor Brackett has always been so incredibly prompt before.

At first, Pamela wasn't even sure that she would be able to see her doctor. Digging into the question with her insurance company revealed that she had a current policy, since there was no record of her having died anywhere in their records. She could only assume that people all over the world were having similar questions answered right now. She shuddered to think what this was going to do to rates everywhere as the industry struggled to make sense of this bizarre time-shift, which so far seemed to be here to stay.

"Right in here," the nurse said. You know the drill. We have a lot of tests to run. You're one of the no longer dead, yes?"

She says this dismissively, as if there have been a lot of these cases in the last 24 hours. Because there have.

"Yes."

"Obviously we have no records of what happened. Can you…"

The nurse pauses. Asking this question still strikes her as absurd every time she asks it.

"Can you tell me what you died of?"

Pamela kicks off her shoes to step onto the scale. "Heart attack, in February. My family tells me that's what it was. I just remember the pain."

"Well then," the nurse says, finally softening with a smile, "let's see what we can do about making sure that doesn't happen again."

Camp Tavala Gaabo
Southwest of Kismaayo
Great East Africa
June 4
6:58 AM

If anything, the rain began to fall even harder the closer they came to the city.

It became increasingly difficult for Major Hamambwe to keep the vehicle on the road. There was a tug of war going on between huge ruts, deep potholes, and large sections of the road itself that were washing out toward the river. In short, the road quickly became impassable.

"A stupid idea," Hamambwe intoned once more, right before it happened.

The flashes the two of them had previously seen up ahead were no longer happening. They had occurred in an area that suggested they had to be the bombing of Wajir's outskirts.

The men had driven on, struggling toward the perceived safety of the pitch dark field of nothing near the road. Only their weak headlamps and the occasional flash of lightning helped to illuminate the way.

Suddenly, there had been a flash and a noise they felt with their entire bodies, and their vehicle became airborne. Unable to hear anything, Colonel Paul Kabinda felt the vibrations of bits of shrapnel peppering the bottom of their vehicle as it rolled in midair, coming to rest on its side several yards from the road.

Then he remembered nothing else as everything went dark. Nothing else until now.

Kabinda wakes up. His analytical mind immediately sets itself to the task of trying to decide what caused the explosion itself. Slowly, his mind reviews the options as he works on opening his eyes.

A mine was unlikely. They had passed through this part of the road only hours before, in the dark and the rain. If there had been a rocket-propelled grenade from the side of the road, they never saw the flash.

The origin of the blast is unimportant, he decides, and he opens his eyes to find himself alone.

Where is Hamambwe?

One minute he and his comrade had been racing toward the Kenyan border...and the next Paul Kabinda finds himself lying on his back in a small, dirty room, on a mattress that stinks of blood. Blood and desperation.

There is shouting on the other side of the room's weakly built wooden door. Someone is barking a sharp set of orders to someone else.

Whoever the person being shouted at is, they are wisely choosing to remain silent.

Kabinda closes his eyes and draws a deep breath as he realizes the words are being shouted in Arabic.

There is a splint on his right arm, which feels painful enough to be sprained but not enough to be broken. Beyond that, he seems to have no further injuries.

Hamambwe is not in the room. There is only him, and a tiny society of spiders in the corner of the barred window. A small window that tells him morning has come and chased away the rain.

There is nothing to do now but pay attention and wait.

Flint
June 4
12:02 AM

The nightmarish parade of frustrating phone calls came to a close as Anne disconnected the call and accessed her wireless printer with her laptop.

"Valerie? Wake up."

Her roommate is now back in place, as Jena and Kyle have packed up most of Jen's things and headed out to try to make sense of the world again, suddenly finding themselves a month removed from their wedding day. Val had fallen asleep reading, the first chance she had allowed herself to relax since the event. She jerks awake with a start.

"Wha?"

Anne points at their printer, which is making warm-up noises. "I got it. We're on a red-eye tomorrow night." She glances at the microwave. "I guess that's tonight now."

Val looks at her phone. "Midnight? You started making calls again at, what, eight?"

"About a quarter to eight, yeah." This had been Anne's fourth attempt at getting a flight to Oregon for the two of them.

The airlines are a mess right now. Most of the world is trying to book a flight back to wherever they were, all at once. Press credentials and a sympathetic booking agent who believed they were with a network, as opposed to an affiliate, had finally won them a pair of seats.

Anne starts talking as she reads something on the screen.

"AP says the entire airline industry might have to shut down and recalibrate this week to try and make sense of everything. We're lucky to be getting out this fast."

She turns her laptop around to face Valerie as she gets up and walks over to the printer, and Valerie sees that she was logged in to the Associated Press website.

"So, telling Ron was the easy part," she says.

"Yeah. Well, telling Ron and deciding which credit card I was going to cripple for our seats."

Valerie purses her lips. "How bad?"

"You don't want to know. Grab your phone and call your Mom. Let her know we're on our way."

His tone is impatient, which is never a good thing.

"Do we have him, or do we *not* have him?"

Benji stares over Roti's shoulder at the Communications Minister after the King says this. As formidable as the King is, his chief bodyguard possesses a menacing stare that pours gasoline on the fire. Then it napalms it.

"It has always been difficult to reach our units in that part of the country on a good day, Your Majesty. This was true even before the event happened, and now the shortwave is filled with madness and noise. We are doing our very best. Somalia has always been a dead zone for most of our methods of communication."

Roti frowns at hearing the word Somalia. As far as he is concerned, that word no longer has any meaning. That land is part of Great East Africa now. He has bigger cats to skin, however, than a simple question of labeling.

"Find me someone more competent then. Someone who can get in touch with them with greater accuracy." He says this to Tafi, the Defense Minister who is also his unofficial heir apparent and oldest friend.

"Your Majesty," Tafi says, jumping to the defense of his fellow appointee. "This is not Jean-Pierre's fault. It is a failure of the technology at use in the most backwards part of our Kingdom. The improvements you made in the last year do not exist. We cannot call on a series of towers and dishes that have not been erected yet."

Roti frowns and heaves a sigh so heavy it raises his shoulders. A chest full of medals clinks as his uniform jacket rests again. It is another hot afternoon, and Roti begins to unbutton his uniform, to shed the jacket.

"Blame the equipment, Sire, not the man," Tafi continues. "He and his staff are doing their very best for you."

Roti says nothing, and leaves the room. Benji follows him, equally silent. He pulls the double doors to the hallway closed with a weighty thump.

The Ministers stare at each other and then stare at the radio as if willing it to spring to life.

Defiant, it sits quietly. The Communications Minister continues to sweat, both from the heat of the afternoon...and the heat from King Roti.

Minneapolis/St. Paul International Airport
June 5
2:34 AM

When they flew out of Flint in the wee hours of late-night, they realized that neither of them had ever seen Bishop International Airport so busy.

Word had it that the same was true at every airport, everywhere. So many people were bitten by the travel bug, and with good reason.

Airlines big and not so big struggled with the world's attempts to get flights back to whatever place where they were supposed to be, wherever they had been before they suddenly appeared someplace else a few days ago. Having found themselves mysteriously transported had been a major inconvenience to people all over the world, some of whom had very serious reasons for needing to get back. At least in America, a lot of people had been home in bed or only just waking up when it had happened.

Their flight to Portland had a stop in Minneapolis/St. Paul. The first leg of the flight had been brief and uneventful. It was, however, only a warm-up for the three and a half hour trip west in the dark of night.

Anne and Valerie sat on the tarmac in their full airplane, unable to sleep, and waiting for it to lift off again and deliver them to Oregon.

Valerie Harrison was tremendously excited. Her mother was alive again. Knowing this would not permit her to focus on her work at all, which had been a major selling point for getting them out of the office and onto the first flight they could get. Likewise, whether she wanted to admit it or not, Anne Ayres was thrilled at the thought that her on-again off-again beau was alive again too, even if he was still in Africa. She was looking forward to seeing Billy's family in Colorado Springs again. And…to a lesser degree…seeing her own family up in the nearby mountains as well.

"Ladies?"

With the majority of the passengers asleep at this ungodly hour, the flight attendants were seeking out the people who were awake to let them know that takeoff was coming.

"Yes," Anne replied, turning her head sharply. She had been staring at the wing from her window, watching the process of refueling.

"Sorry to disturb you, but we wanted to let you know that we'll be taking off in about a minute."

Anne nodded at her.

"Thank you," Valerie said, and she felt her phone vibrate in her pocket. Distracted with thoughts of her mother, the thought of checking her phone while they sat on the runway had never occurred to her.

2 NEW VOICEMAILS

"We'll be taking off shortly, ma'am, I'm sorry."

"I'll be quick," Valerie said, looking to see whom the call was from.

She didn't recognize the first phone number, but the area code was 503.

503 meant *home* to a coastal Oregon girl.

The second call was from her cousin Betty in Portland.

The limited signal fights her first few attempts at accessing her voicemail, but finally Valerie dials in as the plane begins to taxi down the runway. The signal is breaking up and she is only able to make out the words "Looking for" and "of Pamela Harr -" before the connection is gone.

The phone vibrates again. She has lost her voice signal completely, but she remembers hearing once somewhere that texts run on a different signal, something called SMS or C & C or something technical with a similar name.

1 TEXT MESSAGE

The plane is lifting into the air when she presses the message.

Call me asap, can't get through on your phone. IMPORTANT

The display underneath the message reads "Betts" and "02:31 AM."

As the plane climbs into the sky, Valerie is turning her phone off and back on in an attempt to get the signal back.

The screen on her phone just stares back at her blankly.

"What?" Anne asks, suddenly concerned at the flurry of activity.

Valerie looks at her roommate and best friend. She starts shaking, and tears begin to form at the sides of her eyes. They are tears of frustration as she fumbles with the phone.

"I don't know. I...something's going on."

She taps out a quick text to her cousin.

Her thumbs pound out the words *What's going on?*

She sends it, and the phone vibrates again almost immediately.

One new message, her phone says. She opens it.

MESSAGE FAILED. RETRY?

Camp Tavala Gaabo
Great East Africa
June 5
12:34 PM

"The message is incomplete, but I agree with you. It looks like they are telling us the bombing campaign drove Kabinda right to our road."

The man points at the cell block in the direction of the man who looks a little too clean to be the poor civilian he is dressed as.

"That's him. It has to be."

"We have the officer," the director says. "Our rewards will be great. We must take him to the airport at once."

The second-in-command nods, but in the back of his mind, he can't help but think that taking Kabinda to Raibisi, the former warlord of Mogadishu, would be the more beneficial move to his people.

The prison officer is one of the many in this part of the former Somalia who no longer wants anything to do with mad old Roti's Kingdom. Like so many of his fellow citizens though, he is trapped.

Besides, the fiery will to fight Roti has not been stoked here at all since the event happened.

As before, the people of Somalia have discovered that they still have a slightly better life under Roti's renewed Great East Africa. Eating and having a chance to defend themselves with the help of their infidel neighbors in Ethiopia is still preferable to the alternative. The men who had taken control of Somalia after the war had ended and the Kingdom had evaporated have not been able to win the hearts of the people again. The reunion of Great East Africa took hardly any time at all.

"The airport, at once," the man repeats with a sharp salute.

He walks into the cell block and repeats the order.

The prisoner speaks a little bit of Arabic, enough to pick out "officer" and "airport." He braces himself for what he knows is coming.

The dark room is flooded with the light of midday as the heavy latch on the door squeaks up and the door is shoved open.

He sits there quietly. He has been a prisoner of war before, and he understands that being calm and patient is the best way to accomplish one's freedom.

The bulk of these men are not Somalis like the ones in charge seem to be. The foot soldiers guarding the prison are Yemeni or Omani. They speak Arabic far more cleanly than most Somalis or Ethiopians would be able to. They speak it abruptly, devoutly, and cleanly. Chances are they are a new development in the war, hired hands from the other side of the Red Sea. This is an action that had to have happened fairly quickly. Almost as if Roti had been aware that the event was coming and was poised to take advantage of it. Or perhaps these men had been here all along a year ago, but were now being given a greater role in order to keep them in line with Roti's plan to replenish the waters of war. The more the prisoner thinks about it...that seems more likely.

Mere seconds after finding himself squinting in the sunlight, he is hoodwinked and dragged to his feet. The Arabs shuffle him out of the cell, and his feet stumble on the bar at the bottom of its door. No one says a word as he is lifted off his toes and thrown into the back of a truck like a sack of grain.

The director of the camp puffs out his chest, swelling with pride. He is the only Ethiopian here at this transitional prison with a few Somalis acting as general staff over the far more reliable men of Yemen. The Yemenis are sympathetic to Roti's cause for financial reasons. Even in this strange new world, they are finding it profitable to stay in Great East Africa and work with the self-styled King rather than return to their own land and try to figure out what remains of their own lives.

The plane waits for them a few miles from here in the town of Kismaayo along the coast. It has always been a lawless place, a haven for pirates and the perfect place to move things in and out of the country under the nose of whomever might be in power at the time.

The flight to the capital will be brief, but he

will be welcomed as a hero by his King at the end of the journey. He is certain of it.

The driver twists the key in the ignition. The director looks over to his second-in-command.

"Kill the remaining prisoners as soon as we have gone. Take them to the beach. Too many bodies have been left to rot under the sun in these parts already. Go feed the fish."

Sixteen of the men had been prisoners together a year ago, each of them long since dead in the world that had vanished. They had been given a second chance, and the misfortune to have it happen in the same damned prison.

The other man had only just been added to the prison in the last 24 hours. He is another officer who was traveling with the King's prize. Unfortunately for him, he is also wounded and useless. There is no need to keep him around.

It has not occurred to his captors that he might possess any value at all to them.

Allied Command
Nairobi, Kenya
June 5
12:34 PM

"Pemberton!"

Billy drops his spoon and jumps up to salute Major Veracruz.

"Sir?"

"Welcome back, son. Walk with me." The

Major says this with genuine joy to see his junior officer back at the base.

Billy steps away from his bowl of pudding with more than a little sorrow. Pudding is rare here. It will be watery by the time he gets back to it, assuming one of his men hasn't come into their unit's common room by then and commandeered it. Which Crazy does, less than a minute later.

Veracruz has the respect of his men even though they all think he's a hard-ass. Billy can imitate his accent perfectly; though he doesn't dare do it anywhere near the base.

Veracruz closes the door to his office behind them. "Your boys ready to go back out, Billy?"

"Just point, sir," Billy smiles. Veracruz smiles back and moves to a map.

"Good." Veracruz circles an area of the Kenyan-Somali frontier. "We lost a valuable asset right *here*," he taps a spot, "just east of the border. Problem being, we expect this border will move again soon. So we need to extract the asset, and we need to do it fast."

"Who'd we lose?"

"Colonel Paul Kabinda. He's a Congolese but he came to the alliance by way of South Sudan. You remember the name? Were you still alive when he led the advance on the Mog?"

"No sir, but I've heard the name."

"Well he's back, like you are. And he has already disappeared. We need him. Go get him. Briefing in ten for you and Miller. His team's going in, too, south of you. Get your men ready."

"Yes sir."

A mission. That didn't take long. First things first, though. My pudding.

Over Mobridge, South Dakota
June 5
3:32 AM

The only thing that keeps Valerie Harrison from pacing the aisle in her furious anger is the turbulence that keeps her buckled in her seat.

There is absolutely no signal to be had anywhere on the plane, on any device. The airphone system is out of service. There is no WiFi. The cockpit has their radio, but there is an overabundance of chatter going on at all hours on shortwave...even on official channels. She knows better than to try and get a personal message on the ground in Oregon. Soon the radio will be useless, too, as communications issues start to play out like chain-reaction car accidents all over the world.

A dozen scenarios have played themselves out in Valerie's head, none of them offering a positive outcome. Anne is doing her best to comfort her friend, reminding her that she doesn't know anything yet, that she is torturing herself for no good reason.

Several people around them have awakened. They are sharing concerned comments that are only serving to make Valerie more and more angry and impatient. One woman is insisting that

- 224 -

Thank you for answering my question, the prisoner thinks to himself, and he displays a submissive posture, looking away from the guard, who relents.

To the other prisoners beside him in the sand, Paul Kabinda says these words, after looking to see that the Warden is indeed still far from earshot.

"You are all Kenyans? You all speak English?"

"Yes," they respond.

The guards say nothing.

"These men do not understand our words, but our timing will be crucial. So I will only say this once, and I will say it quickly: I do not see why we all have to die. There are three of them. There are 17 of us. They cannot shoot all of us if we attack them together. We will disarm them before they can shoot all of us. A few of us will die, but most of us will live. The ropes on your wrists will give if you stretch them. Try it."

Each of them does.

"Are you with me?"

Everyone nods at him.

Both guards step up to him and shout in Arabic. One spins his rifle around his back on the strap he wears around his shoulder and pulls Kabinda to his feet. The other is watching the action like a voyeur and training the barrel of his gun on the other prisoners.

One of them has just about worked a hand out of the nylon rope that binds his wrists.

The first guard puts his fist in Kabinda's gut.

Paul Kabinda collapses onto his knees again and drops face first to the ground. The guard is laughing as he hovers over him, the sinister laugh of the evil and stupid. He clicks his well-oiled AK-47 and takes aim at Kabinda's head.

The Warden and the boat captain have parked the old truck and are walking up to the edge of the beach. They are about 100 yards away from the shoreline when they see two of the prisoners leap to their feet and rush one of the guards. The other is focused on one prisoner, and the first was busy watching him instead of doing his job.

The guard shoots one of the men down quickly, but the other is on him in a heartbeat. The prisoner's hands are free, and his hands are clawing at the man's eyes in the slit of the face wrappings of his turban.

The gun fires wildly, hitting one of the other prisoners. By now, all of them are starting to rise, wrists unbound. The second guard turns away from the prisoner who lies in the sand facing the water, and as he brings his gun around to take aim at the throng running toward him, the man on the ground knocks his legs out from under him, and he falls.

The prisoners are kicking him repeatedly. The Warden runs to the truck, where his own AK-47 is sitting between the seats. As he touches the door handle he is cut down by a hail of bullets. One of the prisoners with free hands has the second guard's weapon now.

The prisoner makes short work of the boat

captain as well, just to be sure.

Portland International Airport
June 5
3:59 AM

Rain is tapping on the fuselage of the plane as they make their approach. *What a surprise,* Anne thinks to herself, *rain over Portland.*

She glances over at Valerie and is not surprised to find her friend lost in her own thoughts, staring at the approaching surface of the earth. The two of them switched seats when it was decided that Valerie wasn't going to be able to sleep and should therefore at least have a view.

The audio is still turned up on the television as the plane touches down. The flight has been cut off from anything but the in-flight radio signal for much of the trip from Minnesota. Some sort of upper atmospheric disturbance over a good piece of North America has been interfering with a number of signals, digital and analog.

As the wheels touch down and make their high-speed scraping sound on the tarmac, Anne hears the announcer on the still-fuzzy cable news feed say that at this minute, it has now been exactly three days since the event.

There is still nothing but speculation about what has happened. Many experts...

Anne smiles at the thought of that. How could there possibly be an "expert" in this?

...are saying that it seems we will all be repeating the previous year. Which begs the question...to what extent is that true? Already, things have gone very differently all over the world.

The Vatican remains silent on the matter, the other anchor adds, his face next to a screen that is now showing the massive throng at St. Peter's Square in Rome. The shot shows the square ablaze with countless candles last night, as if the faithful were trying to create a new star in the heart of Italy.

Hold to your faith, and pray for the lost, he translates, as the Pope speaks from a thick parchment held in his shaking hand. Anne has seen Pope Leo tremble on TV before, but this time it seems to her that it looks like fear and not age, that causes his hands to move independent of his mind.

As if sensing the time has come to lighten the mood, the bubble-headed co-anchor suddenly bursts out with: *My husband just wants to know if the last World Series counts!*

They share a laugh. It is a genuine laugh, the first either of them has had in a while. There is an underlying nervous energy to the laugh though, and it is short-lived.

Their laugh irritates the hell out of Anne. It seems inappropriate, out of place. Then again, she corrects herself; a world without jokes is hardly a world worth living in.

At this point, the TV goes off. It is finally time to deplane. Valerie is still fighting with her phone, to no avail. Most of the other passengers have watched her drama unfold as they woke up and have silently agreed amongst themselves that the poor woman should be the first one to leave the plane. The door has scarcely clicked into place when she powers through it, Anne in tow. Valerie's bag is bouncing on its little wheels as she hurries along the little hallway.

Aunt Grace is standing at the end of the hall with her daughter Betty. Valerie locks eyes with her cousin.

Betty takes a deep breath, and her chest heaves with a sob she is fighting to keep off of her face, so as not to make it obvious. This is a wasted effort. Valerie understands everything instantly.

Many years ago, Grace and her sister Pamela found themselves married in the same year, and pregnant in the same year. It was an incredibly happy time for the family.

When they both learned they would be having girls, they made a pact to name them Betty and Veronica. They were big Archie's Comics fans, distantly related to the former publisher. Betty was born first. When Valerie was born soon after, Pamela had a sudden change of heart. Grace was angry with her sister for quite a while after that. Eventually she got over it.

Betty and Valerie had been more like sisters than cousins for their entire lives. Valerie knows something has gone wrong before they are even close enough to share words. Betty's face says everything. So does Aunt Grace's.

By the time the three of them have come together and started crying, Anne catches up and just stands off to the side for a moment.

As the other passengers roll past them, they are all looking at the floor, sad to see that the young woman's situation was as bad as she had feared during the flight.

Anne stands her bag up, locks the wheels, and puts a hand on her friend's shoulder as she cries into her family.

There really isn't anything else for her to do.

Washington, D.C.
June 5
7:00 AM

President Guagenti's bedside phone rings. He reaches out and snatches it angrily off the cradle, as if it has offended him by interrupting a particularly wonderful dream, which it has.

Guagenti fancies himself a much better chess player than he actually is. He enjoys the dreams where he is matching wits and strategies with the great grand masters of history. This time it had been the great Cuban master from the 1920s, Jose Capablanca. Often times, the dreams are so detailed that he can remember the moves in the morning, and in more than one case…they have actually been useful to him in matches he has played during his waking hours.

"What," he growls into the receiver, his voice carrying the tone of a starving Kodiak bear.

"Your wakeup call, sir."

The President raises his head high enough off the pillow to see the clock. When he came to bed and looked at it after two very long days with no sleep, it had read 1:55.

"This call was supposed to happen at six."

"The First Lady moved it, Mr. President."

"I see," the President says, because he does.

"You have an intelligence briefing with the Joint Chiefs in 30 minutes, sir," the voice continues, devoid of compassion. His body man, or personal assistant, has grown into the role and knows when to steer the ship in the right direction to avoid the rocks and storms.

"Am I going to enjoy this briefing, Terry?"

"I wouldn't presume to know, Mr. President."

"Are the Joint Chiefs here already?"

Terry pours himself a cup of coffee in his office. "Yes, Mr. President."

The President looks over at the sleeping form of his wife.

"Are the Joint Chiefs smiling?"

Terry puts the coffee pot back on the burner.

"No, Mr. President. But are they ever really smiling?"

Guagenti runs his hand over his face. "No, I suppose not. Wolcott isn't here, is he?"

"No sir."

"Good," the President says. "Tell him I need to see him at 8:30."

Terry looks over the first of what will no doubt be at least five versions of the daily schedule. "Sir, at 8:30..."

"I'm sure," the leader of the free world interrupts, "that whatever I have at 8:30 will understand if I have to give former President Wolcott five minutes of my time this morning. Get his people on the phone." *It's time to put that man back into retirement,* he thinks to himself.

"Yes sir, Mr. President."

Francis Guagenti sits on the edge of his bed and rubs the back of his neck. He stares at the Presidential Seal etched into the glass on the top of his nightstand and wonders just exactly whose stupid idea it was to have him run for President in the first place.

The phone rings again. He sighs heavily and lifts it from the cradle.

"What, Terry?" he asks, more than a little terse.

"General Walters says you should get to the situation room as soon as possible, Mr. President."

He hangs up the phone without another word. A knock at the door and the voice of his Chief of Staff as he does so causes him to start getting dressed as quickly as his hands will allow.

"Mr. President?"

"Walt?" he says, from the other side of the door.

"An urgent update on the Rift Valley, sir. I need you as quickly as you can…"

The President opens the door in his jogging suit because it was faster to put on.

"Let's go."

Hitaddu, Maldives
June 2
4:55 PM
Five minutes before the Event

Basilio Savio is a man who was once known as Vincent Polzonetti. He had a very good reason to become Basilio Savio, a name he crafted for himself before he left Italy.

He pulls off his shirt and strides across the beach like a champion thoroughbred moving to the start-gate. He wades until the water is at his thighs and then dives forward, slipping into the warm waters of the Equatorial Channel.

His most recent island girlfriend was acquired just last night. She is young, firm, and brown, and he has trouble remembering her name at the moment. She sits in a chair on the sand, sipping a drink, enjoying the silent lapping of the waves on the beach as the tanning oil slowly absorbs into her skin under the distant sun. Her eyes, in turn, are absorbing a trashy Indian romance novel from behind a pair of oversized, expensive sunglasses. Her name is actually Kaja, but five minutes from now her name will find a way to be even less important to him than it was last night.

Basilio Savio is a wealthy tourist and island playboy. Vincent Polzonetti, on the other hand, is one of the most wanted men in Italy.

He did not accomplish this notoriety by killing a man or destroying a priceless work of art in Roma. Vincent Polzonetti *stole*.

Eight months ago, back in the proud old city of Siena in the heart of Tuscany, he was a mid-level executive at Monte Dei Paschi.

"Babbo Monte"…Daddy Monte, they call it. Since the late 15th Century the Monte Dei Paschi bank has been a cornerstone of the city, of the region, and of Italy itself. Babbo Monte has always been there for the people of Siena. It is the city's largest employer, and a massive philanthropic hand that supports almost everything in the city. So much money flows in and out of Babbo Monte each year that Vincent Polzonetti was absolutely certain that no one would miss 20 million Euros.

Vincent Polzonetti was, of course, wrong about this. Within hours of his brilliantly untraceable transfer, he discovered it was not so untraceable after all. They did not know where the money went, but there was enough of a digital footprint left in the sand for them to pin the blame squarely on his shoulders.

Polzonetti became a lead story on Italian news. Stealing from Babbo Monte was like stealing from the charities for poor and sick people it supported. It was like stealing from the Palio horse races that happen around the Piazza del Campo every summer. It was like stealing a piece of heritage from their ancestors. It was a much bigger deal to the prideful people of Siena than a mere 20 million Euros.

He was fortunate in a couple of ways. He learned that he was a suspect before they were able to get their hands on him. He had set up the new identity a year in advance, when he had first come up with the idea. He had the accounts where the money would go tucked safely away all over the world and accessible by the new identity. His new persona and passport were a perfect and expensive forgery. They were Slovenian, and he had spent the better part of two years becoming fluent in that barbaric language.

Vincent Polzonetti was also fortunate that he had the kind of easily forgettable face that made it easy to blend into the crowd and slip out of Italy unnoticed hours before his face began appearing on television screens.

Through clever movements and a well-placed bribe, he escaped capture and seemed to disappear off the face of the earth. Not one of his bank accounts has been discovered in the last eight months, 13 days, and three hours since his crime was discovered.

The water is warm. It is always warm in this part of the Indian Ocean, just south of the exact middle of the world. Another golden island sunset is still a couple of hours away, and the view is perfect here on the Addu Atoll. He watches colorful fish dart around in the shallows below him, and he wonders what form dinner should take tonight. Perhaps he will order up the white shark again. The shark is delicious, even though the aftertaste stays with you for a couple of days.

He could ask what's-her-name for an opinion, but she isn't exactly here to offer her opinions on much of anything.

The white shark, definitely. The chef makes it perfectly at the resort.

By the time he finishes his dinner thought, he isn't swimming anymore.

Siena, Italy
June 2
1:00 PM

Polzonetti is on the phone in his office. Not only is he no longer swimming, but he is now completely dry and dressed for work, which is something he has avoided for months.

His brain tells him that he was in the middle of saying something, but he isn't sure what it was. He hears the phone on his desk disconnect without a word as if someone on the other end is as confused as he.

He trails off into silence as he jerks around violently at his sudden surroundings.

This is his former office at Monte Dei Paschi, a place he hasn't seen for some time now except in the confines of the occasional bizarre dream.

The building is old, a stone fortress, the

Palazzo Salimbeni. It has stood strong through plagues, sieges, world wars…and still the statue of Bandini stands out front to welcome the people of Siena into Babbo's loving arms. A truly old structure in the heart of an ancient city.

Polzonetti hangs up the phone, unsure who he was even speaking to or why. He jumps up out of his chair and finds that he is wearing one of his office suits. There are screams from other offices, and from the street below his window. In the distance, he hears a couple of distinct car crashes. A helicopter dips down out of the sky and then fights to climb back up again. Sirens are beginning to fill the air.

People are running in the hallway outside of his old office, and he is thankful for a moment that the door is closed. Back at the bank is the absolute last place Polzonetti would ever choose to be, and yet here he is. His desk calendar shows today's date, but the year is wrong. The new occupant uses the same calendar he did. In fact, very little about the office has changed at all.

He fishes his old cell phone out of his pocket, one that he left behind when he left the city behind. It too shows today's date, but the wrong year.

Impossible, he thinks, and spins around with a start when he hears his door open. He stares at the figure that opened the door, and he is panting wildly as his brain struggles to understand what the hell has happened to him. His mind still remembers the warmth of the sea. Had this happened the other way around, he likely would have drowned.

"You!" shouts the New Business Loans Manager, who was walking down the hallway to the office he had been sitting in only a minute before. After Polzonetti disappeared, the office was assigned to him. He had been sitting there reviewing paperwork when he suddenly found himself transported to his former office, the one down the hall that did not offer a window.

The manager charges into the room and tackles Polzonetti, both men flailing wildly to the floor. One endeavors to free himself while the other seeks to knot his limbs into the other and make an escape impossible.

It is the loan manager who first thinks to throw an elbow, and he plants it cleanly and efficiently. A purple spot appears almost instantly just above the bridge of Polzonetti's nose. Things go a little blurry for a moment. Right before the fugitive loses consciousness as the second blow of the elbow is delivered, he can hear his attacker calling for security.

"It is Polzonetti! Come quick!"

Eight
Mister Kabinda, I Presume

Juba River
Great East Africa
June 5
11:25 PM

Seven men stumbled to the edge of the water, the only survivors of the 17 that had faced a gruesome death in the equatorial coastline of the Indian Ocean, and escaped it.

The truck they had appropriated from their would-be executioners had taken them as far as it could. Sadly, that still wasn't particularly far. They had done a number of miles on foot, which had been even more difficult for the one of them that was shot in the leg. He was slowing them down, and he knew it. Soon they would be in the bush, even more difficult terrain, and he suspected that before long he would become much more of a liability to the group.

Sand had turned to brush. Brush had become slightly greener the closer they came to the river. On the other side of the Juba river the brush quickly turned into something akin to traditional rainforest, although thinner. It was not going to be pleasant to travel through, but they were alive.

Kabinda had been saddened to discover that his friend Hamambwe was not among their group, and he had no way of knowing which direction they should have gone to find him. The four men who had served as their escorts during the diplomatic inquiry were not here either. They were no doubt slain at either the rendezvous point, or at the P.O.W. camp where he had been held.

It was him and a half-dozen of the Kenyans that had been prisoners of war a year ago, each of them quite dismayed to find themselves back in that prison when the event came to pass. They were only too happy to throw their support behind the newcomer's escape plan at the beach, even at the cost of more than half their number.

Now though, they were staring at a sweltering jungle, on a hot night without a moon thanks to thick clouds. There were far too many miles between their group and the hostile border area with Kenya, already teeming with the renewed battles of a confused border war.

Off in the distance, they could hear the shelling of some town or another. They moved in the direction of that noise, in spite of what common sense would tell them to do.

Combat meant a front. A front meant the other side of it would be friendly to them. All they had to do was find their way past the Royal Army regulars who might be holding the line, without getting shot.

Easier said than done with a wounded man, but there weren't a lot of other options available to them.

The seven kept plodding forward into the outer fringes of the jungle, unsure of what might be waiting for them.

Negelli, Great East Africa
June 5
11:39 PM

Even at this late hour and at this altitude, the night air is thick and stifling.

Benji stands on the outer balcony that leads to the King's bedchamber and focuses all of his attention on a small patch of skin in the middle of his back.

A single bead of sweat hangs there. In this heat, wearing his Kevlar body armor, he is summoning all of his mental powers to will the bead back into his pores. He wonders if the mysterious "force" he once saw in an American movie is real, and whether or not he can use it to accomplish this. Thus far, the answer is *no*.

Benji has lived in the heat of Northern Africa his entire life. He knows well that if that first bead of sweat drops, a flood will follow, and he will dehydrate faster. To the south, he sees the first forks of lightning attached to a large storm beginning to slap at the earth.

Hada, the female intelligence officer from

Somalia, walks out onto the balcony with a folded piece of paper. The balcony is shared by three rooms.

"Benji," she says. Her voice is all business but is incapable of hiding the interest she has in him beyond their work. She can pack a lot into two syllables. Words and nuance are her things.

"Hada," he replies. His voice is devoid of emotion. He is the picture of the professional bodyguard. He says little to most people. Mystery and distance are his things.

Hada never hinted about any feelings she might have had for him a year ago, when they had worked together.

Perhaps, coming back to this place and time, Hada has decided that she is going to seize the moment when the right opportunity presents itself. Or so he finds himself hoping.

Hada passes him the note, and he opens it. He closes his eyes and takes a deep breath.

"Wonderful," he says.

"Sorry," she replies, and the apology is packed with empathy. Hada has had to break bad news to Roti in the past. It is never a pleasant process, no matter what it is. Especially when the King has company, which he usually does at this hour when the Queen is not traveling with him.

Benji raps three times on the door and waits to hear the irritation in Roti's voice.

"Come," the King says. The tone Benji anticipated is there.

He opens the door, not happy to be the one who has to deliver this information.

Roti sits up in bed. On either side of him are two young women. Only one of them looks happy to be there.

"What is it, Benji?"

Roti's voice is annoyed and distant. He has obviously been interrupted in the middle of something important. Impatience and ire are usually his things.

"The Somalis brought us Hamambwe, Your Majesty, not Kabinda. It seems they may have had Kabinda but sent him off to be executed."

Roti frowned.

"There is more. We have been told there was an escape, and Kabinda was not among the dead at the beach. They have no idea where he is now, but they are searching for him."

The Somalis. Always the damned Somalis. If he had not needed their strong young men, nothing would have made him happier than to rip their country into a million pieces. *I cannot trust them to accomplish anything but eating and underachieving.*

"I understand," Roti said. For the briefest of moments, as his anger slowly escalated within him...he came within a breath of saying the words *shoot Hamambwe*. He managed not to. Major Hamambwe of the United African Alliance might be useful later on. There was information there. He would find the proper methods to extract it.

Instead of ordering the man's death, he changes the subject.

"The new offensive?"

"Setting up without issue, Your Majesty."

"Good." Roti waves his loyal Benji away.

As the bodyguard closes the door behind him, he shakes his head at the thought of how Roti will take out his frustrations. Obviously, he will do so on the two poor women in the bed beside him.

Worse still, it is his sworn duty to stand out there on the balcony and hear it all.

Portland, Oregon
June 5
7:16 PM

Sleep has still not come to Valerie. Since she got off the plane, her brain has been going a mile a minute trying to adjust to the fact that her mother is dead again.

Her mother had only been back for a few days when she found herself in the wrong place at the wrong time. Val and her mother had spoken on the phone more in those three days than they had in the entire year before her heart attack. It had been a wonderful thing for both of them.

Excited to run to the city and meet Valerie and her friend Anne at the airport, Pamela Harrison drove to her bank to withdraw some cash for the brief road trip. She had always hated carrying plastic, and she was only too happy to discover that being alive again under these strange circumstances meant that she still had a bank account. She had bought herself a few nice things in the last couple of days...and a gift or three for her daughter as well.

She walked into the bank roughly 30 seconds before the desperate young couple who were looking for money to spend on drugs. They ended up killing three people before they were finally shot to death by the security guard they had only managed to wound. Pamela had been the second fatality.

Valerie sat in her mother's empty old house, mourning her for the second time in four months. Anne and Aunt Grace tried but couldn't stay awake. Her cousin Betty was hanging in there, though. At the moment she was pouring each of them a glass of red wine.

"So," Betty began, with her *I'm Going to Be Blunt* tone of voice. It was one that Valerie always found amusing. Even now, in another dark night of her life, it made her give up half a smile.

"This is the part where I say all the crap I told you last year when Aunt Pam died the first time." She pauses, setting the bottle down with tears in her eyes. She grabs the two glasses and gently carries them into the living room. Gently, because they are quite full. She nearly splashes a bit as she clinks her glass into Valerie's.

"Where I say your mom's in a better place." She toasts the air and takes a healthy swallow.

Valerie smiles, says nothing, and hoists her glass before pounding half of it down.

"That-a-girl," Betty says, wiping the corners of her cousin's mouth with her sleeve. "But both of us know that's crap. She's gone. She was gone, and she came back. She came back to us. This was a better place. She had it, and it's gone again. She had it. We had her."

Valerie closes her eyes slowly, as if the eyelids are fighting back something.

"We had her again, and we lost her again."

"It's stupid."

"Stupid," Anne parrots softly from the couch, where she's curled up in a Trailblazers blanket. Anne tends to talk in her sleep when she's over-tired.

"Maybe," Valerie says with her voice numb and nearly devoid of all emotion tonight, "maybe it will happen again. Maybe I'll get her back again. Third time's a charm…that's what they say, right?"

"Maybe," Betty says, and takes another drink.

"Maybe," Anne says softly from the couch.

Faafxadhuun, Great East Africa
June 6
6:20 AM

Following the North Star was not possible on a cloudy night. Neither was remaining in one place when they were most certainly being hunted by now, deep within enemy territory.

They had not wanted to stay along the river, and no one among them possessed navigational devices of any sort. So the survivors made their way through the rain forest as best they could and finally found the road that had eventually led them to this town.

The word *town* is generous. Faafxadhuun is more of a modest collection of abandoned structures and a well that sits dry in spite of the recent rains. The town had been heavily shelled, and the smoldering fires that remain suggested that it happened somewhat recently, perhaps a couple of days before the time-shift had occurred. Somewhat fresh shelling that had now actually taken place over a year ago. *Mind-boggling,* Kabinda thought to himself.

Still, there had been some shelter here, and it had provided ample cover for them to rest for a few hours before the sun rose. Such as the sun was capable of rising on yet another overcast day over Somalia. There is a smell of rain in the air again. It is a specific storm smell, a blending of dust and moisture, of heat and energy, and it was familiar to every African of the Equator.

Kabinda and his fellow travelers are preparing to duck back into the canopy of the bush. They are getting ready to exit the building and follow the thin road out of this town and make for the border.

The Kenyan who has been on watch upstairs appears. He has run down the stairs as quickly as his desire to be silent will permit, and he whispers loudly to Kabinda in English.

"Men are coming in from the Northwest, Colonel! They are dressed as allies, but their leader is a very dark-skinned African."

"So am I," Kabinda replies. Everyone is

speaking English. It seems to be the one language they all have in common, even if some have little ability with it.

"Everyone should relax," Kabinda says. "Stay still and put your rifles down. Except you," he whispers to the man who had been on the top floor. "You take your rifle into the hallway in case I am wrong."

"Smart," Lt. William Pemberton says suddenly from the doorway, smiling. "Optimistic but cautious. I respect that."

All of the men in the room are startled by this except Kabinda. He slowly stands up and extends a hand.

"Hello," he says.

Billy steps into the room, followed by Elvis and Harris.

No one has a weapon raised as Billy grasps the man's hand, and in his best British accent, replies "Mister Kabinda, I presume."

Colorado Springs
June 6
7:01 AM

Helen turns on the news and sips her coffee.

"Good morning," it says to her. "The global financial crisis in the wake of the event four days and two hours ago has resulted in several international markets failing to open today. The New York Stock Exchange has yet to announce its intentions for this morning, after closing early yesterday afternoon amidst continued panic."

Helen puts her coffee cup down and scolds the reporters on the television. "I thought y'all said *good* morning." Her tone and accent always drift back to the Florida Panhandle when she scolds.

The Secretary of Commerce comes on and speaks in a voice that is calm and soothing. A voice the American public can hopefully find a little solace in. It isn't working, especially on Helen, who isn't paying attention to a word he's saying.

The other anchor starts the second top story on the hit parade.

"Still no official word from the Vatican, where Pope Leo the Fourteenth remains cloistered with the Cardinals in the Sistine Chapel. A spokesperson claims a statement from the Pontiff may be coming soon. Meanwhile, the throng at St. Peter's Square continues to..."

"Mom?"

She hasn't heard Sam's voice since Billy's phone call.

"Hey, champ," she says, muting the TV and opting to turn the visual reminder of the mad world completely off. "Why are you up so early?"

"Mom," he says. "I think I did it."

She waves him over, and he sits in her lap on the couch.

"What? You did what, baby?"

Sam holds her close, as if trying to disappear into her embrace.

"I think I broke the world."

Malia's new baby had been smiling at her just seconds ago.

She was taking her little *koulda* for a walk in the middle of Skopje, pushing the squeaky old stroller her parents had given her for their grandchild. She had been thankful that it had a thick hood to protect her baby from the hot sun of Macedonia. Seconds later she found herself here, in the middle of a huge crowd at a music festival she had attended a year ago in Bulgaria. She had blinked in like magic.

Some Swedish metal band was on stage, but their song just fell apart after an initial burst of noise. The screams of 40,000 or so people around her cheering them on also ended abruptly. An eerie mix of silence and feedback erupted after a couple of seconds.

The band, shirtless and long-haired, looked out at the crowd and around at each other. They were every bit as confused as the audience, every bit as confused as the entire world was at this repeated moment in time.

Panic spread through the crowd like a fire in a windswept forest of dry timber. Screams rose again, but they were screams of terror, confusion, anger, sadness.

Malia was wearing a cutoff black T-Shirt with Iron Maiden's *Eddie* mascot on it, dangling the devil from his fingertips like a puppet. Next to her, a former boyfriend named Tino was starting to run away from her, leaving her to face the confusing scene on her own. This was typical behavior from him, as she recalled.

A year ago, she had only stayed with Tino long enough to get to this show. The Foo Fighters were headlining that night and she wasn't going to miss that. She could put up with Tino's fish and cigarette breath long enough to get to and from the show from Macedonia. And she had.

She met Marco a month later, and ten months later found herself having Marco's baby. Her adorable little baby girl.

Right now there was no Marco. There was no precious little Niki. There was only a throng of panicked Eastern European metal heads, and they were beginning to stampede.

Malia only felt the first few boots on her back and neck after she hit the ground. There was screaming and even more feedback from the stage. Those new noises faded out together as the world went black, and she slipped away into final agony as her body was trampled again and again by the panicked sea of people.

Her last thought was of Niki, and wondering where her little baby was right now. Who would care for her now?

Part Two

React,

Reformulate,

Reelect,

Reflect.

Nine
Yesterday's Highway

Portland, Oregon
June 11
8:04 AM

The idea is hardly a new one. Filing audio reports during the segments of her road trip with her little travel-ready Blue Ice microphone hooked up to her laptop. She can email them to the station back in Michigan. A little bit of paid vacation, in other words: A working trip that allows her to contribute to the company's programming on her radio station. Stuff that can also be transcribed for the TV and newspaper sides as well.

Flying home was not an option at the moment. The fleets of every major carrier were in serious mechanical review, since not a single aircraft in the world had a believable service and maintenance record. Additionally, the process of trying to schedule flights when vast numbers of the population wanted to get on a plane as soon as possible, had made for an ongoing nightmare for the FAA and the carriers. The carriers now had no choice but to start shutting down.

Yesterday it had become clear that the airlines were not coming back until later in the month. Anne and Ron cooked up the idea of these road reports over the phone. Turn this into a road trip with stories filed along the way, painting the picture of how things look out West in the aftermath of The Rift. A fresh angle, in other words...something to distract people of the Tri-Cities from the chaos of their own lives for a little while.

All it took was her buying the microphone to go with her laptop. Technology is a wonderful thing. The company would reimburse her the 190 dollars later. She had always wanted one of these little Blue Ice tabletop mics, so she didn't buy the cheap one.

The company would arrange a car for Anne, and she would drive to her father's place in the Rocky Mountains and file reports for a week or so until she could get on a plane and get back to Michigan. Hopefully it wouldn't even be that long.

The thought of driving out alone was not a pleasant one, so it was decided before she left Oregon City that she would be picking up a passenger soon after she got on the road.

Valerie's cousin Betty had an in-law nearby. This in-law had made it clear that she would prefer to ride out whatever this madness was with her son's family in Salt Lake City, as opposed to her lonely apartment in Portland.

As this in-law, whose name was Deb, finished packing, Anne set up her laptop in the living room and recorded her segments for air. It was amusing for Deb, who had no idea a radio show could be recorded in her living room. Anne assured Deb it would only take a few minutes.

She turned on her laptop, configured and tested the microphone with her editing software, and got to work.

There was a pre-recorded introduction that would precede her, so whenever she had voiced these in the past at the studio...she just launched right into it. That's what she did here.

"I heard someone on one of the networks say 'The Rift' yesterday. The Rift? The media took just over a week to give this phenomenon a label, which is *typical* of the media. I suppose in this case though, the label 'The Rift' is accurate enough."

"Usually this kind of labeling sickens me. Like when The Weather Channel made the decision to give ridiculous and clever names to winter storms years ago...you know, like the National Weather Service does with hurricanes. Being a part of the media I think I can mock the media for stuff like this. It's a little like being Jewish, and telling Jewish jokes."

She paused and took a sip of Pepsi. She would edit the pause...and her subsequent tiny belch...out of the file before she mixed it down. She would probably delete the last couple of sentences, as well. She was trying too hard to be funny there. An entire building-full of people in East Michigan would happily remind her that she was *not*. She adjusted her face to a serious place and adjusted the mic position as she continued.

When she did so she lowered her tone, as well.

"Nothing is funny though, not for any of us since this happened. Too many people have died from the shock of The Rift. We've all seen the coverage of the mass funerals that happened all over the world. We've seen them at home, too…so many of them that you almost become numb to them. Almost. Funeral directors are now listed among the wealthiest people in any given town. Everyone either is or knows someone who is mourning a loved one that was lost in the last handful of days. Furthermore, we have the dead who have *returned* to us, without any way to understand the reasons why. None of us do. The Rift has turned our lives into a living nightmare of frightened confusion."

"I am recording this from the road because I find myself having to drive back to Flint from the West Coast. When the airlines shut down last week, I was stuck out here in the Pacific Northwest. My travel partner made the decision to stay, but my life is…was…I guess *is* still in Michigan."

Another sip of Pepsi, another quiet little burp that she would edit out.

"The idea behind these reports is to give you my impressions of what I'm seeing out here in America. Now that I'm starting to send them to you, back home in the Tri-Cities, it occurs to me that there's probably little to tell you that differs from what you're seeing at home. Everyone here is scared, and confused…and wants answers. No one has any answers to give. What I can tell you is that I *do* see people banding together."

She pauses, but not for a drink.

"History tells us that's not always a good thing though. Time will tell."

In the other room, Deb contemplates that comment.

"Okay! I'm wrapping this up on a lighter note. Something trivial. I saw on the news this morning that as soon as the travel restrictions end, professional sports are planning to get back to work. That means baseball, basketball, and for us it means the Stanley Cup for the Red Wings and Winnipeg. So that's something to look forward to again in Southeast Michigan, something that feels like normal life. Of course, since my Avalanche finished with the worst record in the league...I'll have to live vicariously through the rest of you. Again...that, too...is normal."

She glanced down at the length of her audio and gave her standard out.

"Anne Ayres, Three Cities News."

She pressed the space bar and looked at the timing. It seemed long but there were things to fix. The hockey comment stayed, though. It was relatable...and whether people would admit it or not, a lot of people in the region were thinking about it.

After she cut out the sips and burps and insensitive humor...she was looking at a little over 2 minutes. Perfect.

It was edited and sent to Ron within a few minutes, and everything was packed away in no time at all after that.

This was it.

It was time to get on the road.

Anne was not particularly comfortable recording at a lunch stop. The thought of talking to a tabletop microphone in a busy diner felt odd to her. Instead she typed it while it was still fresh in her head and would record it later.

She and Deb commandeered a spot at the counter. The tables were pretty much taken. A lot of people are on the highways right now, probably because there is one fewer option for travel these days.

Deb didn't seem to mind the typing. She wasn't particularly talkative.

LaGrande, Oregon. Greetings from what a travel poster just referred to as 'the heart of the Blue Mountains'. There is still a lot of road ahead of me, unless by some miracle the airlines get rebooted in the next handful of days.

There's little conversation in this place as I type this out in the first café with functioning WiFi I was able to find. It took three tries to find a place that had it. 'Nothin's workin' the way its s'possed to right now,' a handsome young man behind the counter told me a little bit ago. Right now he's wiping the counter down with a damp cloth. The only thing missing is a little hat and we could be in a painting from a much simpler time.

Another man is sitting three seats away, drinking coffee. He blames aliens for everything that's happened. A woman dressed in what has to be the heaviest, most uncomfortable-looking dress I've ever seen is sitting at the next table. She says we are all being punished by God for our wickedness. She's drinking water and eating a very bland-looking chicken breast. She is shaking. She's probably trying to look like she is burning with the fury of The Lord, but I'm pretty sure she shakes because she's scared.

A young couple from Utah is on their way to a friend's place in Canada where they hope things will be simpler. If I had to guess, I'd say they won't be.

I'm sipping a glass of thin tea and listening to them all talk. I don't venture any opinions, and no one asks.

Everyone suddenly went quiet a few minutes ago. President Guagenti was just on TV, telling us he just signed the Emergency Act. As my sandwich arrives, the legislation has become the only topic of conversation.

To start with, everyone who walked away from essential service jobs has been ordered back to them within 24 hours, unless geography makes that impossible. Under the new legislation…failure to do so could result in imprisonment for endangering the public welfare in a crisis.

Opinion is mixed at the café.

"Is he really the President right now?" asks a gruff man in hunter's orange. "It's a year ago, right? So Wolcott should be in that office, making those decisions."

I've heard that opinion a couple of other times in the last week. I'm guessing you have, too.

"You're just saying that because Guagenti won, Dad, and you hate him," says the young man sitting across from him at the table. "We all remember the election. Your guy lost. We all remember that."

"Yeah, but what if we only *think* we remember it,

eh? There's no proof anywhere of anything that happened in the last year. Including the election."

"Dad...seriously..."

The voices start to run together now as I try to block them out and get ready to close the laptop.

"Aliens."

"God."

"Guagenti."

"Magic."

"Wickedness."

"Arabs."

"We're all having a nightmare together."

That last one, uttered by a little girl, is the first one I've heard that makes any sense.

After she says it...the room falls silent for a moment. Everyone clams up and returns to their meals.

"Tonya," the man behind the counter says, nodding toward the little girl. "She died of the pneumonia last winter. She ain't said much since she got back."

I look over at Tonya. She has a far away, almost dead look in her eyes. She is sitting with her mother, who is sitting so closely to her that I wonder how the little girl can breathe.

I can't blame her mother for that one bit.

Salt Lake City, Utah
June 12
7:52 AM

Staying in the guest room of Deb's son's house, Anne woke up to a loud noise that preceded the alarm on her phone and grabbed a quick shower.

After she finished getting dressed, she

flipped on the news and the laptop. She hastily set up the mic and muted the small TV in the room.

"I woke up to a booming noise in the distance. I wasn't sure, but it seemed to come from Great Salt Lake. That was about half an hour ago. I've heard no sirens, and there hasn't been anything on the local news."

"I struck out at the airport last night and was told not to bother this morning either. All flights are still grounded for at least the next 24 hours until the government sorts out the last of the situation and the scheduling issues. There is no wait list yet. There have been no airplanes overhead for the last few days in the United States, except for military flights. It reminds me of 9-11. Eerie."

"I called home, and our news director told me there is no scheduled announcement on air traffic expected today."

"Ron also told me what I'm seeing on the screen right now, something you all saw this morning. The Speaker of the House made some kind of flippant remark about rerunning the election in November. That's all the country needs...more ammunition for people like Old Man Hunter Orange back in east Oregon to fan the uncomfortable flames I'm starting to feel out here in the West. The fire of arguing, of contributing to that most special and uniquely American brand of madness. That wonderful discontent we all have a right to."

"I'm all for having an opinion...but shouldn't we try to find a way to put the world back together before we start arguing about what page we're on? Either way...I'm heading back out before something else blows up."

Cheyenne, Wyoming
June 12
9:32 PM

"You wouldn't think it takes an entire day to drive across Wyoming. You would be wrong. The traffic saw to that."

This recording, it would be noted later back in Michigan, sounded a lot more urgent and nervous than the ones that had come before it.

"I had planned on getting to my Dad's place through Northwest Colorado, taking the backwoods route south, enjoying the scenery. Every single instinct I have said it wouldn't be safe though, given the current situation. So I came the long way around, and I will cross the state line shortly on I-25. I'll be filling up again in Denver if the mileage holds like I think it will in this little car. Eighty-five octane is what you pump in this part of the country, thanks to the altitude and the air purity laws. Seems like the same price though. A lot steeper than it was a week ago. Panic is starting to settle in. Any excuse to push up gas prices. The world hasn't changed *that* much for the oil companies."

Any other time she would have deleted the last part. This was going to be a rush job, though.

"This stretch of I-80 that crosses Southern Wyoming is quite possibly the longest piece of road I've ever been on in my life. It's 9:30 at night, and I just arrived in Cheyenne a half-hour ago to grab a quick dinner and file this before I put in another three hours to get to my Dad's place. Wyoming is beautiful, but it's mind-numbing country when you are still so far from your ultimate destination, and you're doing all the driving by yourself. Admittedly though, I did stop in the late morning to check out Flaming Gorge. How weird is it that I still felt the urge to do the tourist thing in this situation? Am I the only one trying to do something normal this week? God…I hope not."

"Somewhere around the town called Rawling, I started to notice it. More police. More police along the highway. More police in and out of each town. More police looking nervous and jumpy."

"As day became night, I started to see the police less and the military more. None of them looked particularly happy. Likewise, I'm not so sure that I like the situation being one that makes bringing out the military necessary. They have better things to do, right? I guess I'm getting more than a little bit of road paranoia, so I'm signing off and getting back on it right now."

She didn't even bother to record her outcue. Her mind was racing now.

The Internet gave her fits sending the file. The signal was weak. It took several attempts, but her message finally went out.

She left cash on the table and wrapped part of her sandwich in her napkin.

One mile into Colorado on I-25
June 12
9:55 PM

"Where you comin' from, ma'am?"

Anne hands him the license and registration he had asked for before posing that question. He lingers over her picture a bit longer than she would have preferred.

"Displaced in The Rift, were you?"

"No," she replies. "I flew out to Oregon a couple of days later with a friend. Moral support for a family matter."

"What do you do back in Michigan, Miss Ayres?"

"Press."

"Be safe," he says, in a way she finds cryptic. "The highways are getting less and less safe. I wish you weren't traveling alone."

"Yeah," she sighs. "Me too."

About an hour later, she's in the stretch of interstate between Fort Collins and Denver.

She can't help but notice a pair of pickup trucks. They drift in and out of the lanes, intimidating other drivers. They match her speed at one point, and the passenger shoots her a leer that sends shivers down her spine. Thankfully, the police appear and they give up at the Longmont exit.

Anne is certain she saw a shotgun in the hands of the passenger in the second truck.

Riding shotgun, indeed.

On the north side of Denver the situation is deteriorating fast. The smaller highway, 285, is the quicker way home. Traffic signs indicate that it is closed. She has been listening to the radio all day, and a news/talk station out of Colorado Springs on the AM band tells her that multiple incidents have been reported on that road between State Police and locals.

She is only an hour from home when she finds herself having to turn onto the other Interstate, I-70. She really doesn't have any choice if she wants to avoid the areas the authorities say are dangerous.

I-70 can get her to her father's place in the mountain town of Fairplay, but it will add time to her commute and is choked with cars. Hopefully there will be safety in numbers.

She will get there tonight, no matter what the hour. She is even more motivated and determined now as she watches things falling apart.

No matter what station she tunes to, she finds the radio filled with more and more stories of things going horribly wrong across the western states. Here on I-70 she sees enough military and flashing police lights to feel at least a little secure.

One thing she no longer feels at all...is tired. Anne has so much energy flowing through her body right now, so much adrenaline in her bloodstream.

She knows what a toy with a fresh set of batteries feels like now.

Fairplay, Colorado
June 13
2:00 AM

She has been at her family's home for a half-hour now and still can't relax.

Dad is on his way home. He's been working with the Sheriff's Department, helping out with the problems on Highway 285. Her sister Mary finally reached him on his phone to let him know Anne was here, and he is on his way.

Anne has had very little to say since her unexpected appearance at the front door. She had not bothered to let her family know she was coming. The last leg of the trip was particularly stressful, and Anne is just sitting in the family room being unintentionally evasive. Mary is getting frustrated at the lack of answers from her exhausted-looking older sister.

Mary, for her part, was shocked to see Anne when she came to the door. She was armed when she answered it, after seeing an unfamiliar vehicle pull through the trees into their driveway. Mary isn't pushing her to say anything because Anne has never looked quite this out of it. Anne stood there in a sort of ambulatory form of shock, something Mary had never seen on her confident and cocky sister. Possibly because Anne had been in Flint when she found out Billy Pemberton was dead and went into a sort of functional shock at work until Valerie dragged her out of there.

It's late enough that Anne has missed the local news, which is always her preferred way to take the national pulse no matter where she happens to be at the time. It's how the general public sees things, and in her opinion it's an excellent way to gauge public opinion.

One of the 24-hour channels is filling her in. She's staring at the screen, trying to register everything. Mary is watching with her and making unilateral commentary. The door is locked and bolted per their father's instructions. Mary will get a call when he is pulling the truck up the pathway so she can let him in. Most of the lights are off in the house. All of their security measures are active.

Anne starts to reboot her own brain with something tangible that she understands. News coverage.

Item: War has broken out again in the Koreas. *That was probably inevitable,* Anne thinks to herself.

Item: Violence is breaking out pretty much everywhere. Again, this is not a surprise. This second story causes Anne to finally snap out of it and give her sister a hug. She exhales deeply, as if she's been holding her breath since the Wyoming State Line. That concept isn't too far from the truth.

Item: Police and National Guard units have been unable to stop unrest in the Western U.S., especially in the Rockies.

So I've noticed.

Mary brings her a hot cup of tea she didn't ask for but is very happy to see.

What a perfect time for me to spend a couple of days alone on the highways.

Mary sits directly in front of her, between Anne and the television.

"Everything has really been unraveling in the last few hours, Annie. What the hell are you doing out here on the roads? Why are you in Colorado?"

Anne gives her sister a weak smile. "Flew out to Oregon with Val. Her mom passed away again."

"Oh, Jesus."

"Yeah. I couldn't fly back to Flint. Decided to drive it, and I wanted to visit you and Dad on the way back."

The power is fluctuating when their father's truck comes flying through the trees along the rutted path that connects their house to the main road. Mary's cell phone goes off as the truck nearly destroys Anne's rental before it roars to a stop, just in the nick of time.

Fairplay, Colorado
June 13
1:50 PM

She has no signal as she plugs in to charge

her laptop and phone. Neither has a signal at the moment. It's one of the little things about living out here that she does not miss.

She pulls out her mic and records an update anyway. She feels like she's doing it more for herself at this point than the company.

"I don't even know when this file will get to the news room. Internet, cell phones, landlines, TV...everything is especially twitchy here in the Rockies today."

"My family's place in the mountains is in the middle of what you're probably seeing on the news. Communications are down all over the place. I'm not even sure how much of a connection they have at the military bases in Colorado Springs. The fact that we have a formidable military presence in this part of the state, yet we've still had all the chaos we've experienced in the last 24 hours...well, it's just too spooky to think about."

"I assume the military has communications. I'm pretty sure I'd see missiles flying overhead if they didn't."

"I, however, have no cell signal. In this part of the mountains though, that's always kind of been par for the course."

She flips open her little notebook and runs her fingers through her hair nervously.

"The local news out here says there were two killed and six injured in shootings last night on the roads between our little town and Denver. I haven't the slightest idea what anyone is saying about it on the street...because there is no way I'm going out there…"

She starts recording.

"The news is on in about seven minutes, so I'll share my decision with you all. Maybe some day I'll find out if the company aired it."

"I'm resigning."

"I was planning to leave in a few days after I wrap up some personal business in Colorado Springs. Flights are starting to pop up and I had a friend who said he could get me on a flight to Detroit on the 18th."

"Plans change. Sporadic pockets of unrest are still being reported in the area, and I'm safer here. If this lasts for a while…I'm safer here than I would be anywhere, even though I'm in the middle of it. People in this area know my father has one of pretty much every gun in the world. The more I think about it, the more I realize my little mountain hamlet here…the small town Dad retired us to when he finished putting in his time in the Air Force…is where I should be right now."

"I had planned on visiting my family. Now, I want to rediscover them again. Something about hearing gunshots in the distance in the night and sirens in the day does that to you. Terror makes the heart grow fonder."

"I've decided the Tri-Cities can do without me. Like everyone else, I have a life to try and get back on track. Hopefully we'll all have the opportunity to do so. Especially those who had lost their lives before this started and suddenly found themselves back again. I keep thinking of little Tonya, in that restaurant in Oregon. I wonder what happens for her now. She gets to have the childhood that had been taken away from her when she got sick and died. I wonder what she will do with it now that she has a second chance."

"Maybe all any of us gets out of this thing is a second chance. Maybe for some of us that will be enough to make smarter decisions. I hope so anyway."

Anne takes a sip from her water glass and reaches for the remote to the TV. It's time for the news.

"Signing off one last time, this is Anne Ayres, Three Cities News."

Her thumb smacks down on the space bar and the audio file stops recording.

Fairplay, Colorado
June 15
12:09 AM

The Rift.
The ReYear.
The Event.
Every time Anne turns around, it has a new

name. All she knows for sure is that she's tired of it.

She wanted to go for a hike so badly tonight. Black Bear Mountain is perfect for hiking this time of year, but given the current state of things, it just isn't safe enough out there right now.

Besides, part of the appeal of the hike is to get a break from her worried father. And he would insist on going with her. *So much for that idea.*

The television coverage of the unrest is getting hairier. She wonders how Val is doing in Oregon, how Jen is in Flint, what's going on at the news room. She can't reach out to anyone. Communication is still sporadic at best. She hasn't been able to send her resignation letter and broadcast back to Michigan yet. This has allowed her more time to think about that decision...time she did not want.

She especially can't reach out to the person her heart keeps saying it wants to hear from the most.

He's in East Africa, and that seems to be the place he wants to be right now.

A thunderstorm is whipping up in the foothills. Anne's having a smoke on the back porch when the screen door opens and her sister Mary walks out to join her. Their section of the woods has been cleared by the National Guard, and they have been told they are safe enough around their property.

"Can't sleep either?" Anne asks.

"Smokin' again?" Mary replies. The two of

them have always answered each other's obvious questions with another question.

Anne holds the pack and a book of matches out and Mary takes them. *Ray's - Portland OR* is printed thick on the matchbook over a little cartoon of a pig wearing a firefighter's hat holding a beer.

Mary smiles at the little pig as she lights up one of her sister's cigarettes, a scene that has played out many times over the years on this porch. After she exhales, she takes a long deep breath of the mountain air and the impending rain on the wind.

"Danny going over there again?" Anne asks, and her sister rolls her eyes to the left to glare at her.

"He hasn't decided yet," Mary says as she exhales a stream of smoke like a slender brunette dragon in a Broncos jacket. "If things don't fall apart any further we should be able to go into the Springs and see the Pembertons soon. I know they'd love to see you, and I think it would do you some good, too."

"You guys doing okay?"

"Me and Danny?" Again, obvious questions answered with questions. "So far," Mary says with a smile. "We'll see. It's hard wrapping my head around him being alive and back home again."

"Is Dad giving you the same hard time about dating a black boy that he gave me when I dated his brother?"

"Worse," she sighed, "I'm sure."

They listen to the thunder in the distance and

hear the sounds of the rain slowly tapping its way toward them from the woods.

Anne Ayres thinks about the look of utter defeat in the eyes of her friend Valerie when she learned of her mother's second death.

She also thinks of the look of feral wildness in the eyes of the passenger in that pickup, looking over at her on I-25, holding a shotgun as their vehicles ran south at 80 miles per hour.

Mary Ayres thought simply of the rain. It was a great comfort, having her sister back home again, in a trying time.

Then the Civil Defense Siren rang out across the woods, and her comfort was gone.

They shared a wide-eyed look of shock and went back into the house.

Their father stared at the television, which had a screen dominated by a blue screen and the Emergency Alert System.

"Something tells me we aren't going to the city any time soon," Anne mused.

The North Sea
June 2
1:00 PM

The boat rolls gently on the water, which is glassy today.

The painted letters on the stern, in a stout block font, proclaim it to be the fishing vessel DIETERMINED, and underneath the name a home port of CUXHAVEN, in Northern Germany, was given in a smaller, italicized version of the same font. She is not a particularly large boat, just 20 meters long, and she does only a small amount of fishing per year. Still, she is listed as a commercial fishing vessel with the German government with a small quota of cod to bring in each season.

In truth, fishing the North Sea is only a hobby for her master, Dieter Hamlan. He makes his money restoring old timepieces much of the year, a craft and skill and passion he inherited from his father. Dieter leases his boat out to a pair of friends who help him achieve his required quota. This way he can live his life, fish when he feels like it, and keep his charter throughout the year.

Dieter Hamlan makes a comfortable living between the two, fixing everything from wristwatches to the big tower at St. Michaelis for the city of Hamburg. He's done that job six times, and by this point in his life, he almost knows the stoic, copper-plated *Michaeliskirche* better than he does his own pocketwatch.

In the months of late spring and summer though, he spends as much time out on the water as he possibly can.

Dieter is capable of running the boat himself, but usually he has a first mate when he is out here. Enjoying an afternoon nap with him in the hull is that first mate, in every sense of the word, a beautiful Danish girl named Annifrida. They've been together for five years now and share a desire to not be married.

They nap because they spent the morning baiting and setting out their nets, a process interrupted by a power failure that took Dieter about an hour to resolve.

That though, had been a year ago.

A moment before the boat came to rock gently in the waves with her crew dreaming away the mid-afternoon sunshine…the Dietermined had been in two pieces at the bottom of the North Sea, 250 miles south-southwest of Norway off the Northwest Coast of Denmark.

The storm had come up out of nowhere, a bad squall that had rolled down from the Norwegian Sea and the Arctic Circle. The North

Sea was no joke in October, but Dieter had made the decision to drive the boat alone to Oslo rather than fly up.

He had been commissioned to winterize the Akea Brygge Harbor Clock, a beautiful lit timepiece in the center of Oslo's Pipervika Waterfront at the downtown harbor. It was a little late in the season to be working on a job like this, thanks to the city dragging their feet approving the budget. It wouldn't be a pleasant time for him on the boardwalk, but the job would pay for his entire Christmas Holiday. 'Frida wanted to see the Pyramids in Egypt. It sounded like a good enough plan to him, and there would be just enough time to book it. Besides, it was one of the biggest ports in his part of the world, and he had never once sailed into it. He was excited at the prospect, and the forecast was agreeable.

Forecasters were dumbfounded at the rapid deterioration of the skies over the North Sea. By the time Dieter was aware of the change in the weather, it was already too late for him to outrun it on his original course. The Dietermined would have to ride out the storm if he couldn't beat it to Denmark.

His charts suggested that his best possible option would be to make for the Danish port of Hantsholm where he could attempt to get leeward of the worst part of the gale before it reached the shore.

Making 30 knots and peering through the dim fog for any sign of the town's lights, Dieter ran scud ahead of the weather. He struck a meteorological buoy, thanks to its faulty lights. The collision tore a gash along his hull that nearly halved the boat instantly. He had been going way too fast for the conditions.

Dieter had scarcely enough time to issue his emergency message and get into a survival suit before the Dietermined slipped under the waves, and he found himself clamoring aboard his rubber raft in the unforgiving waters of the North Sea, shivering like a wet cat in a kennel full of Rottweilers. The sound of his ship splitting in half under the strain of the water ripping along the new fault line in her hull would stay with him forever, the sound of a forest of metal trees ripped up at the root by an angry god.

Before long though, good fortune smiled on the man. A Danish sword boat had been a mere 20 minutes from his position and responded first to his distress call.

Dieter Hamlan made it to Hantsholm but stepped off of a different boat than his own. He forced himself to pull it together and fly into Oslo to do the job. He would especially need that money now.

Lucky to have escaped from that night with his life, Dieter vowed to someday get back out on the water. There was a peace there, even after what had happened. It was a peace that people who were bound to the land by a silver thread would never completely understand. His friends in Hamburg failed to understand why he would want to save up for another boat and go back out there after nearly losing his life.

Annifrida, however, had the same salt in her veins and understood completely. Together, they had been saving to replace their beloved FV Dietermined. It would be a long road, to be sure, but they were determined to travel it together and reach the destination and set back out on their beloved sea again.

They would wake from their nap in about a half-hour...into what they would, at first, be certain was still a fantastic and wonderful dream.

One from which they never, ever wanted to wake up.

Ten
Falling In Line

It has been nine weeks since the Ayres sisters have been able to follow the trail off their property and down to the main road that led to the town of Fairplay, and beyond.

The rule of law seems to be fully in place across the Front Range of the Rockies, with yesterday marking a full week without an incident being reported in this part of the state. Things seem to be under control again, something that has not been the case since that day two months ago when Anne showed up at her father and sister's front door.

The entire state is not fully sorted out yet. Pockets of violence still remain in the San Juan Mountains in the southern part of the state, as well as in the peaks of the Medicine Bows in the north. For the most part, the Governor says that it is safe for the people to venture outside of their own homes again throughout Colorado. In fact, he is encouraging people to do so. The economy is badly bruised in the Centennial State, as it is in the rest of the nation after these two and a half strange months.

The West was hit especially hard. The U.S. had teetered, like several other nations, on the brink of chaos for weeks until the population finally boiled over. The situation deteriorated to an extent that a number of basic services had been suspended for large swaths of the United States. Life became very difficult for a while for the citizens trapped in the middle.

The news over the last two months had focused on two stories: The virtual anarchy in parts of the American West that the National Guard was doing its best to suppress...and the possible election in the fall.

They needed supplies. They were not as desperate as many of their neighbors on the outskirts of the town because Dad always kept a fully stocked freezer full of meat, and they could collect their own milk and eggs from the animals they had on their acreage. They had put quite a dent in that freezer, and their father would have to have a very successful hunting season or three to restock it. However, they made it through the crisis quite nicely, and were even able to help a couple of neighbors who had braved the trails out of desperation. Now though, the larder was a bit bare.

Despite this, the two of them did not head for the store. Dad would get the supplies. The girls had a road trip planned. They were stir-crazy, to say the least, and Mary needed to see her boyfriend. Last week, she had been desperate enough to see him that she would likely have chewed the arms off any random dissenter that had dared stand in her way on Highway 24. Cooler heads prevailed, especially after word hit the news that night about a robbery on that very road just west of Woodland Park, in which a young woman had been assaulted. Her path to Colorado Springs would have passed right through that area.

The Ayres girls and everyone else in the state had been given the *all clear*, and the roads were choked with traffic.

Their father was not particularly excited to learn where Mary was going, but she was old enough to make her own decisions now. Anne going with her made it more palatable. She could act as something of a chaperone.

The girls drove slowly, in a thick herd of vehicles, through the winding mountain roads that would take them to Colorado Springs.

Colorado Springs
August 18
12:08 PM

The TV signal was actually clear and clean today, and the power wasn't fluctuating at all.

Both had been far more regular in the last few weeks, now that order had been restored in this part of the country. The military had done the job, along with local law enforcement. Many people believed that the Second Chancers were to thank for much of the calm that was finally settling down across the country.

The Second Chancers movement was also very quick to remind people of that. With their efforts to bring together the confused people who had come back to life in the event, they had manufactured a unity that transcended the labels of alive and returned. They banded people together and spread a message of calm. *Destroying ourselves is not the answer.*

This was not a phenomenon exclusive to America either. The Second Chancers movement sprang up quickly and globally. A strong sense of unity existed early on between many of the people who had come back from the dead all over the world. There was a shared experience between them, something that transcended class and position. What's more, it was something the people who had not experienced their own death and rebirth seemed incapable of either fully comprehending or emulating. Eventually, the dissent vanished.

Some of the returned in the world were in positions of power, including the President of France and several high-placed politicians in other countries. They spent the months since The Rift event consolidating a power base for the Second Chancers. A new political force was growing, one without borders. That, too, added enough distraction to stop the chaos in the mountain states.

Chaos that had now been reduced to the lead story on the news, instead of the view from the outskirts of the city.

"Mary and Anne should be here soon, Mom," Daniel said.

Helen looked up from her lunch.

"You should have told me they were coming. I'll make them some lunch when they get here."

Helen and her two boys, Daniel and Sam, sat in front of the flatscreen, which glowed happily under a portrait of Dr. Martin Luther King, Jr.

The Pembertons sipped at tall glasses of apple cider with grilled ham & cheese sandwiches. The sandwiches had two kinds of cheese in them because food was easier to get now on the base. Many things had improved in the last week or so on the base, although the military installations had never quite had it as bad as the towns deep in the mountains like Fairplay.

Still, Helen's family had, like every other on the base, learned to do without in a number of areas. This allowed the meager supplies coming to the base to be more equitably distributed among all the families. Helen had spearheaded the effort, according to Air Force Regulations, and the difficult time had passed.

Fortunately, none of the violence that had plagued other parts of the state had spread to military installations like Peterson Air Force Base, though it had come painfully close in some cases.

Daniel Pemberton, a Second Chancer himself, just wanted to see his Mary and give her sister the latest update on Billy. He was also deeply buried in the decision whether or not to enlist in the Army again. Everyone who had enlisted in the last year was being given their own choice as to whether or not they would do so again, after much debate that had led to a Supreme Court ruling.

There was a sports report on the newscast. Professional baseball had gone through a strange process of difficult math and recollection to try to create statistics for parts of two different seasons that had been erased from the history books. In the end, they came to the decision to rebuild the teams as they had existed when the Event occurred, and by the end of June were doing their best to try and have a season. No one was completely happy with the result, not the players, the fans, or the league. NASCAR had done something similar at first and was now trying to salvage their season instead. The other professional sports faced the same quagmire of record-keeping and statistics, as the summer ticked closer and closer to their own starts.

There were bigger, far more important questions to be answered from the now-absent year.

Foremost was the question of *who* was legally the President right now.

Guagenti had been voted into office during the absent year. Everyone remembered it. The election had been a brutal one that polarized the parties in dramatic ways neither could have seen coming. The extremes became more so.

Now it seemed Francis Guagenti might have to win his election all over again...even though he seemed to be in power right now and had the backing of much of the country.

There was also Great East Africa, and it's Mad King Roti. This was a man who had forged a new nation out of an unlikely pair of countries...one Christian, the other Muslim. He had taken that new nation to war and lost it. Now by the grace of something no one could understand he found himself winning that war. He had learned from all of his mistakes, capitalized on them quickly, and spent the last two months strengthening all but one of his previous partnerships. This helped him turn the tide dramatically in his favor before the forces allied against him could properly react.

Little of the world was making sense in the months since The Rift.

Perhaps that was why people were finally starting to come together again. Perhaps it was a desperate need for strength in numbers.

The wilding packs of malcontents were nearly put down now, with only a few remaining in Colorado, Nevada, Montana, and Idaho. For the most part, after a protracted period of madness, America was back in the America business.

"Pockets of unrest in the west are quickly being blotted out," the network reporter said, standing in front of scenic Glacier National Park. "And this bodes well for the President, who faces a possible election in November that more than a few states are still truly unprepared for...and that no one can say for certain is even legal."

The video cut to a crusty old Senator on the steps of the capital.

"There is no 'according to Hoyle' rule to follow in these circumstances. In politics, that can only breed speculation and resourcefulness in the face of opportunity. The Constitution does not exactly provide a roadmap for the event of time-travel."

A reporter off-camera asks, "So…do you agree with the Speaker of The House that the election should be re-run in November?"

"I say only that Speaker Dumont has seized an opportunity to pose a question no one can answer. Thank you." With that, he held up a hand, and walked away from the press.

Former President Wolcott's party, still reeling from their man's failed attempt at a second term, had made the announcement over the summer. While the people out west were either burning the streets or hiding in their homes, Wolcott's friends used the Fourth of July and the Statue of Liberty as a backdrop for something unprecedented.

It seems that we are destined to repeat the year, so it is only right that we respond to the will of the people and hold the election again on November 4th.

It was not lost on the members of the party in power that the only ones voicing this perceived *will of the people* were from the side that had lost.

Former President Oliver Wolcott, whose loss in the election had been a bitter one, was publicly in favor of the idea, even if someone had forgotten to tell his face. For his part, former Vice-President

Patrick Delahanty put on an equally strong face but seemed to be completely against the idea. Privately, he accused the Speaker of the House and his former boss of attempting to stage a bloodless coup. This was an opinion Delahanty only shared with his wife and with the careful, private notes he kept for his eventual memoirs. For now, he smiled, he waved, and he campaigned for the Vice-Presidency…for the third time in his life. He felt dirty doing it but also felt trapped.

He campaigned, even though no one could say if there would actually be an election in the coming months or not.

What no one expected was the rise of a new political power, a literal personification of the phoenix metaphor. Furthermore…it rose up not only in the United States but everywhere.

The Second Chancers even found a candidate to run in Senator Clark David Brown of Texas. "CDB," as he had always been known, was a well-respected moderate member of the GOP in life. He was serving his sixth term in the Senate when he was lost in a plane crash in the early morning hours of New Years' Day on his way to England.

Before he died, Clark Brown's popularity had made him a favorite to attempt the nomination in the next election to challenge Guagenti, provided Wolcott decided not to try again. His death had been quite a blow to the party.

Now he was alive again.

His name recognition, combined with the respect he had enjoyed in life, gave CDB the support of numerous Second Chancers all over the country, no matter what their party preference had been before their deaths.

The fact that he was from Texas threw a massive monkey-wrench into the proposed election. The Speaker's plan had backfired. Most of the polls showed things in a virtual three-way dead heat with still no decision as to whether or not there would even be an election.

The Supreme Court had debated the matter with fiery arguments and loyalty to the process of democracy. They would continue to do so until they felt they could honor the Constitution…a document that was irritatingly silent on the matter.

"Turning to East Africa," the reporter said, and Danny looked at his brother.

"They'll get it straightened out, Sam," Daniel assured him. "Just wait. They'll do the right thing and make it all okay."

Helen stared at the screen. She never missed a report about the war her eldest was still fighting.

Eating his sandwich, Sam said nothing. Sam did a lot of that.

Sam Pemberton had more than the usual problems of being a young kid in a world that had bumped itself back a year.

Sam was convinced he was at fault for it.

His oldest brother had sent him the magic lamp because they loved Aladdin. Then, he died in the war. Then, his other brother Danny went to the war. When he died too, Sam didn't know what else to do.

He rubbed the lamp and wished for the

Genie in it to find a way to bring his brothers back to life. It worked. However, when it did…it ruined the world for everyone else.

Worst of all, there was no way to take the wish back.

Because the Christmas where he opened the lamp had not come yet. Which meant that Billy hadn't mailed the lamp to him yet. It was still somewhere in Africa.

Sam wondered if Billy would find the lamp again and send it to him again so he could try to fix the world.

Until then, Sam said very little to anyone.

Sam was afraid that somehow he would find a way to make things even worse if he talked.

Juba, South Sudan
August 18
10:08 PM

As his family eats ham & cheese sandwiches half the world away, newly-minted Captain William Pemberton III is having a very late cup of coffee and reviewing the notes he will have to destroy when he finishes with them. The coffee is bitter and grainy, which is to say it resembles his future.

His promotion to Captain was nice, the least his superiors said they could do for him. His family had been proud to hear about it.

They would be less proud if they knew what

had come with it. He was not officially Billy Pemberton any more. He'd had to leave that name behind at headquarters in Kenya, as he embarked on a new assignment that would keep him from returning home. With any luck at all, that will not be indefinite. All indications are though, that this will be a one-way ride.

Billy has no death wish, but he is preparing for the worst.

The worst part of this was lying to his family back home about what he was doing and having to stay out of touch with them.

As he sits at his desk reading the file, Billy wonders how the official account of his death will read if the mission has the outcome everyone expects. Perhaps he will actually be given the credit for the mission, assuming he ends up being successful. Perhaps not.

His training is over, and it is almost time for his placement. He's growing impatient waiting for the South Sudanese President and his Cabinet to finally buy the last of what he's been selling them for so many weeks.

The door opens, spilling more light from the hallway into the dim room. Billy does not overreact at having been seen looking at his top-secret directives. His notes are always coded and sent to him in an official Eyes Only diplomatic folder. This makes it easier to carry them around without fear of intrusion, not even from his superiors. They never know what codes he is currently working with anyway. It's *his* job, not *theirs*.

Not looking up from what he is reading, Billy says, "Yes?"

"Minister Mayuri, I apologize for the lateness of the hour, but you wanted to be told when the order came from the President."

"I did, yes, thank you, Simi."

The man who is using the name Kiir Mayuri closes his Eyes Only diplomatic folder and takes a red plastic one from Simi, the affable office courier.

"That will be all," Billy says dismissively.

His accent is perfect as he says this, of course. He has cultivated it for a while now, and in the three weeks he has been in this particular ministry office, no one has ever questioned him about it. His accent fits perfectly here in the city because his training was every bit as spot-on as his aptitude for picking up linguistics. His is the accent perfect for the center of the Bari tribal lands. He emulates their dialect and mannerisms to the smallest detail after weeks of intensive study.

This will be his finest performance. It has to be.

Everything about Billy now suggests that he is of Privileged Bari stock and not an American military brat. He even had his nose broken before leaving on this assignment so it would be flatter. Colonel Kabinda delivered the blow with his elbow personally at Billy's request. Billy's skin color was already ideal for the tribe of which he was pretending to be a member.

The masquerade was the finest operation of which he had ever been a part. He could not help but feel that he had been born for this purpose, and then brought back to life to carry it out after his premature death in the mountains of Ethiopia. His lifelong ability to imitate accents, which had its roots in his fascination with the speech patterns of his mother's side of the family, finally made sense to him. They were Floridian, yes, but by way of Grenada.

Kabinda was the first to see the potential for this risky endeavor. Billy's dark complexion coupled with his gift for mimicry gave Kabinda an idea on how the war might be won quickly, when every other officer was hell-bent on counterattacks and reacting to the renewed invasion.

Kabinda formulated the plan in short order and was given the go-ahead to have Pemberton reassigned. Billy bought into it right away, even before he was promoted, and even though he knew it was likely a final assignment. He was willing to sacrifice himself if it would make the difference it had the potential to.

With the coming of the new offensive, the campaign to get Roti with missile strikes and bombing runs met with frustration. Roti was a man constantly on the move within his borders. At different times he was said to be deep into Kenya, personally overseeing the occupation. Other times, intelligence had him hiding in neighboring Sudan or in the Saudi desert. He could be hidden anywhere in the world. The allies had no eyes on him, and that was worrisome. It was what Kabinda assumed had led to the approval of his strange plan and the transfer of the American officer to his command.

The architect of the Rift Valley War disappeared without a trace, roughly one week after he had reappeared in his capital building in the former Ethiopia. No intelligence was coming in beyond Roti's occasional video messages to his people. He usually shot these with a fresh copy of The New York Times in front of him, showing that he was very much still alive. To the American people, these videos were reminiscent of the ones Bin Laden had sent out for years after 9-11. It was not an association Roti would have welcomed, but he made it stronger every time he appeared.

As allied frustration grew, Kabinda made his appeal to the top brass to allow him to pursue his strange idea.

"I have met a young officer," he said to them, "an American. He was involved in my rescue from Somalia. This man possesses an incredible talent for languages and accents. He shows far more potential in this area than any of the *mzungu* we have around here," he gestured toward the British playing basketball on the courtyard outside the window as he said this. "Also, none of the Africans that we have access to show *his* potential for this kind of work. I should like very much to send him into special training with a friend in the South Sudanese government."

His idea piqued their interest, and Kabinda detailed his plan to them. This American officer would learn the customs, the idiosyncrasies, and the smallest of nuances that make up a Bari tribesman who had lived in the outskirts of Juba his entire life. He would learn the history of the state, with a particular slant toward the customs of the Equatoria region in the South. He would learn an appropriate amount of the Bari language, no more than most children would have learned before mastering English, which was after all the national language…and had been the preferred tongue of the district before independence. A believable back-story would be planted for him among the heads of the Bari tribe who could be trusted to come aboard. Once he was ready, he would be assigned a diplomatic job in Intelligence. This would be an easy thing to arrange with Kabinda's existing contact in the government, and a simple enough lie to accept in a young country with a history of piss-poor record keeping.

Furthermore, the fact that South Sudan was playing both sides of the war would work to their advantage since Roti was hungry to dominate the region and pull Uganda and the South Sudan back into his web.

After Billy met the right people and displayed the right amount of aptitude for the monumental task that lay ahead, *Project Rich Little* was green lit…and then never referred to by name again. The man who dreamed it up never quite understood the reference anyway.

Captain William Pemberton III called his family with exciting news about his promotion and a new assignment that would send him closer to the border. He promised them that he would be coming home as soon as he was able, once this mission was completed. He did not bother to tell them that he would likely be in a box, if he came home at all.

Then, Billy Pemberton disappeared from the face of the earth, and a man named Kiir Mayuri was transferred into the South Sudan Intelligence Ministry with both a weighty résumé and the backing of Defense Minister Henry Akela, an alleged family friend. *Nepotism*, some cried, but no one could argue that young Mayuri was one of the best intelligence officers to come through the office since its inception.

Billy has been waiting to be activated. Now, here in his hands, the words of President Toburoney on a piece of paper made it official.

Deputy Minister Kiir Mayuri is hereby ordered to report to Addis Ababa and complete the last stages of the recommitment of our Nation to the alliance of Great East Africa. You are to report directly to King Roti and be his connection to our Nation. You will appeal to his Christian nature and express our desire to assist him in his work by whatever means necessary before God.

Billy smiles as he reads the verbiage. The President is always so dramatic.

"Simi? Please arrange for me my car."

Simi nods and leaves the room.

Kiir Mayuri gathers his Eyes Only folder, the red directive folder from the palace, and several others into a leather briefcase that smells of finely oiled leather. He turns off his small desk lamp and reaches for the coffee cup.

Draining it in a single gulp, he wipes the corners of his mouth and remembers how good his mother's coffee tasted so long ago on Peterson

Air Force Base at the front range of the Rocky Mountains.

Kiir Mayuri walks around to the driver's side door and opens it. His driver steps out of the car.

"Sir?"

"You are relieved, Tobias. I feel like going for this drive myself."

"Yes, sir," Tobias says, happy to have the chance to go home before midnight.

Tobias has a new girlfriend, one he is blissfully unaware is a Great East African spy. She is getting excellent information from Tobias every night because he is too chatty about his work. Truth be told, she is the reason why Roti's people already know as much as they do about Deputy Intelligence Minister Kiir Mayuri of South Sudan.

Tobias hopes she might be up for an earlier visit than usual.

Kiir drives in the direction of his apartment along the riverfront. It has only been dark for a few hours, and there are a number of people present. Any one of them could be watching him, he knows, and so he pulls into the parking structure of his apartment complex and uses his security card to open the gate.

A minute later, Billy pulls back out in a different car and doubles back the same way he came, along the river, wearing a hat and clear, horn-rimmed glasses without any prescription to them. He drives to the home of the Defense Minister to share the good news and touch base one final time.

While there, he will also burn the contents of

his Eyes Only folder. The time for preparation is at an end. The fourth quarter is about to begin and he's standing in his own end zone, waiting for the kickoff.

The journey might only be beginning, but at least it has finally begun.

Lilongwe, Malawi
August 19
12:18 AM

Colonel Paul Kabinda opens an eye and looks at his phone as it rings and vibrates at him. Whatever this is, it had better be good.

He reaches over and picks it up, looking at the number before he looks at the time. He has only been asleep for about an hour. He had made it an early night in anticipation of the UAA Conference in the morning at the convention hall.

The number is not a familiar one, which means it is important, and a throwaway phone is being used to place the call.

"Yes," he says, pressing the button to answer the call and putting it up to his ear.

"Our friend is off to see the world."

Kabinda smiles.

"Tell him *bon voyage* for me. I will see you in two days."

The call disconnects, and Kabinda gets out of bed. He has a couple of people to wake up, and he needs to do it in person.

He was not particularly looking forward to this conference anyway.

As he steps out into the waiting car to head for the airport, he passes the cardboard sign at the conference hall. It is painted to read "Through The Past, Together, For The Promise Of Tomorrow."

Kabinda smirks and shakes his head. Most Second Chancers have the same attitude when it comes to the future.

Perhaps it will be there, perhaps it will not.

Windsor, Connecticut
August 18
12:45 PM

Speaker Bruce Dumont entered the office of Oliver Wolcott's family mansion.

Wolcott's office did not resemble the one he had been in the middle of renovating when The Rift happened. That office had been oval-shaped on the inside, to resemble the one he had occupied until January of that year. No, this was every inch his late father's office. It was more or less a cold storage for law books and a great oaken desk. It had been the perfect setting for the private conferences the old man would have from time to time. It had been a place the former President had dreaded entering when he was a child. It was a place where the old son of a bitch could always have the advantage in any meeting.

The former President did not enjoy that same

feeling from the room. It would always be his father's office. This explained why he had ripped out the walls and remodeled it in the shape and likeness of his own legacy when retirement had been thrust upon him in January. Now, he was in the process of doing it all over again, something that had been delayed for various reasons...not the least of which, the Speaker's efforts to put him back in the proper Oval Office.

"Thank you for seeing me on such short notice, Mister President."

"What's on your mind, Bruce?"

"SCOTUS has reached a decision, Ollie. None of my people can find out what it is, but the country will find out in a few hours."

Seattle, Washington
August 19
1:06 PM

Patrick Delahanty stared at the screen and smiled warmly. It was partly for show, and out of satisfaction.

The breaking news of the Supreme Court decision was actually a huge relief for the former Vice President, as it no doubt was for Oliver Wolcott. Delahanty had never quite shared the Speaker's passion for this enterprise, and he had a suspicion that his running mate felt the same way.

The point was moot. The election was not going to happen. Speaker Dumont had stuck his neck out and put all of his political capitol on the line, not to mention that of Wolcott and Delahanty. The Speaker had come up snake eyes when he rolled the dice.

Sitting in the green room of the afternoon news program he was booked on, Delahanty accepted the condolences of his staff. Meanwhile the producers of the show strategized the best way to try to convince him to not back out of his appearance on what had suddenly become a very historic day.

It would not work.

His handler walked up to him with a cell phone. "President Wolcott," he said, holding the phone out to him.

"Mr. President," he said with a smile.

"Mr. Vice-President," Oliver replied. Neither man could help but notice the other's smile on the other end of the phone in just those few words.

"We appear to be off the hook, don't we?"

"Yes sir," Delahanty replied. "On to far more important things."

"Grandchildren."

"Gardening."

"The lecture circuit."

"Your memoirs," Delahanty said. With a smile, he added, "I bet they'll finally be interesting now, sir."

"Interesting? You were the Vice-President, Pat. You shouldn't know the definition of that word." Wolcott laughed.

Both men laughed. Patrick Delahanty laughed loudly and happily enough that, through the door, his security detail allowed themselves smiles and a few small laughs of their own.

"So...statement?"

"We're working on something along the lines of 'A nation united, the unrest is behind us in our own borders, now is the time to rally behind the President, the flag, apple pie and white bread...etcetera.' You should put out one too, of course."

"We'll get on it. Talk to you soon, Mr. President."

"Take care of yourself, Mr. Vice-President."

New York City
August 18
2:00 PM

The applause that greeted him was modest, with very few people in the audience.

"Gentlemen, ladies...you honor me with your presence."

Dr. Karl Stutsman stroked his beard, checked the corners of his immaculate bowtie, and gave his notes a final straightening. He still preferred pen and paper when it came to his presentations.

He was of the old-school, a man who believed computer variables were fine for data. A discussion though...especially one of a highly sensitive hypothesis...should always be more organic, more personal. This was one of the myriad reasons he had insisted this conference should be held face-to-face rather than online.

Twenty-two people sat in the room, an auditorium his backers had reserved at Columbia. Dr. Stutsman was highly respected here, a tenured researcher who had enjoyed having the ear of three former Presidents of the United States, and he tended to get what he wanted.

Getting the lecture hall was easy. Getting his guests here quickly and covertly...*that* had been another matter entirely.

Eleven of the foremost scientific minds of the world were here, accompanied by liaisons that each of their governments had insisted on. They included the President's Chief Science Advisor and the head of a government agency, though Stutsman knew not which. China, Russia, France, India, Britain, Germany, Sweden, Australia, Switzerland, and Brazil rounded out the list of invitees.

Stutsman cleared his throat as they stopped clapping. He stroked the bristling white whiskers on his chin and drew a deep breath to begin his presentation.

"Universal Temporal Contraction. I posit that the universe, which we can all agree is constantly expanding, has stopped. We have reached an apex, the limit of what the physical universe was capable of sustaining, and now it has begun to collapse upon itself."

He paused for a sip of water and cleared his throat.

"This is by no means a new theory, and I claim no singular credit here. However, the incredible physics involved in what we're talking about suggest that the very matter of time itself has been reversed. As to the teleportation issue, we have to think beyond our current definition of what constitutes a dimension. Signals from the probes we have sent into space indicate that they also fell back to a position of 366 days ago. Some sort of hiccup in physical time placed everyone and everything into a position where the halting event occurred, relative to the distance from the event itself. For us, the shock wave of Universal Temporal Contraction happened, against all odds, exactly one year from the amount of time it required..."

Dr. Stutsman began to trail off in the mind of the Australian Foreign Minister. That man scribbled a note in his notepad.

Universal Temporal Contraction = Bullshit.

Everyone in the room suddenly looks to their phones. Text alerts sent to everyone, including the speaker, have interrupted the lecture. When Dr. Stutsman notices that everyone is looking at their phones, he decides to do the same.

SUPREME COURT TO ANNOUNCE RULING ON POSSIBLE ELECTION AT 4PM, EASTERN TIME, Stutsman's phone tells him as he glances at it.

"Well," he says. "I suppose I had better get to the point then."

Eleven
Sense of Duty
(October)

Fairplay, Colorado
October 18
10:09 AM

Saturday morning brings the sound of tires on gravel at the home of the Ayres family.

They are familiar tires, belonging to the old Ford Bronco of Daniel Pemberton. These tires have been common in this driveway...especially in the last two months. The same vehicle made a number of trips in other years, when Daniel's brother Billy had been the one who drove it and made his trips to see Anne.

Two things in particular have changed since Billy's trips to the Ayres house outside of Fairplay. The tires that carried Billy have long since been replaced. Also, Walt Ayres has become a bit more welcoming now to Danny, as opposed to the way he was with the other brother.

Mary and Anne's father has adjusted to the thought of his youngest daughter dating a colored boy. It is not something he had coped with all that well a few years ago when her sister had done so. However, time has changed the man, and the situation has given him the belief that the world has become too strange for many of the old ways that fail to accomplish anything.

Danny though, has made a favorable impression with Walt. Danny shoots, for a start, and they have spent a couple of afternoons together at the gun club shattering clay pigeons and putting holes in targets.

Mary rushes outside to meet him, so excited to do so that she's still holding the kitchen towel she was using to dry dishes. Anne watches from the sink, worrying away at the greasy crust that has formed in the bottom of a pan with a scouring pad.

It is a cool morning in the mountains, so the window is closed. For this reason, Anne has no idea what Danny says to Mary that causes her to throw the dishtowel at him. She is not smiling when she does this.

Anne watches her younger sister ball her fists up and pound at his chest, before pushing him and turning around to run back to the front door.

Mary throws the door open and runs straight upstairs as Anne turns off the water and puts down the dirty pan.

Daniel picks up the dishtowel and walks slowly toward the house. By the time he reaches the porch, where he was going to leave it, Anne is opening the door.

"Hi, Danny."

"Hey."

"Going to Africa, then?" she asks, already knowing what the answer is.

Danny says nothing but nods.

"Tell your folks yet?"

"No."

Anne takes a deep breath and thinks of his mother. She shakes her head. She always liked Helen, who never made an issue about her son Billy dating a white girl. Anne was treated like part of their family from the beginning and straight on through to the end.

"Be careful this time. And bring your idiot brother home with you."

"That's the idea," he says, and he puts his hands in his pockets.

Anne walks over and gives him a hug.

"I mean it."

"I know."

"Come back later. Give her some time to calm down."

"Okay."

Anne takes the dishtowel from him and goes back into the house.

Daniel drops his shoulders and turns to climb back into the truck.

The small voice of doubt in the back of his mind since he made his decision is now screaming as loudly as a desperate murder victim in a darkened alley.

As Anne watches Danny drive away, she looks back down at the sink.

She muses to herself that dishes always seem

to multiply when the person who was helping you is no longer doing so.

Dincha, Great East Africa
October 18
10:36 PM

It has been a long trip and not a very comfortable one.

He makes a mental note to pretend to have difficulty adjusting to the altitude here in the Ethiopian Mountains. Such a thing would be expected of someone from the Nile Valley city of Juba. In truth though, the thin-white tips of the peaks around him remind the man known as Kiir Mayuri of the Rocky Mountain tops of mid-summer back home in Colorado.

He was in these same mountains last November when he died. He tries not to think about that, but he silently fails at it. He remembers all too well the battle for Lake Abaya, a piece of Ethiopian real estate that now lies stretched out below him as his helicopter begins its descent to the waiting truck.

The truck is nondescript. There is nothing identifying it as a military transport vehicle, no official government markings of any kind. It is precisely the kind of understated secrecy he has anticipated.

Kiir/Billy himself is dressed casually as well, making an effort not to appear to be any kind of government official. No one in the city is aware of King Roti's presence beyond the circle of people that Roti wishes to know of it. Such was the life of a fugitive head of state.

"Mister Mah-Yoo-Ree," the Ethiopian driver says to him, struggling with the feel of the words in English. "I am take you to the meeting yes?

"Yes," Kiir says. "And it is May-YUR-ree."

"Apologize," the man says, smiling broadly. Kiir gets a good look at him and realizes he is probably all of 15 years old, at best. The kid double-clutches like a champion though, as they weave through the dirt roads on the way up to the mountain outpost beeping on the boy's GPS. He handles the truck far better than Danny did when he was learning how to drive the Bronco.

"What business you has from to Mister Urragabi?"

"That's between me and Mr. Urragabi, if you don't mind."

"Is cool, boss man," the boy says, shrugging while he drives. "I just wonder what the old man to does. I nostril."

Kiir frowns, trying to interpret this. This boy's English could very well be the most difficult vocalization to mimic that he has ever found. He has forgotten how much fun it is watching these Ethiopian mountain folks struggling with English. Of course, last time he saw them they were welcoming him as a conqueror.

"You…do you mean you are nosy?"

"Ah, nosy. Nosy nosy nosy. Much."

Kiir squirms in his seat. "I would think being

nosy is not such a good idea here."

The boy looks back at him. "It make you rich if you is smart. I is smart, Mister May-yur-ree."

They travel the rest of the way in silence. It only takes about five minutes to get to the outpost that will lead him to his mission.

Kigali, Rwanda
October 20
2:10 PM

The hotel he sits in has a rich history, one he knows well. Not as well as the people who lived through the experience at this hotel so many years ago, but as well as any scholar can.

Colonel Kabinda is a student of history, especially its darker chapters. Perhaps this is why he fights with such fervor against Roti, why he pulled his family out a very good life in Juba, South Sudan to live in exile in Tanzania.

He has traveled all over Africa in the most recent months since his surprising return to life. Today finds him in the dusty river city of Kigali, Rwanda.

Years ago, in a very different time, one of the managers of Kigali's Mille Collines Hotel turned it into a haven. Here there had been relative safety for locals that would have otherwise died under the machetes of mad men. It was a matter of pretending they were guests and borrowing on a number of favors. It was not nearly as simple as it sounds.

While he was a teenager in the country next door, the terrifying acts of genocide that occurred in Rwanda became one of the biggest motivating factors of Kabinda's life. He was still living in the frontier of the Democratic Republic of the Congo. Seeing what happened here when one tribe went after another was a firm reminder of what his early childhood had been like under Mobutu, when his land had been called Zaire.

He and his family had watched Rwanda unravel completely. Paul Kabinda's family could do very little but defend their mountain home from any invaders that might cross the border and work their way into their district. They could hope the chaos would fail to spread to neighboring countries.

That had been a different time. Even with war all around it, it was a quiet and peaceful day today in the city of Kigali.

By his thinking, the push into the final stage of Kabinda's plan could have no greater setting than this hotel. The air here is thick with both humidity and metaphor.

Colonel Paul Kabinda sits by the pool that provided those frightened refugees of the past with a water source and sips a fruity drink that is cool and refreshing. He has no idea what the drink is. The pretty waitress brought it to him when he sat down. A large chunk of fruit he doesn't identify is floating in it.

A man at the table next to him is flirting with a smartly-dressed, pale woman. He is what some would term as "well into his cups," and she is no doubt getting some kind of information from him. This city is always crawling with intelligence people. They crawl all over each other like an incestuous basket of rabbits.

To that end, South Sudan's Minister of Defense Henry Akela is not meeting him at the Mille Collines. He is there, and they are talking. Still, they are not meeting.

Being seen together would not be good for either of them. Officially, they are on opposite sides of the Rift Valley War, and both are no doubt under at least light surveillance. For all Kabinda knows they are being watched by the dark-skinned drunkard and his pale companion, a woman with whom anyone can see the poor bastard has no shot whatsoever.

Kabinda and Akela are sitting in opposite parts of the pool area. They are not even facing each other.

A pretty waitress named Abbi is serving that entire section today. She is actually an intelligence operative from Tanzania; one Kabinda has worked with before. Abbi has been bringing drinks and food to both men while passing a clandestine, continuous note between them.

She is on her fourth trip to Defense Minister Akela's table with the tiny piece of paper. She is good at what she does. Only Akela and the closest of his guards would have noticed the constant arrivals and departures of the piece of paper.

Kabinda and Akela, from either side of the pool area, have filled the scrap of paper with quite a bit of specific information already, though no one who happened to casually read it would know that. Now they are simply chatting for a few strokes in the same vague and secretive code.

Akela's eyes dart to the bottom of the page as it returns.

How did the new fish take to the aquarium?

Akela puts his cigarette in the ashtray on the table and grabs his pen.

Healthy, has not shed a single scale. I am told it will be at least a week before it can be put in the tank with the puffer fish. We don't want it to be eaten.

The waitress brings him a fresh ashtray and writes down another drink order for him. She takes the note from the table and walks toward Kabinda's table. She takes another order from a table in between them before setting the paper in front of Kabinda on her way to the bar.

Kabinda reads, smiles, and takes out his pen.

These things take time. As long as the water is the right temperature, I have no doubt the new fish will flourish. I look forward to hearing how it does in the new tank.

Kabinda rises, leaves a generous tip on top of the note, and walks out of the pool area as soon as he notices that the Tanzanian agent is walking back to his table.

"Thank you, sir. I hope you have enjoyed your stay here at the Mille Collines and will stay with us again the next time you are in Kigali."

"I am certain that I will, thank you." The irony is that his next stop will be her country, about 24 hours from now.

Abbi delivers the note to the South Sudanese Defense Minister with his drink and gives him a smile. After he reads it, he will destroy it before he too prepares to leave the hotel and fly back to Juba. She walks back into the serving area.

"It is hot," she says to one of the other waitresses. "Cover for me a minute, would you? I need to cool off for a moment."

Happy at the possibility to earn a couple of extra tips, the young girl agrees earnestly.

Abbi walks into the cooler with her phone and sends a text to a name in her address book that says Mom.

I met a lovely man from the mountains. We had a pleasant chat with a friend of his. They said the nicest things and they both think the war will end soon. Wouldn't that be nice? My love to father.

Dar Es Salaam, Tanzania
October 20
2:31 PM

The General is at his large Lebanese pine desk composing orders for a training exercise on Zanzibar. He is interrupted by a knock on his door.

"Come," he says. His accent is more England than Tanzania. He was educated in Oxford, his father a professor there from the time the General was a boy of seven. Much of the country speaks Swahili, but most of the official business here is done in English, which is the other official language.

"General?" the aide says, "Admiral Rokiri would like to see you in his office, if you have five minutes. He said to tell you 'Red Sky'."

It is everything the General can do to not jump up as if a large spider has suddenly manifested itself on his chair. He paces himself, rather than blow past the aide and arouse suspicion. He scarcely thinks to apologize to him on the way by, but he does.

The General walks briskly down the hall to the Naval Intelligence Operations Division of their military headquarters. The hall is concrete, and the walls are drab. His footsteps are like a metronome, tapping out an andante beat. He is in a hurry, and he is not doing as well a job of hiding it as he thinks.

He reaches the secure door and is buzzed in by the receptionist, a pretty, young officer who smiles at him and was told to expect him.

He knocks at the Admiral's door and hears "Come," from the other side.

He closes the door behind him after he steps through with a smile. "Lucas?"

"Robert," the Admiral replies. "Call your friend. The sky is a lovely shade of red today."

Alexandria, Virginia
October 20
6:39 AM

- 325 -

This had better be good.

That is the first thought Lieutenant General Harriet Bellingshausen has when she hears it.

Granted, this is a Monday morning, but the General has the day off to try and shake a fever. She is not happy about being denied the chance to sleep in because the phone is ringing.

She pulls the phone into view and peers at the display. She quickly opens her eyes wide and feels a surge of adrenaline as she flips it open.

"Bellingshausen," she says, suppressing a cough. Her voice is gruff and scratchy, and the agent on the other end of the line is unsure if this is from sleep or illness. It isn't relevant to him, so he puts it out of his mind.

"Recorded message on your secure line," he says to her. "Please authenticate."

She rubs her sweaty forehead and rattles off 13 numbers and letters from memory, followed by a code word. Both will now be different the next time she needs to use them.

"One moment," the agent says. A series of encoded beeps and tones follow.

"Harry," an Oxford-sounding voice says. "Lovely red sky this afternoon out here."

The recording ends. General Bellingshausen punches a code to shake the line and hangs up.

She crawls out of bed, her muscles aching with what is starting more and more to feel like the flu. She closes her robe over herself and moves to the window. She squints as she watches the morning sunlight break through the trees.

Red Sky this morning, she thinks with a smile. *Roti take warning.*

The General just lost her day off.

Washington D.C.
August 22
10:09 AM

"The Canadians are onboard as well. They have no shortage of sites where they can build."

The Director nods at her and smiles. "Good. I have authorization here for six dedicated sites, which will thin-out the facilities we've been using since the project began. Yours will be this one."

He points at a spot on the map surrounded the mountains.

"You have one month to get it fully up and running, including staff."

"One month is a little difficult in that spot." The spot was in the part of the country where the violence had only recently ended. "Getting people in an area this remote will be a challenge."

The Director gives a shake of his head and smirks at her. "There is no town anywhere near this area, and part of your construction began a month ago. It's very inaccessible and presents exactly the sort of privacy you will need to get things set up. We have the means to deliver the rest of the raw materials you'll need, don't worry about that. We should even be able to get the last of it in without attracting too much attention."

"And if you do? Isn't it going to be fairly obvious what's being built out there?" she counters.

The Director smiles, "That's a fair question. The cover story is that extra 'detention centers' had to be built to house the worst of the regional rioters and separatists. As bad as things became out there, no one will argue that. And given the remote location we've selected, we run very little risk of NIMBY."

"Nimby?"

"Not in my backyard. I have every faith that you'll get this done in the time allotted to you. We all do. You should be ready to receive by..." he fingered a wall calendar..."October one."

She blinks, tilts her head, and looks again at the topmost map.

GEM LAKE, it says, at the farthest reach of a river.

She studies the maps carefully. As much as she hates to ever admit this, the director is right. This spot is way the hell out in the middle of nowhere with no real access roads.

It's a perfect place to stick a prison you don't want anyone to find.

Chapter Twelve
The Leopard's Spots

Gatelo, Great East Africa
October 20
2:31 PM

The car pulls into the capital on a cool afternoon, the clouds hanging in the Ethiopian sky pregnant with rain. The rain will refuse to fall, however, until these clouds have moved further toward the Red Sea. Rainclouds have always seemed to enjoy being cruel to the people of this country, even here in the mountains.

It is a nice car that waits for him, one of the official cars from the palace in distant Addis Ababa. Urragabi explained that they would be traveling in style today, in one of the cars from Roti's personal fleet.

It seems to Billy...who is now quite used to answering to the name Kiir Mayuri...that while the cat is away, the mice enjoy the chance to play with his many fine things.

Kiir Mayuri of the South Sudanese Intelligence Directorate has had a long couple of days.

The journey to the town called Dincha was

difficult enough, though nothing like his 100-plus mile run right after he came back to life a few months ago. The journey to the remote town was immediately followed by a boat ride across Lake Abaya to the little town of Gatelo, on the other side of yet another mountain, which they half-climbed and half-skirted.

The duration of the trek was spent with a small entourage of armed guards and two other diplomats. The diplomats were obviously not used to back-country life, and Kiir Mayuri did what he could to not show his amusement at this.

For the entire journey…Urragabi grilled him.

Tell me, Mr. Mayuri…what do you miss most about your country?

Which tribe do you hail from again?

Tell of your people's customs, for they very much interest me as a man of the world.

How many languages do you speak?

When independence came…how did it feel for you to have a new country suddenly birthed around you?

Were you conflicted with loyalties to your former regime in Khartoum?

Was there much influence involved in getting you into such an important office at such a young age?

Their arrival at Gatelo was a relief. The pair of diplomats conferred secretly with Urragabi during dinner, talking about their impressions of the young Intel officer from the wavering neighbor-state that suddenly sought to get back on the winning side.

Kiir Mayuri ate alone; quiet and friendless, pretending not to notice that he was the subject of such obvious consternation. Inside, he was smiling at the performance he had given them in his newly-mastered accent. Kabinda would have been proud. So would his family, if he had been able to tell them about any of this.

He took a deep breath after the meal and looked at the flat and flavorless landscape. In the distance was the place where he had died in November. He paused for a moment as he did so, remembering every detail…every sharp, white-hot moment of that experience. It was a sharp memory, like a raw nerve. He had done everything possible not to irritate that nerve.

That had been yesterday. Today, he is waiting for the brown-nosing Urragabi to finish with the other diplomats so they can get back on the road already. Whatever business they are conducting has already taken three hours more than it was supposed to have.

Kiir Mayuri feigns irritation, displaying annoyance at being kept waiting. He isn't a soldier anymore. He's an intelligence diplomat. Playing the part involves more than an accent and tribal nuances.

One of the armed men from their travel party approaches him.

"Mister Mayuri? Are you…"

"Is that our car then?" he asks abruptly, cutting the man off.

"It is, sir. Mister Urragabi apologizes for the delay and says we will be on the road in about ten minutes. I have tea for you in the commissary."

"Fine, that will be fine…Mister…?"

"I am called Edward, sir."

"Thank you, Edward." Kiir Mayuri stomps off toward the commissary building. He does so not in the manner of a petulant child, but like an important man who does not feel he is being *treated* like an important man.

Edward follows quickly, stuffing a wad of khat in his mouth to enjoy a little bit of a buzz.

For a moment, he debates whether or not to offer a bit to the South Sudanese who has just swept through the door ahead of him. Then he thinks the better of it. It would only serve to stimulate the man. He seems stimulated enough at the moment, basking in the warm glow of his own impatience and self-importance.

The man is a typical diplomat.

Colorado Springs
October 20
9:42 AM

Daniel has been the unofficial therapist for his brother Sam for a couple of months. This morning though, Sam has finally opened up about what's been on his mind.

The Colonel is glad that he is home for the reveal. Being the Base Commander in a time of great international crisis and uncertainty has meant he has spent far too much time away from family. He has felt powerless to deal with his youngest son's emotional issues for far too long.

None of them but Daniel have really been able to penetrate the shield Sam has put up. The boy is as stubborn as their oldest was at that age.

Daniel has managed to push him just far enough over the edge today to start sharing. All the while, he has been convincing Sam that no one is upset with him about anything, just worried about him.

Young Sam remains convinced that somehow he is the one that caused the Rift event by making a wish.

"I made a wish on the lamp he sent me at Christmas. I wished everything was back the way it was, so you would both be back alive again."

"Let me see the lamp, Sammy."

"I...I don't..." Sam looked devastated all of a sudden.

"It isn't here, is it?" Helen said softly, understanding all at once. "Because he sent it to you a couple of months from now."

Danny and The Colonel closed their eyes, comprehending at last how heavily this has been weighing on the boy's conscience.

"It isn't here. I can't wish for the world to be fixed again. I ruined the world for everyone but us, and I can't fix it now. I don't have the djinni lamp."

"Did you ever see the djinni? Did you talk with him?"

"I didn't see him, but I talked to him."

"Talked *to* him, or *with* him?" Helen asked.

"To him."

"He never talked back?" Danny asked.

- 335 -

"No."

"Wishes don't really work like that," Daniel tells him, and their parents back him up with smiles. "It's the kind of thing that only happens in stories or dreams."

"And this is neither," the Colonel says.

"Then how did it happen?" Sam asks.

"No one knows, baby," Helen says, holding her boy close. "But I like to think of it as a dream come true. Your brothers are both alive again, and when Billy comes home...we'll all be together again."

"When is he coming home?"

The Colonel sighs. "We don't know. Hopefully before Christmas. He volunteered for a new assignment."

Sam tears up. "Why? Why did he do that?"

Daniel looks at his parents as he hugs his brother. "For the same reason I'm probably going to go back. Because there is a job to do, and it's something we feel we have to do."

The statement hangs in the air as if it had been written in granite and chained from the ceiling.

Helen closes her big brown eyes and fights back the flood of tears that rushed toward them.

So, she thinks to herself...as did her husband. *Daniel has made up his mind about going back.*

Colonel William Pemberton feels a chill, thinking the worst, already blaming himself for potentially blazing the trail that two of his sons might possibly have followed to their deaths...twice.

Dinner is eaten late at a rickety table in a simple resort that overlooks the calm waters of Lake Zwai.

"I was born here," Urragabi says, his mouth full of slightly scorched chicken. The meal is over-cooked and represents more food than the average family around here likely sees in the course of a week. The man answering to Kiir Mayuri has spent enough time in this country to know that. Over the recent course of two different lives now.

"Is that so?" Kiir replies, politely. "Where I was born, there are not such wonderful mountains. There was only the Nile, which was loaded with crocodiles...and the grassy foothills that we could not play in for fear of the big cats."

"Ah, yes. The big cats. One advantage to the drought we always had to contend with here was that there was not much of interest for the leopard or the lion or the cheetah or tiger. They left our part of Africa be."

"I see," Kiir says.

He takes another bite of chicken. Each bite is loaded with thin spices and thick guilt.

They have been working their way up the road that snakes through the mountains, along the valley of lakes that create a watery spine along the rift valley in the center of the Ethiopian midlands.

Earlier in the evening, they passed the road to Sodo. Although, he referred to it as *Soddu*, like the natives would. He is supposed to be Sudanese, not Ethiopian, but he would still be from the region. He has studied these details to the minutest detail. Either way, using the same name the West uses would send up a red flag.

His eyes lingered on the road as they passed it, and despite his best efforts, his mind drifted for a moment to his final trip down the mountain. To the day he died, nearly a year ago now...even though by the calendar of the physical world, it was a month away yet.

After they left this place and left this beautiful water behind them, they would be finished with the series of lakes and only a short distance from the end of their journey. Late tonight they would be pulling into the capitol. Tonight, he has been told, he will be sleeping in the King's palace. He will meet Roti's wife, Queen Fedens, and up to three or four of their many spoiled children. They are briefly at home to handle a vague situation that Kiir has only described to him as "something domestic."

Roti will not be there.

Kiir is fine with that. He is in no hurry. He has no intention of appearing overeager to meet the man.

He knows he has to take this process slowly. He is never going to get close enough to do what he has to do if he does not manage to win the King's trust.

He knows that he could, in the parlance of back home, find himself waxing these skis for months before he has the chance to try and take to the slopes.

He has plenty of wax and plenty of patience.

Colorado Springs
October 20
7:42 PM

Danny Pemberton, unaware that his brother Billy is currently pulling the proverbial wool over the eyes of the upper echelon of Great East Africa, stands on a rainy street in the downtown area. He is in the part of town that was once called Colorado City. Early in the State's existence, it had served as the capital of the Territory. A solitary building from that era still exists in the park, and a huge festival happens here every summer. One of his favorite restaurants is here, a place where some of the best local microbrews are on tap.

This is also the part of town where the recruiting stations for Army, Navy, Air Force, and Marines do a booming business in this confluence of so many military bases. Colorado Springs is within immediate distance of four Air Force installations and an Army Base.

The rain is a soaker today. Not especially hard, but constant. A wet rain, most likely an Albuquerque Low meeting up with a wet pile of air from the mountains. It's a constant occurrence at the edge of the Rockies, especially as the weather begins to turn colder. People huddle into the collars of their jackets and rush to wherever they are going.

Daniel does not rush anywhere at the moment, nor does he make any effort to hide from the rain. He stands there, getting wetter and wetter until he cannot possibly become any more wet. He lingers at the door of the business next door, a musty-smelling bookstore his brother's ex-girlfriend Anne used to work at.

He shifts his weight back and forth, left foot to right foot.

He considers whether or not he is going to walk through that door again, like he did the last time this part of this same year came up.

Addis Ababa, Great East Africa
October 21
8:03 AM

Queen Fedens is pacing, looking for something to complain about.

On the one hand, the staff is fortunate that they have kept the Palace up so well. They have done such a fine job of keeping things spot-on that she has found the place to be immaculate after her prolonged absence.

On the other though, they have left her nothing to complain about, therefore robbing her of one of the greatest pleasures in her life.

They count their lucky stars that she and the youngest of the children will only be here for one day.

The staff hasn't really formed much of an opinion about the newest member of the group that is traveling on to King Roti. They find Kiir Mayuri from South Sudan to be quiet and unassuming. Much the same as his new country has been since the ReYear happened. Neither he nor his country seems to be in a hurry to commit to much of anything. How very typical and predictable of them, so milquetoast in their support of the cause of war. Still, this man may show promise. He already looks smarter than the last one Juba sent their way.

Urragabi and the butler who serves as the Head of House open the doors to the main hall, where Fedens is carefully examining a few portraits of her husband. They were all commissioned to grace the halls of the government buildings in the former capitals of Somalia and Kenya. Roti feels that these cities are secure enough now. The flag of Great East Africa was raised in Nairobi without incident long enough ago that he can start moving his staff into permanent positions in the outer territories. Urragabi is to oversee Northern Kenya, where Roti expects the most difficulty. The Somalis seem to be more or less in line now.

"A strong face," she says, beaming. "The sort of face to launch the future, do you not think, Urragabi?"

Urragabi is quickly at her side. "Yes, Your

Majesty." He gestures at the butler in the doorway. "Our breakfast appears to be ready. May I accompany you to the dining hall?"

He extends an elbow, like a gentleman, and his Queen accepts it.

In the hallway, fresh from his room, Kiir Mayuri is standing there at the window, watching thin clouds stretch themselves even thinner in the upper atmosphere. It is cold and dry here. The air is a strange mingling of livestock and European perfumes.

"Mr. Mayuri? Join us! Chef has prepared something special for us to eat before we get on the road."

"Excellent," Mayuri replies, his voice devoid of emotion. "Just exactly where are we off to today?"

"There is much of our beautiful Kingdom to see today before we begin the real journey. Best we fuel up properly first, yes?"

"Agreed," Mayuri says. It continues to amaze him how well the Palace eats while the majority of their subjects starve. *Regimes change quite often in this part of the world,* he thinks to himself, *but they always manage to stay the same.*

"I do hope he hasn't over salted again," Fedens says, "I positively *hate* when he does that…"

"If he did," one of the children says, her face tightened into a frown with her tongue sticking out, "I'm not eating."

Urragabi and Fedens say nothing. Kiir Mayuri manages to not shake his head.

She's about seven minutes early. Not too bad.

It's a chilly Tuesday, slowly working its way into the afternoon, and the promise of a cool autumn rain. Cold, rainy days at the edge of the mountains can come hard and fast, and this one looks like it wants to gather quickly.

Anne Ayres has a lunch meeting with a radio station in Colorado Springs, the news station she interned at when she was in high school.

She doesn't really feel like she has the "in" she was hoping for. The News Director is not the one she worked with before. Like most radio companies, this one has had an awful lot of turnover. The General Manager remembers her though, as does the morning host. Both have given glowing recommendations of her to the News Director. She put in a lot of hours of good work as an intern when she was a teenager and showed great potential. No one was surprised to hear she found a job right away in Michigan when she started looking during her college years.

Ron and the people back in Flint have long since gotten on with their lives, and her father has finally made it clear to Anne that she needs to do the same. There had been a long conversation about Billy and sitting around becoming a hermit waiting for word about him. It wasn't so much that her father wanted her to contribute around the house...it was that he wanted her to get off her ass like she was raised to do.

So, there would be a lunch meeting today.

The News Director came out and introduced himself. She was delighted and amused to learn that his name was Ron.

They decided to run to a pub near the mall that housed the radio station, on the north side of the city.

"So," he said, breaking the ice once they had ordered, "other than you're the right person for the job...tell me why I should hire you."

She relaxed after that. She was going to be a reporter again.

Zanzibar, Tanzania
October 22
8:35 AM

"Welcome, ladies and gentlemen, to the First Conference of the African Second Chancers."

There was vigorous applause, and the speaker paused and smiled.

She was the formerly late First Lady of Zimbabwe, a woman called Nadia Wasata. She had been a fashion model before she had married the President and had died in a traffic accident in South Africa between Christmas and New Year's of the now absent year.

"Our first order of business is to fill the final seat on our Advisory Council. Yes…one of you is about to be dragooned into service, to use a phrase the British were once so fond of saying when they occupied this island."

The hall fills with laughter. Pretty young women, each of them pages for the assorted politicians and other leaders assembled here in the hall, are handing out ballots with four names on them.

Colonel Paul Kabinda takes a sip of his water with a lemon wedge and nearly spits it back out immediately as he sees the name at the top of the page.

Kabinda, Paul…Colonel, UAA (South Sudan)

He looks up at the lectern and sees that Mrs. Wasata is looking directly at him and smiling.

Hardly anyone in the hall wastes any time voting, and Kabinda notices that everyone at his table checked the first box. Including Thomas Piquesse.

He looks at his ballot again and notices the name under his.

Piquesse, Thomas…Surgeon (Mozambique)

Kabinda checks Thomas' name in an effort to negate at least one of their votes and throws a smile at the man. He knows Thomas fairly well, having helped establish hospital units in Kenya with him at the onset of the war.

Piquesse notices this, to the amusement of the other people at the table.

"It isn't going to save you, Colonel."

The comment is overheard by a nearby table,

which shares in the laughter.

The other members of the council sort the ballots at the head table while the lovely Mrs. Wasata continues with her opening remarks. Kabinda cannot help but notice that everyone in the room, at one point or another, seems to be throwing him a glance and a smile.

He sighs with acceptance before his name is even announced.

"Ladies and gentlemen, may I present Colonel Paul Kabinda of the Congo, by way of the South Sudan, Kenya, and his heroic service to the cause of freedom in the wilds of Somalia. We are proud to have him as one of the strongest voices for Reborn Africa."

The hall erupts into applause. Kabinda rises, acknowledges them, and sees Wasata motioning him to the podium.

As he passes the table, he notices that his pile of votes dwarves the others. He received perhaps 90 to 95% of the vote.

It would appear that he has no choice but to accept. Most of the senior officers he works for are already in the room, applauding his new lot in life.

Colorado Springs
October 20
7:58 PM

When the world changed for everyone a few months ago, it stayed the same for Ashley Gordon.

The only change was Ashley finding herself back in it...the same miserable person she had been. With the same miserable problems.

She woke up this morning to her stuffy, quiet apartment. The radio and television were off, and they would stay that way. The curtains in her apartment would stay drawn, with the bright Colorado sunlight trying vainly to bend itself around the edges and provide a little light into the dismal place.

There is no cat, no dog...not even a plump goldfish or a stinky hamster. No companion had been left to suffer alone in this sad place when she took her own life.

That had happened one year ago, on this very date. A date that had now come back on the calendar all over again to haunt her like a banshee with an icy stare.

Ashley dropped a couple of Pop Tarts in her shiny silver toaster that morning, and sat at her table in silence, waiting. There was only the low hum of her old refrigerator to keep her company while she waited, lost in her thoughts.

There had been counseling sessions in June after she woke up in bed that morning, surprised to find herself still alive. She went to the counselor in order to keep her job, and for her mother's sake, but Ashley's heart was never in it.

She felt her heart leap at the noise of the toaster pastries popping up, nice and warm. The sound had filled the tiny kitchen and given her more of a shock than it should have. This was going to be a day on-edge. She could tell right at the beginning. However, she had expected that would be the case today.

After breakfast Ashley brushed her teeth and took a very long shower. For a full five minutes of it, she stood still as a statue under the pulsating hot water. It turned her flesh a stinging red as she tried to feel something.

She called her mother, which she had promised to do, and spoke to her over the speakerphone while she dressed for work.

This is a Monday, and Ashley had to catch the bus that took her up Union and Academy to her job at the bank. The job is new, but a few of the managers there are aware of what happened to her a year ago at her former job, and they no doubt intended to watch her closely today. For her part, Ashley had made a decision, but she was not exactly religious about it.

If she lives today or dies today, she will greet her fate with the same indifference. She certainly does not intend to try anything again today.

The workday goes just fine. In fact, it turns out to be a good day. She doesn't have to force the smile when she talks to a customer who gives her one first. Still, there is an emptiness gnawing away at her insides, and it would not be denied.

It's raining fairly hard and the bus is crowded as she climbs aboard it to go home. She has an anxiety about sitting next to men, but the only seat is next to a young black man in a second-hand suit. The man and his suit are both very wet.

She takes the seat without a word or a nod…and then it finally happens.

The weight of this dreadful anniversary lands a series of blows on her emotional state, and she begins to cry.

Her tears are soft and silent and seem not to attract any attention. She wasn't looking for any. In fact, she is embarrassed by them.

The part of her mind that has always told her the world is too difficult, too cold to live in, not a place where she belongs…that part is screaming at her right now in her head. *Nothing has changed! No one loves you! No one ever will! Toxic! Toxic!* That part of her has the face of her father. She glances up and sees him sitting in the seat opposite her. He is always there when she has these days, even though he's been dead since she was in the fifth grade.

Her thoughts evaporate at once when she suddenly feels a hand on hers. The first instinct is to pull it away, but she can't. She quivers and looks at the man seated next to her.

The man looks back.

She sees something in his eyes, something deep and complex. His eyes house a phalanx of conflicting emotions, the ones shared by everyone who has been given a second chance; a mix of pain, terror, confusion, relief...and gratitude.

It's the same combination of feelings she sees in her own eyes every day in the mirror.

The young black man notices the look in her eyes, and without a word, his other hand is there. Both of the stranger's hands now cradle her own, and they look at each other for a moment.

It only feels awkward for a couple of seconds. She tenses up, nervous, uncertain what's about to happen next.

No one else on the bus seems to notice the two of them. They are all lost in the screens of their phones and tablets or reading a book or staring out of the windows as the bus rocks back and forth on the busy street.

Ashley says nothing. He says nothing.

He rubs her hands, softly, lovingly. He squeezes and caresses...moving in ways far more personal than a stranger probably would or should.

He himself isn't even sure why. Danny just senses that she needs the human contact and doesn't understand why he felt the need to provide it. He just did.

Shocked, Ashley feels tension leave her body. Parts of her hand she wasn't even aware ached are soothed by this strange man who has brashly inserted himself into her evening commute.

He says nothing, but watches her eyes close. Her shoulders drop a little, as if she had been ridden by stress that had been digging its spurs into her sides for some time now. That stress has now dismounted and retreated, and her free hand rises up to wipe tears from both of her eyes.

The brakes of the bus pull it to a stop and air hisses from them as the doors swing open.

The strange man releases her hand and stands up. Ashley feels him give her a kiss on the top of her head as he pats her shoulder. Then he steps off, disappearing from her life as quickly as he entered it.

As he steps off the bus, Daniel Pemberton isn't entirely sure what prompted him to do that. Now though, he feels that somehow he had been meant to have a flat tire after he walked away from the recruiting office. He walks over to the garage where his friend from high school will be waiting for him with the jack he had lacked in the Bronco. The rain has finally, mercifully stopped.

Back on the bus with a last wipe of her eyes, uncertain what to do or say, she looks up as the bus jerks back to movement.

Her father is still sitting in the seat opposite her, a shocked look on his face.

"There is kindness and love in this world, you bastard" she mutters under her breath, "even for me." No one else could have heard it.

Her father dissipates before her eyes, a stern frown in his eyes, his mouth still agape.

Ashley turns to face the window and feels herself smiling for the first time in many years.

Fine. If the world is so damned determined to give her a second chance, then she'll take it.

Chapter Thirteen
Trust

Al Qadarif, Sudan
October 21
7:36 PM

Their arrival was low-key and appeared as nothing special to the handful of people at the border checkpoint. The armed Sudanese soldiers did not know who they were when they presented their papers for the crossing.

There had been an abandoned village a mile ago, on the GEA side of the border, where the two cars and the fine clothing were left behind for a return trip to the palace. Urragabi now assumed the role of patriarch of a family of travelers crossing the border on foot with Sudanese passports. Wealthy dissenter refugees bribing their way across the border were common at these checkpoints. The Royals posed as his wife and children with Kiir Mayuri and the four armed guards as their servants.

As near as Mayuri could tell, Urragabi's role and that of his Queen were not so far from the truth. There was closeness between the two of them that no one else had seemed to notice. At the very least, no one had ever dared comment on it.

Now that they had crossed the border, and the traveling party was down to just the nine of them, Kiir Mayuri began the process of implementing the specifics of his plan. There was no way to communicate back to the people who had sent him here without running the risk of the signal being intercepted and decoded. He was on his own now and left to his own devices. This was the way he preferred it.

Now, he would begin to warm even more to Urragabi. He would start to display even more of the qualities that had gotten him this far. He would make it known that he was not just another pushover South Sudan diplomat. He was here to conduct business, and he possessed more than ample value to Roti's cause. If they would trust him, he could deliver almost anything to them. He would have an incredible amount of intelligence about the remaining American, British, and Qatari troops in Kenya. He would offer them the key to the heart of South Sudan, and all of the necessary support to enable that front of the war to be fortified without the effort and expense of using GEA troops. This meant those troops could find greater purpose elsewhere.

In essence, he would prove to Urragabi that he had something to offer, that he was not merely biding his time.

The foremost question now for Billy was this: why was Roti hiding in the Sudan?

Sudan was not particularly an ally. It was

more along the lines of what Spain was to the Nazis in World War II. Great East Africa's alliance with South Sudan made any formal alliance a cultural impossibility for the General that served as Sudan's President. There was, after all, still an uneasy cease-fire in place between Sudan and their Southern neighbor. Many in the capital city of Khartoum still viewed South Sudan as 10 states in the South that had forgotten their place in recent years. A temporary cessation of hostilities existed between them at best.

Honestly, the more Kiir Mayuri thought about it...it made perfect sense. The process of trying to locate Roti had involved numerous agents planted throughout the man's kingdom. These same people were also carefully measuring the dissent and doing what they could to foster more of it wherever and whenever possible.

The Allies were firm in their conviction that Roti was going to lose all over again. Roti was not going to be able to win over the many tribes of Kenya. Kenya's own government had barely been able to do that, and they had not done so using force and intimidation. The Somalis loyalty would run out when the food did, and then they would go back to supporting whichever warlord was able to supply it. Uganda, which had been so incredibly gung-ho for the war the first time around, was sitting it out entirely this time. Roti had been smart and lucky since the Rift event, but it would not last.

This is what they told themselves anyway.

The reality was somewhat different. The

Ethiopian and Somali soldiers, wiser the second time around, were very happy with their renewed success. By all appearances, they were determined to hang on to their territorial gains this time to the last man.

"This is where we say goodbye then, my Queen." Urragabi says. He is feigning...no, he is *selling*...nonchalance. Kiir-Billy is not buying it for a second, though. It has all the resonance of his last goodbye with Anne Ayres. It is a loaded farewell, hopeful that things will not go horribly wrong and find one of them dead before they have a chance to hold each other again.

"I will see you soon," she says, and two of the guards guide her to the door of a very nice car of European origin that Kiir does not recognize. The other two remain with him and Urragabi.

Kassala, Sudan
October 25
4:52 PM

Determined to never be a prisoner again, Roti does not enjoy staying in one place for very long. The irony of this is that he has now become a prisoner of the road itself.

Still, this is one of the pivotal points on the map where refugees are likely to stream out of Eritrea if his invasion plan is to come to fruition. He likes to imagine the people who have long refused to admit that they were Ethiopian pouring in to the Sudan from the east. He imagines them panicking and without hope. He imagines the children crying. He enjoys that image in particular.

His own children...or at least the three youngest of the ones he has fathered with his wife...are squabbling in the bedroom he has arranged for them to share upstairs. Fedens, his glorious and magnificent Queen from the fragrant waters of the Blue Nile, is ignoring the sounds of their bickering as she reads a book. The book is in French, which she has been endeavoring to learn. She is not doing very well with it. For the sake of appearance though, she is convincing herself that she not only understands the book but is enjoying it.

Benji appears holding a cell phone.

"Urragabi," he says, and he hands the phone over without expression.

"Tell me of our friend," Roti says, "and whether I should bother to hear anything he has to say."

"He is a difficult man. I like that. Chances are you would, as well."

Roti is smiling. "So, where does he stand on November?"

On the other end of the phone call, it is Urragabi's turn to smile. "He has suggestions on how the plan for November can be improved. He does not think the current situation is being properly interpreted to you. He feels he can help us change that."

Roti thinks for a moment. Urragabi is well

versed in this particular bit of silence, and he says nothing so as not to interrupt it. There is static enough to indicate that the call has not disconnected. The moment grows while the King contemplates all of the variables.

A full 60 seconds pass before Roti breaks the silence with a curt, "Site 5 in 24 hours," and disconnects the call before Urragabi can say another word.

Washington, D.C.
October 25
9:02 AM

The situation room is dark with maps of eastern Africa dominating the main wall. President Guagenti and the Joint Chiefs take their seats.

"Zanzibar is on the line, Mr. President." The uniformed General who says this presses a button on the phone and hangs up the receiver.

"Go ahead, Colonel," the President says. General Bellingshausen flips open a notebook to take a few notes as they talk.

"Good morning, Mr. President, ladies and gentlemen," the voice of Kabinda through the phone is smiling an infectious smile. None of the people in Washington is aware that he is relishing the opportunity to dodge out of what he keeps thinking of as The Conference of the Living Dead.

"What do you have for me, Colonel?" the

President says, hopeful the news will be good today. Good news days from the Great Rift Valley have been infrequent lately.

"Operation Diamond is over, Mr. President. Defense Minister Tafi is in custody."

Kabinda's smile spreads around the table quickly.

"And Operation Rich Little, excuse me...Operation *Vorpal*?" inquires the Army three-star at Bellingshausen's left.

"I have no update, sir, and I don't expect one," Kabinda says.

"That's kind of the point, Nate," General Bellingshausen says. Her smile has faded rather quickly. "None of us will know until it's over."

The Army three-star, annoyed at being corrected by the Air Force three-star, nods and says nothing more for the moment.

Guagenti closes his eyes for a moment. It would appear that Nathan Fisher's recent promotion was not green-lit for the man's vast reserves of patience.

"Please continue, Colonel. How did you get him?"

"It was an inspection tour of Mt. Kenya, Mr. President. Tafi got a little too bold, came a little too far south. Thought he was Hitler in Paris or something. Roti did not sanction his trip as far as we are able to tell. We heard about it through a plant and intercepted his convoy in a town called Nyeri."

"Took him alive?" Guagenti asks.

"We did, sir. Tafi is on a plane and should be

arriving at the agreed-upon location within the next three hours."

"Excellent work, Colonel. My congratulations to you and the rest of the UAA. I look forward to finally meeting with you in person."

"And I you, Mr. President. Thank you."

The call disconnects.

"That'll be all, everyone," the President says, rising, "I'd like the room. Nate? Stick around, would you?"

Everyone else in the room leaves without a word but filled with the gleeful thought that the new kid is finding himself charged with the task of banging erasers by the teacher.

"Vorpal is never discussed," Guagenti begins, lighting a cigarette he borrowed from one of the Marine's outside the Oval before he left for the Sit room. "It especially isn't discussed on an overseas line."

"I'm sorry, Mr. President."

"I like you, Nate. You came highly recommended to take this seat from the asshole that kept it warm before. That asshole was and is a close, personal friend. His endorsement sealed the deal to move you in here and put that other star on your shoulder."

"And I appreciate that, Mr. President."

"Take the time to listen and learn, General. You'll get the hang of it."

Guagenti pauses and takes a long drag of the cigarette. He is already imagining Mrs. Guagenti smelling it on him later. He can already see the disdain in her gaze. He enjoys that look.

"As for when Vorpal comes to an end…who knows? We may not know until the media does. It's a delicate situation and a whole new world."

Even if the calendar looks the same, he manages not to add.

"And if it fails?" General Fisher asks.

"Then I suppose we'll know much faster."

The President stubs out his cigarette and gives the man a nod as he collects his folder from the desk and steps to the door.

Atbara, Sudan
October 26
5:02 PM

Roti is right on time and pleased to see that Urragabi and the man from South Sudan are already there and waiting.

The man introduced to the King as Kiir Mayuri is prepared to dazzle him. Mayuri strides forward with total confidence and grasps his hand firmly, but not too firmly.

"Mister Mayuri," the King says, grinning like a hyena in the Katanga Plateau. "Give me your assessment of the situation as it stands today."

Mayuri nods. "The hold on Nairobi is tenuous, and it is likely to be retaken in the coming weeks. You already know this, Your Majesty. It is in your best interest to focus on central Kenya, fortify your position there while you still have the manpower. If you are spread too thin you will be unable to make any kind of meaningful move along the coast...which would be your next objective if you want to be taken seriously."

Roti purses his lips for a second before responding. He liked that the man called him "Your Majesty" without being one of his subjects. "Uganda?" he asks.

"Forget Uganda," Kiir Mayuri advises. "They have never had the heart for war unless it is with themselves. Your master plan for East Africa was nothing but a chance for them to try and absorb the rest of Lake Victoria's northern shore."

"True enough," Roti says. "Go on."

"The South Sudan is prepared to stand with you again. I bring you the word of our Defense Minister. We will spread south from the Elemi Triangle as we did before. Once we grasp the attention of the piece of the Alliance now focused west of Lake Turkana, there will be a shift. This will give you the opportunity to redouble your efforts elsewhere across the North, and hold the center. Bring in some of the Somalis you enjoy employing as cannon fodder to hold the East, which is thin and easily controlled anyway. Once you have established a stronger position, you can begin to move troops back across the old border and prepare an assault on Eritrea." *Like at the end of a turn playing Risk,* he didn't add. That board game reference would not make sense in East Africa and might give him away.

Urragabi winced a little. No one was ever this straight with Roti.

Kiir Mayuri noticed this and knew what Urragabi was thinking. *Perhaps,* Kiir thought, *if his advisors were not merely sycophantic Yes Men you idiots might have done better in the war the first time around. Hell, you might have even won yourselves Northern Kenya. At least for a while.*

Roti's face turned stern as he stared into Mayuri's eyes.

"You know of the Cataracts, yes?"

Kiir nodded. "Of course. Some of them are quite scenic, I understand. I admit having never seen them in person before."

"How unfortunate," Roti says, a note of sadness in his words.

"To be completely honest, Your Majesty, my family never had much opportunity to come this far down the river when I was younger."

He gave himself points for remembering that the river flowed south to north. He had nearly said *up the river* instead.

His words also rang with truth: The Pemberton family had never visited the Nile Cataracts.

"The Fifth Cataract is not far from here. Meet me there tomorrow at noon, and we will talk again."

Roti turned and walked away before the young man could respond.

That was that. Captain William Pemberton had experienced his first conversation with Mad King Roti. Like so many who had done so before him, he had also experienced how abruptly every conversation with the man ended: quickly and unilaterally.

No one had anticipated that the conference would run into the weekend, but everyone had made it work into their schedules. The agenda was indefatigable.

This obviously reflected the gravity of the last item on the agenda, which took a full day to explore.

Rumors were beginning to spread in Asia and South America about a series of what were, for lack of a better label, new "detention camps." The actual purpose these facilities served was not clear, nor did anyone have any evidence yet that they were in fact targeting Second Chancers, as rumors also suggested.

It was agreed that the situation bore attention, and it was left at that.

Paul Kabinda stood at the bar, having surrendered his seat to an Egyptian woman who served with him on the African Second Chancers Council. She was an executive at a shipping firm.

Kabinda replayed the last few days over and over again in his mind, thinking about the work that now lay before him, and how it might affect his military career.

He had worked hard to get where he was,

and he was loathe to giving up on everything he had built for himself.

Still, as his wife had told him over the phone several times this week, sometimes the man is defined by the circumstances and not by who he once was.

It annoyed him how wise his wife could be sometimes.

North Hollywood, California
July 11
6:00 AM
Five weeks after the Event

Carlos Perez has the day off today, which is unusual for a Friday. The Dodgers are starting a three-game home stand with the Cubs today, and he has not been able to go to a game since the league started back up. He's been a little busy going to therapy proving that he can be a contributing member of society this time.

Major League Baseball just came back into existence a few weeks ago, and the crazy, sometimes violent reactions to the ReYear thing last month are starting to fade into the usual psychotic haze of the City of Angels.

He is working in the city's Sanitation Department now, with coworkers who were unaware of his history…or, rather, possible future.

Last night, Perez laid out his faded blue Beltre jersey to put on after he finishes toweling off from his shower. His first alarm is set to go off in an hour, and the sun promises a beautiful summer day today. The sort of day that is perfect for a baseball game. For now, though, he sleeps peacefully. He is the portrait of stillness. He does not even snore.

The government is thrilled that a number of cities have had nice weather since the games have been restarted. America needs a distraction. The hope is that getting things going again in the major and minor leagues will be a big help in keeping people calm. Nothing makes the government happier right now than the thought of people like Carlos Perez heading to ballparks across the country this past week and cheering loudly. Drinking overpriced beer. Eating overpriced hot dogs. Exchanging high fives with all of the complete strangers within reach after someone scores a run for the home crowd.

The government, however, does not intend to let Carlos Perez enjoy his beloved Dodgers this afternoon.

Carlos had a difficult year last year, which he would freely admit. However, he has gone to great lengths to keep himself from making the same mistakes again.

Last summer was a mistake, but now it's like it never happened. He is going to have a better year. Yolanda moving out was the first step in that direction; something they agreed on after they had both suddenly appeared in the apartment again a couple of weeks ago.

That might sound peaceful, but it was anything but.

Yolanda's reaction to waking up next to

Carlos again was a scream of stark terror, a hasty grabbing of purse and car keys from the dinner table, and running for her life in her Red Hot Chili Peppers t-shirt and panties.

In the weeks that followed, the strange set of circumstances faced by the entire world went from bad to worse to complete chaos. After a time, the situation became clearer, as did everyone's heads.

Yolanda took him to court and filed a protective order. It was granted, however the courts decided there was no crime for which to punish Carlos Perez. After all, the crime had not happened yet. Courts across the country…indeed, the world…were finding themselves in situations where they had to make similar decisions.

Yolanda was not happy to hear that he could not be arrested again for a crime he technically had yet to commit. Especially, she argued without success, considering what the crime had been. She was so uncomfortable at the thought of even returning to their former place that she had to be talked out of the decision to let him keep her things.

Angry, defeated, and still terrified, Yolanda eventually arranged to visit their former place to get a few of her things that were of vital importance to her.

She will be coming today actually, with a police escort. She is doing this with the understanding that the man who murdered her in August would not be home. That much, the police were able to arrange on her behalf. Carlos has assured the LAPD that he will be at the Dodgers game.

Carlos does not hear anyone enter his home. He is a heavy sleeper. His eyes finally open when a weapon in his bedroom clicks while being drawn into fire-ready position.

He wakes up to find the barrel of that rifle staring at him. His instinct is to struggle as his wrists are drawn together and bound, but only for a second. The rifle has convinced him to be still after that.

"Mister Carlos Federico Perez," says a woman standing next to the man with the rifle, and she follows his name with his Social Security Number. "You are being taken into protective custody by the Department of Homeland Security. If you are willing to cooperate and discuss your case in a rational manner, this will go easier for you. Will you comply?"

A violent outburst is the absolute last idea Perez would entertain at the moment. He nods at the woman, who drops the stern face and smiles at him.

"Thank you, Mister Perez."

It is not entirely accurate to claim that they are from Homeland Security. This arrest is the seventh in the Los Angeles area this week for an extremely covert group that has no official name. They are akin to the foot soldiers of the classic Black Helicopters. They do not exist.

In the hallways of the few places that even know of their existence, they are referred to as the Department of Preventive Criminology.

Not even the people who work within the

department are aware which branch of the government tree they are hanging from. They have a duty to perform. They do it without asking questions. As for how deep these roots might run, no one is certain. You only know the person to whom you report.

Before the majority of his neighbors are even awake, Carlos Perez is in custody and led out to a car in silence.

North Hollywood, California
August 19
5:08 PM
9 ½ Months before the Event

The bus pulls into the stop at Griffith Park. It sheds six passengers and gains four. One of them has a cowboy hat on, pulled low over much of his face. The brim hides a face that is twisted in pain, anguish, and confusion. The cowboy stays near the front of the bus choosing a seat in the second row with no one seated too closely to him.

There is a woman, Yolanda, in the back of this city bus. She is wearing Cowboy Hat Man's engagement ring on one slender finger of her left hand. She has worn it for exactly three weeks today. She is sitting next to a tall man and holding his hand while they talk closely and intimately with one other. She has been having regular sex with this man for eight weeks. He is *not* the man she promised to marry. That would be the man sitting in the front of the bus wearing a borrowed cowboy hat.

The bus gets up to speed as it passes the Hollywood Bowl, and Carlos Perez stands up and starts moving toward the back of the bus.

"Yo, John Wayne. Wait for the stop," the driver says haphazardly. He is required to say it. He doesn't really have any energy behind it because he doesn't really care if the guy falls down in the aisle or not. He doesn't make enough money to care.

Yolanda and Tall Guy, whose name Carlos does not know and never will, are so wrapped up in each other that she fails to notice he is standing there until he pulls the gun out and a woman screams.

Tall Guy takes the first bullet. He's shot point-blank in the face, the bullet tearing through his left eye socket and taking everything in its path on the way out.

Would-Be Hero Guy is shot second. He's a young white kid from the suburbs with sandy blond hair in an expensive shirt. He jumps out of a nearby seat and tries to save the day. Carlos shoots him in the chest. He'll be hospitalized for four weeks before he's well enough to be released. He faced a future full of constant pulmonary issues until the ReYear happened. At that point, Would-Be Hero Guy will suddenly be given a world where every physical trace of his near-fatal chest wound has been taken away, right down to the scar.

The bus slams to a violent stop after the

second shot, and Carlos grabs Yolanda by the hair. He pulls her from the bus as the back doors open up, and people stream toward the front of the bus. He hurls her onto the street, and her knees and elbows scrape against the pavement. People on the bus continue to scream.

He fires two shots into Yolanda, and she stops screaming. Instead, she groans and writhes.

He fires one more, this time at her head.

She stops moving.

Carlos Perez begins to run.

He has one bullet left and isn't going to waste it. He just wants to be alone when he does it.

The next twenty minutes of his life are a blur. There are fences and yards. There are dogs and pointing bystanders. There is an inexhaustible series of police sirens. In those 20 minutes, he comes to realize just what he has done. It fills him with a strange mixture of emotions. There is a bit of remorse, panic, and even delight. It manifests itself in nervous, manic laughter. It makes what he has to do all the easier to face, and he finally comes to a stop.

His whirlwind afternoon ends with him wedging himself tightly between the rusty metal beams under an overpass. For the moment, he feels that he is safely hidden from the world and ready to take one last shot with his stolen six-shooter. Deciding to steal his friend Walt's cowboy hat as well had been a last-second decision.

The gun fails to fire. He pulls the trigger repeatedly, and nothing happens.

He hears the sirens, the roar of the approaching high-tuned engines, and the expletive-laden shouts of the LAPD. No one can swear like a frightened L.A. cop.

Pulling himself back out of the tight spot he was content to die in, Carlos holds the useless gun out in front of him as he slips down the concrete embankment.

The gun can still serve a purpose.

Suicide by cop will work just fine.

Until next spring. When it suddenly doesn't.

Chapter Fourteen
Burning the Grasses

Fifth Cataract of the Nile River
Northeast Sudan
October 26
12:07 PM

The Atbarah River pours into the Nile here. It is a smaller, thinner blood brother of the Nile. A tiny hand mingling its veins with those of the majestic titan that winds up through the heart of Africa on its journey to the Mediterranean.

The Atbarah is slow here, whereas the Nile runs swift and proud, like a gazelle on the open plains. The Nile stirs around small islands of rock in this place, flat stretches of sandy slab that rise from what passes for rapids here.

The Fifth Cataract is not as impressive as the other ones farther downstream, but it provides a nice visual in the midst of the desert nevertheless.

So much of the Nile seems long, sandy, and desolate. At the Cataracts, however, the water seems to teem with youthful enthusiasm and energy. People travel to see the Cataracts from all over East Africa. It is one of the few things this part of Egypt and the Sudan have going for it, so far as tourism is concerned.

The man being thoroughly searched for a weapon though, has not come here for the waters or the view. He has come here because he has been ordered here. Knowing he would be searched, he has brought nothing with him that would arouse suspicion. This is, after all, still early in the process. He is still building trust. He has no need for a weapon.

Toward that end, Kiir Mayuri walks with a man he has not yet figured out. Roti stares out at the bubbling, frothing water from behind the silver lenses of his prescription sunglasses.

"Mister Mayuri...you have never been here before I take it?"

"No," Billy responds. "My family never made it this far along the Nile, Your Majesty. No farther than Khartoum."

"We are in the farthest reaches of the Nubian Swell," Roti says, gazing into the wriggling waters of the river. "If we were to follow it deeper into the Sudan, around the two bends, we would come to a rise at the Third Cataract."

Roti pauses for a moment and breathes deep before he continues.

"The Third is volcanic, mysterious. The Earth shifts and shakes there at a great arch of weighty hills. Cross the border into Egypt, and the river drops into a trough at The Great Cataract. That one is forever lost to us beneath the surface of Lake Nasser, but make no mistake, it is still there. Surely as the gods of old."

"As with the Rift Valley," Kiir offers. "Such instability."

"As with time itself, it would seem," Roti offers. "The geology of this part of the world is just as unpredictable as the geography."

Kiir tilts his head slightly, thinking. "The November earthquake."

"Exactly," Roti replies, finally breaking his gaze and looking over at the young man. "And will it not be interesting to see if the earthquake happens again, when the date comes back around next month?"

"Indeed," Mayuri says, and he means it. Already so many things have been different in the repeated year. Who's to say the earthquake that ripped through the Rift Valley and disrupted the war in the weeks before his death will happen again? In the long run, it proved helpful in bringing the war to a swift end. Perhaps history will repeat itself.

"Perhaps by then, I will be a step closer to securing the Kingdom."

"How will you do that?"

King Roti stares at the young man who has just overstepped his bounds.

"I like you, Mayuri. You are an exceptional tactician. You show great promise and have a future in my service. Do not presume that I will share more with you than you need to know."

Oops. "I am sorry, Your Majesty. I was simply curious about your endgame."

"My endgame is to bring back the golden era, my boy. The world was far more entertaining when two sides were clinched in a true stalemate."

Nukes? He wants nukes?

"You are a young man, Mister Mayuri. The world is a very small place for you. You lived on this river for your entire life, yet you had never seen this part of it before."

"This is true," Mayuri says. Two of the four things he had just said actually were true.

"I have seen much more of this world than you could even imagine," Roti says.

The King stares out at the water and softly sighs. The two of them look across to the other side where children wash clothing in the river, not far from the crocodiles that sunned themselves near the surface of the silt-laden water.

"This is why I want to watch it burn."

Fairplay, Colorado
October 26
2:11 AM

She was happy and excited to be working in a newsroom again, but for some reason tonight the weight of the world decided to come crashing down on Anne Ayres.

Now and then, the heaviness of everything that has happened slams into the brain of everyone. For nearly five months now, the entire world has had to come to grips with how different things are since the Rift Event. Everyone tries to live his or her life as best they can. Everyone is looking to make the most of this bizarre second chance.

Anne has filed her cleverly written news stories about this situation for weeks and weeks now online for her limited personal audience. She did this just to "keep her chops up" and stay in the habit. Now however, when she has a job once again in news...she finds herself tired of it.

Anne is tired of approaching the world like a reporter, hammering a story that gets deeper and deeper. The story is being told every day without her in the expansive world of social media by the people living it...also known as *everyone*. She is tired of not dealing with the hand the ReYear has dealt her in her own life.

Within the first week of this stupid situation, her best friend's mother came back from the dead and they flew out to see her. When they arrived, she was suddenly dead again, and her best friend flipped her lid. One of the sharpest people she has ever met became a quivering, withdrawn rag doll.

Anne found herself with no real option but to extricate herself from the situation. On some level, she still kicked herself for abandoning her friend. She still called her every couple of days for a fresh dose of morose. Almost five months later, and Valerie is still destroyed about it, still wandering around a house in Oregon.

In her own case...the only man Anne ever loved was among the recent "undead." That wasn't the right term though. They all seemed to prefer the tag "Second Chancers."

He was a good man, and they would always

have a connection with each other. She assumed he would come home after he returned to life, that he would return to his life here, his parents...*her*. Instead, her dashing young officer made the decision to stay in the place that had killed him. Africa was what he chose, rather than return to the Rockies to try and repair their relationship.

Now it has been more than a month since she has been able to get any kind of message to him, let alone hear his voice. Absence has made the heart grow fonder. She waited too long to tell him she even wanted the two of them to be together, to mold their own "second chance." With this new super-secretive mission he seems to be on, she is not entirely sure she will get the chance any time soon.

If the opportunity never comes, she will blame herself for failing to change his mind.

There is more to the emotional weight on her shoulders. The recent unrest, which was especially bad up here in the Rockies, turned her father into a borderline survivalist psychopath. He has enough weapons and clean water and tinned food stowed away in the old bomb shelter to last the three of them the better part of two years. He has become twitchy and nervous. He bought a lot of gold in case currency becomes useless. He has stopped shaving and is scaring the crap out of his daughters. Everything he says is tainted with the sort of phrases that would make the most hardcore ultra-conservative Tea Partier cringe with a bit of discomfort.

Deep down, she wrestles with the desire to

know *how* this damn thing happened, let alone *why*. That question has been asked repeatedly by several billion people.

Colorado Springs
October 26
2:11 AM

Sleep also has Daniel Pemberton on ignore tonight.

Tonight has been Daniel's night to ask the bigger question as well.

Why?

Danny gave it a lot of thought, but his decision about Africa, and his enlistment, still weighs heavily on his mind.

The next difficult decision will be how to tell his brothers. Sam will be happy; he has no doubts about that. His mother will, too. Billy…he is not so sure that Billy will support the idea. He is convinced his father will be disappointed.

Danny looks at the clock.

2:12.

He decides to tell Billy first.

He and his brother have always been close. If he writes him a letter, he can rehearse how he will tell the rest of the family. Billy will be the first he tells. Thanks to where he is, he will also be the last to find out.

Billy, he begins, writing a hand-written letter for the first time since he was overseas half a year ago in the days before his death. *We miss you, you asshole.*

I don't know what super-secret mission you're on right now or even what part of the stupid theater you're in. I don't really care. I just know we all need you to come home in one piece. So after you finish doing whatever the hell it is you're doing, put in for your home leave. No one can say you aren't overdue for it, not with the time you've put in.

So: I'll be here when you get here.

I'm not enlisting. They gave me the option, and I've made up my mind. I don't know if you heard or not, but all of us new recruits who had died and suddenly showed up back home previous to our enlistments were not required to sign up again. I took the option. I hear a lot of us have.

I'm sorry if you're disappointed in us, disappointed in me. You're a Second Chancer too though, so I hope you get it. I don't want to lose this life now that I have it back. It wasn't wasted but it wasn't complete, either.

It isn't a question of "not our war" or anything like that. We're soldiers. We get told what our war is, and we go fight it. We do it with pride. We do it for a reason. We do it because that's who we are. We are the best in the world at what we do.

But I feel like it isn't who I am anymore. Do you understand that? By the time you read this, I'll know whether or not Dad will understand that.

I really have no idea what he's going to think. Dad is still impossible to get a read on, man. But I know I feel good about it. And since I can feel something, that's good enough for me.

Sam is getting better, but he needs you. He thinks this is all his fault somehow.

Come home. Everybody's waiting for you.

Washington D.C.
October 26
4:15 AM

President Francis Guagenti wakes up in a cold sweat.

He can swear that he read somewhere once that you have to be asleep for a certain number of hours before your brain is capable of entering the dream part of REM sleep. He watched the clock flip over to two a.m. before he fell asleep. Two hours should not have been enough for him to have had a dream.

Nevertheless, he had dreamed. One of those especially vivid dreams, the ones that hit you so hard they leave you breathless and convinced the universe is trying to tell you something.

He was back in the military, which he hadn't been a part of for more than ten years. The dream began with him putting on his dress whites. It seemed that he was going to some kind of event and had to wear his full dress uniform. The not-yet First Lady however, had no gown hanging on the hooks in the closet door. Whatever this was, she wasn't a part of it.

She laid atop the covers on their king size bed, nose deep in a book of Chinese philosophy, and paid him no mind.

There were no sly little comments about loving a man in uniform, which she had made for two decades every time he'd had to put on the monkey suit. In fact, she scarcely seemed to notice he was in the room at all.

"So, okay," he said. "I'm heading out."

"Mmm," she replied, as if acknowledging this bit of news with a full *Mmm hmm* wasn't worth the effort.

"I'm really going. I...I guess I'll be back later."

He turned, and she sighed. "You're wearing *that?*"

He looked back at her, and the bedroom changed. She was older, the age she is now. Still lovely and classy, something she couldn't help but radiate. Oddly, she still read the same book and she appeared as she looked tonight...more silver and wizened.

He looked down and saw that he was wearing his tuxedo now. The cufflinks were the jade set he had been given by the Sultan of Brunei, the ones he saved for special occasions.

"You know it's going to be a long time before we see each other again," he said. "Are you sure you want to be this way about it?"

"Not really," she says, and she is suddenly in her twenties, reading the same book. Her hair is a fiery red and pulled back in a headband to keep it out of her face. A baby sleeps in a bassinet next to their small bed in the bedroom of their first apartment at Pearl Harbor, shortly after he joined the Navy, before he was transferred to go to law school.

"What time is it?" he asks, confused. He looks down at the watch on his wrist and notices the second hand moving counter-clockwise.

His wife sighs from behind her book. "Christ, Frank, I don't know. Does it really matter?"

The room shakes as if an earthquake has struck the base. He reaches for his wife to pull her to the relative safety of the doorframe, but as he makes contact with her arm, his hand passes through her. Like a ghost, she just fades away, turning a page with a moistened thumb.

The apartment falls away below him, and he waits to fall.

He does not fall.

Frances Guagenti hangs in mid-air for a moment, suspended above the sinking rubble of the building that crumbles away below him. His hands are balled into fists which flank either side of his face, his arms involuntarily pulling themselves into a defensive posture when he felt the building go and realized his wife was not really there.

After a handful of heartbeats, looking down at the destruction below him...he feels himself yanked violently up into the air.

Falling up, his limbs begin to flail as the Hawaiian Islands drop away below him. The air grows thin and cold and he realizes he's back to his older, Presidential self again. The chilled metal clasps of the jade cufflinks are uncomfortable as they touch his wrists.

He watches the world stop spinning and come to a complete stop. As it does so, he hears a sound like the squeaking of air brakes on a school bus.

The blue planet beneath him suddenly starts spinning in the wrong direction. Slowly at first, then quickly...far faster than the world should be turning no matter which way it goes.

It spins for a bit then stops again with another squealing of bad brakes. He hadn't counted, but it had rotated the wrong way 366 times. Somehow he knows this.

President Guagenti can feel the thin air failing to satisfy his lungs, and each icy breath brings only more and more of a dry, freezing sensation to them. His heart begins to pound, and the gentle Earth below him starts to slowly spin in the correct direction again as he wonders how long it will take him to die.

He begins to fall, this time in the proper direction.

He remembers watching a man covered in energy drink logos. He made a free fall from some stratospheric height years ago, setting a number of records on his way back to terra firma and somehow *not* managing to break any of his bones in the process. It captivated the entire world that October weekend, and he has never forgotten it.

Now, he is living it.

His fall is not aligned with the Pacific Ocean, as his ascent had been. Instead, the clouds part to reveal the Eastern seaboard of the United States. Thin cirrus clouds are being disrupted by his rapid drop as he rips through them, watching with wide-eyed terror as the Chesapeake Bay region becomes larger and clearer as the seconds drag themselves past him with the whipping volume of the wind.

Soon, it is clear that Washington D.C. is where he is falling to, and he recovers his extremities well enough to start clawing at the very air. He is a giant bird given human form, which suddenly finds itself unable to fly.

He is plunging faster now, not slowing down in the slightest. Further, he has no mechanism at hand that might make that happen for him. The roof of the White House awaits him, and he closes his eyes, knowing that he will crash into it in one of the imminent seconds of his life. One of those seconds will be his last. It is likely going to be that same second.

He was no longer cold, but his blood certainly felt like it was. He could feel it rolling through his circulatory system like a thick barbeque sauce, the kind that ruined brushes.

He winced as the whistling of the air became even louder as the wind grew thicker and heavier. With a crash and an abrupt stop he found himself seated in his huge black chair behind the Resolute Desk in the Oval Office.

An ornate grandfather clock sat in the corner in a spot where it could always be read as clear as day from his chair.

The hands swung back and forth at the bottom of the face, like three pendulums of various thicknesses, moving out of unison from each other like the drumming of fingers on a desk.

Everything in the room seemed hazy, out-of-focus to him, with the exception of that clock. His vision seemed to pull him toward it, the clock suddenly becoming the center of his universe.

All at once, the clock exploded in a mushroom cloud, vaporizing everything in the office, including him.

The President sat up and looked at the digital clock beside the bed.

4:15.

Not too early to get up and start the day. Of course, the same was true for him no matter what day it was.

This was one of the hazards of deciding to run for President…and then winning because you did an exceptional job of running.

Colorado Springs
October 26
5:17 AM

Colonel Wild Bill Pemberton smells the familiar scent of frying bacon floating up the stairs.

He gets dressed, and he thinks. He thinks long and hard.

He's due to re-up soon, if he chooses to put in another four years in the Air Force. He has a meeting scheduled with his presiding General today, and he is certain that he'll hear two of three pieces of news.

The first piece is that someone else is going to become Base Commander. The new military has a new way of doing things. It started even before the Rift Event, and the shift in time only made the brass more interested in new ideas.

Colonel Pemberton is an old-guard career soldier. He isn't interested in new ideas. He's interested in efficiency, reliability. He can adapt with the best of them, but he knows as well as the General does that he isn't the guy to pull Peterson Air Force Base into the future. This despite how grand a steward he has been of its past.

That last point will count against him. Being a part of the past means that the third piece of news he might hear today is more likely than the second.

The second piece of possible news is long-awaited promotion to Brigadier General. The news that he will finally, *finally* put that star on his shoulder that he has coveted for so many years would be a relief.

The third piece of news though, is what he expects.

You've been stuck at rank too long, Bill, is how the conversation will begin. As he says it, the General will hand him a drink. Wild Bill doesn't care for Jim Beam but he'll accept it. He'll accept it just as he has in a number of late morning meetings with the General over the years. *You know as well as I do that it's not our Air Force anymore. Things have changed and people like you and me, we don't belong now.*

Colonel Wild Bill Pemberton will listen politely while his old friend tells him that when it comes time for him to re-up next spring, he will likely get rifted.

Officers who reach a peak always run the risk of what they call the rift...especially when they stay in beyond what the top brass consider to be their shelf life. They get rifted down, usually to enlisted rank, to serve out their time. If this happened to Pemberton, chances are he would be reassigned somewhere else. It would be awkward to have a former base commander serve in the same post, especially when he is now a highly placed Master Sergeant. Upon his retirement he would go out with the benefits and pension of his former, higher rank. Nice though that is, it hardly makes most of the former officers feel any better about the change of status they had endured. To be un-promotable in the military is the same as it is in any walk of life. It leads to being cast aside. It leads to soul-shattering depression in the strongest of men.

Wild Bill knows his best option in that scenario would be to retire.

I've carried ya as far as I can, Bill, he can hear the general say, most likely right after draining his highball glass and pouring another two fingers of his favorite bit of his old Kentucky home into it, *but this is where the ride stops and we gotta get off. Hell, I'll prob'ly join ya year after next. They ain't gonna gimme that third star. We're antiques, Bill, you an' me. We're museum pieces. Different world now. It ain't just about us an' the Reds, like it used to be. It's us and the crazy desert people, and the North Koreans, and the bat-shit crazy bomb makers in Montana and Texas and Boston. People like us, we get to talk on Fox News during military exercises or new wars. We get to teach military history at colleges. We're not field guys anymore...hell...you an' I never were.*

Wild Bill smells the bacon as he moves into the hallway. He really enjoys that smell.

Daniel's door isn't closed all the way, and he peeks in at his son. He is proud of his son for wanting to do his duty, something they've always tried to do in this family. Even when it wasn't a popular idea for a black man in the country to become a soldier, the Pembertons have always signed up. Far too many of them have paid with their lives. Two of them were his sons.

The Colonel can't help but think that road is coming to a close at he looks at his second son, sleeping quietly in the light from the hallway.

He steps into Daniel's room.

Two of his sons were dead, and he got them back. Rather than come home...one stayed at war because of duty and loyalty. Now this one has expressed a desire to do the same.

He spots a handwritten letter on his son's desk and picks it up when he sees Billy's name on it. He turns toward the light from the hall and reads it, even though he knows he shouldn't.

A minute later he puts it down and smiles.

There is pride in that smile, pride that would have been there no matter what. Pride that doesn't take its cues from what his sons do, but rather what and who his sons *are*.

Wild Bill Pemberton closes the door behind him and walks down the hall to peek at young Sam. Young Sam is talking in his sleep, mumbling nothing in particular. He does this a lot.

The Colonel leaves the room quietly and wanders downstairs to have breakfast with his beautiful wife.

No matter what the meeting turns out to be, this already has the earmarks of a good day.

Coral Sea
June 1st
9:59 PM
One minute before the event

Commander Stuart Brant has hit the mother lode.

The wreck of the *Darling Marie* has yielded even more treasure than he expected. He isn't picking the bones of the vessel for gold or anything like that. Commander Brant is looking for navigational charts, and he has found them.

He has actually found *three dozen* of them. And all in remarkable condition, considering the ship went down in a bad tempest in the early 1960s.

The large blue and yellow dory fish are darting around him like big, beautiful aquatic mosquitoes as he works. He loves them for their bright colors and their curious nature, which keeps them around his head. His daughter loves them because she is convinced they all speak with the voice of Ellen DeGeneres.

He is removing the first stack of the maps.

They are ornate, detailed, and more magnificent than he could have hoped. He begins placing them into the first set of protective sleeves, when he suddenly is not there anymore.

London
June 2nd
Noon

Commander Brant appears at a table in a mess hall. There is a beverage and a menu on the table before him, but they are the least of his concerns.

Brant begins to convulse violently, falling out of his chair and onto the cool tiled floor, scuffed and marked by the footwear of countless sailors and marines over the years.

Everyone around him is confused, disoriented. It takes them a few seconds to realize where they all are, and another few seconds to discover the commander on the floor in serious distress.

"Doctor!" shouts a junior officer. His voice is familiar, but Brant cannot focus on anything at the moment. He begins to fade fast; first his vision, then hearing, his senses are shutting themselves down in rapid succession.

He dies somewhat quickly. This happens because, despite their best efforts to treat him, no one in the room could have guessed that he was suffering from the bends.

The bends are a dangerous problem in the blood, having to do with nitrogen, and pressure, and a rapid rise from the depths of the sea to sea-level.

In Commander Brant's case, that rise had been instantaneous.

Chapter Fifteen
Kings and Vultures

Colorado Springs
October 31
5:45 PM

He is swathed in synthetic zebra and lion furs, sporting a crown ringed with false stones and carrying a gold-colored scepter.

He is an African King, a noble lord of the savannah. He struts proudly, and hopes the night has brought him many Milky Ways. For Milky Ways are the finest confections in all the land.

The King has deemed it so.

His Majesty's bag is heavy. Sam has made quite a haul this year, and is walking the neighborhood with his older brother Danny and a small group of kids that live on the command circle. Safety in numbers is the rule of thumb, even when you are walking on a safe, secure military base.

Halloween is always host to an interesting anomaly. That odd situation of seeing neighbors whom you typically never see. On a military base, in a world where time has hiccupped and a number of people who had died in war are suddenly back alive again...it adds an extra dimension of awkwardness to conversations to have someone answer a door that you had heard was dead.

As he walks his brother and the little ones around the neighborhood, Daniel sees six faces that he knows had died when a supply flight went down over Tanzania during the war. He himself having experienced the same "good fortune," and finds it amazing that everyone who has seems to be able to recognize it in others.

It is something in the eyes. An unspoken nod of understanding passes between them. A nod speaks volumes about just how *good* their good fortune can sometimes actually feel.

Those who have returned from the dead do not always feel welcome.

Not all of those who were given a second chance on June 2nd...wanted one.

Daniel smiles though. He walks with the children while dressed in the costume of a zombie.

He smiles at the fact that he walks in irony.

Halaib, Sudan
November 1
3:45 AM

As Sam enjoys the warmth of his thick Halloween costume as he walks door-to-door collecting his candy, his eldest brother fails to sleep half a world away.

The man who is currently known as Kiir Mayuri is not the only one in the safe house who is awake right now.

It is hot.

The stars bake in the night sky over coastal East Africa on the leading edge of morning.

It has been especially warm on the coastline of the Red Sea. It is the driest autumn anyone can remember, far worse than it was last year...the year the world is supposed to be repeating. It would seem Mother Nature did not get that message.

It is still dark as Benji wakes up, 15 minutes before his alarm is due to go off. This is how his day usually begins. He shakes the cobwebs from his mind and begins his morning routine.

He is not comfortable having Roti here in an actual town. Tents in the desert are easier to defend and less likely to draw attention. Benji does not trust these Sudanese, and he does not like Roti playing both sides of the confederacy between these two dirty countries.

As much of an asset as Kiir Mayuri has been, he and the rest of the South Sudanese are even more useless in his mind than these other disorganized Sudanese chimpanzees currently playing host to them. Benji yearns for the day that his King tells him they are going home. These are low people.

Benji prays this morning, as he does for one minute every morning. He prays for the strength and courage to perform his duty before God. He prays for a simple day. He prays for the armistice that will allow them to return to Addis Ababa.

At the very least, he prays there will be a swift resolution to all of this. The cause seems strong now, but Roti's sanity is far afield. Without a strong king to hold it all together, this war is likely to collapse quickly and the kingdom along with it.

Hada stirs in his bed. Benji's efforts to be quiet this morning have not been successful, but she needs to return to her room anyway. She stretches and props her head up on her palm, an elbow bent beneath it on the thin pillow.

"Good morning," he says to her with a soft smile.

She smiles and takes a deep and cleansing breath. "Good morning," she replies.

There is wind outside the window. The Somali woman climbs out of the bed and scratches her shoulder as she walks to the thin curtain and pulls it aside. A pair of vultures is out there, approaching an untended ostrich nest. She stares at them for a moment before she speaks.

"I should get back to my room before…"

"…yes," Benji says, cutting her off. This is only the third night they have spent together, and neither of them is sure how this relationship…if that's truly what it is…will be received. Roti is unlikely to be happy about his bodyguard beginning a relationship with the Intelligence Chief from Somalia. Or rather *The East Farthing*, as Roti refers to her homeland. Roti loves his Tolkien.

Benji gets dressed and removes something else from his bag for the trip downstairs. Hada steps away from the birds outside the window, pulls her clothes on rather hastily, and waits for Benji to check the hallway. There are only six rooms in this house, and Roti is snoring loudly from the one across the hallway from the room they had shared this morning.

Benji's number two man, Robert, is standing outside of the door. Hada nods at him as she walks to the room at the end of the hallway.

In the room between Hada's and Benji's, Kiir Mayuri is not sleeping.

Mayuri heard both doors open and close. He sits at his bedroom window, listening closely.

In the thin light of the pre-dawn he watches vultures on the ground below. They are squawking and spitting rocks at the large eggs in an ostrich nest.

It takes him a moment to figure out why.

Once they have broken through the protective shell, the vultures are able to dip their beaks into the eggs and eat what's inside.

Get past the defenses first. That's the key. It is a strategy he knows all too well this morning. He has been at that very thing for many weeks now.

He takes the vultures as a sign. Today is the day. He was already feeling it, but this has clinched it.

This is the first trip with His Royal Highness for which Kiir has been invited to stay with them. He knows that it is because he has finally achieved a level of trust with King Roti, and it makes him smile. It did not take nearly as long as he had expected it to. Only a couple of rocks had to be spat against the shell before the whole thing crumbled before him.

Kiir has been aware of the chief bodyguard's relationship with the Somali Intelligence consultant since it began on Monday. He finds it amusing, having watched the two of them dance around each other in the last handful of weeks.

Benji is unaware of this as he escorts his lady-friend to her room. He looks back at Robert, who gives him the "nothing to report" nod.

Benji goes down the creaking wooden stairs to put a small pot of clean water on a hotplate to heat it.

Roti's tea is a process, something Benji takes very seriously. For starters, no one but he is permitted to make the King's tea. He steeps a mix of Chinese black tea leaves and Indian chai at 200 degrees for three and a half minutes, and stirs in a teaspoon of cane sugar. He carries all of these ingredients with him when they travel in a small case. Roti is very particular about his tea.

He pours it into a mug with a lid that he keeps in the same case with bottles of spring water. The stairs creak again as he carries it back upstairs. This safe house is very old and has been hammered by a combination of desert sands and sea winds for many years.

Benji walks back to Roti's door, and Robert knocks three times before turning the knob for him. Benji steps through.

"Good morning, Your Majesty. It is 4:20. I

have your tea."

Roti rises. For once, he is alone in his bed. There is no young woman or women to hurry out of the door. Their group arrived very late last night, and there had not been time to dragoon a woman into service. Roti had been too tired for company anyway, for once.

"Thank you, Benji. Tell me about my day." He takes a sip of the tea and burns his tongue a bit. The tea is hot but it is perfect. Benji's tea is always perfect.

Benji continues to stand at attention. "The intelligence briefing is at 6:30. Hada, Mayuri, and DeTress will present the latest on our losses in Kenya."

"Tafi?"

"Still no word on his whereabouts, Sire. At this point I am afraid we have to assume the worst."

Roti frowns. "I see. When is the strategy meeting?"

Benji looks the King in the eyes. Roti does not care for it when people do this. He knows that when Benji does it, he does it to emphasize a point.

"It has been moved to tonight, Your Majesty. The generals and the Ministers will be waiting for us at the next location."

"And where is this next location? Further from the desert, I hope."

"Closer, sir."

Roti rolls his eyes to the ceiling at this, and Benji is quick to amend it.

"However, I have been talking to Advance and we will be getting closer to home again in the next couple of weeks."

Roti frowns. "Fine. The desert it is. Leave me so I can shower and get dressed."

"As you wish," Benji says.

He leaves the room and stops at the door, looking straight ahead.

"You are relieved, my friend," he says to Robert. "Sleep well."

Robert, who is happy to see his boss finally having an opportunity to start up with the woman he had spent this repeated summer pining over, smiles and hands over the radio. He walks to his room without a word.

Benji stands perfectly still for about an hour. At 5:35 in the morning, Roti steps out into the hallway dressed in a common robe and a turban.

"Let us go."

Outside of his window as they pass the hall, Kiir Mayuri has been watching a small family of cheetahs. There are five of them, on the opposite side of the house from the vultures, at the edge of the high grass. Cheetahs are a rare sight in this part of Africa, especially so many of them in one place. They are all lean and gaunt, because the summer was long and cruel here in this part of the Sudan. The eldest male wears a lot of silver in his coloring, and he stares at the house as if he is waiting for a meal to present itself. The alpha cheetah seems completely unaware of the birds on the other side of the house, as do the rest of his small coalition.

He leaves the room and joins the breakfast table where the other two Intel people sit with Roti and Benji. Hada, the Somali woman, does a terrible job of not looking at Benji every now and then. She has the appearance of someone every bit as tired as Billy's men were at the end of their 100-mile run. Her exhaustion however, comes from frustration. It cannot be easy being the voice of Somalia when the man who rules you seems to have little use for you or your people, despite his many promises.

Benji stays by Roti's side all through breakfast, and when the meal is over, the intelligence officers are dismissed before any business has had the chance to be discussed.

"Eight," Benji says to Urragabi, and he nods. The door closes and their strange guide leads the three of them outside.

"The King spends two hours after breakfast and dinner practicing his Arabic, Mister Mayuri. Just he and Benji."

"I understand," Kiir Mayuri says.

For the next two hours the four of them explore the sandy grasses near the house. When the big cats begin sniffing around again, they return to the house to wait out the remainder of the time there.

Kiir Mayuri does his level best to not attract any undue attention to himself. He reads in the sitting room beside the dining room and turns the pages gradually on a dog-eared copy of a cheap pulp novel he found in the house. He had been surprised to find one in English in a small house on the edge of the Nubian Desert. The book had the look of one that had been there for a very long time, perhaps since the British dominated this part of the continent. The price on the cover was very low, and in pence.

Arabic practice continues in the other room. Mayuri can hear it through the thin walls.

Roti feels it important to practice his Arabic every day. He wants to blend in with his surroundings during their time here. Additionally if he has reason later to cross the Red Sea and hide on the Arabian Peninsula, he wants to be prepared. Roti has the words down, but he has trouble with the pronunciations and nuances.

Hearing Roti struggle with something he loves most about learning languages and accents amuses the man known as Kiir Mayuri. He finds it difficult to stifle the smile and remain serious.

Benji is the one person in the world who can correct Roti without incurring his wrath. The sad truth is that the man on the other side of the wall would have been a much better teacher.

Finally, a few minutes before eight o'clock, Urragabi pokes his head in the sitting room.

"Ah. Mister Mayuri. I believe His Majesty is ready for you now."

"Thank you," Kiir replies. He sets the book down on the arm of the chair and walks back into the dining room.

Benji and Roti have already been rejoined at the table by the other two intelligence officers when Mayuri walks in.

Roti rises from the table to stretch his back as

Benji walks to the door to whisper something to Urragabi.

In the two seconds Benji is not looking in the direction of his King, Captain William Pemberton III of the United States Army has pressed the barrel of a small pistol to Roti's temple and squeezed off two very loud and very sudden shots.

The pistol was mostly plastic actually, hastily put together in his room this morning by candlelight and the light of the moon. Many of the pieces had been a cigarette case and a pen, the sort of weapon that Q Branch would have given to James Bond. The bullets had been hidden in his shoes, one in each. The opportunity to use it never presented itself during breakfast. Billy had been forced to hide this makeshift gun far longer than he had intended.

Hada screams and Benji feels the blood drop out of his own face as he watches Roti fall to the floor under an arc of spurting blood. DeTress is reaching for Billy's odd-looking gun.

Benji rips his own sidearm out of the folds of his heavy robes and pumps four shots in the direction of the man he knows as Kiir Mayuri. As he fires, he runs toward him swelling with rage. Two of the shots make their mark. Another slug strikes Colonel DeTress in the shoulder, as he has inadvertently placed himself in the path of the shots. The fourth bullet embeds itself deep in the plaster wall.

Mayuri and DeTress hit the floor together. Hada has the clarity of mind to dive atop them both and wrestle the weapon away from Mayuri. Urragabi bursts into the room and Roti writhes on the floor for a second. Benji rushes to his side.

Benji glances over his shoulder for a moment to make sure Kiir Mayuri is not moving. Hada has him duly pinned.

The bodyguard sinks to his knees and cradles the head of his King in his lap.

"Roti! Roti! Speak to me!"

Roti whispers his final words, weakly.

"Burn the world," he struggles to say, and then he stares into the wall.

Benji is still holding Roti when Robert and the rest of the security team rush in. He pulls himself to his feet while the rest of the men attend to Roti, who is no longer responsive.

With the fury of a desert storm, Benji rounds on the assassin and kicks him sharply in the head. Billy grimaces weakly, and his head snaps back very slowly.

"This dog is alive," Benji says to his team.

One of the bullets has hit Billy in the arm. He can feel it buried in the muscle. The other grazed his side. That wound is bleeding hard but he can tell it looks far worse than it is.

"We will take him out into the sands and tear him into pieces too small for the buzzards," Benji says. His words are almost detached from any thought process as he lingers over Roti.

"Please," Urragabi pleads suddenly as he shoulders a canvas bag. "Allow me, my old friend. I owe him."

Benji is too stunned by what has happened to

disagree.

"See to it that he suffers, Urragabi. And walk him away from the house."

Billy Pemberton feels hands lift him up from the floor under his shoulders. His gunshot wounds cause him to wince in pain.

Urragabi says something in Arabic to the guards that drag him out of the house and points to the sandy hills to the east of the house.

Billy quietly accepts his fate. He has reached the end of his journey and will die as Kiir Mayuri. He has always known this mission was likely a one-way proposition. He feels a strange smile move across his face, even finds himself oddly at peace as the men carry him out of the house. His feet drag behind him in the sand; making twin trails out beyond the spot where the big cats had been earlier. He feels that he could walk if he had to, but he is enjoying the thought of making his murderers work for it by dragging him across the course sand.

A grin is painted on his face as Billy thinks to himself that he could do with a cyanide capsule about now. It would be a wonderful irritation to these men if he could die before they could punish him. It would be a fun way to spite his executioners.

They carry him over one last sand dune in the area where the brush ends and the sand dominates underfoot.

Urragabi barks an order. The two men carrying Billy stop walking and dump him unceremoniously to the ground.

Urragabi pulls out a gun and shouts at the men. Billy hears their footsteps walking away, and he is suddenly alone in the desert with a man whose trust he has betrayed. He takes a glance and watches the tops of their heads disappear as they walk away.

"Your luck has changed, Mayuri." Urragabi clicks open the mechanism of the pistol and blows. A few grains of sand are cleared out of it. The Ethiopian stands before him, and takes aim.

As the men reach the house, they hear a gunshot ring out across the field.

The vultures begin to shout at one another in the heat of the early morning.

Colorado Springs
November 1
12:17 AM

There is no school tomorrow, and like every other child of Trick-or-Treating age...Sam is not ready to surrender his bag just yet.

His haul was decent this year. The 13 bite-size Milky Ways were, of course, the stars of the bag. There are 12 now because he had to have one right away. The remaining dozen will be saved for last. Sam has always done this. Billy always used to commend him for the incredible restraint he has shown with this tradition.

While digging around in his bag, trying to figure out what the last piece will be before he finally succumbs to the sugar crash and gets some sleep…it hits him.

He feels a deep shiver run down his spine.

Almost immediately, he knows something horrible has happened. He does not know what, or to whom, but something has gone very wrong.

He rolls up his bag of candy. Suddenly, Sam Pemberton doesn't want any more of it tonight.

He buries himself in the blankets on his bed and hopes he's just imagining it. There is no denying that he has a sinking feeling about Billy right now.

Outskirts of Cairns, Australia
June 5
6:14 PM
A few days after the Event

Garrett Auburn is drunk and angry.

He is drunk and angry for a number of reasons.

His house, for a start, was full of beer. Six crates of Victoria Bitter to be accurate. It had been ordered for a huge wake he hosted on June 6th, when it came around the first time. Either a year ago or tomorrow. Whichever. He hasn't given that much thought at this point.

All of his friends came to his house on that night to mourn two other friends. They had died in a small plane crash on May 31st on their way to a holiday in Indonesia.

The date gnawed at him. As the situation had become more and more clear in the last couple of days…and they realized that they had gone back in time to a date so very close to the one that had taken their friends…his anger about it grew. His friends had missed their shot at resurrection by less than 48 hours. Rotten bloody luck and more than a little unfair.

There are a number of other reasons he is drunk and angry. His girlfriend, Ashley Hudson, is technically still Mrs. Ashley Beems of Perth, living way over on the side of the country. Whether she wants to be there or not, she is unable to fly out and doesn't have the money to travel out any other way yet. Her husband is making a desperate attempt to rebuild their marriage...and Garrett is getting the impression that she is openly negotiating the possibility. Possibly, she does this because the bizarre circumstances the world is facing have pushed her and her ex back together. They'd been married for six years after all. Familiarity in the face of desperation breeds comfort and solace. It can be a powerful eraser as well as bonding agent.

He had also made considerable progress in the last year trying to gain the upper hand on the population of invasive cane toads around his home. He lives on the western outskirts of the city, in the woods, not far from where the species was introduced more than 70 years ago in an attempt to control the cane beetle population. His efforts are now for naught: all of his progress has been lost. They chirp in the early evening twilight. They chirp very bloody loudly.

Time deciding to move back one exact year without giving any hint of an explanation *why* has plucked every nerve in his scientific body. The same is true of nearly every mind in the world.

These are all things that bother him tonight

as he drinks and he fumes. None of the questions though, bristle with the magnitude of the one foremost fact that is bothering him.

The fact is that Garrett Auburn has one particular reason to be pissed off, and it is the primary reason he has gotten drunk tonight. It eclipses his dead friends who just missed the deadline, his poisonous toad problem, the great cosmic mystery…even the bitch who claimed she loved him now appears to be a lot less sure about that claim.

Since the event, which struck at 10 o'clock in the evening during another late-night of working with the pigs in Lab D2 at the facility, he's been looking for it all.

And he hasn't been finding it.

The last year has been a crucial one for Dr. Auburn and his team. He has managed to unlock several keys to the kingdom, as it were, in his research. He felt that he was starting to truly get close to a clinical trial of something that showed real promise in the fight against a previously untreatable, unbeatable cancer. An announcement in the next couple of weeks was not out of the question, depending on the last round of swine tests.

Then the world decided to back up a year.

Everything is gone from that year, except the cruel, taunting memory of it.

The world's chronological shift took data with it. It took data from everyone, everywhere.

Computer files are gone, irretrievable because they never existed. Hard copies that were made to back up computer files were never printed. Handwritten notes in his books have become blank pages. Everyone in the world has this problem. Not everyone in the world however had a cure for cancer.

So many experiments have come and gone in the last year that his mind has trouble remembering exactly which mixtures of what had gotten him to the point he was at before.

He and his team, which consists of two other researchers, have spent the last 24 hours trying to use the same equipment and the same combinations of the same rudiments and drugs that they knew they had been working with.

None of the combinations have shown the same promise. They are not necessarily back to square one, but they are a substantial number of steps back from where they were.

So Garrett came home and checked all of his personal files, hoping to uncover some clue that would lead him in the right direction.

He has found nothing. No research, no Ashley Hudson...nothing but six large, inviting crates of Victoria Bitter.

There is no cure for cancer here at the house. There is only a cure for sobriety and the clicking and croaking of hundreds of god damned cane toads on his rain-strewn back lawn.

The beer is nowhere near as bitter as his frustrated tears.

Dr. Garrett Auburn is drunk and angry.

Chapter Sixteen
Headless

Addis Ababa, Great East Africa
November 1
9:45 AM

"I understand, Benji."

On the other end of the phone call, Benji heaves a sigh and says "That makes one of us, my old friend. There is little here that I can truly understand. The throne is empty and we can only hide that fact for so long. Tafi will need to…"

"Tafi is gone, Benji. Roti did not tell you that he was captured?"

"Then you are in power now, General. You were the next man in line."

Dikir allows himself a sad smile. "This is the situation, yes."

"What are your orders? I can be home in…"

General Dikir interrupts him. "Honestly Benji, I think you should go back to what you were doing in Ghana."

"Ghana?" Benji laughed. "I'm afraid that ship has sailed, General. They will know who I am now, especially after I failed to come back to them after the Event. I will have to find something else to do if it is truly your desire that I disappear. Are you certain there is no place for me with you?"

"You are loyal Benji, perhaps to a fault. You avoided the tribunal once," Dikir replies, "but I do not believe you can be so fortunate a second time. I am certain that *I* cannot. I have made far too many mistakes since we won back the kingdom. I cannot hide the actions I was able to hide last time, and I have no desire to face a war crimes tribunal again."

"You are leaving too then."

"I am already packing, Benji. Great East Africa dies with Roti. That is my decision."

Benji shakes his head in disgust. "We are winning the war this time, General. How can you…"

"I have seen the loose nature of the federation in Somalia, Benji. You have not. They will turn on us. That process has already begun."

Benji looks over to Hada as the general continues in his ear. Hada, who cannot hear the other end of the conversation, gives Benji a sad smile.

"Once we lose the Somalis we lose any hope of holding on to Kenya. We are winning the war today. By the end of the day or the end of the week…however long it might take the world to find out Roti has been assassinated…we will have lost any real grasp we have on the South."

They are silent for a beat. Both of them know that to be true. Africa has an amazing ability to right itself when the balance is upset.

Benji stares at the box that contains the body of his King.

"You are right. What am I to do with the body?"

"Bury him in the desert, Benji. In secrecy, put him in the ground. Kill the guards to make sure no one will talk. If you cannot trust Detress, Hada, and Urragabi…kill them as well. We will keep this quiet for as long as we can, and let the world discover it much later when his lack of orders leads to the inevitable leak from the Capital."

Benji closed his eyes slowly as he contemplated this. He opened them again as he said "What of his things?"

"Send them to me in a secure way, but not through official channels where they could be intercepted. You're on the Red Sea. Find a ship. Send them slowly by boat rather than air. A boat flying our flag so that we need not worry it will be stopped in the Bāb al Mandab or attacked by the pirates in the Gulf of Aden."

Benji frowns. "I don't like it. If the allies…"

"So what? Let the Alliance intercept his things if they are so clever. Sail his belongings to our coastal base at Bender Cassim. A direct flight from there to here would be the most simple to arrange without suspicion. Port Sudan isn't that far from you, but an international flight from up there would raise too many suspicions and the allies would learn the truth faster."

Suddenly Benji understands. "You are trying to get a head start, yes?"

"Exactly. We cannot hide this news, but we can be far afield when the story spreads. I will see to it that Fedens is made aware of what has happened, when the time is right."

"Fedens. Yes. Has she returned home yet?"

Dikir was already starting to put papers together. "No. I believe she is actually still on your side of the border."

"Urragabi has volunteered to drive out and find her to deliver the news in person."

The General smirked. "Yes. I am certain he has. What of the traitor?"

"Ah," Benji says. "The traitor. Let us say only that the desert is a place of many secrets, general."

"This is true."

"Good luck to you, brother," Benji says sadly. Everything in his life made so much more sense a few hours ago.

General Dikir squeezes the handset of the phone a little, the grief of the news finally overtaking him. Through it all, Roti had been his friend and Benji had always been there, keeping him safe. "And you, brother. God save the King."

He chokes a little on the last word. He is the leader of his people now, and the only thing he wants to do is find himself anywhere else.

Dikir wishes with all his heart that the ReYear would strike again, right now. He isn't sure where he was last November 1st, but it had to be somewhere better than this place, at this moment.

In a small town in the Sudan Benji closes his phone and looks again at the body of Roti, laid out on the floor of the sitting room Kiir Mayuri had been sitting in.

"God save the King," he says quietly with a smile.

He shouts in Arabic. "Robert! Have everyone attend me!"

He looks over at Hada.

"We have work to do."

The Olduvai Gorge, Tanzania
November 2
7:45 AM

The caravan comes to rest at the southern edge of the fault line, a line of yellow Humvees that have left the main road along the gorge. They have come this way intentionally to find this place. It is a village that has no name. It only appears on half of the maps of the country. This is in spite of the fact that it predates nearly every community within a thousand kilometers of it.

The Humvees bear the logo of the United African Alliance, but they have been appropriated for Colonel Kabinda's other cause. They also bear the unofficial seal of the African contingent of the Second Chancers movement, a Roman numeral "II" imposed over an outline of the continent, which is filled in with a brilliant sun rising over a grassy plain that bears a giraffe, and a single, thin tree.

Kabinda is the first to put his boots on the

ground, folding up the map and placing it in the front passenger's seat he has just vacated. As he does so, the others dismount from their own steely steeds and wait to follow the Colonel's lead.

The people of the village are primitive by any standard. They do not have much use for the modern world, nor do they venture far from their home. Only occasionally do they find themselves spotted by the scant number of tourists and research anthropologists that venture to this south westernmost portion of the gorge.

When the people of the village make their way to this part of the gorge, it is to perform their sacred ceremonies with the bones of their ancestors. The majority of the fossilized remains that can be found in the area are of some of the earliest known hominids, dating back a couple of million years.

The famous anthropologists, the Leakeys, have been here, unraveling the mysteries of early man. They were among the very few outsiders who have ever been accepted by the natives of the gorge. The village does not acknowledge much of the outside world.

Kabinda notices the tribe's Shaman walking toward him. The man is older than anyone else around him, which makes sense for a tribe that is not hostile. A hostile tribe would have a younger, more virile leader. This is a tribe that respects wisdom and experience. Mind over muscle. This is the sort of tribe that will communicate with a man like Kabinda. A man who comes armed only with knowledge and reason.

The Colonel waves the interpreter over. Kabinda has studied many of the tribes of the Rift Valley, but this tribe has an incredibly unique language. It took some time to find a man in Mwanza who spoke both English and something akin to the unusual tongue of the villagers. Jean is his name, and he will try his very best to interpret for Kabinda. The colonel isn't even certain what the language is called.

Jean's success carries the promise of a new house for him to share with his wife, their coming child, and his mother. It's a child his wife has already given birth to once before, and one strange afternoon she suddenly found herself pregnant with the child again as the Event hit the world.

The home they had built together is gone now. It was suddenly reoccupied by people who had moved and regretted it. They refused to give it up. A year ago Jean and his bride were freshly married and expecting. They were living with his mother, and looking for a new home.

In this new world though, his mother has fallen ill and no longer has a home. It was burned in the lootings and other violence that rolled around the southern coast of Lake Victoria in mid-June, as it did in much of the world. They have nothing.

The Shaman approaches. He walks with a limp, his leg gnarled from an accident among these rocks many years ago that never properly healed.

Kabinda approaches to a point, then stops. At a certain distance, a man who continues to walk toward a Shaman of this ritual-rich tribe is a man who considers himself to be of equal footing with him. And the Shaman is a man worshipped as a living god. Kabinda wants the Shaman to know which of them has the power in this conversation. To emphasize the point, Colonel Kabinda raises both of his hands in front of him, his palms out. Jean stands beside him and does the same after observing Kabinda's movements. The two of them appear to have pleased the Shaman.

"Tell him I wish him respect and life, and I have come to him with counsel."

Jean nods and speaks a few strange words. A couple of glottal clicks accompany them.

The Shaman clicks back and speaks abruptly, curtly. Kabinda has no idea what the man says, but he understands the tone perfectly.

"He wanna know what advice you could possibly give that he must to hear."

Kabinda looks the old man in the eye. The Shaman is sizing him up like a lion staring down a cornered wildebeest. The Colonel thinks he recognizes something in that stare, and takes a chance.

"Jean, ask the Shaman if he remembers dying."

"Sir?"

"Ask him. Use that exact phrase."

Jean closes his eyes and sighs. He poses the question.

The Shaman's face remains stony, but Kabinda, who continues to hold eye contact with the man, sees a glint of something inside the man begin to soften. The Shaman stares at Kabinda, a stare both men know all too well. It is the stare of someone who understands death from the inside of it.

Language barrier aside, these two men now understand each other a little better.

The Shaman says nothing but nods.

"The valley opened beneath you," Kabinda says, taking a pause every few words so Jean can figure out how to translate it. Jean is not a fluent expert in this language. The only experts live *here* in this tribe and speak it every day. "You and your people were swallowed."

Jean shakes his head before continuing. "Swallowed?"

"Say *eaten*."

Jean does so.

"Eaten by the soil."

The Shaman listens and nods again. He responds with clicks and words. Kabinda listens, wondering how the young man from America would enjoy hearing this language. It has beautiful nuances. It is fascinating. Captain Billy Pemberton would eat this language up and ask for seconds. It is a crying shame that he will never have a chance to hear it. If he isn't already, the young man will be dead soon enough. A sacrifice on the altar of peace sent to his death by Colonel Paul Kabinda.

Perhaps he is trying to atone for that now.

"Our fathers called us all to join them," Jean interprets, after the Shaman speaks.

Kabinda shakes his head.

"But your fathers sent you back to live again."

Jean raises an eyebrow and works the sentence into the ancient tongue.

The Shaman nods but puffs out his chest and bellows his response. Jean strains to make sense of it because it is long.

"Our fathers...have...purpose?...for us. We have work...no...uh...we have *ritual* that we have not...made for them. They are not pleased with us. We have...made shame for them."

Kabinda smiles. "The ground will open for your people again. Are you prepared to face them now?"

The face of the Shaman indicates that he is not, long before Jean has passed the man's response along.

Kabinda puts his hands together, hoping to show emphasis, rather than aggression.

"You must leave the soil before it opens again. We will bring you back to it when it is safe."

He pauses for Jean's sake. Jean struggles greatly to find a word for *safe*. He manages, finishes, and looks at Kabinda. Jean is in awe of Kabinda right now as the pieces of what the man is doing here start to fall into place for him.

"You will live to do your rituals and please your fathers. They will come to understand you left here for a brief time in order to live, to carry on honoring them. There will be no shame for your people. The fathers will know you to be wise sons and daughters. Worthy children of their great family."

Hearing this, the Shaman is silent for some time, staring into the eyes of this strange man from the yellow trucks.

Then he turns his back on Kabinda and Jean and stares at the canyon. He feels the wind blow past his face and smells the Serengeti on the back of it.

He turns to Kabinda again and simply nods.

The Shaman limps back to his people to inform them of the man's offer, and of his decision to accept it. He knows the decision will not be a popular one among his rival elders, but all will comply with his wishes because of who he is.

As the man is walking away, Kabinda's aide solemnly walks up to him.

"Headquarters on the radio, Colonel," he says. "They have been trying to contact us, but we are out of range for normal relays. They would also like to know where you are and what you are doing."

Kabinda says nothing, but smiles.

"Contact the liaison office. I want a safe house set up for this man in Mwanza." He gestures to Jean. "The cost is to be covered by my special military stipend from the UAA. See to it."

Within the hour, all 42 people will have cleared out of the village and piled into the pair of lumbering troop transports at the back of the convoy.

The earthquake does, in fact, strike the Olduvai Gorge again on November 6th. It hits the region in the exact same spot as it did before, and unleashes the exact same level of power and destruction. However this time a tribal village will not lose a single life. None of the nearby settlements, in fact, take a single casualty.

Kabinda had first suggested to the UAA and the Tanzanian Government that they should make an effort to evacuate the indigenous population before the 6th, in case the quake returned. He took matters into his own hands when both dragged their feet.

Though his actions angered the UAA, they made him a hero to the Second Chancers of the world, and the United Nations.

As soon as the word spread about what has happened here and in the other affected cities, Colonel Paul Kabinda will become the face of that movement in Africa. His actions immediately served as a demonstration of the ultimate expression of what the Second Chancers movement claimed to be all about.

Quickly the name Paul Kabinda was widely discussed in powerful circles with the phrase *Nobel Peace Prize*.

More importantly, a small tribe survived. A tiny group of 42 souls, whose traditions and language and only bloodline had been erased from the Earth would live on.

For now though, Colonel Kabinda was content with the last thought. It was the only one that concerned him.

Coming back to this world was not enough.

He needed to find ways to make it better. It was not a want.

It was a need.

Kabinda took a short nap after he checked in with UAA Headquarters by radio and received his scolding for absconding with their trucks for his heroic joyride.

He wakes to the first knock on the door. One thing he has noticed in the months since his miraculous return to life is that he does not sleep particularly deeply anymore.

"Yes?" Colonel Kabinda asks.

"Colonel?" It is a familiar voice.

"Come," he says, and he sits up in bed, squinting in the thin light of the hall.

The man comes in and shuts the door behind him.

"What is it, Captain Qasir?"

The man crosses his arms and stands in the darkness.

"You wanted to know the specifi – "

"What *is* it," he repeats impatiently, "*Captain.*" He says the last word as if it seems to be a little too lofty for the moment if the man delays any further.

"He is gone. Someone in Dikir's office says that a Sudanese infiltrator was allegedly the trigger man. They have also heard that the man is

- 429 -

dead. I am sorry."

Kabinda frowns. "It was necessary, and our man knew it. He knew the chances of executing his mission in a way that permitted his own escape were meager at best. What is the official word the rest of the world is hearing?"

"There is none. No indication has been made that anything has happened. Roti was already in hiding somewhere. Therefore his absence has yet to be felt. There are reports that many of his top advisors are disappearing all over Addis Ababa."

"The rats deserting the ship, Qasir."

"So it would appear, sir."

The Colonel swings his legs over the opposite side of the bed from the Captain.

"I am not sorry, but I am sad to hear the gunman has died. You did not know him...I scarcely knew him myself. But he was a good young man, and we have lost too many of those."

Kabinda had hoped the boy would find a way to survive his mission.

"Will the war end, sir?"

Kabinda pulls his weary bones up out of the bed. Time and abuse have made most mornings a slow process, one for which there was typically no witness other than himself. He hides the usual grunts and groans from his attending officer.

"It already has. By the time the earthquake strikes...assuming it does so again...there will be a very small number of Ethiopians and Somalis in Kenya. Except," he adds, walking to his bathroom, "for those who are in custody."

"You think so?"

Kabinda splashes a little water on his face from the sink. "The GEA finds itself headless now. Tafi was the only one who could have possibly held it together, and he belongs to us now. Urragabi is missing and would not have been able to command the respect necessary to take over. And Dikir does not possess the fortitude. There is no one else who has a chance of keeping Somalia in step. Without Somalia for the dirty work, Great East Africa is only Ethiopia, a hungry people who have not been a power in their own right for many generations."

"Your orders?"

"What time is it in Washington right now? I can never remember the time zones there."

"Washington is Eastern American, sir. It is eight hours earlier there than here. It is almost 10 this morning there."

"I will need a secure line to make a phone call in the next hour. Can you do this?"

Captain Qasir tightened his lips. "It will be difficult here, but I will make it so, Colonel."

"Excellent. First, I need you to inform headquarters that I will be returning there as soon as possible."

"As you wish."

What the Captain would not be able to tell them was that Kabinda intended to resign his commission once he arrived there. The Colonel wanted to tell his right-hand man that this was the case, but this was not the time to do so. He was uncomfortable having shared as much about the secret operation with the American as he'd had to.

It had been necessary to get the information without going through the UAA channels. That would have made it far too public, and even less under his control.

Washington D.C.
June 2
7:13 AM
Thirteen minutes after the Event

He woke to a shout.

"Okay," the voice bellowed, *"what* the *hell?!?"*

Senator Clark David Brown of Texas sat up in bed in a panic, totally confused and horrified. He drew a sharp breath and let out a moist but shallow cough.

She stood in the doorway and he sat up in bed…and they stared at each other in shock.

Like everyone else on earth in the seconds before this one, the two of them had been in completely different circumstances.

Moments ago the Senator had been clutching the hand of the passenger next to him on the plane, watching the Atlantic Ocean rush up at their aircraft as it dove for the frigid, choppy waters below.

Noise from the failing engine outside the fuselage filled the ears of the passengers as their shared terror swept through the cabin like a specter.

The woman beside him was a Senate Page that Senator Brown had known for about a year. He knew her well enough to know that she was looking forward to seeing her boyfriend while they were in London, that her parents did not know she was still dating the young Brit, and that they weren't even aware that she had been assigned to the Senator's entourage. This news was going to come as a complete shock to them.

Harriet was her name. She was named for her maternal Grandmother, a D.A.R. stalwart in Connecticut. The senior Harriet would also take the news hard. The girl was her pride and joy and the first thing she boasted about at their meetings.

He held her hand to offer her a tiny bit of comfort in their final moments. His relationship with young Harriet was innocent and platonic. He was older than the girl's Grandmother.

The next thing the Senator knew he was waking up to the screams of his former nurse in the doorway of his bedroom.

Brown was 70 years old when that plane went down, one of the more senior members of the Senate, a body he had served in for 33 years. He was thought of as every bit as much a Texas tradition as chili, football, and gun racks in the back windows of pickup trucks were. *CDB*, they called him. His colleagues, his constituents, the press, and several presidents had all referred to him by that name.

CDB's loss over the Atlantic on a New Years'

Eve flight to Britain made world headlines. He was a respected moderate voice, a common sense politician who though like the 19th Century, argued like a man who helped shape the end of the 20th, and felt quite at home in the 21st.

However, he had spent his last summer on the earth suffering from a nasty bout of pneumonia. A fiercely independent man, CDB had to eventually bow to his doctor's wishes and permit a nurse to keep a constant eye on him in his Washington apartment.

At 7 in the morning on June 2nd...about seven months before his death...Senator CDB was asleep in his bed. His body did battle against the tide of muck in his chest, with a massive assist from his medication. He had been down for some time with it but was finally making strides in the last 48 hours. The worst summer illness of his long and robust life was coming to an end, at last.

When he returned to life he had been blissfully unaware of it for 13 minutes.

Julia Handy was not as fortunate as that.

At seven in the morning on that day, she had been walking up the steps to the Senator's building, pulling her purse around to fish out her keys. She had already been there that morning to check on him before running out to arrange some breakfast for the two of them. The Senator had shown further signs of improvement and he needed to eat.

A year later Nurse Handy was in bed herself, sleeping in after pulling a late shift.

Suddenly she was dressed for work and

walking up to a Federal apartment complex in D.C., the city she had not worked in for eight months now. She was working in a cardiac ward in Boston these days.

From asleep and dreaming to dressed and walking in an instant. She froze at first and just listened.

Two cars collided further up the street in a symphony of screeching rubber and twisting metal. They were joined seconds later by a third that just barely ran out of space for its brakes.

Overhead an aircraft roared and wobbled a bit before correcting itself. She looked back down after watching it for a second, mesmerized by the absurdity of this. She became quickly convinced she was still dreaming.

As she looked away from the plane she saw faces in almost every window of the building before her.

The scene was ethereal and did little to form any kind of proper argument against this being a shift in her dream.

Julia stood there for a full minute drinking it all in, waiting to see what else might happen.

Nothing really did. She followed her instincts and stepped away from the building.

There was work waiting for her, and she had already wasted a minute. A minute she had felt every second of. She walked over to the auto accident, hearing the crisp ring of her footsteps on the cobblestone street.

"Incredibly realistic," she remarked to herself.

The people involved in the accident were all okay, miraculously. One had a minor scrape.

"You," she said to one of the other drivers, "call 9-1-1."

Dazed and confused, the man complied. He did so almost on autopilot. Julia took a good look at the wound.

"Hang on a sec," she said. She ducked her head in through the ruined passenger side window and opened the glove box. She fished some fast food napkins out of it and brought them to the driver side.

"You'll be fine," she said. She followed that up with a stern nurse's command.

"Hold these over it until help gets here." She looked up at the man who was shutting off his phone. "They on their way?"

"I'm rebooting. No connection. 9-1-1 was tied up. It was busy."

"It was busy? 9-1-1 was busy?"

"What am I doing here?" he asked. He looked extremely lost, his thumb lifting up from the power button as the phone came back to life in his hand.

"Relax. We'll figure everything out. Call 9-1-1 again."

"Okay," he said, hitting his dial button.

Rebooting it would not help. Every phone circuit in the world had overloaded with the volume of calls in the last few minutes.

Julia looked back up the street at the apartment building and opened her purse. She dug around for a moment and came up with a fistful of keys.

"Really?" she asked no one in particular.

She walked up to the building again, hesitating for a few breaths before climbing the stone steps. She sank the brass-colored key into the lock and twisted it to the right.

The lock slid to one side with a tiny, mechanical crash. She pulled and stepped inside.

The guard was not at his post, which never happened. In truth, the old man had bolted out in confusion while she was walking up to the car accident. He had no idea why he had suddenly been there any more than anyone else on the face of the Earth.

Nurse Julia walked to the elevator and thumbed the up-arrow. The bell dinged and the doors opened at once, and she stepped in.

As she turned to look at the numbers, her hand hovered over the buttons for a few heartbeats. It was more muscle memory than anything that caused her to press the 6 button and wait for the doors to close. This job had ended 11 months ago.

Still, she managed to recognize the building. As the elevator doors dinged and parted once more, she recognized the hallway. Suite 602 was her destination: Senator Brown.

Why she was dreaming about this job was beyond her. Except that the Senator had been famous…even before he died in that plane crash at New Year's…the job hadn't been particularly remarkable. Pneumonia, it had been. And a nasty case of it too, for a 70 year-old patient. The Senator bounced back from it well. His recovery displayed the same strong will his reputation carried while he was kicking hornets' nests on Capitol Hill.

Now, he sat up with that old familiar rattle in his chest, and looked at his former nurse.

"This is the strangest dream I've ever had," Julia Handy said, leaning against the doorframe.

"You're telling *me*," the Senator replied. "This is the first dream I've had in heaven."

"Is that so?" she replied. "Well, I guess I'm flattered to be in it then, Senator."

He gave her an innocent smile and another chesty cough.

"So," he asked, "any idea why we're both having the same dream?"

Chapter Seventeen
Election Day

Washington D.C.
November 4
12:12 AM

"Say that again?"

"It's only a rumor at this point sir, but it's from a trustable source." This is the reply of Lieutenant General Ken Franklin. He stands at attention with three stars and a number of colorful ribbons on his nice clean uniform. He has been wearing it all day, appreciative that he works in a series of heavily air-conditioned rooms. The fabric is as weighty as the sensitive material he handles in his job.

"I want confirmation from the UAA before I take this to the President."

"We're efforting that now, sir. This would explain the sudden about-face on the ground in Kenya."

"Well *that's* for damn sure. Thanks, Ken."

Walter Randall reaches into his desk and pulls out his bottle of ibuprofen. It is a large bottle because he goes though a lot of it. Randall rarely drinks but he is fairly certain he will suffer liver problems in his golden years thanks to the number of pain relievers he has taken in his life. Assuming the planet doesn't reverse itself again and keep him from getting any older. That idea might appeal to most people, but most people don't have his job.

The coffee he uses to push down the analgesics is cold, but he doesn't care. The last time he remembers getting coffee was four hours ago when he had failed to show up at dinner.

This is what it is to be the Chief of Staff at the West Wing of The White House. There was lunch with the British Ambassador, and there had been a special Saturday Breakfast with the First Lady's favorite charity before that. Otherwise, there had been coffee and coffee alone since he woke up at four o'clock this morning. Except now, that was actually *yesterday* morning. The days didn't run together in this job so much as the *weeks* did.

His secretary appears in the doorway, looking every bit as tired as he himself feels.

"Zanzibar is on the line, Walt."

"Jesus, Jenny...you're still here too?"

"I leave when you do. You haven't noticed that?"

He smiles as he picks up the phone. "This is Walter Randall at the White House, to whom am I...?"

He listens for several seconds after being interrupted.

"Okay, and what's happening in Kenya?"

He listens again, and eventually repeats one of the words he heard.

"Equator. That's fantastic news. Thank you, Colonel. Have a great..."

He looks up at the clock and does some quick math in his head...

"...day today, sir."

He hangs up the phone. "Jenny? Is the President in the residence?"

"I believe so."

"I need to see him right now. Call in the rest of the Joint Chiefs, too, please. It's time to wake everybody up."

The Chief of Staff grins with the broad smile of the Cheshire Cat.

Just after midnight.

This is a hell of a great way to start a new day. Today he gets to deliver good news to his President for the first time in a very long time. Actually, it could be argued that it's the best news he's given him since the day they found out there wasn't going to be another Presidential Election tonight.

He rises from his chair and buttons his jacket.

UAA Headquarters
Zanzibar, Tanzania
November 4
8:20 AM

Paul Kabinda hangs up the phone and walks down the hallway to await the Prime Minister of

Tanzania, who is not in his office yet.

A pair of generals is walking down the hallway, and Kabinda snaps to attention. He throws them a salute as they pass. They return it, and one of them says "Colonel," as he does so. Two aides walking behind them, junior officers both, carry *Eyes Only* folders and salute Kabinda. He returns their salutes. Every one of them, regardless of rank, was smiling. Everyone in the building this morning is aware that the GEA is quitting Kenya at an unexpected rate of speed.

The Prime Minister's secretary greets Kabinda at the door.

"He's running late, Colonel, but should be along presently. Tea?"

"Please," he says with a smile. "Two sugars."

She pours hot water in a cup and reaches for a teabag. "It's a new day for Africa, Colonel. Things are changing again, but for the better this time...don't you think?"

"I do indeed."

"It is good to have men like you on our side, Colonel."

He takes the cup that she hands him, and stirs it. "I'm just a soldier, miss. One of many."

"And a bit of a pencil-pusher these days, at that." Admiral Lucas Rokiri says this from the doorway with a smile. "Good morning, Nina. Good morning, Paul."

Kabinda salutes. "Good morning, sir. He isn't in yet."

The Admiral waves off the salute. "You've placed your other phone call this morning, I assume?"

"Yes, sir. Minutes ago."

"Your tea, Admiral," Nina says. She hands the man his usual. Admiral Rokiri has been a frequent visitor to this office during the war.

The Prime Minister walks through the door. He wears a smart blue suit, a matching hat, and a smile as wide as the Nile.

"Good morning, Nina. Gentlemen."

"Good morning, Prime Minister," his secretary says with her usual smile. "Your coffee is nearly ready, sir."

"Thank you, Nina. It is a good day, is it not?"

"It is," she says. "The war will be ending soon, will it not?"

"I certainly hope so, Nina. See to it no one disturbs us for the next 30 minutes, yes?"

"Certainly, Mister Prime Minister."

He walks briskly to his office, the officers trailing him quickly.

"So," Rokiri says as he closes the door behind them. "Ten Downing Street first, or the United Nations? I assume Kabinda, you have already taken care of the Americans?"

"Yes, Mr. Prime Minister. They've been given the information we agreed upon this morning. All of it."

"Excellent. The British and the UN will have to wait to hear about King Roti until we are informed by an official source. I expect that will happen in the next 24 to 48 hours. We will tell them, however, of our *suspicion* that he might be dead."

"Underpromise," Admiral Rokiri says, "and overdeliver."

A knock at the door causes the First Lady to look up from her book. She glances over at the President.

For the first time in recent history, he has fallen asleep before she has. She smiles. The man doesn't sleep enough. It's likely he never will in this room. This job does not lend itself to proper sleep patterns.

She pivots herself out of bed and plants her feet in her slippers. Another light knock at the door comes before she arrives at it, but she is hesitant to say anything for fear of waking her husband.

She opens the door slightly and looks expectantly at the Secret Service agent in the hallway.

"What is it, Bicks?"

Senior Agent Bickell frowns at her. "I'm sorry, ma'am, but the Chief of Staff needs a minute."

She ties her robe and pulls the door open a bit more. Walter Randall is standing in the hallway outside the bedroom.

"Evening, Walt. He's sleeping. Why are you

- 446 -

going to ruin it this time?"

"Kenya. It's good news. But it really can't wait until morning."

She pursed her lips in defeat and held up her index finger. "Give me a minute. I'll wake him up."

Colorado Springs
November 4
1:00 PM

Anne Ayres spent most of her morning interviewing people on the street downtown. She asked them about the election that didn't happen today. That had been her plan for today since Friday.

Thanks to the news that broke this morning she was also able to gauge public opinion while she was on the street about the Kenya pullout. The answers to both questions were predictable for a city with such a heavy military presence on every side of it.

She is putting the finishing touches on the script for the election story, and getting ready to begin the Kenya reaction story, when she glances up at the TV in her office and it grabs her attention.

The bottom of the screen says *Statement from Kenyan President expected at 1:30 ET.* She thumbs the MUTE button on her remote to turn the volume back on.

"We will carry the live statement from the newly-reinstalled President of Kenya in a half-hour," the doe-eyed blond cable newscaster says.

Anne clicks mute again, and decides to wait to write the other story.

Nairobi, Kenya
November 4
9:30 PM

The formerly-exiled Kenyan President is indifferent to the international spotlight. His statement fits on a single sheet of paper, which is smoothed out on the desk before him as he sits at his desk.

Before the camera in his office turns on, most of the news outlets in the world are showing the Kenyan flag being raised over the building again. It is up there for the first time since The Rift event, when it was suddenly missing. The shield and spears wave in the wind in the corner of most of the screens as the President begins to speak.

"Good evening. Kenya is free. With great pride and the most humble of thanks to our allies, the people of our great republic proclaim ourselves to be free of the yoke of our oppressors. A new day is dawning for us all, and as we wake up to it...a nightmare is ending for the African community."

The President folds his hands on the desk in front of him.

"I say to the people of Ethiopia: We have had

many difficulties over the course of our histories. Freedom has come to Kenya. It can come for you, as well. Your Pretender King is not the master of our fate, or yours. Already we have seen our neighbors in Uganda and the South Sudan turn away from their relationships with him. Rise up against him and regain your dignity."

He lays his hands flat.

"Thank you."

No one watching can help but notice that there is no message to the people of Somalia.

A year and a half has done little to erase the memory of mass graves.

There remains a possibility that peace may be fleeting in the region.

Colorado Springs
November 4
5:25 PM

Sam throws his duffel bag out of his bedroom window.

He digs his football out of the closet and thumps down the stairs. Once he hits the last step, he sits on it and pulls his high top sneakers on.

He grabs his coat and hat and announces his intentions as his hand grabs the doorknob.

"Heading over to Darren's house to play football."

"Wait," Helen says from the kitchen. "Homework done?"

"Yes," Sam replies. It's on the dinner table.

"Okay. Dinner is at seven," she replies. "Don't be late."

"All right, mom."

He starts to pull the door shut behind him then pauses for a moment. The corners of his mouth are turned down as he adds, "Love you."

"Love you too, baby," she says absent-mindedly.

Sam walk out of the house and walks around to the back. He stashes his football in the bushes and grabs the bag.

He takes a deep breath and throws the strap over his shoulder.

He takes off running in the direction of the next street over.

Forty minutes later Helen is clearing off the dining room table when she hears the knock at the door. Her husband is upstairs changing after what is going to be one of his last days as Base Commander at Peterson.

"Danny, get the door, baby," she shouts. Daniel has been destroying Texas A&M on his X-Box in the living room. He pokes the button to pause the game and gets up from the couch.

With his father's footsteps coming down the stairs, Danny opens the front door.

"Uh," he says, taken aback, "good evening, General Gilmour."

"Good evening, Danny." He doesn't add anything to that as the colonel comes around the corner of the stairs.

"Gil?" he says, puzzled. Helen hears this and

drops a plate on the table with a clang. It does not break, but it tilts back and forth on the bottom rim for a second before it comes to a rest.

"Come in," the colonel says, and Danny holds open the door.

From the other room, Helen is less welcoming, and her southern is showing.

"You are not welcome in this house if you're bringin' me bad news, Gil. Choose your words carefully."

An awkward silence chills the air in the house, making the Colorado November outside seem warm by comparison. General Gilmour stands in the hallway with his hat in his hand, saying nothing.

His face says everything.

Helen's shoulders drop.

"He's M.I.A., they won't tell me exactly where, just that he is presumed dead. I'm…"

She is holding a plate in her right hand, and she sends it flying against the opposite wall in the living room. The shrapnel dances in every direction, raining down shards around Duke the dog, who jumps up and runs upstairs, yelping like his tail was on fire.

Helen slams her fists down on the dining room table, drops to her knees, and begins sobbing uncontrollably. Her husband runs to her side and starts rubbing her back in large, sweeping circles.

She is doubled over and shrieking in agony. It's as if a white-hot blade has been inserted between two ribs and left there to temper. Danny instinctively closes the door so the neighbors won't hear it, and then sinks to the floor with his back against the door. He bangs his head against it three times, and then looks down. He stares a hole in the floor between his knees.

As Danny's fingers meet behind his head, he is filled with thoughts that it should have been him. For the first time since he returned to life, he feels that he should have gone back to Africa to face the war with his brother.

"Where is Sam?" he asks, still looking at the hallway throw rug. No one but the general could have possibly heard him over his mother.

Danny leaps up to his feet and walks into the living room. Helen has just gotten back up to her feet with help from the colonel, and she reaches out and absorbs Danny when he approaches.

"Mom," he says. He pulls back with some effort and looks into her eyes. They are ruined with tears and darting around the room in madness. He tries again.

"Mom!"

She looks up at him, finally seeing him.

"Where is Sammy?"

Helen holds him close again. She is shaking like a machine separating gold from silt. Wild Bill pulls her over to his chest.

"Sam's playing football over at Darren's."

"I'll go." He had to get out of the house. He was certain of that. In less than one minute he breezes past the general in the hallway and jumps in his SUV.

General Gilmour's nose takes control and

turns his entire head. Whatever Helen had walked away from in the kitchen in order to set the table has reached a moment where it needs immediate attention. He steps into the kitchen, lays his coat across a chair at their kitchen table, and gets his bearings on whatever she had going. He's no chef but at least he can keep their house from catching fire.

Two minutes go by when the house phone rings. General Gilmour answers it.

"Pemberton residence."

"Hey…it's Danny. Let me talk to my mo…my dad."

"Hold on, Danny."

The general holds out the phone to Bill, who has managed to get his wife to sit in a chair at the dining room table. He steps into the kitchen and takes the receiver.

"What is it, boy?"

"Dad…Darren said he never made any plans to play with him today, and no one over here has seen him."

Khartoum, Sudan
November 5
1:30 AM

Urragabi enters the city with the swagger of a victorious pirate. He stops himself emotionally before he walks up to the third of the GEA safe houses that was established for the Royal Family in Sudan's capital, not far from the confluence of the White and Blue Niles.

He focuses his efforts on putting on the emotionless face he is best known for displaying. The circumstances behind his visit are not known to the guards, and he does not want to betray any information. Appearing to be mournful...or incredibly happy...would only raise more questions and turn this enterprise into a far more difficult one.

He turns to the first guard as he walks up. They know him by sight and do not make any attempt to stop him as he approaches.

"Replace my vehicle with a newer one, please. Find me something that can give me some distance."

"As you wish, Minister."

"On your way."

The two remaining guards nod at him as he passes between them. There is nothing written on his face whatsoever. He is sure of this.

Fedens and the children she typically travels with are asleep upstairs in a room protected by two more armed men. They know Urragabi by sight from the list of people who make up the upper echelon, but they still require the Minister to produce an official order to go into the bedchamber.

The house is a nice one. It belongs to a sympathizer to Roti's cause, a wealthy businessman with interests that align with great East Africa's. A lot of them sprang up in neighboring countries a couple of years before the war, when rich new deposits of gold were discovered in the mountains of the Oromia region of Ethiopia. This gold finally fed a people who had starved for generations. This gold forged a union with Somalia to secure both a coastline and a cheap workforce. Later, it would also provide cannon fodder.

Lya, the youngest of her daughters, has climbed into bed with Fedens. Lya is actually Urragabi's child, a well-kept secret known only to her biological parents. Urragabi touches the child's cheek and she stirs slightly but does not wake. His eyes wander to her mother, who is looking up at him and smiling. Feeling her child shift woke her and she is pleased to see who was behind it.

"Is it done?" she whispers.

"It is," he whispers in reply, "but I dare not give you any of the details here and now. We need to get ourselves on the road quickly and far away from this place."

Colorado Springs Airport
November 4
7:59 PM

The two of them sit in the security office, utterly dejected.

It had made sense to Sam, and it had been a simple enough matter to get the tickets. Getting the flight was the easy part.

Brianna goes to school with Sam Pemberton and is very fond of him in the way only another 11 year-old girl could possibly understand. She has filled more than a few pages of her little pink pony diary with the words Mrs. Brianna Pemberton.

Sam has encouraged this because none of his friends have any girls hanging around, and it made him cool to kiss her after school in front of people. That decision was made only a month ago. He has grown to really appreciate the situation for more than purposes of looking cool to the other kids.

When he found out her mother was a travel agent, Sam decided to use her devotion to his advantage. He felt a little bad about that, but he had no other options at his disposal.

Hacking into her mother's system was far easier than it should be. Brianna, like most tweens, is a very tech-savvy kid.

Within 48 hours of sharing his desire to go overseas with Brianna, Sam had a ticket. He had a gluten-free meal. He even had a window seat. He also had special dispensation to travel abroad without an adult, and she arranged for the airport shuttle to pick him up at her house so as not to arouse any suspicion.

New York to Lisbon to Lagos, and then on to Dar Es Salaam...which was as close to Ethiopia as the current flight restrictions would permit her to get him. Dar Es Salaam had a large American Base on it. He would be able to track down Billy there and find out where they could find the lamp with the djinni.

That would fix everything.

Attempting to board the flight that would lead him to the first stop, airport security ran his name. Chances are it was his final destination, though several steps in his itinerary threw up red flags because several travel agent steps were incomplete. It turned out that the boy had been reported missing only fifteen minutes earlier from one of the Air Force bases.

Ten minutes later, Sam and his first girlfriend (this had been part of the bargain) sat in the security office of the airport, waiting for the hammers of parental justice to come down hard upon them.

Sam would just have to hope that Billy would find the lamp all over again and send it to him. He knew now that he had to destroy it, in order to make sure no one else ruined the world with it ever again.

Wild Bill and Helen have been frantic trying to find him in the last two hours.

When the airport called, Danny decided to give his parents some space to deal with the situation.

"While you're getting him, I have to take a drive up into the mountains," he told them. Today's was not the sort of news he was going to give Anne over the phone.

The colonel nodded in agreement.

Helen remained numb and silent. Chances are she wouldn't be making the drive to the airport, either. She was sitting quietly in her living room, her best friends sitting around her like a nice warm blanket of people. They were doing their best to get her to respond to them, but she couldn't do anything. Wild Bill was glad to have them there for her.

One more person had to be told what had happened. Sam had no idea his brother was dead again.

Fairplay, Colorado
November 4
10:37 PM

She has always muttered under her breath when she is *really* into what she is typing.

This has driven three roommates crazy, as well as her on-again, off-again boyfriend Billy. Not to mention a number of people in the newsrooms she has haunted over the years that have sat within earshot of her work stations.

She is trying to make sure this piece isn't a rip-off of one she wrote a couple of years ago for her newspaper boss at Three Cities. She had written a brief feature on the history of what had sparked The Rift Valley War for the paper...even though she technically belonged to the radio side of the company. *A Match To Old Parchments*, she called it. It won her three local awards and made her a finalist for a state honor.

This piece was not flowing nearly as easily as that one had. She had pages of research to refer to for that one, and two days to write her draft. This assignment had a much tighter deadline and little to build from, as the situation continued to unfold layer by layer.

She was being asked to state a point of view, and that's what she was going to do.

The withdrawal of Great East Africa from Kenya likely signals its death knell. Already there is an uprising in what passes for major cities in Somalia, and there are reports of pirates striking at Ethiopian ships in the Gulf of Aden. The breakdown of the G.E.A. alliance is quickly re-forging the former border between the former countries...the area where King Roti was born and raised on the Ethiopian side. The fault lines run deep there.

Grimly, she mused that *that* would play especially well if the earthquake hit the region again on Thursday, as it had the first time the year came around. There was no cruelty in the thought. The news has a way of desensitizing the people who report it. She expanded on the thought as she kept going.

They are religious and cultural cracks as sure as the ones in the Earth that form the Rift Valley itself. Ethiopia and Somalia will likely be independent again by the end of the month, if the withdrawals continue at their current pace. There remains no word from Roti himself, and no video update from the man has been filed in two weeks.

She stops and reads, checking her syntax and spelling. Spellcheck is turned off. She doesn't trust Spellcheck.

Tuesday was to have been an Election Day here in the United States again, had the Supreme Court ruled a different way. Instead we find ourselves in a freshly optimistic situation. With the troop movements confirmed by satellite flyovers, victory can be claimed again in The Rift Valley War. The Kenyan people can once more embrace their

A sharp rap at the door interrupts her thought process. She can quite literally feel the next few words fly out of her head like a mist and float away. She hates when that happens.

"Damnit!"

She needs to get this piece for the website done quickly. New Ron has trusted her with a big feature for the first time and she needs to really nail it.

She sets her laptop down and walks over to the front door, boiling over with irritation at having been article-blocked so abruptly.

Danny Pemberton is standing on the other side of the door, but he isn't facing it. He knocked, he turned around, and he stared out at the mountains, smoking a cigarette.

Anne Ayres opens the door, and finds herself unable to use any of the smart-ass comments she would typically hurl at the young man when he shows up at her house. She isn't sure why.

"Mary's not home," she says.

He says nothing.

Something doesn't feel right. Perhaps it's the fact that he's smoking, which she doesn't typically see him do. Or maybe it's the fact that he still hasn't turned around as she steps out onto the porch with a creak of the boards underfoot.

No. It is most definitely the way he holds out

the cigarettes without looking at her and passes her a lighter when she takes one.

Anne Ayres feels her heart rate skyrocket as she lights it and stands next to him.

She takes a long, deep drag and exhales with a shudder that has nothing to do with the temperature. There can only be one reason why he would come here, looking this distraught, and not be looking for Mary.

"You're kidding me," she says, and she says it with disappointed anger.

"All we know is it was a couple of days ago, and they're sending us an empty box. Missing in action, presumed dead. I don't know where, I don't know how. I...I don't know." He chokes on the words.

Anne Ayres does not cry.

She drops the cigarette in the short instant before she faints and falls to the deck.

Daniel Pemberton lurches to catch her and fails to do so.

Approaching Bîr Shalatein, Egypt
November 5
6:02 AM

The border crossing happened under cover of darkness, several miles to the west of the thin road that followed the coast up from Marsa Sha'ab, the last piece of the Sudan before the border. The waters of the Red Sea pounded at the coastline a few miles to his right. The air here was rich with the smells of seagulls, dead fish, and of the gulls that pecked relentlessly at their tiny bodies along the beaches.

The night was favoring him. Only stars were out tonight. No moonlight bounced off the shifting sands to betray his position to anyone or anything that might be patrolling the frontier in the old Treaty Zone. He hoped he was not throwing any scents inland that might attract any wildlife. He knew he was too weak to defend himself, and knew also that he was upwind.

For days he has pulled himself along in silence. Around gritty mountains and naked animal bones and fat, shifting dunes bleached white by the blank stare of the sun.

Somewhere around Mount Farâid, within sight of the coast of Foul Bay, the British maintained an outpost. He had to be within distance of it soon. There had to be a patrol along the border at some point.

These things had to be true because if they weren't...he would die.

Failing that, he might make the town itself if he could just keep his feet under him for a little longer. He was not sure he could, but he would certainly try.

An antiquated form of tracked vehicle appeared over the next sand dune, heading just to the right of his location.

Once he saw it turn in his direction, Captain William Pemberton III dropped to his knees, and thanked whatever god might be listening for delivering him from the desert.

Amarillo, Texas
November 4
11:25 PM

"Had things turned out differently, Senator, we might be toasting your election to the Presidency right now."

CDB sips at his beer. "I'm a patient man, Ari. I can wait."

The Saudi smiles in response.

Senator Brown stands up. "Gentlemen, can I interest you in a tour of the place? Feel free to bring your drinks."

Five men rise to follow him around the mansion.

"It's been in my family for generations," CDB says as they move down the hallway. "My granddaddy added this wing after double-ya-double-ya two. I grew up here," he taps a security code into a silent panel hidden in a fake book in the bookcase. A whisper-quiet secret door opens in the wall under the grand staircase.

"And I know every inch of this house."

He gestures for his guests to follow him into the room. As the last guest walks through the opening, CBD presses a button under his desk and the door slides shut without so much as a click.

"Gentlemen, this is the most secure room you will ever be in. We could shoot Uzis at a gong in here and no one on the outside would ever hear a thing. Let's have a seat and get to our business."

The six of them sit at a table in the center of the room. The seats are plush and comfortable. The table is onyx trimmed with gold. The whole thing seems a little gauche to a couple of his guests, who have more simple tastes. The Saudi Prince however, feels right at home. Oil bought this. He can relate.

"There is no way we can build any facilities in Europe," one man says. He has a German accent, Bavarian to be precise. He has a thick moustache and beard and is just an old tweed suit removed from being the spitting image of the photos one usually sees of Otto von Bismarck. "There would be no way to hide the activity required to build them. Your..." he imitates the accent as best he can... "Dubble-yah-dubble-yah two saw to that. All of central and eastern Europe is trained to spot the slightest signs of such activity. The era of social media would be the ruin of any project."

"Spoken like a cautious German," CDB says.

"Asia can shoulder much of the load," a soft-spoken man with a slightly Russian accent says. "There are a number of sites in Kazakhstan that would be perfect for what has been proposed. I am certain that I can bring Siberia on board, as well. There is no need for us to struggle to meet the Chinese price."

"We can put at least two up in the Outback by March," says an Australian woman. "Working through the hot summer will not be easy."

"It would be less easy putting any up on the peninsula," the Arab says suddenly. "We are under far more satellite scrutiny than even the Senator is likely aware."

"I don't doubt that. My country has quite a hard-on for you boys. Beggin' your pardon, ladies."

The last woman, an olive-skinned Brazilian in a smart purple suit, smiles at the Texan.

"We can build two, perhaps three. It will be difficult to get the materials into the areas they will be needed, though."

"Well that's where the Prince and the German come in. They can't build, but they can sure as hell fund. We have enough covert government backing between us that we can build ten or eleven facilities and have them up and running by April. Here in the States, over in Kazakhstan and Russia, in Brazil and in Australia. Report back to your people that we're a go, and we'll begin putting together the first steps of Remora through the usual channels before Christmas. Anything else?"

No one says a word.

"Good luck, ya'll." He hits another button under the desk, and the door reopens.

After they've all stepped back into the hall,

CDB closes the door with the fake book panel, and smiles.

"And that was the last time that old dog chased after an armadillo in the yard, I'll tell you that!"

His guests share a polite laugh.

The CIA operative makes a note that the party dropped out of audio range for about a minute, and there might be an issue with one of the microphones in the Senator's house.

Chapter Eighteen
The Third Time Is a Charm

Though the British have maintained a military presence in the city for decades, this hospital has only been here since the beginning of the Rift Valley War.

It has served a role as the primary regional medical center for British Troops in the Northern Theatre. It is of good size, as big as the one the Americans have in Mombasa, Kenya. It is a permanent structure that will be left behind for the city of Aswan after the war is over, something that has granted the British certain special favors regarding the facility.

The building is only a few years old: New enough to still smell of fresh timber and antiseptic, and old enough to smell of blood and heartbreak.

The duty nurse has learned not to question orders. The first time she mentioned something when an Ethiopian was brought in, she was quickly reminded by the Chief Surgeon that the uniforms come off when they come through the door, and only the men and women remain. Therefore the unconscious, dark-skinned young man with the somewhat flattened nose they carry through the doors on a moonless night could be anyone, from anywhere.

The ID Biopsy turns up something really interesting.

"Key-er Mayuri," the duty nurse says in a thin northern brogue. It's precisely the sort of accent that would have fired up the brain of their patient. "From South Sudan. Diplomat, no less...have a look then!"

She holds up the ID to her supervising officer. She takes it with a smile.

"A diplomat. Well, at least it should be a simple matter to contact his people. That's not always the case with that country."

Two doctors respond urgently to a beeping noise coming from the patient's room.

The duty nurse frowns.

"Hopefully we'll be able to give them good news when we phone them up."

Aswan, Egypt
November 6
12:05 PM

"Poor bastard," noted one.

"Hardly," replied the other. "I'd say he's one

lucky bastard."

"Look at 'im twitch. That man's dreamin'."

The nurses worked in time-practiced tandem, changing the bandages and delivering a sponge bath at the same time. They did their best to be careful not to disturb him, even though Kiir Mayuri was in a shallow coma while his tissues rehydrated. The jury was still out as to whether or not he would suffer any permanent brain damage from his ordeal in the desert.

In truth he *was* dreaming.

His dream was a memory, one he was replaying over and over again. It was the last time he had interacted with other people before he was discovered by the British unit at the border.

"You have done me a great favor, Mr. Mayuri," Urragabi said to him once the other guards had gone. "And for that reason, I will do this favor for you."

The Ethiopian pulled out a carbon-bladed knife that looked big enough to carve a Thanksgiving turkey with, and stuck it into the sand next to Billy.

As the prisoner prepared to reach out and grab it out of the sand, he jumped involuntarily at the sound of a very loud gunshot.

Urragabi lowered the pistol and said nothing at first. Billy looked behind him at the far dune, and saw that a big leopard lay dead in the sand.

"So long as you can move quickly, the animals in the area will be more interested in the cat than in you. You can run away. The cat cannot. Do you understand what I am telling you?"

Billy nodded, a little confused.

"You will take the knife to protect yourself, but you will not find any men between here and Egypt. You will find no boats at the shoreline, only sharks that love to pick off bathers in the shallows. You can make the border in a few days if you are smart. No matter how much you thirst do *not* drink from the Red Sea. Stay away from the shore and keep moving north. Perhaps you will survive. Perhaps you will not."

He helped Billy to his knees and quickly worked on his gunshot wounds.

"And I did not set you free. You found a way to escape after you shot him. Is that understood?"

"It is," Billy said. "Unfortunately that means I can't thank you, because you didn't help me."

Urragabi finished tying a bandage on his arm.

"I will get over it," Urragabi said. "Now go."

Juba, South Sudan
November 8
9:01 AM

The secretary closes the door behind her after she enters the office. "It has been three days, Mister Vice President. We have not been able to find the records."

Vice President Kerek looks up from what he was reading.

"Mm?"

"I'm sorry sir...I should have been more specific. The Diplomat. The one in the hospital in Egypt. We cannot locate his records."

South Sudan is a proud and independent country. However it is not a particularly tech-savvy one, and it still stores much of its record-keeping in thick manila folders locked up in a huge steel shed in the federal block.

Kerek tapped a folder on his desk. "My office has located one of them. We are already trying to find a relative. The man does not appear to have any."

The secretary's face sank. "So sad. Well at least you have something to start with. I don't remember him at all. What division was he in?"

"He wasn't in our office," the Vice President says, and he leaves it at that.

No one from Intelligence has returned his call yet. This is not unusual. His office is never particularly high on anyone's return call list.

The Vice President returns to his Ian Fleming novel, the best use of his day.

Denver International Airport
November 10
9:45 AM

Anne is running a little late, but since most flights do the same, she is certain she is okay for time.

The call from Valerie had been a pleasant

surprise. The cryptic request to pick her up at the Denver Airport Monday morning around 9:40 was curious, especially when coupled with Valerie's refusal to discuss why over the phone.

Valerie is walking out of the terminal doors into the main part of the airport when Anne is walking toward the terminal, having just tucked her car into the *Hourly* lot. They run up to give each other a hug, having not seen each other since Anne hit the road in Oregon City.

She makes it all the way to the outer doors of the airport, walking to the lot, when she can't take it anymore.

"So...what the hell? What's going on that got you on a plane?"

"I'm on an assignment," she says, and suddenly Anne understands the subterfuge.

Valerie has been doing stringer work for The Eye. It's a muckraking magazine out of Tacoma known for its work exploring questionable moves, scandals, and anything else that might irritate the hell out of the government. In other words, she does precisely the sort of work Anne has always sworn she herself would never do. She doesn't condemn Val for going in that direction, but it just isn't her thing.

"And your work has brought you to Colorado?"

"I want to see if you're interested in helping me with something. I'm willing to share the byline. I have a fat expense account to get the gear I'm going to need, and I need someone who knows their way around mountains better than I do. That's you."

Valerie spends the drive to Fairplay detailing the story that landed on her desk, something that would have usually ended up in the crank file of most places.

There had been not one, but four different accounts of a secret prison that had been hastily built somewhere in the Rockies. It was allegedly one of at least a few across the United States and Canada, along with a number of them in other parts of the world.

Supposedly, these facilities were stocked with people who had committed violent crimes in the missing year. Some faction of the government, and no one at The Eye had any idea which it might be, seemed to be running their own department of "Repeat Crime Prevention." She had no idea what it might actually be called, or if it was even attached to the government.

For that reason, Valerie had no idea who to trust in an official capacity.

Valerie had only one name for a clue: Gem Lake.

In a situation such as this, she had not gone to any authorities. How could she possibly know whom to trust? You ask a question to the wrong person, and you find yourself disappeared. There was no way to try and have someone in the government look into what she suspected without worrying that she might end up a guest of the little maximum security hotel…if it existed.

Anne listened intently and wheels began to turn in her mind.

"I've never been, but years ago Billy went on some kind of Boy Scout trip to a Gem Lake upstate, by Wyoming."

She couldn't finish her thought. She started to cry, wiping the tears away with the back of her hand to keep a view of the road.

Sensing the subject needed to change quickly, Valerie returned to the original topic.

"Do you think your new Ron will let you go?

Anne took a sharp breath and wiped her nose. "Only one way to find out."

Kinshasa, D.R. Congo
November 15
5:45 AM

This would be the first morning that would see him wake up in his former homeland since he was a teenager. He would be gone by the end of the evening, on a plane back to the country that welcomed his family when they fled.

His benefactors claimed he was safe here. He was obligated to meet with the Congo's Second Chancers leadership. His wife and children remained in Tanzania, wrapping up their lives there before they returned to South Sudan to meet up with him. There again, he had been assured that his family would be safe. None of them were particularly certain about that.

Kabinda had intentions to change that.

Paul Kabinda wakes to a knock at his door.

Instinctively his hand reaches under the pillow as he opens an eye. He wraps his hand around the cold handle of the pistol he keeps there.

A slender young woman opens the door. It is Abbi, the Tanzanian operative he worked with in Rwanda. The United African Alliance has tasked her with serving as his personal assistant, and the last line of defense for his protection detail. There are many eyes on the situation in the Congo, as there are in other potential hot spots across the continent. Kabinda needs to get used to her because she is going to be a part of his life for a long time. He is more concerned about Mrs. Kabinda getting used to her.

He lets go of the gun. "Yes, Abbi?"

"There is a call for you, Bwindi, that you will want to take." He smiles as she addresses him by his clan name. Most people never use it.

She gestures at the phone at his bedside, which has one light blinking on the secure line.

He lifts the receiver, stifling a yawn. "This is Colonel Kabinda."

"Security code, please."

Kabinda sighs and drags his hand across face. "Jolly Roger 53."

"Please hold for General Robert Erbe," a pleasant young voice says.

"Good morning, Colonel," says a man with a very notable tinge of England in his Tanzanian accent. "I've just been on a very pleasant phone call with Vice President Kerek."

"Ah," says Kabinda. "I thought you said the call had been a pleasant one."

"Yes," Erbe says, with a bit of light laughter, "but the content of the call is what made it pleasant."

"He's decided not to run for President?" Kabinda says hopefully.

"He's been in contact with the Brits in Egypt. It seems they've picked up a young Intelligence Officer named Mayuri near the border with Sudan."

Paul Kabinda is now awake for the day. Wide awake.

"Call him back. Tell him I'll collect the man."

"I already have, old friend. You will need to stop in Juba to get his file and make it all look official. They'll expect you in the morning."

"They will get me tonight," Paul says. He makes a triumphant fist and holds it over his head in celebration.

His young American is still alive.

Fairplay, Colorado
November 15
7:34 AM

"I don't like not knowing where you're going."

"We don't know either, Dad," she lies.

Anne hated lying to her father and had developed a long history in her teenage years of being very bad it. This one however, seems to be plausible.

The reasons for the trip have been kept vague. The only thing her family knows for sure is that she will be in parts of the mountains where she will be out of reach for several weeks. She is planning to be home before Christmas.

Anne has made that assurance even though she has no way of knowing for sure if she can keep it. She intends to do her best to be truthful about that. Christmas is a big deal in their house.

Either way, Walt Ayres will have to wait to hear from his daughter again until *she* reaches out to him. Not unlike when she had first moved to Michigan.

"I promise I'll check in when I can, but I just…"

Her words catch in her throat, and her father bails her out, the way of parents everywhere.

"You have to get away from here. I get it. Just be careful and don't get into any trouble, okay?"

"Okay."

He holds his oldest daughter, and within a few seconds his youngest joined in.

"Be safe, nag," Mary whispers in Anne's ear.

"We will, mule," her sister responds.

With that, Anne and Valerie climb into Val's rented 4x4 and pull out of the Ayres property.

Watching them go, Mary reaches down and takes her father's hand.

"She needed a road trip, Dad. She's been here for months without being able to go any further than the Springs. She hasn't been right since she found out Billy died again."

"I know," Walt says. "I just don't think we

know everything that's going on here."

"Well, she's an adult now. We both are. We've been hiding shit from you for years."

Two horses nickered and paced at the fence line in the thin light of morning.

Walt gave his daughter a playful smack on the backside.

"You two only *think* you've been hiding shit from me. Come on, help me feed the horses."

Aswan, Egypt
November 15
4:34 PM

His car is pulling up to the military hospital as the wind picks up and bends the tops of the palms that line the street.

The Nile is pleasant and fragrant here, despite the city's best efforts to corrupt the waters. It reminds him of his former home in Juba, to which he looks forward to returning soon.

It smells nothing like the waters of his childhood, some distance to the south in the Congo. That was the smell of rotting vegetation and simian feces. This was far preferable.

He's in his uniform and he looks important, so it is a simple matter to rush through security without too many questions. Besides, there are few people in this part of Africa that do not know his face from the news. He is the Liberator of Mogadishu, the man who died and came back to serve an even more heroic purpose by rescuing an entire tribe in Tanzania.

Abbi stops to register him with the duty nurse as Kabinda walks directly into the hospital room to see the unconscious man.

A young nurse is tapping data onto a tablet when he walks in.

"Has he wakened at all?" Kabinda asks.

"No," she says, scarcely looking up.

"I will be back."

Abbi is walking in as he steps back out of the room.

"I will be back shortly. I need to call Minister Akela."

Alexandria, Virginia
November 15
9:40 AM

Harriet Bellingshausen has been awake for about an hour. She enjoys sleeping in on Saturdays.

Saturday is her day to watch movies. She selected one at random after her shower, barely registering what it was, and is listening to it from the kitchen as she puts a ton of effort into breakfast for one.

Her plate is finished, and perfect. Two people in the western she had put on are trading gunshots from behind inadequate, but camera-friendly cover.

She pulls a TV tray around with her plate on it, takes her usual spot on the couch...and her phone rings.

"Of course."

She thumbs the pause button on the remote and grabs her phone.

INTERNATIONAL CALL.

She straightens her spine a bit before hitting the button.

"This is General Bellingshausen."

"General? This is Henry Akela."

"Minister," she says. "To what do I owe the pleasure?"

"Are you sitting down?"

"Yes, sir. Why?"

"It would appear that our earlier assessment regarding Captain Pemberton was in error. The Brits have him in a hospital in Egypt."

Harriet pumps her fist in victory.

"That's fantastic. Send the report to my office. I'll be there in an hour and I'll take it from there. Thank you for the call, Minister."

"It is my pleasure, General."

Harriet disconnects and looks at the breakfast she had devoted 20 minutes of her morning to.

She sighs. It smells fantastic. She doesn't cook very often, and she hates having anything get in the way when she does.

This however is a happy exception.

Besides, most of it looks like it could be reheated later without being too worse for wear.

Except for the bacon. That is coming with her.

She calls her office and sits the bacon on a paper towel. She hears her assistant pick up the line.

"Geoff? I need to see General Gilmour in an hour. Tell him we need to be wheels up in two. Tell him to dress warmly."

Aswan, Egypt
November 15
9:12 PM

He walks across the desert sands, listening carefully for anything in the area that might want to make a meal of him.

The Red Sea is off to his right, lapping at the African shoreline, its breezes mingling with the thin fronds of the plants below the embankment.

He can hear the carrion eaters overhead. There are no settlements here and few animals come to this place to die. Billy Pemberton is a welcome attraction. The killers on the wing are the first to have noticed him, but likely won't be the last. Other creatures will follow once they notice the buzzards are circling something. He has to get out of here quickly.

A mirage is forming up ahead of him. He knows it isn't water, even if it looks like it. What's unusual about this one is that someone is in it, moving toward him. It takes a step when he takes one.

Closer and closer they come to one another,

until he can see the man more clearly.

The man is roughly his own height, and appears to be staggering with the same difficulty he is. He's very dark in complexion, like Billy is, but the same is true of most of the people who live in this part of Africa.

The closer he comes, Billy realizes they are dressed exactly the same.

Minutes later they are face to face, and it becomes obvious that they are wearing the same one.

"Billy Pemberton," he says, extending his hand.

"Kiir Mayuri," says the other man. "What are you doing here, Billy Pemberton?"

Billy shakes his head. "You wouldn't believe me if I told you."

"No," Kiir says. "What are you still doing in Africa? Why are you *here?*"

Billy thinks for a moment. "I had a job to do."

Kiir Mayuri smiles at him. It's his own smile. He's never really seen it outside of a mirror. Billy has never realized how nice his own smile is before this moment, how soothing and full of joy it is.

"The job is finished. Wake up and go home."

Paul Kabinda is sitting in a hospital room in Egypt, listening to the wind whistle across the Nile, and reading a book. It's a book Abbi had with her and is the first bit of extracurricular reading he has done since the war began. He has forgotten how much he enjoys fiction. Even horrible vampire-related fiction.

One of the machines beeps in a new way, and he looks up at it. As he does, he happens to see Captain Billy Pemberton III open his eyes.

"Welcome back," Kabinda says with a smile.

Somewhere in Northern Colorado
November 15
12:31 PM

"I think it's time to find a spot for lunch, don't you?"

Anne nods in agreement. "No phones."

"No phones," Valerie says. "In fact, gimme."

Val takes Anne's phone and switches it off. She does the same to her own, and puts them in the glove box.

"There," she says. "We're free. I say we stay that way until we figure out if there's anything going on at Gem Lake."

"I agree if we get burgers."

"Burgers it is."

Colorado Springs
November 15
6:10 PM

Dinner has begun. There is no prayer. There has been no prayer at mealtime for almost two weeks now.

Helen Pemberton claims that she has nothing further to say to God.

Aunt Tara is visiting from Panama City. She hasn't been able to sustain Helen's mood. Pharmaceuticals have done a decent job though, and she is at least holding it together enough to eat dinner with the family tonight. Tara made their mother's gumbo recipe with what passes for fresh seafood out here in the Rocky Mountains.

The doorbell nearly causes Helen to jump out of her skin. Everyone at the table looks at everyone else at the table. Danny is the one who wipes his mouth with his napkin while getting up out of his chair.

The family hears him open the door and say the next three words with almost no emotion.

"Well, come in."

Helen is facing away from the hall their visitors enter the room from, but she gauges her husband's response and figures out it is someone in a uniform. She is used to that. Her husband is, for the time being, still the Base Commander here.

When she hears General Gilmour's voice however, she starts to get up.

"I don't want to hear from you, Gil. I..." she starts to shake... "I can't talk to you, Gil."

"Helen, Bill...just look at this."

He finds a spot on the table next to Helen's seat and puts a folder down on the table. She pulls her hands up to her face and starts to turn around.

General Gilmour puts a hand on Helen's shoulder, and General Bellingshausen opens the folder.

Sitting on top of the papers in the folder is a picture of her son in a hospital bed.

"That was taken yesterday, in Egypt. As we speak we're moving him to Italy, because we've been assured he's well enough to make the trip."

Everyone at the table gasps.

Bellingshausen asks her. "How quickly can you be ready to fly out?"

She's not the least bit surprised when this woman she has never met gives her the biggest hug she's had in years.

Aviano AFB, Italy
November 16
8:13 PM

Colonel Bill Pemberton and his wife Helen are walked quickly through the hallways. Every single person in the hospital knows who they are, and why they are there, and wants them to get to their son's room as quickly as possible.

When they arrive at their son's floor, a man in scrubs greets them.

"Lieutenant Colonel Hildebrandt," he says. "I'm your son's doctor. Please come with me."

"Is he…"

"He's bouncing back very well, Ma'am. We're fighting an infection in one of his wounds, but we're getting the better of it. He's past the worst of it. Chances are you'll have him home in time for Thanksgiving dinner."

Wild Bill is walking briskly to keep pace with his wife. "Seriously?"

"He's a hell of a healer, your son. He's been trying to stay awake because he knew you were coming, but his meds keep him fairly sedate."

They come to the door and Helen pushes past both of them. She then stops suddenly when she sees the face she's been waiting to see again for the two longest years of her life.

"Hi, mom."

Somewhere in Northwest China
June 2
7:59 PM
One minute before the Event

Pai Mei sits in evening prayer.

He is devout in his fealty before Allah and prays at the end of each day's toil on his quiet farm in the Tien Shan Mountains. His land is remote and tranquil. It is not easy to till and sow from. Still, he has had a number of successful years here.

There have been far more good years here than bad ones, even when droughts have come. It is one of the many things he thanks Allah for when he hits his knees.

What he lacks in companions, he makes up for in his energy. He has lived 70 summers, and has spent most of them tending his crops and caring for his chickens.

Pai has never seen a city; he has never traveled beyond the mountains to see the yellow plains of the steppe or smell the vast stretch of an ocean. His contact with the outside world is minimal at best, coming only when he has need for something for the farm and has to make his way to the closest village, which is two days away by foot, or about a day on the back of his stubborn, braying ass.

As he prays, he feels a warm feeling wash over him all at once. He opens his eyes and finds that the sky has grown suddenly cloudy with the setting of the sun.

His prostrations completed, Pai Mei rises to his feet and rolls up his mat. He tosses seed to his chickens and makes a mental count of them. There is one more than he remembered having, a large one that resembles a great egg-layer he had last year before it was taken by a wild dog. He shrugs it off without another thought.

A short supper of rice and bread is his plan for this evening until he is pleasantly surprised to find that there was still a fish in the larder from his last trip to the river with his net. He was certain that the last one had been eaten the night before. The fish is salty and warm, and it feels good on a stomach that has grown tight in the fields, keeping the weeds out of his vegetables and harvesting the overgrowth from the large area that brings him his rice.

He has no television or radio, he certainly has no computer. There is no newspaper, no library of classic books in his tiny home.

There is only contemplation, and the sounds of the mountain side. There is the breeze blowing through his white beard. There are stars in the sky, too many to count or name. There are the dreams of attaining a personal center within himself that will please the spirits of his ancestors.

Pai Mei lies on a mat behind his house that he rests on when separating his rice and folds his hands behind his head to support the weight of his thoughts.

He stares at the sky and watches galaxies spin around one another because Allah decrees it should be so.

Pai Mei will never know what has just happened to the world. The event will never affect him in the slightest except to put an extra fish in his belly and return a chicken to him. He will have to repair a broken latch again that the dog had used last year to steal his fat hen, but he will do so without a second thought. This is the country. Things wear out here.

It has always been so and will always be so.

Some things never change.

- THE END -

Epilogue
Horizon

It is a Friday morning, and the temperature is an unusually warm 60 degrees. The sun is shining over Colorado Springs, and the flight is on final approach.

Local schoolchildren have been let out to attend this homecoming, to cheer on the soldier that their parents have been buzzing about for days. Many of them have made signs.

One of those schoolchildren is the youngest brother of the soldier, a boy named Sam. He is standing with his brother and Aunt on the flight line. His girlfriend, watching from the grandstand, wishes they were already married so she could be down there, too, with a better view.

The Air Force Band is playing. There is a generous number of Generals on-hand to greet him, along with the Mayor, Senators, members of Congress, and the Governor of Colorado.

The C-130 touches down, and Billy walks down the ramp that drops down from the back of the aircraft. He is flanked on either side by his parents.

The force of the cheer that meets him at the end of the ramp is almost powerful enough to knock him back into the cargo bay. He is wearing his dress uniform, although he has one arm bandaged from the gunshot wounds he sustained the day he ended the life of King Roti.

His Aunt and brothers rush forward to embrace him, and the moment is captured by a number of news cameras.

Captain Pemberton has been trumpeted as a hero of the last days of the Rift Valley War, a man who was directly involved in the last push that led to the expulsion of GEA troops from Kenyan soil. There have been no details released beyond that. The only person there who knows anything more is the Captain's father. He only knows the truth because of who his friends are in Washington.

Billy scans the sea of nearby faces, the next stack of people he needs to be greeted by who will squeeze his arm and make his shoulder ache. He spots Mary Ayres there.

He gives his brother's girlfriend a hug, and asks a question while his lips are directly next to her ear.

"Where's Anne?"

He feels her tighten a little.

Acknowledgements

I told far too many of you about this book.

On a number of levels, this book has intimidated the hell out of me since the idea came up in 2008. It loomed large enough that it took another year for me to finally start writing out the notes for it.

I spent more than four years being afraid to write this book, to the point that every time I was ready to work on it...I wrote three other novels and about a dozen short stories instead. I would visit this idea every now and then but really only in thin sketches and fat notes.

I was in a perpetual state of research when it came to this story, always keeping an eye out for things I could use to expand on the ideas. The actual writing though, was always something I wasn't ready to begin yet. It was always a project for *a couple of years from now*. It wasn't so intimidating if I kept it there, in the future. It wasn't so damn scary.

The scope of what I always called *my ReYear*

Project was more than I could wrap my head around in one sitting. Then I started talking it out with several of you that (hopefully) bought this. All of you said the same thing.

"That is so deep. I can't wait to read it!"

Suddenly, this book had found an entirely new way to intimidate me. Oh good.

Hopefully, the small collective community of you who kept telling me how much you were looking forward to reading this, found it worth the wait. It certainly felt worth the wait while writing it.

Thank yous. There are several. Kim, Emily, and Skylar, as always. Kim had more input in both my editorial and creative processes than ever. Whenever the book started to intimidate me again, she ended up hearing far more about this story than she had the others. She helped shape it and give it clarity. Even in the situations where all she had to do was listen and nod because I worked it out myself while talking. Yeah. She had to put up with a lot of that this time around. Thank you, Beautiful.

My brother Frank Jasper-Stump, who years ago was one of the first people I bounced the idea off of, and who started raving about how interesting the premise was. It was a fun night of conversation and whisky. Yes, he is my brother...I don't care that we don't actually share any parents.

My sister that I share actual biology with, Hollie Ayres, remains my first line of grammar defense. I can't make these without her. The heroine of this story had to have her last name, because she helps me save every one of my stories in the end.

My dear friend Carl Stutsman helped me realize that one part of the storyline deserved to be an entirely separate book…and eventually it will be, with any luck. Another pair of friends, namely Andrew Witkowski and Tori James, made great efforts to steer me in the direction of research assistance that for one reason or another never quite panned out.

Trent Rentsch was on the other end of a couple of conversations during the embryonic stages of this story, and his enthusiasm to read it pushed many of the first sketches into being many years ago.

Jon Zimney is more than my boss, he's my friend. He put the final polish on *A Match To Old Parchments* for me, despite having less free time than any human being who has ever walked the earth. Thank you so much, *O Captain! My Captain!*

My mother and father fueled everything I wrote when I first tried creating stories as a teenager. As always, I owe them a debt of thanks for every spine out there with my name on it. They have always encouraged me to do this. They have always been proud of me no matter what I've done in my life, even when I've fallen on my ass and made the exact wrong decisions. I've done a lot of that, actually.

Also, Kristin Blitch. We may not have the lines of communication open like we did in the past, thanks to our differing schedules. That does not change the fact that she was the one who said to me, upon seeing a rough early version of *Mulligan,* "you should really do something with this. You *wrote a book.*"

Speaking of which, I would like to thank a book none of you are allowed to read. Without having typed the words "the end" on something horrible called *The Christmas Project* way back in 1991...I would never have believed I could finish one of these...let alone five of them.

Finally...thank you to YOU, for taking a chance on this book. With any luck at all, we'll pick up where we left off in the story very soon.

This book was written without an active connection to the internet, or even a smart phone that would permit me to do instant research. Which was a pain in the ass, to be honest with you. All of the research for this book came from maps, my beloved almanacs, and from other books.

That is to say...except for certain situations where I needed to know something specific that would be a simple matter of a tiny search engine query. Which I could not do on my crappy cell phone. Which was very irritating.

In those moments, and there were more than a few, I picked up my crappy cell phone and asked someone to jump online and find out stupid little things for me like "Is there an Air Force Base in New Jersey?"

That someone always pulled his laptop over without hesitation...no matter what he was doing...and looked it up for the guy who had no active internet connection at home. This is sort of an irresponsible way to write a novel these days, actually. Especially when you've always been a research guy.

That someone was my father, every time. Thanks for the assist, Dad. I really, deeply appreciate it.

From the Keep on the Borderlands,
July 2013

About the author

Tommie Lee is the Afternoon News Anchor at Michiana's News Channel in South Bend, Indiana. He has worked in radio since Halloween, 1988. It was a bad decision, sure, but he was very young when he made it.

Before that, he thought he was a musician. It turned out he wasn't. Before any of that, he was writing fiction in his bedroom on his mother's old typewriter and then on a Commodore 64. You have apps with more power than that computer. Now he is married with two teenagers, a cat, and a dog. They all tolerate his occasional bouts of incessant typing.

This is his fifth novel. He wants a brand new laptop to use to write the sixth one. Assuming he has any energy left after completing this one. It was a lot more draining than the ones that came before.

Connect with the author

You can find Tommie online at tkcbooks dot com, and his narcissistic ramblings on Twitter (@tlcjr and @AuthorTLee), as well as on Facebook. You are encouraged to find and like Books By Tommie Lee on Facebook.

When this went to press, he was the afternoon news anchor at News/Talk 95.3 Michiana's News Channel, perhaps the last signal on the South Bend, Indiana FM dial anyone ever expected him to work at again.

He welcomes your feedback emails about the story at tlc@tealsea.com. He writes back.

If you liked this book, tell people by posting a review of it somewhere. Every time he notices that someone has bought one of his books, he does a disturbing little "Sales Dance" that freaks out his dog, Duchess. He enjoys freaking Dutchie out whenever possible...

http://www.tkcbooks.com
http://www.facebook.com/tkcbooks

A Match to Old Parchments:

Roti, Great East Africa, and the Roots of Conflict in The Rift Valley War

Anne Ayres
Three Cities News

- FIRST DRAFT -

It is said that when one considers North Africa, one must consider thirst. This is true.

Equally true is that to consider *East* Africa, one must consider hunger.

The people in that forgotten corner of the world hunger for more than food. They hunger for knowledge, for stability, and also for technology. As is true of any society, East Africans hunger for the opportunity to make a better life for themselves.

Unfortunately, they lack the necessary raw materials for this. These are a people that suffer the disadvantages of scant resources, minimal infrastructure, and the disinterest of most of the world.

From such circumstances, strange bedfellows are made. When ethnicity and tribal loyalties mean everything to a people, religion cannot hope to have the power to divide. At the very least, differences in faith do not carry the same sway they do in the more "civilized" parts of the world.

As conditions worsened in East Africa, the

Christians of Ethiopia and Muslims of Somalia came together in their efforts to survive. The decades-old problems of both nations made each of them ideal prey for the right predator.

In the closing years of the last century, Ethiopia became the thin, emaciated face of famine. At least one million people died of disease and starvation. Only a handful of years before this, a rebellion in the Ogaden region resulted in a million Ethiopians fleeing over the border into Somalia after a failed attempt to ignite a civil war. The Somalis had quietly supported the rebel effort, the last time the two nations had faced off against each other.

Most of the one million refugees that slipped into Somalia were women and children. The men remained in Ethiopia to fight against the army. In 1978 many of these same freedom fighters had, with help from the Cubans and Soviets, fought a war against the very Somalis they now trusted with their families.

One of these soldiers was the man the world now knows as Roti.

Roti began life as Michele Salim Uaroti, the son of a Muslim father and Christian mother in Domo, Ethiopia. He was raised within sight of the Somali border, and spent a great deal of his time on both sides of that frontier. Roti was the youngest of eight children, and more importantly, the only *son* of an elderly father who passed away before he reached the age of ten. Soon after, Roti took his father's place in the army.

Educated in Cairo after his service, Roti returned home and entered politics. In this he displayed astounding charisma and charm, as well as an aptitude for bringing people around to a unified way of thinking. It was only a matter of time before he ascended to Ethiopia's Presidency.

As his power base solidified, he first reached

out to Ethiopians in Somalia and invited them home. He promised amnesty to those who chose to return. He worked tirelessly to keep the peace at home as they resettled. He began sweeping reforms that turned the tide for Ethiopia's outlook, and his people began to find themselves fed by their own hand, guided by the man whose smile was as infectious as their own optimism.

When rich new deposits of gold were found in the mountains of the Oromia region, Ethiopia suddenly found itself flush with new friends all over the world. Roti became the face of African pride and potential to the entire world. To his own people Roti became the face of hope and promise, the man who would give them a place in the global consciousness again. This time, not as victims.

Rather than squander his nation's new riches, he extended the hand of friendship to Ethiopia's former enemies. These included the warlords of Somalia whose population he was thinning, and the far more legitimate heads of state in Djibouti and Eritrea. Of course, a number of wars had been fought with the latter, but Roti dreamed of a united Ethiopia.

Eritrea politely declined anything more than an agreement in principle to maintain peace in the region, as did Djibouti. Both countries are far more politically attached to Saudi Arabia than Ethiopia. Somalia, however, was another matter.

Somalia was a mess, as it had been for some time. Ethiopia's powerful renewal was like a lightning strike to a country that had been bereft of anything resembling a functioning government for a couple of decades. Within six months of bloody fighting the Somali people had toppled the most corrupt of the warlords, and Roti began to collect the remaining brokers of power in Somalia. The provincial warlords of Somalia soon became little more than puppets in the hands of their neighbor, the man who had shown an entire nation the way to a brighter future. Those who didn't agree with him, pretended to do so. Failure to side with Roti was the best way to find oneself stripped of power in the new Somalia.

The call for unification was sudden and overwhelming. "History," Roti thundered to both sides on the radio, "compels us to face the future together, just as we faced our distant past." Within a month, the two nations had merged into his new Great East Africa. Again invitations were extended to the former territories of Djibouti and Eritrea. Again both refused to join them in the new experiment. Firmly emboldened by their alliances with the Muslim powers in the Middle East – which eyed the new G.E.A. and their leader with great suspicion – the two coastal nations remained untouched and independent.

It was soon after his new nation was formed that Roti began to change. Like his hero Napoleon, he elevated himself to King, and a new Kingdom was born in the ancient land of Axum. In his first year on his new throne, King Roti began what his detractors called a descent into eccentricities that bordered on madness. His subjects all went along for the ride.

Roti became known for sleeping through most of the daylight hours, running the country from behind a closed door until evening. He would emerge only after dark, and his first priority would be the broadcasts of his rambling speeches. They would stagger from treatises on patriotism to tirades about "the enemies of the Kingdom, who would have us starving and covered in flies once more, begging for scraps from their dinner plates."

Before long, it became clear that the chief enemy had a local face. It was Kenya, preached Roti, who would hold the grip of the rifle when the Kingdom was threatened.

A series of attacks, which the Kenyans continue to maintain were staged, occurred on the border region. Great East Africa responded in kind, crossing the frontier and beginning the slaughter of the people of Northern Kenya.

Amped up with rhetoric and fresh atrocities, the situation led to a number of diplomatic collapses. Here were sown the seeds of war.

As has been the case for centuries in the region, the impetus for disaster came down to one thing over all others.

Water.

At the insistence of the fragile Egyptian government, a package of dramatic amendments were proposed to clean up the Nile River Usage Acts. In Entebbe, Uganda, a meeting was held for representatives of the Nile Basin Commission. At this meeting the member nations lined up on two very clear sides of the argument.

Egypt, the two Sudans, and Eritrea had a very clear desire to see sweeping reforms in the current agreements, citing increased deposits and diversions of the river that contradicted previous agreements. The offending actions had resulted in several adverse effects on their sections of the Nile. Everyone in the hall knew they were pointing fingers at the Ethiopians, whose increased mining activity was taking quite a toll on many parts of their ecology. Eventually the Northern nations were able to win over the Rwandans, Burundis, and Tanzanians to the side of greater enforcement – citing the need to keep the waters of Lake Victoria as healthy as possible, too. Uganda stood with Roti and the G.E.A., and all of the Congolese delegates abstained.

This left Kenya as the swing vote on the Commission. They were in possession of the last votes needed for ratification or refusal by percentage. Kenya themselves were guilty of numerous pollution violations, owing to increased mining activity in their own highlands that came quickly after the Ethiopian Gold Rush. Eventually, the Kenyans proffered their mea culpa and sided with the Egyptian Plan.

Kenya's mistake ran deeper than simply going against Roti. They went a step further, publicly humiliating him and painting him as the primary element of destabilization in the region.

The mistake here was that to his subjects, King Roti enjoyed (and still does) a cult of personality unprecedented in the region for decades. It was a simple matter for Roti to use Kenya's words as justification for invasion. It was more food on his plate to satiate his hunger for empire.

The shaky, young government of South Sudan complicated things further by diverting a small number of the troops that held their former Sudanese countrymen at bay in the north, and chose this moment to strike at Kenya. They quickly managed to retake the natural gas-rich swamps of the Elemi Triangle, before crossing the hundred year-old Maud Line that had been hotly debated for some time.

This of course, came to pass only a month ago. Sudan has since reacted by attacking them from the north, and at the time of this writing the South Sudanese are fighting for their lives on two fronts. A harsh payment for a rash mistake.

Old alliances are already being pulled into this conflict. The United States and United Kingdom swept into Kenya to stop the advance of G.E.A., Ugandan, and Southern Sudanese troops that poured over the Boran region borderlands. When things went poorly for Kenya very quickly the West stepped up their efforts. American troops attached to the intervention have nicknamed the dusty place "The Bor".

In particular, the United States was perhaps

motivated by previous missteps in East Africa in the 1990s. Somalia, an all-but-forgotten dark chapter in our nation's history from 1993, looms like a dark-skinned specter in the halls of power in Washington. Additionally, there is the glaring lack of action on our part a year later, as nearly a million Rwandan Tutsis were murdered under the machetes of their fellow citizens, the Hutus. Those memories served as a stinging reminder that a similar fate should not befall another people in the same part of the world

Of course, the disastrous terrorist attack at our embassy in Nairobi just two months ago left the American public hungry for Ethiopian and Somali blood.

Gingerly, the American military committed thousands of troops to the situation as borders began to be redrawn throughout the Great Rift Valley. Escalation gave Roti the fuel he needed to step up his cruelties in Kenya.

The Americans would not have to go it alone, however. The British stepped up, much to the chagrin of many subjects of the United Kingdom. The British have a history in Kenya, one that does not make them particularly popular. Many pundits believe the UK will spend only a limited amount of time in country before they are forced to cease their efforts. They are there in the shadow of the Mau Mau Revolt of the 1930s, where the shattering of their great empire began in the years before the Second World War.

Qatar, a nation with extensive business investments in Kenya, has also committed troops. This is an uncharacteristic activity for Qatar, and their effectiveness is a question mark that only time will be able to provide an answer to.

The Russians and Italians sent aid to the G.E.A. early on, and the world drew a deep breath. Italy, in particular, suffers the same image problem in both Ethiopia and Somalia that Britain faces in Kenya. Fortunately the involvement of those two countries has gone no further than that, and a heightened conflict on a global scale seems to have been avoided. China, it seems, has decided to sit this out, as have the Muslim powers in the Middle East...save perhaps Yemen. No one wants to turn East Africa into a Crusade for either side of the equation.

Roti has made it to the equator, and as far south as Mt. Kenya. It seems unlikely that he can maintain such a large swath of land, given the forces that have rallied against him. Ultimately, he must know that he cannot win, but how long he can prolong the agony is the key question.

Where this conflict will take the United States, its allies, and the people of the region remains to be seen. It is my considered opinion that men like Roti eventually fall victim to their own hubris. History is littered with such self-inflated despots. The sad truth is that Roti had the potential to bring positive revolution to all of the troubled lands in the region, of which there are many. He was unable to maintain himself after he gained his dreams of empire.

Roti cannot placate the Somali people for much longer, and they will eventually break up the Kingdom. Ethiopia's new wealth cannot support a war against the forces allied against them, especially one being fought with soldiers who still do not eat well enough to be particularly effective. Already the Ugandans who slipped so cleverly around Lake Victoria and captured the Kenyan city of Kisumu are being driven back across the water. And the refugees that have crossed into Tanzania will likely force that nation's hand at some point, as well. There is talk of an African alliance already beginning to form against Roti.

Then there is the question of the Ethiopian

people. For so long they were viewed as the victims of the world. Now they are seen as an aggressor. A peaceful people have hungrily followed Roti into madness, touching a series of lit matches to many old agreements that kept a peace in place in a shaky region for generations.

One can only hope that their fate, when the end of this bloody conflict finally comes, will be kinder than that which led them to this place in their history.